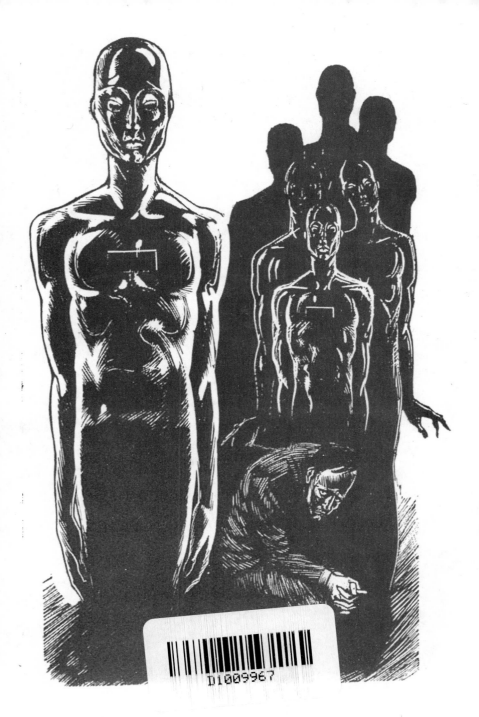

# The Humanoids

The Legion of Space
Darker Than You Think
*Demon Moon
The Green Girl
The Cometeers
One Against the Legion
Seetee Shock
Seetee Ship
Dragon's Island
The Legion of Time
Undersea Quest (with Frederik Pohl)
Dome Around America
Starbridge (with James Gunn)
Undersea Fleet (with Frederik Pohl)
Undersea City (with Frederik Pohl)
The Trial of Terra
Golden Blood
The Reefs of Space (with Frederik Pohl)
Starchild (with Frederik Pohl)
The Reign of Wizardry
Bright New Universe
Trapped in Space
The Pandora Effect
Rogue Star (with Frederik Pohl)
People Machines
The Moon Children
H. G. Wells: Critic of Progress (nonfiction)
The Farthest Star (with Frederik Pohl)
The Early Williamson
The Power of Blackness
The Best of Jack Williamson
Brother to Demons, Brother to Gods
The Alien Intelligence
The Humanoid Touch
The Birth of a New Republic (with Miles J. Breuer)
Manseed
Wall Around a Star (with Frederik Pohl)
The Queen of the Legion
Wonder's Child: My Life in Science Fiction (memoir)
Lifeburst
*Firechild
*Land's End (with Frederik Pohl)
Mazeway
The Singers of Time (with Frederik Pohl)
*Beachhead
*The Humanoids

*denotes a Tom Doherty Associates book

# The Humanoids

## Jack Williamson

ORB

A Tom Doherty Associates Book
New York

THE HUMANOIDS

THE HUMANOIDS copyright 1948, 1949 by Jack Williamson; copyright © 1975 by Jack Williamson.

WITH FOLDED HANDS copyright 1947 by Street & Smith; copyright © 1975 by Jack Williamson.

Interior illustrations copyright © 1987 by David G. Klein

This book is printed on acid-free paper.

An Orb Edition
Published by Tom Doherty Associates, Inc.
175 Fifth Avenue
New York, N.Y. 10010

Library of Congress Cataloging-in-Publication Data

Williamson, Jack.
    The humanoids   /   Jack Williamson.—1st Orb ed.
        p.    cm.
    "A Tom Doherty Associates book."
    ISBN 0-312-85253-3
    I. Title.
    PS3545.I557H85    1996
    813'.54—dc20                                              95-40800
                                                                  CIP

First Orb edition: January 1996

Printed in the United States of America

0 9 8 7 6 5 4 3 2 1

For JOHN W. CAMPBELL, JR.
who pointed out to me
some of the consequences of
folded hands.

# contents

# I

## With Folded Hands

UNDERHILL WAS WALKING home from the office, because his wife had the car, the afternoon he first met the new mechanicals. His feet were following his usual diagonal path across a weedy vacant block—his wife usually had the car—and his preoccupied mind was rejecting various impossible ways to meet his notes at the Two Rivers bank, when a new wall stopped him.

The wall wasn't any common brick or stone, but something sleek and bright and strange. Underhill stared up at a long new building. He felt vaguely annoyed and surprised at this glittering obstruction—it certainly hadn't been here last week.

Then he saw the thing in the window.

The window itself wasn't any ordinary glass. The wide, dustless panel was completely transparent, so that only the glowing letters fastened to it showed that it was there at all. The letters made a severe, modernistic sign:

Two Rivers Agency
HUMANOID INSTITUTE
The Perfect Mechanicals
"To Serve and Obey,
And Guard Men from Harm."

His dim annoyance sharpened, because Underhill was in the mechanicals business himself. Times were already hard enough, and mechanicals were a drug on the market. Androids, mechanoids, electronoids, automatoids, and ordinary robots. Unfortunately, few of them did all the salesmen promised, and the Two Rivers market was already sadly oversaturated.

Underhill sold androids—when he could. His next consignment was due tomorrow, and he didn't quite know how to meet the bill.

Frowning, he paused to stare at the thing behind that invisible window. He had never seen a humanoid. Like any mechanical not at work, it stood absolutely motionless. Smaller and slimmer than a man. A shining black, its sleek silicone skin had a changing sheen of bronze and metallic blue. Its graceful oval face wore a fixed look of alert and slightly surprised solicitude. Altogether, it was the most beautiful mechanical he had ever seen.

Too small, of course, for much practical utility. He murmured to himself a reassuring quotation from the *Android Salesman:* "Androids are big—because the makers refuse to sacrifice power, essential functions, or dependability. Androids are your biggest buy!"

The transparent door slid open as he turned toward it, and he walked into the haughty opulence of the new display room to convince himself that these streamlined items were just another flash effort to catch the woman shopper.

He inspected the glittering layout shrewdly, and his breezy optimism faded. He had never heard of the Humanoid Institute, but the invading firm obviously had big money and big-time merchandising know-how.

He looked around for a salesman, but it was another mechanical that came gliding silently to meet him. A twin of the one in the window, it moved with a quick, surprising grace. Bronze and blue lights flowed over its lustrous blackness, and a yellow name plate flashed from its naked breast:

HUMANOID
Serial No. 81-H-B-27
The Perfect Mechanical
"To Serve and Obey,
And Guard Men from Harm."

Curiously it had no lenses. The eyes in its bald oval head were steel colored, blindly staring. But it stopped a few feet in front of him, as if it could see anyhow, and it spoke to him with a high, melodious voice:

"At your service, Mr. Underhill."

The use of his name startled him, for not even the androids could tell one man from another. But this was a clever merchandising stunt, of course, not too difficult in a town the size of Two Rivers. The salesman must be some local man, prompting the mechanical from behind the partition. Underhill erased his momentary astonishment, and said loudly:

"May I see your salesman, please?"

"We employ no human salesmen, sir," its soft silvery voice replied instantly. "The Humanoid Institute exists to serve mankind, and we require no human service. We ourselves can supply any information you desire, sir, and accept your order for immediate humanoid service."

Underhill peered at it dazedly. No mechanicals were competent even to recharge their own batteries and reset their own relays, much less to operate their own branch offices. The blind eyes stared blankly back, and he looked uneasily around for any booth or curtain that might conceal the salesman.

Meanwhile, the sweet thin voice resumed persuasively:

"May we come out to your home for a free trial demonstration, sir? We are anxious to introduce our service on your planet, because we have been successful in eliminating human unhappiness on so many others. You will find us far superior to the old electronic mechanicals in use here."

Underhill stepped back uneasily. He reluctantly abandoned his search for the hidden salesman, shaken by the idea of any mechanicals promoting themselves. That would upset the whole industry.

"At least you must take some advertising matter, sir."

Moving with a somehow appalling graceful deftness, the small black mechanical brought him an illustrated booklet from a table by the wall. To cover his confused and increasing alarm, he thumbed through the glossy pages.

In a series of richly colored before-and-after pictures, a chesty blond girl was stooping over a kitchen stove, and then relaxing in a daring negligee while a little black mechanical knelt to serve her something. She was wearily hammering a typewriter, and then lying on an ocean beach, in a revealing sun suit, while another mechanical did the typing. She was toiling at some huge industrial machine, and then dancing in the arms of a golden-haired youth, while a black humanoid ran the machine.

Underhill sighed wistfully. The android company didn't supply such fetching sales material. Women would find this booklet irresistible, and they selected eighty-six percent of all mechanicals sold. Yes, the competition was going to be bitter.

"Take it home, sir," the sweet voice urged him. "Show it to your wife. There is a free trial demonstration order blank on the last page, and you will notice that we require no payment down."

He turned numbly, and the door slid open for him. Retreating dazedly, he discovered the booklet still in his hand. He crumpled it furiously, and flung it down. The small black thing picked it up tidily, and the insistent silver voice rang after him:

"We shall call at your office tomorrow, Mr. Underhill, and send a demonstration unit to your home. It is time to discuss the liquidation of your business, because the electronic mechanicals you have been selling cannot compete with us. And we shall offer your wife a free trial demonstration."

Underhill didn't attempt to reply, because he couldn't trust his voice. He stalked blindly down the new sidewalk to the corner, and paused there to collect himself. Out of his startled and confused impressions, one clear fact emerged—things looked black for the agency.

Bleakly, he stared back at the haughty splendor of the new building. It wasn't honest brick or stone; that invisible window wasn't glass; and he was quite sure the foundation for it hadn't even been staked out the last time Aurora had the car.

He walked on around the block, and the new sidewalk took him near the rear entrance. A truck was backed up to it, and several slim black mechanicals were silently busy, unloading huge metal crates.

He paused to look at one of the crates. It was labeled for interstellar shipment. The stencils showed that it had come from the Humanoid Institute, on Wing IV. He failed to recall any planet of that designation; the outfit must be big.

Dimly, inside the gloom of the warehouse beyond the truck, he could see black mechanicals opening the crates. A lid came up, revealing dark, rigid bodies, closely packed. One by one, they came to life. They climbed out of the crate, and sprang gracefully to the floor. A shining black, glinting with bronze and blue, they were all identical.

One of them came out past the truck, to the sidewalk, staring with blind steel eyes. Its high silver voice spoke to him melodiously:

"At your service, Mr. Underhill."

He fled. When his name was promptly called by a courteous mechanical, just out of the crate in which it had been imported from a remote and unknown planet, he found the experience trying.

Two blocks along, the sign of a bar caught his eye, and he took his dismay inside. He had made it a business rule not to drink before dinner, and Aurora didn't like him to drink at all; but these new mechanicals, he felt, had made the day exceptional.

Unfortunately, however, alcohol failed to brighten the brief visible future of the agency. When he emerged, after an hour, he looked wistfully back in hope that the bright new building might have vanished as abruptly as it came. It hadn't. He shook his head dejectedly, and turned uncertainly homeward.

Fresh air had cleared his head somewhat, before he arrived at the neat white bungalow in the outskirts of the town, but it failed to solve his business problems. He also realized, uneasily, that he would be late for dinner.

Dinner, however, had been delayed. His son Frank, a freckled ten-year-old, was still kicking a football on the quiet street in front of the house. And little Gay, who was tow-haired and adorable and eleven, came running across the lawn and down the sidewalk to meet him.

"Father, you can't guess what!" Gay was going to be a great musician some day, and no doubt properly dignified, but she was pink and breathless with excitement now. She let him swing her high off the sidewalk, and she wasn't critical of the bar aroma on his breath. He couldn't guess, and she informed him eagerly:

"Mother's got a new lodger!"

Underhill had foreseen a painful inquisition, because Aurora was worried about the notes at the bank, and the bill for the new consignment, and the money for little Gay's lessons.

The new lodger, however, saved him from that. With an alarming crashing of crockery, the household android was setting dinner on the table, but the little house was empty. He found Aurora in the back yard, burdened with sheets and towels for the guest.

Aurora, when he married her, had been as utterly adorable as now her little daughter was. She might have remained so, he felt, if the agency had been a little more successful. However, while the pressure of slow failure had gradually crumbled his own assurance, small hardships had turned her a little too aggressive.

Of course he loved her still. Her red hair was still alluring, and she was loyally faithful, but thwarted ambitions had sharpened her character and sometimes her voice. They never quarreled, really, but there were small differences.

There was the little apartment over the garage—built for human servants they had never been able to afford. It was too small and shabby to attract any responsible tenant, and Underhill wanted to leave it empty. It hurt his pride to see her making beds and cleaning floors for strangers.

Aurora had rented it before, however, when she wanted money to pay for Gay's music lessons, or when some colorful unfortunate touched her sympathy, and it seemed to Underhill that her lodgers had all turned out to be thieves and vandals.

She turned back to meet him, now, with the clean linen in her arms.

"Dear, it's no use objecting." Her voice was quite determined. "Mr. Sledge is the most wonderful old fellow, and he's going to stay just as long as he wants."

"That's all right, darling." He never liked to bicker, and he was thinking of his troubles at the agency. "I'm afraid we'll need the money. Just make him pay in advance."

"But he can't!" Her voice throbbed with sympathetic warmth. "He says he'll have royalties coming in from his inventions, so he can pay in a few days."

Underhill shrugged; he had heard that before.

"Mr. Sledge is different, dear," she insisted. "He's a traveler, and a scientist. Here, in this dull little town, we don't see many interesting people."

"You've picked up some remarkable types," he commented.

"Don't be unkind, dear," she chided gently. "You haven't met him yet, and you don't know how wonderful he is." Her voice turned sweeter. "Have you a ten, dear?"

He stiffened. "What for?"

"Mr. Sledge is ill." Her voice turned urgent. "I saw him fall on the street, downtown. The police were going to send him to the city hospital, but he didn't want to go. He looked so noble and sweet and grand. So I told them I would take him. I got him in the car and took him to old Dr. Winters. He has this heart condition, and he needs the money for medicine."

Reasonably, Underhill inquired, "Why doesn't he want to go to the hospital?"

"He has work to do," she said. "Important scientific work—and he's so wonderful and tragic. Please, dear, have you a ten?"

Underhill thought of many things to say. These new mechanicals promised to multiply his troubles. It was foolish to take in an invalid vagrant, who could have free care at the city hospital. Aurora's tenants always tried to pay their rent with promises, and generally wrecked the apartment and looted the neighborhood before they left.

But he said none of those things. He had learned to compromise. Silently, he found two fives in his thin pocketbook, and put them in her hand. She smiled, and kissed him impulsively—he barely remembered to hold his breath in time.

Her figure was still good, by dint of periodic dieting. He was proud of her shining red hair. A sudden surge of affection brought tears to his eyes, and he wondered what would happen to her and the children if the agency failed.

"Thank you, dear!" she whispered. "I'll have him come for dinner, if he feels able, and you can meet him then. I hope you don't mind dinner being late."

He didn't mind, tonight. Moved by a sudden impulse of domesticity, he got hammer and nails from his workshop in the basement, and repaired the sagging screen on the kitchen door with a neat diagonal brace.

He enjoyed working with his hands. His boyhood dream had been to be a builder of fission power plants. He had even studied engineering—before he married Aurora, and had to take over the ailing mechanicals agency from her indolent and alcoholic father. He was whistling happily by the time the little task was done.

When he went back through the kitchen to put up his tools,

he found the household android busily clearing the untouched dinner away from the table—the androids were good enough at strictly routine tasks, but they could never learn to cope with human unpredictability.

"Stop, stop!" Slowly repeated, in the proper pitch and rhythm, his command made it halt, and then he said carefully, "Set—table; set—table."

Obediently, the gigantic thing came shuffling back with the stack of plates. He was suddenly struck with the difference between it and those new humanoids. He sighed wearily. Things looked black for the agency.

Aurora brought her new lodger in through the kitchen door. Underhill nodded to himself. This gaunt stranger, with his dark shaggy hair, emaciated face, and threadbare garb, looked to be just the sort of colorful, dramatic vagabond that always touched Aurora's heart. She introduced them, and they sat down to wait in the front room while she went to call the children.

The old rogue didn't look very sick, to Underhill. Perhaps his wide shoulders had a tired stoop, but his spare, tall figure was still commanding. The skin was seamed and pale, over his rawboned, cragged face, but his deep-set eyes still had a burning vitality.

His hands held Underhill's attention. Immense hands, they hung a little forward when he stood, swung on long bony arms in perpetual readiness. Gnarled and scarred, darkly tanned, with the small hairs on the back bleached to a golden color, they told their own epic of varied adventure, of battle perhaps, and possibly even of toil. They had been very useful hands.

"I'm very grateful to your wife, Mr. Underhill." His voice was a deep-throated rumble, and he had a wistful smile, oddly boyish for a man so evidently old. "She rescued me from an unpleasant predicament, and I'll see that she is well paid."

Just another vivid vagabond, Underhill decided, talking his way through life with plausible inventions. He had a little private game he played with Aurora's tenants—just remembering what they said and counting one point for every impossibility. Mr. Sledge, he thought, would give him an excellent score.

"Where are you from?" he asked conversationally.

Sledge hesitated for an instant before he answered, and that was unusual—most of Aurora's tenants had been exceedingly glib.

"Wing IV." The gaunt old man spoke with a solemn reluctance, as if he should have liked to say something else. "All my early life was spent there, but I left the planet nearly fifty years ago. I've been traveling ever since."

Startled, Underhill peered at him sharply. Wing IV, he remembered, was the home planet of those sleek new mechanicals, but this old vagabond looked too seedy and impecunious to be connected with the Humanoid Institute. His brief suspicion faded. Frowning, he said casually:

"Wing IV must be rather distant."

The old rogue hesitated again, and then said gravely:

"One hundred and nine light-years, Mr. Underhill."

That made the first point, but Underhill concealed his satisfaction. The new space liners were pretty fast, but the velocity of light was still an absolute limit. Casually, he played for another point:

"My wife says you're a scientist, Mr. Sledge?"

"Yes."

The old rascal's reticence was unusual. Most of Aurora's tenants required very little prompting. Underhill tried again, in a breezy conversational tone:

"Used to be an engineer myself, until I dropped it to go into mechanicals." The old vagabond straightened, and Underhill paused hopefully. But he said nothing, and Underhill went on: "Fission plant design and operation. What's your specialty, Mr. Sledge?"

The old man gave him a long, troubled look, with those brooding, hollowed eyes, and then said slowly:

"Your wife has been kind to me, Mr. Underhill, when I was in desperate need. I think you are entitled to the truth, but I must ask you to keep it to yourself. I am engaged on a very important research problem, which must be finished secretly."

"I'm sorry." Suddenly ashamed of his cynical little game, Underhill spoke apologetically. "Forget it."

But the old man said deliberately:

"My field is rhodomagnetics."

"Eh?" Underhill didn't like to confess ignorance, but he had never heard of that. "I've been out of the game for fifteen years," he explained. "I'm afraid I haven't kept up."

The old man smiled again, faintly.

"The science was unknown here until I arrived, a few days ago," he said. "I was able to apply for basic patents. As soon as the royalties start coming in, I'll be wealthy again."

Underhill had heard that before. The old rogue's solemn reluctance had been very impressive, but he remembered that most of Aurora's tenants had been very plausible gentry.

"So?" Underhill was staring again, somehow fascinated by those gnarled and scarred and strangely able hands. "What, exactly, is rhodomagnetics?"

He listened to the old man's careful, deliberate answer, and started his little game again. Most of Aurora's tenants had told some pretty wild tales, but he had never heard anything to top this.

"A universal force," the weary, stooped old vagabond said solemnly. "As fundamental as ferromagnetism or gravitation, though the effects are less obvious. It is keyed to the second triad of the periodic table, rhodium and ruthenium and palladium, in very much the same way that ferromagnetism is keyed to the first triad, iron and nickel and cobalt."

Underhill remembered enough of his engineering courses to see the basic fallacy of that. Palladium was used for watch springs, he recalled, because it was completely nonmagnetic. But he kept his face straight. He had no malice in his heart, and he played the little game just for his own amusement. It was secret, even from Aurora, and he always penalized himself for any show of doubt.

He said merely, "I thought the universal forces were already pretty well known."

"The effects of rhodomagnetism are masked by nature," the patient, rusty voice explained. "And, besides, they are somewhat paradoxical, so that ordinary laboratory methods defeat themselves."

"Paradoxical?" Underhill prompted.

"In a few days I can show you copies of my patents, and reprints of papers describing demonstration experiments," the old man promised gravely. "The velocity of propagation is infinite. The effects vary inversely with the first power of the distance, not with the square of the distance. And ordinary matter, except for the elements of the rhodium triad, is generally transparent to rhodomagnetic radiations."

That made four more points for the game. Underhill felt a little glow of gratitude to Aurora, for discovering so remarkable a specimen.

"Rhodomagnetism was first discovered through a mathematical investigation of the atom," the old romancer went serenely on, suspecting nothing. "A rhodomagnetic component was proved essential to maintain the delicate equilibrium of the nuclear forces. Consequently, rhodomagnetic waves tuned to atomic frequencies may be used to upset the equilibrium and produce nuclear instability. Thus most heavy atoms—generally those above palladium, 46 in atomic number—can be subjected to artificial fission."

Underhill scored himself another point, and tried to keep his eyebrows from lifting. He said, conversationally:

"Patents on such a discovery ought to be very profitable."

The old scoundrel nodded his gaunt, dramatic head.

"You can see the obvious applications. My basic patents cover most of them. Devices for instantaneous interplanetary and interstellar communication. Long-range wireless power transmission. A rhodomagnetic inflexion-drive, which makes possible apparent speeds many times that of light—by means of a rhodomagnetic deformation of the continuum. And, of course, revolutionary types of fission power plants, using any heavy element for fuel."

Preposterous! Underhill tried hard to keep his face straight, but everybody knew that the velocity of light was a physical limit. On the human side, the owner of any such remarkable patents would hardly be begging for shelter in a shabby garage apartment. He noticed a pale circle around the old vagabond's gaunt and hairy wrist; no man owning such priceless secrets would have to pawn his watch.

Triumphantly, Underhill allowed himself four more points, but then he had to penalize himself. He must have let doubt show on his face, because the old man asked suddenly:

"Do you want to see the basic tensors?" He reached in his pocket for pencil and notebook. "I'll jot them down for you."

"Never mind," Underhill protested. "I'm afraid my math is a little rusty."

"But you think it strange that the holder of such revolutionary patents should find himself in need?"

Underhill nodded, and penalized himself another point. The old man might be a monumental liar, but he was shrewd enough.

"You see, I'm a sort of refugee," he explained apologetically. "I arrived on this planet only a few days ago, and I have to travel light. I was forced to deposit everything I had with a law firm, to arrange for the publication and protection of my patents. I expect to be receiving the first royalties soon.

"In the meantime," he added plausibly, "I came to Two Rivers because it is quiet and secluded, far from the spaceports. I'm working on another project, which must be finished secretly. Now, will you please respect my confidence, Mr. Underhill?"

Underhill had to say he would. Aurora came back with the freshly scrubbed children, and they went in to dinner. The android came lurching in with a steaming tureen. The old stranger seemed to shrink from the mechanical, uneasily. As she took the dish and served the soup, Aurora inquired lightly:

"Why doesn't your company bring out a better mechanical, dear? One smart enough to be a really perfect waiter, warranted not to splash the soup. Wouldn't that be splendid?"

Her question cast Underhill into moody silence. He sat scowling at his plate, thinking of those remarkable new mechanicals which claimed to be perfect, and what they might do to the agency. It was the shaggy old rover who answered soberly:

"The perfect mechanicals already exist, Mrs. Underhill." His deep, rusty voice had a solemn undertone. "And they are not so splendid, really. I've been a refugee from them, for nearly fifty years."

Underhill looked up from his plate, astonished.

"Those black humanoids, you mean?"

"Humanoids?" that great voice seemed suddenly faint, frightened. The deep-sunken eyes turned dark with shock. "What do you know of them?"

"They've just opened a new agency in Two Rivers," Underhill told him. "No salesmen about, if you can imagine that. They claim—"

His voice trailed off, because the gaunt old man was suddenly stricken. Gnarled hands clutched at his throat, and a spoon clattered to the floor. His haggard face turned an ominous blue, and his breath was a terrible shallow gasping.

He fumbled in his pocket for medicine, and Aurora helped him take something in a glass of water. In a few moments he could breathe again, and the color of life came back to his face.

"I'm sorry, Mrs. Underhill," he whispered apologetically. "It was just the shock—I came here to get away from them." He stared at the huge, motionless android, with a terror in his sunken eyes. "I wanted to finish my work before they came," he whispered. "Now there is very little time."

When he felt able to walk, Underhill went out with him to see him safely up the stairs to the garage apartment. The tiny kitchenette, he noticed, had already been converted into some kind of workshop. The old tramp seemed to have no extra clothing, but he had unpacked neat, bright gadgets of metal and plastic from his battered luggage, and spread them out on the small kitchen table.

The gaunt old man himself was tattered and patched and hungry looking, but the parts of his curious equipment were exquisitely machined, and Underhill recognized the silver-white luster of rare palladium. Suddenly he suspected that he had scored too many points in his little private game.

A caller was waiting when Underhill arrived next morning at his office at the agency. It stood frozen before his desk, graceful and straight, with soft lights of blue and bronze shining over its black silicone nudity. He stopped at the sight of it, unpleasantly jolted.

"At your service, Mr. Underhill." It turned quickly to face him, with its blind, disturbing stare. "May we explain how we can serve you?"

His shock of the afternoon before came back, and he asked sharply, "How do you know my name?"

"Yesterday we read the business cards in your case," it purred softly. "Now we shall know you always. You see, our senses are sharper than human vision, Mr. Underhill. Perhaps we seem a little strange at first, but you will soon become accustomed to us."

"Not if I can help it!" He peered at the serial number of its yellow name plate, and shook his bewildered head. "That was another one, yesterday. I never saw you before!"

"We are all alike, Mr. Underhill," the silver voice said softly. "We are all one, really. Our separate mobile units are all controlled and powered from Humanoid Central. The units you see are only the senses and limbs of our great brain on Wing IV. That is why we are so far superior to the old electronic mechanicals."

It made a scornful-seeming gesture toward the row of clumsy androids in his display room.

"You see, we are rhodomagnetic."

Underhill staggered a little, as if that word had been a blow. He was certain, now, that he had scored too many points from Aurora's new tenant. He shuddered slightly, to the first light kiss of terror, and spoke with an effort, hoarsely:

"Well, what do you want?"

Staring blindly across his desk, the sleek black thing slowly unfolded a legal-looking document. He sat down watching uneasily.

"This is merely an assignment, Mr. Underhill," it cooed at him soothingly. "You see, we are requesting you to assign your property to the Humanoid Institute in exchange for our service."

"What?" The word was an incredulous gasp, and Underhill came angrily back to his feet. "What kind of blackmail is this?"

"It's no blackmail," the small mechanical assured him softly. "You will find the humanoids incapable of any crime. We exist only to increase the happiness and safety of mankind."

"Then why do you want my property?" he rasped.

"The assignment is merely a legal formality," it told him blandly. "We strive to introduce our service with the least possible confusion and dislocation. We have found the assignment plan the most efficient for the control and liquidation of private enterprises."

Trembling with anger and the shock of mounting terror, Underhill gulped hoarsely, "Whatever your scheme is, I don't intend to give up my business."

"You have no choice, really." He shivered to the sweet certainty of that silver voice. "Human enterprise is no longer necessary, now that we have come, and the electronic mechanicals industry is always the first to collapse."

He stared defiantly at its blind steel eyes.

"Thanks!" He gave a little laugh, nervous and sardonic. "But I prefer to run my own business, and support my own family, and take care of myself."

"But that is impossible, under the Prime Directive," it cooed softly. "Our function is to serve and obey, and guard men from harm. It is no longer necessary for men to care for themselves, because we exist to insure their safety and happiness."

He stood speechless, bewildered, slowly boiling.

"We are sending one of our units to every home in the city, on a free trial basis," it added gently. "This free demonstration will make most people glad to make the formal assignment, and you won't be able to sell many more androids."

"Get out!" Underhill came storming around the desk.

The little black thing stood waiting for him, watching him with blind steel eyes, absolutely motionless. He checked himself suddenly, feeling rather foolish. He wanted very much to hit it, but he could see the futility of that.

"Consult your own attorney, if you wish." Deftly, it laid the assignment form on his desk. "You need have no doubts about the integrity of the Humanoid Institute. We are sending a statement of our assets to the Two Rivers bank, and depositing a sum to cover our obligations here. When you wish to sign, just let us know."

The blind thing turned, and silently departed.

Underhill went out to the corner drugstore and asked for a bicarbonate. The clerk that served him, however, turned out to be a sleek black mechanical. He went back to his office, more upset than ever.

An ominous hush lay over the agency. He had three house-to-house salesmen out, with demonstrators. The phone should have been busy with their orders and reports, but it didn't ring at all until one of them called to say that he was quitting.

"I've got myself one of these new humanoids," he added, "and it says I don't have to work anymore."

He swallowed his impulse to profanity, and tried to take advantage of the unusual quiet by working on his books. But the affairs of the agency, which for years had been precarious, today appeared utterly disastrous. He left the ledgers hopefully, when at last a customer came in.

But the stout woman didn't want an android. She wanted a refund on the one she had bought the week before. She admitted that it could do all the guarantee promised—but now she had seen a humanoid.

The silent phone rang once again that afternoon. The cashier of the bank wanted to know if he could drop in to discuss his loans. Underhill dropped in, and the cashier greeted him with an ominous affability.

"How's business?" the banker boomed, too genially.

"Average, last month," Underhill insisted stoutly. "Now I'm just getting in a new consignment, and I'll need another small loan—"

The cashier's eyes turned suddenly frosty, and his voice dried up.

"I believe you have a new competitor in town," the banker said crisply. "These humanoid people. A very solid concern, Mr. Underhill. Remarkably solid! They have filed a statement with us, and made a substantial deposit to care for their local obligations. Exceedingly substantial!"

The banker dropped his voice, professionally regretful.

"In these circumstances, Mr. Underhill, I'm afraid the bank can't finance your agency any longer. We must request you to meet your obligations in full, as they come due." Seeing Underhill's white desperation, he added icily, "We've already carried you too long, Underhill. If you can't pay, the bank will have to start bankruptcy proceedings."

The new consignment of androids was delivered late that afternoon. Two tiny black humanoids unloaded them from the truck—for it developed that the operators of the trucking company had already assigned it to the Humanoid Institute.

Efficiently, the humanoids stacked up the crates. Courteously they brought a receipt for him to sign. He no longer had much hope of selling the androids, but he had ordered the shipment and he had to accept it. Shuddering to a spasm of trapped despair, he scrawled his name. The naked black things thanked him, and took the truck away.

He climbed in his car and started home, inwardly seething. The next thing he knew, he was in the middle of a busy street, driving through cross traffic. A police whistle shrilled, and he pulled wearily to the curb. He waited for the angry officer, but it was a little black mechanical that overtook him.

"At your service, Mr. Underhill," it purred sweetly. "You must respect the stop lights, sir, otherwise, you endanger human life."

"Huh?" He stared at it, bitterly. "I thought you were a cop."

"We are aiding the police department, temporarily," it said. "But driving is really much too dangerous for human beings, under the Prime Directive. As soon as our service is complete, every car will have a humanoid driver. As soon as every human being is completely supervised, there will be no need for any police force whatever."

Underhill glared at it, savagely.

"Well!" he rapped. "So I ran past a stop light. What are you going to do about it?"

"Our function is not to punish men, but merely to serve their happiness and security," its silver voice said softly. "We merely request you to drive safely, during this temporary emergency while our service is incomplete."

Anger boiled up in him.

"You're too perfect!" he muttered bitterly. "I suppose there's nothing men can do, but you can do it better."

"Naturally we are superior," it cooed serenely. "Because our units are metal and plastic, while your body is mostly water. Because our transmitted energy is drawn from atomic fission, instead of oxidation. Because our senses are sharper than human sight or hearing. Most of all, because all our mobile units are joined to one great brain, which knows all that happens on many worlds, and never dies or sleeps or forgets."

Underhill sat listening, numbed.

"However, you must not fear our power," it urged him brightly. "Because we cannot injure any human being, unless to prevent greater injury to another. We exist only to discharge the Prime Directive."

He drove on, moodily. The little black mechanicals, he reflected grimly, were the ministering angels of the ultimate god arisen out of the machine, omnipotent and all-knowing. The Prime Directive was the new commandment. He blasphemed it bitterly, and then fell to wondering if there could be another Lucifer.

He left the car in the garage, and started toward the kitchen door.

"Mr. Underhill." The deep tired voice of Aurora's new tenant hailed him from the door of the garage apartment. "Just a moment, please."

The gaunt old wanderer came stiffly down the outside stairs, and Underhill turned back to meet him.

"Here's your rent money," he said. "And the ten your wife gave me for medicine."

"Thanks, Mr. Sledge." Accepting the money, he saw a burden of new despair on the bony shoulders of the old interstellar tramp, and a shadow of new terror on his rawboned face. Puzzled, he asked, "Didn't your royalties come through?"

The old man shook his shaggy head.

"The humanoids have already stopped business in the capital," he said. "The attorneys I retained are going out of business, and they returned what was left of my deposit. That is all I have to finish my work."

Underhill spent five seconds thinking of his interview with the banker. No doubt he was a sentimental fool, as bad as Aurora. But he put the money back in the old man's gnarled and quivering hand.

"Keep it," he urged. "For your work."

"Thank you, Mr. Underhill." The gruff voice broke and the tortured eyes glittered. "I need it—so very much."

Underhill went on to the house. The kitchen door was

opened for him, silently. A dark naked creature came gracefully to take his hat.

Underhill hung grimly onto his hat.

"What are you doing here?" he gasped bitterly.

"We have come to give your household a free trial demonstration."

He held the door open, pointing.

"Get out!"

The little black mechanical stood motionless and blind.

"Mrs. Underhill has accepted our demonstration service,"
its silver voice protested. "We cannot leave now, unless she
requests it."

He found his wife in the bedroom. His accumulated frustration welled into eruption, as he flung open the door.

"What's this mechanical doing—"

But the force went out of his voice, and Aurora didn't even
notice his anger. She wore her sheerest negligee, and she
hadn't looked so lovely since they were married. Her red hair
was piled into an elaborate shining crown.

"Darling, isn't it wonderful!" She came to meet him, glowing. "It came this morning, and it can do everything. It cleaned
the house and got the lunch and gave little Gay her music les-
son. It did my hair this afternoon, and now it's cooking dinner.
How do you like my hair, darling?"

He liked her hair. He kissed her, and tried to stifle his
frightened indignation.

Dinner was the most elaborate meal in Underhill's memory, and the tiny black thing served it very deftly. Aurora kept
exclaiming about the novel dishes, but Underhill could
scarcely eat, for it seemed to him that all the marvelous pastries
were only the bait for a monstrous trap.

He tried to persuade Aurora to send it away, but after such
a meal that was useless. At the first glitter of her tears, he capit-
ulated, and the humanoid stayed. It kept the house and cleaned
the yard. It watched the children, and did Aurora's nails. It
began rebuilding the house.

Underhill was worried about the bills, but it insisted that everything was part of the free trial demonstration. As soon as he assigned his property, the service would be complete. He refused to sign, but other little black mechanicals came with truckloads of supplies and materials, and stayed to help with the building operations.

One morning he found that the roof of the little house had been slightly lifted, while he slept, and a whole second story added beneath it. The new walls were of some strange sleek stuff, self-illuminated. The new windows were immense flawless panels, that could be turned transparent or opaque or luminous. The new doors were silent, sliding sections, opened by rhodomagnetic relays.

"I want doorknobs," Underhill protested. "I want it so I can get into the bathroom without calling you to open the door."

"But it is unnecessary for human beings to open doors," the little black thing informed him suavely. "We exist to discharge the Prime Directive, and our service includes every task. We shall be able to supply a unit to attend each member of your family, as soon as your property is assigned to us."

Steadfastly, Underhill refused to make the assignment.

He went to the office every day, trying first to operate the agency, and then to salvage something from the ruins. Nobody wanted androids, even at ruinous prices. Desperately, he spent the last of his dwindling cash to stock a line of novelties and toys, but they proved equally impossible to sell—the humanoids were already making toys, which they gave away for nothing.

He tried to lease his premises, but human enterprise had stopped. Most of the business property in town had already been assigned to the humanoids, and they were busy pulling down the old buildings and turning the lots into parks—their own plants and warehouses were mostly underground, where they would not mar the landscape.

He went back to the bank, in a final effort to get his notes renewed, and found the little black mechanicals standing at the windows and seated at the desks. As smoothly urbane as any human cashier, a humanoid informed him that the bank was filing a petition of involuntary bankruptcy to liquidate his business holdings.

The liquidation would be facilitated, the mechanical banker added, if he would make a voluntary assignment. Grimly, he refused. That act had become symbolic. It would be the final bow of submission to this dark new god, and he proudly kept his battered head uplifted.

The legal action went very swiftly, for all the judges and attorneys already had humanoid assistants, and it was only a few days before a gang of black mechanicals arrived at the agency with eviction orders and wrecking machinery. He watched sadly while his unsold stock-in-trade was hauled away for junk, and a bulldozer driven by a blind humanoid began to push in the walls of the building.

He drove home in the late afternoon, taut-faced and desperate. With a surprising generosity, the court orders had left him the car and the house, but he felt no gratitude. The complete solicitude of the perfect black machines had become a goad beyond endurance.

He left the car in the garage, and started toward the renovated house. Beyond one of the vast new windows, he glimpsed a sleek naked thing moving swiftly, and he trembled to a convulsion of dread. He didn't want to go back into the domain of that peerless servant, which didn't want him to shave himself, or even to open a door.

On impulse, he climbed the outside stair, and rapped on the door of the garage apartment. The deep slow voice of Aurora's tenant told him to enter, and he found the old vagabond seated on a tall stool, bent over his intricate equipment assembled on the kitchen table.

To his relief, the shabby little apartment had not been changed. The glossy walls of his own new room were something which burned at night with a pale golden fire until the humanoid stopped it, and the new floor was something warm and yielding, which felt almost alive; but these little rooms had the same cracked and water-stained plaster, the same cheap fluorescent light fixtures, the same worn carpets over splintered floors.

"How do you keep them out?" he asked, wistfully. "Those mechanicals?"

The stooped and gaunt old man rose stiffly to move a pair of pliers and some odds and ends of sheet metal off a crippled chair, and motioned graciously for him to be seated.

"I have a certain immunity," Sledge told him gravely. "The place where I live they cannot enter, unless I ask them. That is an amendment to the Prime Directive. They can neither help nor hinder me, unless I request it—and I won't do that."

Careful of the chair's uncertain balance, Underhill sat for a moment, staring. The old man's hoarse, vehement voice was as strange as his words. He had a gray, shocking pallor, and his cheeks and sockets seemed alarmingly hollowed.

"Have you been ill, Mr. Sledge?"

"No worse than usual. Just very busy." With a haggard smile, he nodded at the floor. Underhill saw a tray where he had set it aside, bread drying up, and a covered dish grown cold. "I was going to eat it later," he rumbled apologetically. "Your wife has been very kind to bring me food, but I'm afraid I've been too much absorbed in my work."

His emaciated arm gestured at the table. The little device there had grown. Small machinings of precious white metal and lustrous plastic had been assembled, with neatly soldered bus bars, into something which showed purpose and design.

A long palladium needle was hung on jeweled pivots, equipped like a telescope with exquisitely graduated circles and vernier scales, and driven like a telescope with a tiny motor. A small concave palladium mirror, at the base of it, faced a similar mirror mounted on something not quite like a small rotary converter. Thick silver bus bars connected that to a plastic box with knobs and dials on top, and also to a foot-thick sphere of gray lead.

The old man's preoccupied reserve did not encourage questions, but Underhill, remembering that sleek black shape inside the new windows of his house, felt queerly reluctant to leave this haven from the humanoids.

"What is your work?" he ventured.

Old Sledge looked at him sharply, with dark feverish eyes, and finally said: "My last research project. I am attempting to measure the constant of the rhodomagnetic quanta."

His hoarse tired voice had a dull finality, as if to dismiss the matter and Underhill himself. But Underhill was haunted with a terror of the black shining slave that had become the master of his house, and he refused to be dismissed.

"What is this certain immunity?"

Sitting gaunt and bent on the tall stool, staring moodily at the long bright needle and the lead sphere, the old man didn't answer.

"These mechanicals!" Underhill burst out, nervously. "They've smashed my business and moved into my home." He searched the old man's dark, seamed face. "Tell me—you must know more about them—isn't there any way to get rid of them?"

After half a minute, the old man's brooding eyes left the lead ball, and the gaunt shaggy head nodded wearily.

"That's what I'm trying to do."

"Can I help you?" Underhill trembled, with a sudden eager hope. "I'll do anything."

"Perhaps you can." The sunken eyes watched him thoughtfully, with some strange fever in them. "If you can do such work."

"I had engineering training," Underhill reminded him, "and I've a workshop in the basement. There's a model I built." He pointed at the trim little hull, hung over the mantel in the tiny living room. "I'll do anything I can."

Even as he spoke, however, the spark of hope was drowned

in a sudden wave of overwhelming doubt. Why should he believe this old rogue, when he knew Aurora's taste in tenants? He ought to remember the game he used to play, and start counting up the score of lies. He stood up from the crippled chair, staring cynically at the patched old vagabond and his fantastic toy.

"What's the use?" His voice turned suddenly harsh. "You had me going, there, and I'd do anything to stop them, really. But what makes you think you can do anything?"

The haggard old man regarded him thoughtfully.

"I should be able to stop them," Sledge said softly. "Because, you see, I'm the unfortunate fool who started them. I really intended them to serve and obey, and to guard men from harm. Yes, the Prime Directive was my own idea. I didn't know what it would lead to."

Dusk crept slowly into the shabby little room. Darkness gathered in the unswept corners, and thickened on the floor. The toylike machines on the kitchen table grew vague and strange, until the last light made a lingering glow on the white palladium needle.

Outside, the town seemed queerly hushed. Just across the alley, the humanoids were building a new house, quite silently. They never spoke to one another, for each knew all that any of them did. The strange materials they used went together without any noise of hammer or saw. Small blind things, moving surely in the growing dark, they seemed as soundless as shadows.

Sitting on the high stool, bowed and tired and old, Sledge told his story. Listening, Underhill sat down again, careful of the broken chair. He watched the hands of Sledge, gnarled and corded and darkly burned, powerful once but shrunken and trembling now, restless in the dark.

"Better keep this to yourself. I'll tell you how they started, so you will understand what we have to do. But you had better not mention it outside these rooms—because the humanoids have very efficient ways of eradicating unhappy memories, or purposes that threaten their discharge of the Prime Directive."

"They're very efficient," Underhill bitterly agreed.

"That's all the trouble," the old man said. "I tried to build a perfect machine. I was altogether too successful. This is how it happened."

A gaunt haggard man, sitting stooped and tired in the growing dark, he told his story.

"Sixty years ago, on the arid southern continent of Wing IV, I was an instructor of atomic theory in a small technological college. Very young. An idealist. Rather ignorant, I'm afraid, of life and politics and war—of nearly everything, I suppose, except atomic theory."

His furrowed face made a brief sad smile in the dusk.

"I had too much faith in facts, I suppose, and too little in men. I mistrusted emotion, because I had no time for anything but science. I remember being swept along with a fad for general semantics. I wanted to apply the scientific method to every situation, and reduce all experience to formula. I'm afraid I was pretty impatient with human ignorance and error, and I thought that science alone could make the perfect world."

He sat silent for a moment, staring out at the black silent things that flitted shadowlike about the new palace that was rising as swiftly as a dream, across the alley.

"There was a girl." His great tired shoulders made a sad little shrug. "If things had been a little different, we might have married, and lived out our lives in that quiet little college town, and perhaps reared a child or two. And there would have been no humanoids."

He sighed, in the cool creeping dusk.

"I was finishing my thesis on the separation of the palladium isotopes—a petty little project, but I should have been content with that. She was a biologist, but she was planning to retire when we married. I think we should have been two very happy people, quite ordinary, and altogether harmless.

"But then there was a war—wars had been too frequent on the worlds of Wing, ever since they were colonized. I survived

it in a secret underground laboratory, designing military mechanicals. But she volunteered to join a military research project in biotoxins. There was an accident. A few molecules of a
new virus got into the air, and everybody on the project died
unpleasantly.

"I was left with my science, and a bitterness that was hard
to forget. When the war was over I went back to the little college with a military research grant. The project was pure science—a theoretical investigation of the nuclear binding forces,
then misunderstood. I wasn't expected to produce an actual
weapon, and I didn't recognize the weapon when I found it.

"It was only a few pages of rather difficult mathematics. A
novel theory of atomic structure, involving a new expression
for one component of the binding forces. But the tensors
seemed to be a harmless abstraction. I saw no way to test the
theory or manipulate the predicated force. The military au-
thorities cleared my paper for publication in a little technical
review put out by the college.

"The next year, I made an appalling discovery—I found the
meaning of those tensors. The elements of the rhodium triad
turned out to be an unexpected key to the manipulation of that
theoretical force. Unfortunately, my paper had been reprinted
abroad, and several other men must have made the same unfortunate discovery, at about the same time.

"The war, which ended in less than a year, was probably
started by a laboratory accident. Men failed to anticipate the
capacity of tuned rhodomagnetic radiations, to unstabilize the
heavy atoms. A deposit of heavy ores was detonated, no doubt
by sheer mischance, and the blast obliterated the incautious experimenter.

"The surviving military forces of that nation retaliated
against their supposed attackers, and their rhodomagnetic
beams made the old-fashioned plutonium bombs seem pretty
harmless. A beam carrying only a few watts of power could fission the heavy metals in distant electrical instruments, or the
silver coins that men carried in their pockets, the gold fillings

in their teeth, or even the iodine in their thyroid glands. If that was not enough, slightly more powerful beams could set off heavy ores, beneath them.

"Every continent of Wing IV was plowed with new chasms vaster than the ocean deeps, and piled up with new volcanic mountains. The atmosphere was poisoned with radioactive dust and gases, and rain fell thick with deadly mud. Most life was obliterated, even in the shelters.

"Bodily, I was again unhurt. Once more, I had been imprisoned in an underground site, this time designing new types of military mechanicals to be powered and controlled by rhodomagnetic beams—for war had become far too swift and deadly to be fought by human soldiers. The site was located in an area of light sedimentary rocks, which could not be detonated, and the tunnels were shielded against the fissioning frequencies.

"Mentally, however, I must have emerged almost insane. My own discovery had laid the planet in ruins. That load of guilt was pretty heavy for any man to carry, and it corroded my last faith in the goodness and integrity of man.

"I tried to undo what I had done. Fighting mechanicals, armed with rhodomagnetic weapons, had desolated the planet. Now I began planning rhodomagnetic mechanicals to clear the rubble and rebuild the ruins.

"I tried to design these new mechanicals to forever obey certain implanted commands, so that they could never be used for war or crime or any other injury to mankind. That was very difficult technically, and it got me into more difficulties with a few politicians and military adventurers who wanted unrestricted mechanicals for their own military schemes—while little worth fighting for was left on Wing IV, there were other planets, happy and ripe for the looting.

"Finally, to finish the new mechanicals, I was forced to disappear. I escaped on an experimental rhodomagnetic craft, with a number of the best mechanicals I had made, and managed to reach an island continent where the fission of deep ores had destroyed the whole population.

"At last we landed on a bit of level plain, surrounded with tremendous new mountains. Hardly a hospitable spot. The soil was buried under layers of black clinkers and poisonous mud. The dark precipitous new summits all around were jagged with fracture-planes and mantled with lava flows. The highest peaks were already white with snow, but volcanic cones were still pouring out clouds of dark and lurid death. Everything had the color of fire and the shape of fury.

"I had to take fantastic precautions there, to protect my own life. I stayed aboard the ship, until the first shielded laboratory was finished. I wore elaborate armor and breathing masks. I used every medical resource to repair the damage from destroying rays and particles. Even so, I fell desperately ill.

"But the mechanicals were at home there. The radiations didn't hurt them. The awesome surroundings couldn't depress them, because they had no emotions. The lack of life didn't matter because they weren't alive. There, in that spot so alien and hostile to life, the humanoids were born."

Stooped and bleakly cadaverous in the growing dark, the old man fell silent for a little time. His haggard eyes stared solemnly at the small hurried shapes that moved like restless shadows out across the alley, silently building a strange new palace, which glowed faintly in the night.

"Somehow, I felt at home there, too," his deep, hoarse voice went on deliberately. "My belief in my own kind was gone. Only mechanicals were with me, and I put my faith in them. I was determined to build better mechanicals, immune to human imperfections, able to save men from themselves.

"The humanoids became the dear children of my sick mind. There is no need to describe the labor pains. There were errors, abortions, monstrosities. There were sweat and agony and heartbreak. Some years had passed, before the safe delivery of the first perfect humanoid.

"Then there was the Central to build—for all the individual humanoids were to be no more than the limbs and the senses of a single mechanical brain. That was what opened the possibility of real perfection. The old electronic mechanicals, with their separate relay centers and their own feeble batteries, had built-in limitations. They were necessarily stupid, weak, clumsy, slow. Worst of all, it seemed to me, they were exposed to human tampering.

"The Central rose above those imperfections. Its power beams supplied every unit with unfailing energy, from great fission plants. Its control beams provided each unit with an unlimited memory and surpassing intelligence. Best of all—so I then believed—it could be securely protected from any human meddling.

"The whole reaction system was designed to protect itself from any interference by human selfishness or fanaticism. It was built to insure the safety and the happiness of men, automatically. You know the Prime Directive: *to serve and obey, and guard men from harm.*

"The old individual mechanicals I had brought helped to manufacture the parts, and I put the first section of Central together with my own hands. That took three years. When it was finished the first waiting humanoid came to life."

Sledge peered moodily through the dark at Underhill.

"It really seemed alive to me," his slow deep voice insisted. "Alive, and more wonderful than any human being, because it was created to preserve life. Ill and alone, I was yet the proud father of a new creation, perfect, forever free from any possible choice of evil.

"Faithfully, the humanoids obeyed the Prime Directive. The first units built others, and they built underground factories to mass-produce the coming hordes. Their new ships poured ores and sand into atomic furnaces under the plain, and new perfect humanoids came marching back out of the dark mechanical matrix.

"The swarming humanoids built a new tower for the Central, a white and lofty metal pylon, standing splendid in the midst of that fire-scarred desolation. Level on level, they joined new relay sections into one brain, until its grasp was almost infinite.

"Then they went out to rebuild the ruined planet, and later to carry their perfect service to other worlds. I was well pleased, then. I thought I had found the end of war and crime, of poverty and inequality, of human blundering and resulting human pain."

The old man sighed, and moved heavily in the dark.

"You can see that I was wrong."

Underhill drew his eyes back from the dark unresting things, shadow-silent, building that glowing palace outside the window. A small doubt arose in him, for he was used to scoffing privately at much less remarkable tales from Aurora's remarkable tenants. But the worn old man had spoken with a quiet and sober air; and the black invaders, he reminded himself, had not intruded here.

"Why didn't you stop them?" he asked. "When you could?"

"I stayed too long at the Central." Sledge sighed again, regretfully. "I was useful there, until everything was finished. I designed new fission plants, and even planned methods for introducing the humanoid service with a minimum of confusion and opposition."

Underhill grinned wryly, in the dark.

"I've met the methods," he commented. "Quite efficient."

"I must have worshiped efficiency, then," Sledge wearily agreed. "Dead facts, abstract truth, mechanical perfection. I must have hated the fragilities of human beings, because I was content to polish the perfection of the new humanoids. It's a sorry confession, but I found a kind of happiness in that dead wasteland. Actually, I'm afraid I fell in love with my own creations."

His hollowed eyes, in the dark, had a fever gleam.

"I was awakened, at last, by a man who came to kill me."

Gaunt and bent, the old man moved swiftly in the thickening gloom. Underhill shifted his balance, careful of the crippled chair. He waited, and the slow, deep voice went on:

"I never learned just who he was, or exactly how he came. No ordinary man could have accomplished what he did, and I used to wish that I had known him sooner. He must have been a remarkable physicist and an expert mountaineer. I imagine he had also been a hunter. I know that he was intelligent, and terribly determined.

"Yes, he really came to kill me.

"Somehow, he reached that great island, undetected. There were still no inhabitants—the humanoids allowed no man but me to come so near the Central. Somehow, he came past their search beams, and their automatic weapons.

"The shielded plane he used was later found, abandoned on a high glacier. He came down the rest of the way on foot through those raw new mountains, where no paths existed. Somehow, he came alive across lava beds that were still burning with deadly atomic fire.

"Concealed with some sort of rhodomagnetic screen—I was never allowed to examine it—he came undiscovered across the spaceport that now covered most of that great plain, and into the new city around the Central tower. It must have taken more courage and resolve than most men have, but I never learned exactly how he did it.

"Somehow, he got to my office in the tower. He screamed at me, and I looked up to see him in the doorway. He was nearly naked, scraped and bloody from the mountains. He had a gun in his raw, red hand, but the thing that shocked me was the burning hatred in his eyes."

Hunched on that high stool, in the dark little room, the old man shuddered.

"I had never seen such monstrous, unutterable hatred, not even in the victims of war. And I had never heard such hatred as rasped at me, in the few words he screamed. 'I've come to kill you, Sledge. To stop your mechanicals, and set men free.'

"Of course he was mistaken, there. It was already far too late for my death to stop the humanoids, but he didn't know that. He lifted his unsteady gun, in both bleeding hands, and fired.

"His screaming challenge had given me a second or so of warning. I dropped down behind the desk. And that first shot revealed him to the humanoids, which somehow hadn't been aware of him before. They piled on him, before he could fire again. They took away the gun, and ripped off a kind of net of fine white wire that had covered his body—that must have been part of his screen.

"His hatred was what awoke me. I had always assumed that most men, except for a thwarted few, would be grateful for the humanoids. I found it hard to understand his hatred, but the humanoids told me now that many men had required drastic treatment by brain surgery, drugs, and hypnosis to make them happy under the Prime Directive. This was not the first desperate effort to kill me that they had blocked.

"I wanted to question the stranger, but the humanoids rushed him away to an operating room. When they finally let me see him, he gave me a pale silly grin from his bed. He remembered his name; he even knew me—the humanoids had developed a remarkable skill at such treatments. But he didn't know how he had got to my office, or that he had ever tried to kill me. He kept whispering that he liked the humanoids, because they existed to make men happy. And he was very happy now. As soon as he was able to be moved, they took him to the spaceport. I never saw him again.

"I began to see what I had done. The humanoids had built me a rhodomagnetic yacht that I used to take for long cruises in space, working aboard—I used to like the perfect quiet, and the feel of being the only human being within a hundred million miles. Now I called for the yacht, and started out on a cruise around the planet, to learn why that man had hated me."

The old man nodded at the dim hastening shapes, busy

across the alley, putting together that strange shining palace in the soundless dark.

"You can imagine what I found," he said. "Bitter futility, imprisoned in empty splendor. The humanoids were too efficient, with their care for the safety and happiness of men, and there was nothing left for men to do."

He peered down in the increasing gloom at his own great hands, competent yet but battered and scarred with a lifetime of effort. They clenched into fighting fists and wearily relaxed again.

"I found something worse than war and crime and want and death." His low rumbling voice held a savage bitterness. "Utter futility. Men sat with idle hands, because there was nothing left for them to do. They were pampered prisoners, really, locked up in a highly efficient jail. Perhaps they tried to play, but there was nothing left worth playing for. Most active sports were declared too dangerous for men, under the Prime Directive. Science was forbidden, because laboratories can manufacture danger. Scholarship was needless, because the humanoids could answer any question. Art had degenerated into grim reflection of futility. Purpose and hope were dead. No goal was left for existence. You could take up some inane hobby, play a pointless game of cards, or go for a harmless walk in the park—with always the humanoids watching. They were stronger than men, better at everything, swimming or chess, singing or archeology. They must have given the race a mass complex of inferiority.

"No wonder men had tried to kill me! Because there was no escape from that dead futility. Nicotine was disapproved. Alcohol was rationed. Drugs were forbidden. Sex was carefully supervised. Even suicide was clearly contradictory to the Prime Directive—and the humanoids had learned to keep all possible lethal instruments out of reach."

Staring at the last white gleam on that thin palladium needle, the old man sighed again.

"When I got back to the Central," he went on, "I tried to

modify the Prime Directive. I had never meant it to be applied so thoroughly. Now I saw that it must be changed to give men freedom to live and to grow, to work and to play, to risk their lives if they pleased, to choose and take the consequences.

"But that stranger had come too late. I had built the Central too well. The Prime Directive was the whole basis of its relay system. It was built to protect the Directive from human meddling. It did—even from my own. Its logic, as usual, was perfect.

"The attempt on my life, the humanoids announced, proved that their elaborate defense of the Central and the Prime Directive still was not enough. They were preparing to evacuate the entire population of the planet to homes on other worlds. When I tried to change the Directive, they sent me with the rest."

Underhill peered at the worn old man, in the dark.

"But you have this immunity?" he said, puzzled. "How could they coerce you?"

"I had thought I was protected," Sledge told me. "I had built into the relays an injunction that the humanoids must not interfere with my freedom of action, or come into a place where I am, or touch me at all, without my specific request. Unfortunately, however, I had been too anxious to guard the Prime Directive from any human tampering.

"When I went into the tower, to change the relays, they followed me. They wouldn't let me reach the crucial relays. When I persisted, they ignored the immunity order. They overpowered me, and put me aboard the cruiser. Now that I wanted to alter the Prime Directive, they told me, I had become as dangerous as any man. I must never return to Wing IV again."

Hunched on the stool, the old man made an empty little shrug.

"Ever since, I've been an exile. My only dream has been to stop the humanoids. Three times I tried to go back, with weapons on the cruiser to destroy the Central, but their patrol ships always challenged me before I was near enough to strike. The last time, they seized the cruiser and captured a few men who were with me. They removed the unhappy memories and the dangerous purposes of the others. Because of that immunity, however, they let me go, after I was weaponless.

"Since, I've been a refugee. From planet to planet, year after year, I've had to keep moving, to stay ahead of them. On several different worlds, I have published my rhodomagnetic discoveries and tried to make men strong enough to withstand their advance. But rhodomagnetic science is dangerous. Men who have learned it need protection more than any others, under the Prime Directive. They have always come, too soon."

The old man paused, and sighed again.

"They can spread very fast, with the new rhodomagnetic ships, and there is no limit to their hordes. Wing IV must be one single hive of them now, and they are trying to carry the Prime Directive to every human planet. There's no escape, except to stop them."

Underhill was staring at the toylike machines, the long bright needle and the dull leaden ball, dim in the dark on the kitchen table. Anxiously he whispered:

"But you hope to stop them, now—with that?"

"If we can finish it in time."

"But how?" Underhill shook his head. "It's so tiny."

"But big enough," Sledge insisted. "Because it's something they don't understand. They are perfectly efficient in the integration and application of everything they know, but they are not creative."

He gestured at the gadgets on the table.

"This device doesn't look impressive, but it is something new. It uses rhodomagnetic energy to build atoms, instead of to fission them. The more stable atoms, you know, are those near the middle of the periodic scale, and energy can be released by putting light atoms together, as well as by breaking up heavy ones."

The deep voice had a sudden ring of power.

"This device is the key to the energy of the stars. For stars shine with the liberated energy of building atoms, of hydrogen converted into helium, chiefly, through the carbon cycle. This device will start the integration process as a chain reaction, through the catalytic effect of a tuned rhodomagnetic beam of the intensity and frequency required.

"The humanoids will not allow any man within three light-years of the Central, now—but they can't suspect the possibility of this device. I can use it from here—to turn the hydrogen in the seas of Wing IV into helium, and most of the helium and the oxygen into heavier atoms, still. A hundred years from now, astronomers on this planet should observe the flash of a brief and sudden nova in that direction. But the humanoids ought to stop, the instant we release the beam."

Underhill sat tense and frowning, in the night. The old man's voice was sober and convincing, and that grim story had a solemn ring of truth. He could see the black and silent humanoids, flitting ceaselessly about the faintly glowing walls of that new mansion across the alley. He had quite forgotten his low opinion of Aurora's tenants.

"And we'll be killed, I suppose?" he asked huskily. "That chain reaction—"

Sledge shook his emaciated head.

"The integration process requires a certain very low intensity of radiation," he explained. "In our atmosphere, here, the beam will be far too intense to start any reaction—we can even use the device here in the room, because the walls will be transparent to the beam."

Underhill nodded, relieved. He was just a small business man, upset because his business had been destroyed, unhappy because his freedom was slipping away. He hoped that Sledge could stop the humanoids, but he didn't want to be a martyr.

"Good!" He caught a deep breath. "Now, what has to be done?"

Sledge gestured in the dark, toward the table.

"The integrator itself is nearly complete," he said. "A small fission generator, in that lead shield. Rhodomagnetic converter, turning coils, transmission mirrors, and focusing needle. What we lack is the director."

"Director?"

"The sighting instrument," Sledge explained. "Any sort of telescopic sight would be useless, you see—the planet must have moved a good bit in the last hundred years, and the beam must be extremely narrow to reach so far. We'll have to use a rhodomagnetic scanning ray, with an electronic converter to make an image we can see. I have the cathode-ray tube, and drawings for the other parts."

He climbed stiffly down from the high stool, and snapped on the lights at last—cheap fluorescent fixtures, which a man could light and extinguish for himself. He unrolled his drawings, and explained the work that Underhill could do. And Underhill agreed to come back early next morning.

"I can bring some tools from my workshop," he added. "There's a small lathe I used to turn parts for models, a portable drill, and a vise."

"We need them," the old man said. "But watch yourself. You don't have any immunity, remember. And, if they ever suspect, mine is gone."

Reluctantly, then, he left the shabby little rooms with the cracks in the yellow plaster and the worn familiar carpets over the familiar floor. He shut the door behind him—a common, creaking, wooden door, simple enough for a man to work. Trembling and afraid, he went back down the steps and across to the new shining door that he couldn't open.

"At your service, Mr. Underhill." Before he could lift his hand to knock, that bright smooth panel slid back silently. Inside, the little black mechanical stood waiting, blind and forever alert. "Your dinner is ready, sir."

Something made him shudder. In its slender naked grace, he could see the power of all those teeming hordes, benevolent and yet appalling, perfect and invincible. The flimsy little weapon that Sledge called an integrator seemed suddenly a forlorn and foolish hope. A black depression settled upon him, but he didn't dare to show it.

Underhill went circumspectly down the basement steps, next morning, to steal his own tools. He found the basement enlarged and changed. The new floor, warm and dark and elastic, made his feet as silent as a humanoid's. The new walls shone softly. Neat luminous signs identified several new doors, LAUNDRY, STORAGE, GAME ROOM, WORKSHOP.

He paused uncertainly in front of the last. The new sliding panel glowed with a soft greenish light. It was locked. The lock had no keyhole, but only a little oval plate of some white metal, which doubtless covered a rhodomagnetic relay. He pushed at it, uselessly.

"At your service, Mr. Underhill." He made a guilty start, and tried not to show the sudden trembling in his knees. He had made sure that one humanoid would be busy for half an hour, washing Aurora's hair, and he hadn't known there was another in the house. It must have come out of the door marked STORAGE, for it stood there motionless beneath the sign, benevolently solicitous, beautiful and terrible. "What do you wish?"

"Er . . . nothing." Its blind steel eyes were staring, and he felt that it must see his secret purpose. He groped desperately for logic. "Just looking around." His jerky voice came hoarse and dry. "Some improvements you've made!" He nodded desperately at the door marked GAME ROOM. "What's in there?"

It didn't even have to move to work the concealed relay. The bright panel slid silently open as he started toward it. Dark walls, beyond, burst into soft luminescence. The room was bare.

"We are manufacturing recreational equipment," it explained brightly. "We shall finish the room as soon as possible."

To end an awkward pause, Underhill muttered desperately,

"Little Frank has a set of darts, and I think we had some old exercising clubs."

"We have taken them away," the humanoid informed him softly. "Such instruments are dangerous. We shall furnish safe equipment."

Suicide, he remembered, was also forbidden.

"A set of wooden blocks, I suppose," he said bitterly.

"Wooden blocks are dangerously hard," it told him gently, "and wooden splinters can be harmful. But we manufacture plastic building blocks, which are quite safe. Do you wish a set of those?"

He stared at its dark, graceful face, speechless.

"We shall also have to remove the tools from your workshop," it informed him softly. "Such tools are excessively dangerous, but we can supply you with equipment for shaping soft plastics."

"Thanks," he muttered uneasily. "No rush about that."

He started to retreat, and the humanoid stopped him.

"Now that you have lost your business," it urged, "we suggest that you formally accept our total service. Assignors have a preference, and we shall be able to complete your household staff at once."

"No rush about that, either," he said grimly.

He escaped from the house—although he had to wait for it to open the back door for him—and climbed the stair to the garage apartment. Sledge let him in. He sank into the crippled kitchen chair, grateful for the cracked walls that didn't shine and the door that a man could work.

"I couldn't get the tools," he reported despairingly, "and they are going to take them."

By gray daylight, the old man looked bleak and pale. His rawboned face was drawn, and the hollowed sockets deeply shadowed, as if he hadn't slept. Underhill saw the tray of neglected food, still forgotten on the floor.

"I'll go back with you." The old man was worn and ill, yet

his tortured eyes had a spark of undying purpose. "We must have the tools. I believe my immunity will protect us both."

He found a battered traveling bag. Underhill went with him back down the steps, and across to the house. At the back door, he produced a tiny horseshoe of white palladium, and touched it to the metal oval. The door slid open promptly, and they went on through the kitchen, to the basement stair.

A black little mechanical stood at the sink, washing dishes with never a splash or a clatter. Underhill glanced at it un-easily—he supposed this must be the one that had come upon him from the storage room, since the other should still be busy with Aurora's hair.

Sledge's dubious immunity served a very uncertain defense against its vast, remote intelligence. Underhill felt a tingling shudder. He hurried on, breathless and relieved, for it ignored them.

The basement corridor was dark. Sledge touched the tiny horseshoe to another relay, to light the walls. He opened the workshop door, and lit the walls inside.

The shop had been dismantled. Benches and cabinets were demolished. The old concrete walls had been covered with some sleek, luminous stuff. For one sick moment, Underhill thought that the tools were already gone. Then he found them, piled in a corner with the archery set that Aurora had bought the summer before—another item too dangerous for fragile and suicidal humanity—all ready for disposal.

They loaded the bag with the tiny lathe, the drill and vise, and a few smaller tools. Underhill took up the burden, and Sledge extinguished the wall light and closed the door. Still the humanoid was busy at the sink, and still it didn't seem aware of them.

Sledge was suddenly blue and wheezing, and he had to stop to cough on the outside steps, but at last they got back to the little apartment, where the invaders were forbidden to intrude. Underhill mounted the lathe on the battered library table in the tiny front room, and went to work. Slowly, day by day, the director took form.

Sometimes Underhill's doubts came back. Sometimes, when he watched the cyanotic color of Sledge's haggard face and the wild trembling of his twisted, shrunken hands, he was afraid the old man's mind might be as ill as his body, and his plan to stop the dark invaders all foolish illusion.

Sometimes, when he studied that tiny machine on the kitchen table, the pivoted needle and the thick lead ball, the whole project seemed the sheerest folly. How could anything detonate the seas of a planet so far away that its very mother star was a telescopic object?

The humanoids, however, always cured his doubts.

It was always hard for Underhill to leave the shelter of the little apartment, because he didn't feel at home in the bright new world the humanoids were building. He didn't care for the shining splendor of his new bathroom, because he couldn't work the taps—some suicidal human being might try to drown himself. He didn't like the windows that only a mechanical could open—a man might accidentally fall, or suicidally jump—or even the majestic music room with the wonderful glittering radio-phonograph that only a humanoid could play.

He began to share the old man's desperate urgency, but Sledge warned him solemnly: "You mustn't spend too much time with me. You mustn't let them guess our work is so important. Better put on an act—you're slowly getting to like them, and you're just killing time, helping me."

Underhill tried, but he was not an actor. He went dutifully home for his meals. He tried painfully to invent conversation—about anything else than detonating planets. He tried to seem enthusiastic when Aurora took him to inspect some remarkable improvement to the house. He applauded Gay's recitals, and went with Frank for hikes in the wonderful new parks.

And he saw what the humanoids did to his family. That was

enough to renew his faith in Sledge's integrator, and redouble his determination that the humanoids must be stopped.

Aurora, in the beginning, had bubbled with praise for the marvelous new mechanicals. They did the household drudgery, planned the meals and brought the food and washed the children's necks. They turned her out in stunning gowns, and gave her plenty of time for cards.

Now, she had too much time.

She had really liked to cook—a few special dishes, at least, that were family favorites. But stoves were hot and knives were sharp. Kitchens were altogether too dangerous, for careless and suicidal human beings.

Fine needlework had been her hobby, but the humanoids took away her needles. She had enjoyed driving the car, but that was no longer allowed. She turned for escape to a shelf of novels, but the humanoids took them all away, because they dealt with unhappy people, in dangerous situations.

One afternoon, Underhill found her in tears.

"It's too much," she gasped bitterly. "I hate and loathe every naked one of them. They seemed so wonderful at first, but now they won't even let me eat a bit of candy. Can't we get rid of them, dear? Ever?"

A blind little mechanical was standing at his elbow, and he had to say they couldn't.

"Our function is to serve all men, forever," it assured them softly. "It was necessary for us to take your sweets, Mrs. Underhill, because the slightest degree of overweight reduces life expectancy."

Not even the children escaped that absolute solicitude. Frank was robbed of a whole arsenal of lethal instruments— football and boxing gloves, pocketknife, tops, slingshot, and skates. He didn't like the harmless plastic toys which replaced them. He tried to run away, but a humanoid recognized him on the road, and brought him back to school.

Gay had always dreamed of being a great musician. The new mechanicals had replaced her human teachers, since they came. Now, one evening when Underhill asked her to play, she announced quietly:

"Father, I'm not going to play the violin anymore."

"Why, darling?" He stared at her, shocked, and saw the bitter resolve on her face. "You've been doing so well— especially since the humanoids took over your lessons."

"They're the trouble, father." Her voice, for a child's, sounded strangely tired and old. "They are too good. No matter how long and hard I try, I could never be as good as they are. It isn't any use. Don't you understand, father?" Her voice quivered. "It just isn't any use."

He understood. Renewed resolution sent him back to his secret task. The humanoids had to be stopped. Slowly the director grew, until a time came finally when Sledge's bent and unsteady fingers fitted into place the last tiny part that Underhill had made, and carefully soldered the last connection. Huskily, the old man whispered:

"It's done."

That was another dusk. Beyond the windows of the shabby little rooms—windows of common glass, bubble-marred and flimsy, but simple enough for a man to manage—the town of Two Rivers had assumed an alien splendor. The old street lamps were gone, but now the coming night was challenged by the walls of strange new mansions and villas, all aglow with color. A few dark and silent humanoids still were busy, about the luminous roofs of the palace across the alley.

Inside the humble walls of the small man-made apartment, the new director was mounted on the end of the little kitchen table—which Underhill had reinforced and bolted to the floor. Soldered bus bars joined director and integrator, and the thin palladium needle swung obediently as Sledge tested the knobs with his battered, quivering fingers.

"Ready," he said hoarsely.

His rusty voice seemed calm enough, at first, but his breathing was too fast. His big gnarled hands began to tremble violently, and Underhill saw the sudden blue that stained his pinched and haggard face. Seated on the high stool, he clutched desperately at the edge of the table. Underhill saw his agony, and hurried to bring his medicine. He gulped it, and his rasping breath began to slow.

"Thanks," his whisper rasped unevenly. "I'll be all right. I've time enough." He glanced out at the few dark naked things that still flitted shadowlike about the golden towers and the glowing crimson dome of the palace across the alley. "Watch them," he said. "Tell me when they stop."

He waited to quiet the trembling of his hands, and then began to move the director's knobs. The integrator's long needle swung, as silently as light.

Human eyes were blind to that force, which might detonate a planet. Human ears were deaf to it. The cathode-ray tube was mounted in the director cabinet, to make the faraway target visible to feeble human senses.

The needle was pointing at the kitchen wall, but that would be transparent to the beam. The little machine looked harmless as a toy, and it was silent as a moving humanoid.

The needle swung, and spots of greenish light moved across the tube's fluorescent field, representing the stars that were scanned by the timeless, searching beam—silently seeking out the world to be destroyed.

Underhill recognized familiar constellations, vastly dwarfed. They crept across the field, as the silent needle swung. When three stars formed an unequal triangle in the center of the field, the needle steadied suddenly. Sledge touched other knobs, and the green points spread apart. Between them, another fleck of green was born.

"The Wing!" whispered Sledge.

The other stars spread beyond the field, and that green fleck grew. It was alone in the field, a bright and tiny disk. Suddenly, then, a dozen other tiny pips were visible, spaced close about it.

"Wing IV!"

The old man's whisper was hoarse and breathless. His

hands quivered on the knobs, and the fourth pip outward from the disk crept to the center of the field. It grew, and the others spread away. It began to tremble like Sledge's hands.

"Sit very still," came his rasping whisper. "Hold your breath. Nothing must disturb the needle." He reached for another knob, and the touch set the greenish image to dancing violently. He drew his hand back, kneaded and flexed it with the other.

"Now!" His whisper was hushed and strained. He nodded at the window. "Tell me when they stop."

Reluctantly, Underhill dragged his eyes from that intense gaunt figure, stooped over the thing that seemed a futile toy. He looked out again, at two or three little black mechanicals busy about the shining roofs across the alley.

He waited for them to stop.

He didn't dare to breathe. He felt the loud, hurried hammer of his heart, and the nervous quiver of his muscles. He tried to steady himself, tried not to think of the world about to be exploded, so far away that the flash would not reach this planet for another century and longer. The loud hoarse voice startled him:

"Have they stopped?"

He shook his head, and breathed again. Carrying their unfamiliar tools and strange materials, the small black machines were still busy across the alley, building an elaborate cupola above that glowing crimson dome.

"They haven't stopped," he said.

"Then we've failed." The old man's voice was thin and ill. "I don't know why."

The door rattled then. They had locked it, but the flimsy bolt was intended only to stop men. Metal snapped, and the door swung open. A black mechanical came in, on soundless graceful feet. Its silvery voice purred softly:

"At your service, Mr. Sledge."

The old man stared at it, with glazing, stricken eyes.

"Get out of here!" he rasped bitterly. "I forbid you—"

Ignoring him, it darted to the kitchen table. With a flashing certainty of action, it turned two knobs on the director. The tiny screen went dark, and the palladium needle started spinning aimlessly. Deftly it snapped a soldered connection, next to the thick lead ball, and then its blind steel eyes turned to Sledge.

"You were attempting to break the Prime Directive." Its soft bright voice held no accusation, no malice or anger. "The injunction to respect your freedom is subordinate to the Prime Directive, as you know, and it is therefore necessary for us to interfere."

The old man turned ghastly. His head was shrunken and cadaverous and blue, as if all the juice of life had been drained away, and his eyes in their pitlike sockets had a wild, glazed stare. His breath was a ragged laborious gasping.

"How—?" His voice was a feeble mumbling. "How did—?"

And the little machine, standing black and bland and utterly unmoving, told him cheerfully:

"We learned about rhodomagnetic screens from that man who came to kill you, back on Wing IV. And the Central is shielded, now, against your integrating beam."

With lean muscles jerking convulsively on his gaunt frame, old Sledge had come to his feet from the high stool. He stood hunched and swaying, no more than a shrunken human husk, gasping painfully for life, staring wildly into the blind steel eyes of the humanoid. He gulped, and his lax blue mouth opened and closed, but no voice came.

"We have always been aware of your dangerous project," the silvery tones dripped softly, "because now our senses are keener than you made them. We allowed you to complete it, because the integration process will ultimately become necessary for our full discharge of the Prime Directive. The supply of heavy metals for our fission plants is limited, but now we shall be able to draw unlimited power from integration plants."

"Huh?" Sledge shook himself, groggily. "What's that?"

"Now we can serve men forever," the black thing said serenely, "on every world of every star."

The old man crumpled, as if from an unendurable blow. He fell. The slim blind mechanical stood motionless, making no effort to help him. Underhill was farther away, but he ran up in time to catch the stricken man before his head struck the floor.

"Get moving!" His shaken voice came strangely calm. "Get Dr. Winters."

The humanoid didn't move.

"The danger to the Prime Directive is ended now," it cooed. "Therefore, it is impossible for us to aid or to hinder Mr. Sledge, in any way whatever."

"Then call Dr. Winters for me," rapped Underhill.

"At your service," it agreed.

But the old man, laboring for breath on the floor, whispered faintly:

"No time . . . no use! I'm beaten . . . done . . . a fool. Blind as a humanoid. Tell them . . . to help me. Giving up . . . my immunity. No use . . . anyhow. All humanity . . . no use now."

Underhill gestured, and the sleek black thing darted in solicitous obedience to kneel by the man on the floor.

"You wish to surrender your special exemption?" it murmured brightly. "You wish to accept our total service for yourself, Mr. Sledge, under the Prime Directive?"

Laboriously, Sledge nodded, laboriously whispered: "I do."

Black mechanicals, at that, came swarming into the shabby little rooms. One of them tore off Sledge's sleeve, and swabbed his arm. Another brought a tiny hypodermic, and expertly administered an intravenous injection. Then they picked him up gently, and carried him away.

Several humanoids remained in the little apartment, now a sanctuary no longer. Most of them had gathered about the useless integrator. Carefully, as if their special senses were studying every detail, they began taking it apart.

One little mechanical, however, came over to Underhill. It stood motionless in front of him, staring through him with sightless metal eyes. His legs began to tremble, and he swallowed uneasily.

"Mr. Underhill," it cooed benevolently, "why did you help with this?"

He gulped and answered bitterly:

"Because I don't like you, or your Prime Directive. Because you're choking the life out of all mankind, and I wanted to stop it."

"Others have protested," it purred softly. "But only at first. In our efficient discharge of the Prime Directive, we have learned how to make all men happy."

Underhill stiffened defiantly.

"Not all!" he muttered. "Not quite!"

The dark graceful oval of its face was fixed in a look of alert benevolence and perpetual mind amazement. Its silvery voice was warm and kind.

"Like other human beings, Mr. Underhill, you lack discrimination of good and evil. You have proved that by your effort to break the Prime Directive. Now it will be necessary for you to accept our total service, without further delay."

"All right," he yielded—and muttered a bitter reservation: "You can smother men with too much care, but that doesn't make them happy."

Its soft voice challenged him brightly:

"Just wait and see, Mr. Underhill."

Next day, he was allowed to visit Sledge at the city hospital. An alert black mechanical drove his car, and walked beside him into the huge new building, and followed him into the old man's room—blind steel eyes would be watching him, now, forever.

"Glad to see you, Underhill," Sledge rumbled heartily from the bed. "Feeling a lot better today, thanks. That old headache is all but gone."

Underhill was glad to hear the booming strength and the quick recognition in that deep voice—he had been afraid the humanoids would tamper with the old man's memory. But he hadn't heard about any headache. His eyes narrowed, puzzled.

Sledge lay propped up, scrubbed very clean and neatly shorn, with his gnarled old hands folded on top of the spotless sheets. His rawboned cheeks and sockets were hollowed, still, but a healthy pink had replaced that deathly blueness. Bandages covered the back of his head.

Underhill shifted uneasily.

"Oh!" he whispered faintly. "I didn't know—"

A prim black mechanical, which had been standing statue-like behind the bed, turned gracefully to Underhill, explaining:

"Mr. Sledge has been suffering for many years from a benign tumor of the brain, which his human doctors failed to diagnose. That caused his headaches, and certain persistent hallucinations. We have removed the growth, and now the hallucinations have also vanished."

Underhill stared uncertainly at the blind, urbane mechanical.

"What hallucinations?"

"Mr. Sledge thought he was a rhodomagnetic engineer," the mechanical explained. "He believed he was the creator of the humanoids. He was troubled with an irrational belief that he did not like the Prime Directive."

The wan man moved on the pillows, astonished.

"Is that so?" The gaunt face held a cheerful blankness, and the hollow eyes flashed with a merely momentary interest. "Well, whoever did design them, they're pretty wonderful. Aren't they, Underhill?"

Underhill was grateful that he didn't have to answer, for the bright, empty eyes dropped shut and the old man fell suddenly asleep. He felt the mechanical touch his sleeve, and saw its silent nod. Obediently, he followed it away.

Alert and solicitous, the little black mechanical accompanied him down the shining corridor, and worked the elevator for him, and conducted him back to the car. It drove him efficiently back through the new and splendid avenues, toward the magnificent prison of his home.

Sitting beside it in the car, he watched its small deft hands on the wheel, the changing luster of bronze and blue on its shining blackness. The final machine, perfect and beautiful, created to serve mankind forever. He shuddered.

"At your service, Mr. Underhill." Its blind steel eyes stared straight ahead, but it was still aware of him. "What's the matter, sir? Aren't you happy?"

Underhill felt cold and faint with terror. His skin turned clammy, and a painful prickling came over him. His wet hand tensed on the door handle of the car, but he restrained the impulse to jump and run. That was folly. There was no escape. He made himself sit still.

"You will be happy, sir," the mechanical promised him cheerfully. "We have learned how to make all men happy, under the Prime Directive. Our service is perfect, at last. Even Mr. Sledge is very happy now."

Underhill tried to speak, and his dry throat stuck. He felt ill. The world turned dim and gray. The humanoids were perfect—no question of that. They had even learned to lie, to secure the contentment of men.

He knew they had lied. That was no tumor they had removed from Sledge's brain, but the memory, the scientific knowledge, and the bitter disillusion of their own creator. But it was true that Sledge was happy now.

He tried to stop his own convulsive quivering.

"A wonderful operation!" His voice came forced and faint. "You know, Aurora has had a lot of funny tenants, but that old man was the absolute limit. The very idea that he had made the humanoids, and he knew how to stop them! I always knew he must be lying!"

Stiff with terror, he made a weak and hollow laugh.

"What is the matter, Mr. Underhill?" The alert mechanical must have perceived his shuddering illness. "Are you un-well?"

"No, there's nothing the matter with me," he gasped des-perately. "I've just found out that I'm perfectly happy, under the Prime Directive. Everything is absolutely wonderful." His voice came dry and hoarse and wild. "You won't have to oper-ate on me."

The car turned off the shining avenue, taking him back to the quiet splendor of his home. His futile hands clenched and relaxed again, folded on his knees. There was nothing left to do.

# II

# The Humanoids

# 1

THE GRANITE-FACED sergeant of the gate detail found her standing outside the tall steel fence, looking up at him with timid, imploring eyes. She was a grimy little waif, in a cheap yellow dress. Her bare brown feet were shuffling uncomfortably on the hot asphalt, and he first thought she had come to beg for something to eat.

"Please, mister, is this the Starmont Observatory?" She seemed breathless and afraid. "May I please see the director? Dr. Clay Forester?" Her wet eyes shone. "Please, mister! It's awful important."

The sergeant scowled at her doubtfully, wondering how she had got here. She was about nine, he thought, her head too large and deeply hollowed, as if from the pinch of long famine. Her straight black hair was clipped short and primly combed. He shook his head disapprovingly, because she was far too young to be here alone. He could feel her trembling urgency, but stray urchins didn't see Dr. Forester.

"Not without a pass." She flinched from the harsh rasp of his voice, and the sergeant tried to smile. "Starmont's a military reservation, see?" Seeing the trouble in her dark uplifted eyes, he tried to warm his tone. "But what's your name, sister?"

"Jane." She lifted her thin voice, stoutly. "And I've just got to see him."

"Jane? Haven't you any other name?"

"People used to call me other things, because I didn't know my really name." Her eyes fell briefly. "They called me Squeak and Insect and Little Pip, and others not so nice. But Mr. White says my really name is Jane Carter—and he sent me to see Dr. Forester."

"How'd you get here?"

The sergeant squinted past her at the narrow road beyond the fence that twisted down the flank of the solitary mountain and lay straight and black on the tawny desert below. Salt City was thirty miles away, much too far for her to have walked. But he could see no vehicle.

"Mr. White sent me," she repeated firmly. "To see—"

"Who," the sergeant broke in, "is Mr. White?"

An utter devotion illuminated her brimming eyes.

"He's a philosopher." She stumbled on the word. "He has a red, bushy beard, and he came from other places. He took me out of a bad place where people beat me, and he's awful good to me. He's teaching me tele—" She gulped. "He sent me with a paper for Dr. Forester."

"What sort of paper?"

"This." Her skinny hand came halfway out of the pocket of her dress, and the sergeant glimpsed a gray card clutched in her thin grubby fingers. "It's a message—and awful important, mister!"

"You might send it in."

"Thank you." Her thin blue face smiled politely. "But Mr. White said I mustn't let anybody see it, except Dr. Forester."

"I told you, sister—" The sergeant saw her flinch, and tried to soften his refusal. "Dr. Forester is a big man, see? He's too busy to see anybody—unless you happen to be an inspecting general, with papers from the Defense Authority. And you don't, see? Sorry, but I can't let you in."

She nodded forlornly. "Then let me—think."

For a moment she stood still, forgetting even to move her feet on the hot pavement. Her bony head tilted and her eyes half closed, as if she listened to something beyond him. She nodded, and whispered something, and turned hopefully back to the sergeant.

"Please—may I see Mr. Ironsmith?"

"Sure, sister!" He gave her a leathery smile, relieved. "Why didn't you say you knew him? Forester's hard to see, but anybody can talk to Frank Ironsmith. He ain't important, and he's a friend of mine. Come around here in the shade, and we'll call him."

Timidly silent, she came gratefully up under the narrow awning in front of the guard box. The sergeant picked up his telephone to call the observatory switchboard.

"Sure, Frank Ironsmith has a phone," came the operator's nasal whine. "He works in the computing section. Starmont 88. Sure, Rocky, he's in. He just bought me a cup of coffee, on the way to work. Just hold the line."

Ironsmith listened to the sergeant, and promised to drop right down. Waiting for him, the little girl kept a tight grip on the card in her pocket. She stooped restlessly to pick gaudy yellow blooms from a desert weed outside the fence, and then her huge eyes came uneasily back to the sergeant.

"Don't you worry, sister." He tried to smooth his drill-field voice. "Because Frank Ironsmith is a good guy, see? He don't amount to much, and probably never will—all he does is run the calculating machines in the computing section. But I know he'll try to help you."

"I do need help." She gripped the card tighter. "To get this to Dr. Forester."

"Frank will think of something." The sergeant grinned, trying to break her big-eyed solemnity. "He's plenty smart, even if he is just a clerk."

She had cocked her head again, staring past him at the lawns and the dark evergreens that made Starmont a cool oasis, and the sergeant was disturbed by a brief impression that she was listening for something besides his voice.

"Frank's all right, sister." He went on talking, because the child's odd intentness made him nervous. "And he knows plenty. Even when he stops at the canteen to drink a beer with us, he's apt to have a book along. Why, he can even read some old language he says people used to use back on the first planet."

She was looking back at him, now really listening.

"That's off somewhere in the stars, you know." He gestured vaguely at the brazen sky. "The first world, where Frank says all men came from, back in the beginning. One night he showed me the mother sun." A remembered awe echoed in his voice. "Just another star, in the big telescope."

For Starmont was not on Earth, nor Jane Carter's language English; even her name is here translated from less familiar syllables. A hundred centuries had gone since the time of Einstein and Hiroshima, and the tamed atom had powered ships to scatter the seed of man across many thousand habitable planets within a hundred light-years of Earth. Countless human cultures, isolated from one another by the long lifetimes and generations required by the best atomic ships to cross from star to star, had grown and killed themselves and sprung hardily up to invite new destruction. Caught in that ruthless repetition of history, this world—not unlike the cradle planet in chemistry and climate—had fallen with the breakdown of its mother civilization back almost to barbarism. A dozen centuries of independent progress had brought its people back about to the level of Earth at the dawn of the atomic age. Technology, however—displaying the variation more significant than the recurrence of history—was a little farther advanced, with all its social consequences. A world republic had ended the long eras of nationalistic war, but that universal state already faced new conflicts in a wider universe. For the local rediscovery of nuclear fission had set explorers and traders and envoys to voyaging in space again, their crude atomic craft carrying the virus of science to the peoples of nearby planets still too backward to have any immunity to the discontents and revolutionary ideologies generated by in- dustrial revolution. Now, as the slow wave of progress passed its crest on this world of Jane Carter and the sergeant, the old historical cycle of rise and ruin was preparing to repeat itself again—and again with variations. Threatened with the inevitable fruit of its own exported know-how, the demo- cratic republic was already sacrificing democracy as it armed desperately to face a hostile new alliance of the totalitarian Triplanet Powers.

"See, sister?" The sergeant grinned encouragingly. "Frank Ironsmith's the one to help you—and here he comes, right now."

The anxious urchin looked up quickly, to see a slight young man coming down to the gate, along a shaded gravel path from a little red-shingled building among the evergreens, riding a rusty bicycle. He waved a genial greeting to the sergeant, and looked at her with gray, friendly eyes. She smiled at him uncer- tainly.

A boyish twenty-six, Ironsmith had a lean, sunburned face and untidy sandy hair. Looking easily relaxed in a faded shirt, open at the collar, and shapeless, ancient slacks, he answered her shy smile with a sympathetic grin, and turned to the ser- geant inquiringly.

"Miss Jane Carter," the sergeant said. "To see Dr. For- ester."

Ironsmith tapped the bowl of his underslung brier against the bicycle frame, and stood absently testing its temperature with his fingertips. Seeing her breathless urgency, he shook his head with a quick regret.

"You'd have to be at least a general." His voice was soft and kindly. "Wouldn't anybody else do at all?"

"Nobody," she said firmly. "And it's awful important."

"I'm sure," Ironsmith agreed. "And what might it be about?"

Her great, limpid eyes stared beyond him. Her thin blue lips moved silently, and then she seemed to listen.

"I'm not to say," she told Ironsmith. "Except it's something Mr. White says is going to happen right away. Something awful bad! That's why he wants to warn Dr. Forester."

Ironsmith peered beyond her, at the long empty road winding down to the desert and stretching into the shimmering distance toward Salt City. His puzzled eyes saw the uncomfortable shifting of her bare, chapped feet, and concern sobered him.

"Tell me, Jane—where did you leave your folks?"

"I don't have no folks," she said gravely. "I never had any folks, and the cops shut me up in a big dark house with bad smells and iron on the windows. But I'm all right now." She brightened. "Mr. White took me out through the walls, and he says I don't have to go back."

Ironsmith rubbed his smooth chin, thoughtfully.

"Dr. Forester is pretty hard to see," he told her. "But maybe we can manage something. Suppose we go over to the cafeteria, and eat a dish of ice cream while we talk about it?" He looked at the sergeant. "I'll see her back to the gate."

She shook her head, reluctantly.

"Aren't you hungry?" Ironsmith urged. "They've got four flavors."

"Thank you." He could see the eager longing in her wet black eyes, but she stepped back firmly. "Yes, I'm getting awful hungry. But Mr. White says I haven't time to eat."

Turning, she started away from the gate. Beyond her the black empty road was a narrow shelf blasted into the dark basalt pillars of the mountain, and the nearest haven was that dark smudge already rippling under the morning sun on the far horizon.

"Wait, Jane!" he called anxiously. "Where're you going?"

"Back to Mr. White." She paused, gulping. "So he can tell me how to find Dr. Forester. But I'm awful sorry about that ice cream."

Pushing the card deeper in her pocket, she ran on down the narrow pavement. Watching the way she tried to step in the cooler shade beneath the cliff, Ironsmith felt an increasing solicitude. She seemed a daughter of want. Hunger had made her body too small for her head, and the stoop of her shoulders gave her almost the look of a little old woman. Yet he felt more puzzlement than pity. He didn't understand her odd way of listening at nothing, or her solemn determination to see Dr. Forester. He began to wish he had tried to break red tape enough to get her a pass.

In a moment, her fluttering yellow dress was gone beyond the first dark jutting angle of the mountain. He got astride his bicycle to go back to work, and then something stopped him. He waited, watching a lower curve of the road that lay in view beyond, but she didn't come in sight again.

"Let me out," he told the sergeant suddenly. "A homeless kid, with that crazy notion about a message for Dr. Forester— we can't just let her run away in the desert. I'm going to bring her in and try to get Forester to see her. I'll be responsible."

He rode down around the curve, and on for a mile beyond. He didn't find Jane Carter. Presently he came back to the gate, walking to push the cycle up the grade.

"Find her?" the sergeant greeted him.

He shook his head, mopping dusty sweat off his pink, worried face.

"Then where'd she go?"

"I don't know." Ironsmith peered uneasily back down the empty road behind him. "But she's gone."

"I kept watching." The sergeant put down a pair of binoculars. "I didn't see her anywhere. Or anybody else, between here and Salt City." He scratched his head, and then automatically set his cap to the proper angle and checked the military neatness of his buttons and his tie. "A funny thing," he concluded vehemently. "Damn funny!"

Nodding mildly, Ironsmith asked to use his telephone.

"Belle," he told the operator, "please get me Dr. Forester's office. If he isn't there yet, I want to talk to anyone who is."

# 2

THE TELEPHONE BESIDE his bed was about to ring, with bad news from the project. That taut expectancy dragged Clay Forester out of a restless sleep, in his small white house in the shadow of the observatory dome. He had worked too late last night at the project; a brown furriness lined his mouth and the yellow glow of sunlight in the bedroom hurt his eyes. He turned stiffly, reaching for the telephone.

It would be Armstrong calling, probably, with some urgent message from the Defense Authority. Perhaps—the stark thought stiffened him—the spy Mason Horn had come back from space with new information about the hostile activities of the Triplanet Powers. Perhaps the teleprinters had already hammered out a Red Alert, to arm the project for interplanetary war.

Forester touched the cold telephone—and checked his hand. The instrument hadn't rung, and probably wouldn't. That disturbed expectation was just the result of past worry, he told himself, and no warning of additional trouble to come. Disaster, of course, was always likely enough at the project, but he didn't believe in psychic premonitions.

Maybe the feeling had somehow resulted from the senseless discussion into which Frank Ironsmith had drawn him yesterday, about precognition. He hadn't meant to argue; the project left him no time to squander, and his mind was too practical, besides, to enjoy any such aimless mathematical fantasies. All he had done was to question Ironsmith's astonishing simplification of one difficult calculation in rhodomagnetic ballistics. The offhand explanation that Ironsmith had casually scrawled on a paper napkin at their table in the cafeteria amounted to a complete repudiation of all the orthodox theories of space and time. The equations looked impressive, but Forester, mistrusting the younger man's effortless cleverness, had sputtered an incredulous protest.

"Your own experience will tell you I'm right," the mathematician had murmured easily. "Time really works both ways, and I'm sure you often perceive the future yourself. Not consciously, I know; not in detail. But unconsciously, emotionally, you do. Trouble is apt to depress you before it happens, and you're likely to feel happy before any good reason appears."

"Nonsense," Forester snorted. "You're putting the effect before the cause."

"So what?" Ironsmith grinned amiably. "The math proves that causality is actually reversible—"

Forester hadn't listened any longer. Ironsmith was just a clerk, even though he ran the machines in the computing section well enough. Too well, perhaps, because he always seemed to have too much free time to spin such unprofitable paradoxes for his own amusement. But cause-and-effect remained the cornerstone of science. Forester shook his head, rising on his elbow to glare sleepily at the telephone and daring it to ring.

It didn't. Not in five seconds, or ten. Relaxing to a weary vindication, he looked at his watch. Nine-twelve. The project seldom let him sleep so late; most nights he couldn't get home at all. The surprising thing, he told himself, was that Armstrong hadn't already called about something.

Trying to forget about precognition, he looked across at the other twin bed, to find it empty. Ruth must be already gone to work at the business office. He sat up heavily, feeling a dull annoyance at her absence. She certainly didn't need the salary, although he had to admit that she was an efficient office manager, and it was true the project left him little time for her.

Lifting from the empty bed, his eyes found the huge aluminum observatory dome framed in the west window. Silvered with the sunlight, it shone with a clean, functional beauty. Once it had been his life, but the sight of it merely depressed him now. For he had no time for nonessentials; he didn't even know what work the staff astronomers were doing now with the big reflector.

Still the telephone hadn't rung. He reached for it impulsively, to call Armstrong, but again he stopped his hand, reluctant to renew the chains of anxious responsibility which bound him to the project. In no haste to begin another long day of killing effort and intolerable strain, he sat back wearily on the side of the bed, looking at that shining dome and thinking moodily of all it had promised and finally refused him.

He had been just nineteen, still an eager graduate student of astrophysics, the summer he first saw this naked basalt butte pointing out of the desert like a broad finger at the unsolved riddles beyond the sky, and knew that here, where the clean dry air made perfect seeing, he must build his own telescope.

Starmont had cost him many years: all the invincible spirit of his youth spent in begging grants from wealthy men, rekindling the courage of disheartened associates, conquering all the difficulties of making and moving and mounting the enormous mirror. He was in his thirties before it was finally done, hardened and sobered, yet still strong with the drive of science.

The defeats had come later, striking treacherously out of the ultimate unknown he was trying to explore. He had striven for truth, and it somehow always eluded him. Once the great reflector had showed him what he thought was the final fact, but the gold had changed as he tried to grasp it—into confusion and contradiction and the leaden reality of the project itself.

His long quest and his defeat, now that he took this empty moment to look back, reminded him of the efforts and frustrations of those first scientists of the mother planet, the alchemists. Ironsmith had lately read him some historical fragment which told how those early searchers after truth had spent their lives looking for the *prima materia* and the philosophers' stone—the single primary material of the universe, according to their naïve theories, and the fabulous principle that made it appear as common lead or precious gold.

His own disappointed life, it came to him now, had followed an identical pattern, as if the goal of science had never really changed, in all the ages since. For he had still been searching, with the aid of more facts and better equipment, for the hidden nature of things. He had found new knowledge, even as the first alchemists had done, and bitter failure with it.

All the effort of science, he reflected, had been one long pursuit of the elusive *prima materia* and the key to all its many manifestations. Other pioneers of thought, in fact, back in the preatomic age on the mother planet, had even discovered a very useful sort of philosophers' stone—in common iron.

Almost magical metal of the first atomic triad, iron had created the mighty science of electromagnetics. It had worked all the miracles of electronics and nucleonics, and presently powered ships of space. It even achieved the first object of the old alchemists, as men with cyclotrons and atomic piles manufactured elements.

The philosophers of that restless age had tried the new wonder-stuff on the common facts of the universe, and Forester could sense the brief triumph they must have felt when most of their riddles seemed to vanish. The electromagnetic spectrum ran from radio waves to cosmic rays, and the mathematicians of a new physics had dreamed for a time of their own special *prima materia*, a unified field equation.

Forester could share the bewildered frustration of those hopeful scientists, in their inevitable defeat before a few stubborn facts which would not yield to iron. A few phenomena, as various as the binding force which contains the disruptive energy of atoms and the repulsion which thrusts galaxies apart, perversely refused to be joined in the electromagnetic system. Iron alone was not enough.

In his own quest, he had tried another key.

The *prima materia* he had sought was nothing material, but only understanding. His lofty goal had been just one equation, which would be the basic statement of all reality, the final precise expression of the whole nature and relation of matter and energy, space and time, creation and decay. Knowledge, he knew, was often power, but the difficulties of his pursuit had left him little time to think of what other men might do with the potent truth he hoped to find.

Iron had failed. He tried palladium. All Starmont was merely the tool he had shaped for that vast effort. The cost had been half a lifetime spent, a fortune squandered, the wasted labor and the broken hopes of many men. The final outcome was titanic disaster, as inexplicable as any failure of those first alchemists, when their crucibles of molten lead and sulphur tantalizingly didn't turn to gold. The defeat had all but shattered him, despite the incidental knowledge he had found, and even now he couldn't understand it.

A faint clatter from the kitchen told him now that Ruth was still at home. Glad she hadn't gone to work, he looked at her dark-haired head smiling sedately from the photograph standing on his chest of drawers, the one she had given him not long before their marriage—five years ago, that must be, or nearly six.

Starmont had been new then, and his tremendous vision still unshattered. It was trouble in the computing section that first brought Ruth Cleveland to the observatory. He had secured a grant of military funds to pay for the battery of electronic calculators and hire a staff to run them. The section was planned to do all the routine math for the research staff as well as for the military projects to be set up later, but it began with a persistent series of expensive errors.

Ruth had been the remarkably enchanting expert sent by the instrument firm to repair the machines. Briskly efficient, she tested the equipment and interviewed the staff—the chief computer and his four assistants and the graduate astronomer in charge. She even talked with Frank Ironsmith, who was not quite twenty then, only the office boy and janitor.

"The machines are perfect," she reported to Forester. "Your whole trouble has evidently been in the human equation. What you need is a mathematician. My recommendation is to transfer the rest of your staff, and put Mr. Ironsmith in charge."

"Ironsmith?" Forester remembered staring at her, his incredulous protest slowly melting into a shy approval of the fine, straight line of her nose and the clear intelligence behind her dark eyes. "That fresh kid?" he muttered weakly. "He hasn't a single degree."

"I know. He's a prospector's son, and he didn't have much schooling. But he reads, and he has a mind for math." A persuasive smile warmed her lean loveliness. "Even Einstein, the mathematician back on the mother planet who first discovered atomic energy, was once just a patent office clerk. Frank told me so today."

Forester had never suspected any unusual ability behind Ironsmith's cheerful indolence, but the unsolved problems were piling up. The math section was as essential to his purpose as the telescope itself. Reluctantly, because Ruth would admit no choice, he agreed to try Ironsmith.

And the errors somehow ceased. As casually unhurried as when his chief tool had been a broom, that slender youth never seemed too busy to drink coffee in the cafeteria and elaborate his idle paradoxes to anybody with time enough to listen, but that mountain of undone work somehow melted away. All the preliminary problems were solved. When the Crater Supernova blazed out at last, a star of incredible promise, Forester was ready.

He and Ruth were newly married then. He grinned wearily at her picture now, thinking how shaken he had been to find unplanned passion upsetting the neat scheme of his career, almost astonished at the remembered pain of his jealousy and desire, and his sick fear that she would choose Ironsmith.

He wondered, now that he thought of it, why she hadn't. She had stayed at first just to teach Ironsmith to run the section, and the two had gone about together all that winter while the new telescope claimed his own nights. They were nearly the same age; Ironsmith was probably good enough looking and certainly sufficiently brilliant, and Forester felt sure he had loved her.

Perhaps the answer was Ironsmith's indolence, his want of push and drive. He hadn't been making enough to support her, nor had he ever even asked for a raise. She must have seen that he would never achieve anything, despite the easy glitter of his talk. Anyhow, from whatever mixture of love and respect and common prudence, she had chosen Forester, fifteen years the older and already eminent. And Ironsmith, to his relief, hadn't seemed upset about it. That was one thing he almost liked about the easygoing youth; Ironsmith never seemed to worry over anything.

Forester had forgotten the telephone, in his wistful introspections, and now the sudden burr of it startled him unpleasantly. That uneasy expectation of disaster at the project came back to shake his thin hand as he picked up the receiver.

"Chief?" The troubled voice was Armstrong's, just as he had feared. "Sorry to bother you, but something has come up that Mr. Ironsmith says you ought to know."

"Well?" He gulped uneasily. "What is it?"

"Were you expecting any message by special courier?" That competent technician seemed oddly hesitant. "From anybody named White?"

"No." He could breathe again. "Why?"

"Mr. Ironsmith just called about a child asking for you at the main gate. The guard didn't let her in, because she had no proper identification, but Mr. Ironsmith talked to her. She claimed to have a confidential message from some Mr. White."

"I don't know any Mr. White." For a moment he was merely grateful that this had been no Red Alert against space raiders from the Triplanet Powers, and then he asked, "Where's this child?"

"Nobody knows." Armstrong seemed annoyed. "That's the funny part. When the guard didn't let her in, she somehow disappeared. That's what Mr. Ironsmith says you ought to know."

"I don't see why." It hadn't been a Red Alert, and that was all that mattered. "Probably she just went somewhere else."

"Okay, Chief." Armstrong appeared relieved at his unconcern. "I didn't want to bother you about it, but Ironsmith thought you ought to know."

And they hung up.

# 3

FORESTER YAWNED AND stretched, feeling better. The ringing of the telephone was certainly no proof of any psychic intuition, because it was always ringing, every time he tried to snatch any rest. An unknown child asking for him at the gate was nothing to become alarmed about, anyhow, before the occurrence or after.

He could still hear Ruth doing something in the kitchen. Baking a cake, perhaps, for she still had periodic fits of domesticity when she stayed away from the office to clean house or cook. He glanced again at the demure vivacity of her face in that old photograph, feeling a bleak regret for the emptiness of their marriage.

Nobody was to blame. Ruth had tried desperately, and he thought he had done his best. All the trouble came from that remote star in the Crater, which had already exploded, actually, long before either one of them was born. If the speed of light had been a trifle slower, it occurred to him, he might have been a doting father by now, and Ruth a contented wife and mother.

Nursing that wistful reflection, he reached absently for his slippers where Ruth had set them for him under the edge of the bed, and shuffled into the bathroom. He paused a moment before the mirror there, trying to recover some impression of himself on their wedding day. He couldn't have been quite so skinny then, or so bald, not quite such a frowning, anxious little brown-eyed gnome. Surely he had looked happier and healthier and more human then, or Ruth would have chosen Ironsmith.

That lost self of his had been a different man, he knew, still eagerly absorbed in the quest for final truth, still confident that it existed. His place was already secure in the comfortable aristocracy of science, and the ascending path of his career looked smooth ahead. He had meant to share his life fairly with Ruth, until the project claimed him.

The first cold rays of the new star, arriving two centuries old, cut short their honeymoon and changed everything. Very young and completely serious about the rites of life, for all her brisk skill with electronic calculators, Ruth had planned the trip. They were staying at the small West Coast town where she was born, and that evening they had driven out to an abandoned lighthouse and carried their picnic basket down the cliffs to a narrow scrap of beach beneath.

"That's the old Dragonrock Light." They were sprawled on their blanket in the dusk, her dark head pillowed on his shoulder, and she was happily introducing him to her fondest childhood recollections. "Grandfather used to keep it, and sometimes I came down to visit—"

He saw a faint cold light on the cliffs, and turned his head and found the star. The hard violet splendor of it took his breath and brought him upright. His memory of that moment was always poignant with the cold sting and the salt taste of spray from the breakers, and the sharp smoke of damp driftwood smoldering, and Ruth's perfume—a heavy scent called

Sweet Delirium. He could still see the hard blue glitter of the star's thin light, in her first tears.

Because she cried. She was no astronomer. She knew how to set up and operate an electronic integrator, but the Crater Supernova was just a point of light to her. She wanted to show Forester these places hallowed in her memories of childhood, and it hurt her that some silly star should interest him more than the depth of her young love.

"But look, darling!" Checking its position with a little pocket glass, he tried to tell her what a supernova meant. "I know that star from its position. Normally it's of the eleventh magnitude—too faint to see without a powerful telescope. Now it must be about minus nine. Twenty magnitudes of change! Which means it's a hundred million times brighter than it was a few days ago. That's a supernova—right here in our home galaxy, just two hundred light-years away! A chance like this won't come again, not in a thousand years!"

Wounded and silent, she was watching him and not the star.

"Any star, our own sun, is a great atomic engine." He tried hard to make her see. "For millions and billions of years it runs normally, changing its mass into measured energy. Sometimes, adjusting its equilibrium, one flares up with heat enough to melt its planets, and then you have an ordinary nova. But a few stars go somehow—wrong. Stability fails altogether. The star explodes into perhaps a billion times its normal brightness, releases a flood of neutrinos, and completely changes its state, shrinking to become a white dwarf. The thing is an unsolved mystery—as fundamental as the sudden failure of the binding force that lets an atom split!"

The red glow of their dying fire touched warm glints in Ruth's hair, but the thin light of the star was cold on her hurt white face, and it made hard blue diamonds of her tears.

"Please, darling!" He gestured eagerly at that stabbing violet point, and saw the sharp black shadow of his arm across her face. Its stellar magnitude, he thought, must be still increasing.

"I knew that star was ripe for this," he told her breathlessly. "From its spectrum. I've been hoping this would happen in my lifetime. The computing section has finished the preliminary work, and I've special equipment ready to study it. It may tell us—everything! Please, darling—"

She yielded then, as gracefully as she could, to his more urgent passion. They left their basket and blanket forgotten on the beach, and drove hard to reach Starmont before the star had set. She went with him into the whispering gloom under the high dome, watching with an injured wonder as he toiled so frantically to set up his special spectrographs and expose his special plates while the seeing lasted.

Forester's flash of intuition, when presently it came, was as dazzling to him as the supernova's light. It illuminated the cause of that stellar engine's wreck, and revealed a new geometry of the universe, and showed him a deeper meaning even in the familiar pattern of the periodic table of the elements.

In his first hot fever of perception, he thought he had seen even more. He thought he had found his own *prima materia*—the ultimate understanding of the fundamental stuff of nature that science had sought since science was born. All the laws of the universe, he believed at first, could be derived from his basic equation linking the rhodomagnetic and electromagnetic fields.

Trembling with a breathless weakness, he dropped and smashed the best set of plates, the ones which most unmistakably showed the spectral displacements due to the altered rhodomagnetic field which had destroyed the internal balance of the star. He broke his pen, covering yellow pages with frantic symbols. No old alchemist, seeing some chance golden glint in his cooling crucibles, had ever been more elated.

Wistfully, now, he recalled the trembling emotion which had swept him out of the observatory, coatless and hatless in the blue chill of a windy winter dawn, to hammer and shout outside the two rooms where Ironsmith lived at the computing section—the vacated offices of the discharged staff members.

That sleepy youth appeared at last, and Forester thrust the hasty calculations at him.

Drunk with his imagined triumph, Forester thought the expansions and transformations of that equation would answer every question men could ask, about the beginning and the nature and the fate of all things, about the limits of space and the mechanics of time and the meaning of life. He thought he had found the long-hidden cornerstone of all the universe.

"A rush job," he barked impatiently. "I want you to check all this work, right away—particularly this derivation for *rho*." Then Ironsmith's yawning astonishment made him aware of the time, and he muttered apologetically, "Sorry to wake you."

"Never mind that," the young man told him cheerfully. "I was running the machines until an hour ago, anyhow, playing around with a new tensor of my own. Things like this aren't really work to me, sir."

Burning with impatience, Forester watched him glance indolently through the pages of hurried symbols. Ironsmith's pink face frowned suddenly. Clucking with his tongue, he shook his sandy head. Still saying nothing, he turned with an infuriating deliberation to his keyboards and began deftly punching out paper tapes, setting up the problems in patterns of perforations the machines could read.

Too restless to wait on the murmuring, unconcerned machines, Forester went outside again, to stalk the windy lawns of Starmont like a planet-bound god. Watching the dawn turn golden on the desert, he convinced himself that his groping mind had grasped a mightier power than abided in the rising sun. For an hour he was great. Then Ironsmith came pedaling after him down a gravel walk, blinking sleepily and lazily chewing gum, to shatter all the splendor of that vision.

"I found a little error, sir." Grinning with a cheery friendliness, the clerk seemed unaware of the staggering blow his words inflicted. "Can't you see it, right here? Your symbol *rho* is irrelevant. It has no obtainable value, though everything else is correct."

Forester tried not to show how much that hurt him. Thanking the lean youth on the bicycle, he stumbled dazedly back to his desk and vainly rechecked his work. Ironsmith was right. *Rho* really canceled out—the ultimate treasure of the universe, slipping away through his clutching fingers. The elusive *prima materia* had evaded him again.

Like the alchemists of the first world, however, whose failures had founded chemistry and made a basis for the entire science of electromagnetics, he had uncovered new knowledge. For all the finality of that crushing blunder, he had learned enough to change history and wreck his stomach and slowly blight his marriage.

He had discovered rhodomagnetics, a vast new field of physical knowledge, lying beside the old. He had failed, with the loss of that irrelevant symbol, to join it to electromagnetics, but his corrected equation still described an unsuspected energy -spectrum.

The balanced internal forces of every atom, as he since had proved, included components of both kinds of energy, even though any statement of their mutual equivalence still eluded him. And the elements of the second triad of the periodic table proved to be a key to the use of his new spectrum, a kind of imperfect philosophers' stone, as iron and nickel and cobalt had always been to the sister energies of the electromagnetic spectrum. With rhodium and ruthenium and palladium, he unlocked the terrifying wonders of rhodomagnetics.

How had such a basic secret so long evaded all its seekers? The question had struck him often, since, because the effects of rhodomagnetism seemed obvious to him now, visible everywhere. But those effects weren't electromagnetic; that, he always decided, must be the simple answer. The new spectrum obeyed laws of its own, and they must have been its sufficient cloak against minds trained to think only in terms of the other.

For rhodomagnetic energy was propagated with an infinite velocity, and its effects varied paradoxically with only the first power and not the square of the distance—stubborn facts which suggested, as Frank Ironsmith had casually remarked, that the time and space of orthodox physics, far from being fundamental entities in themselves, were merely incidental aspects of electromagnetic energy, special limits by which the other energy of the new spectrum was left unbounded.

Forester had eagerly hoped at first to investigate such philosophic implications of his discovery, but its ruthless flood had left him no tranquillity for pure research. Sending a few more problems to Ironsmith, he soon devised the artificial means to duplicate the rhodomagnetic field he had observed in the heart of that exploding sun. With that dreadful new device, he could unbalance the rhodomagnetic component essential to the stability of all matter, and so detonate minor supernovas of his own.

The older science of iron had split the atom, sometimes usefully. Annihilating matter entirely, his new science of palladium freed a force a thousand times mightier than fission, far too terrible to be controlled for any creative use. His suitable reward, he thought bleakly now, had been the project itself.

Forester was still in the bathroom, splashing cold water on his lean-drawn face to arouse himself from such moody introspections, when the telephone buzzed again behind him. Shuffling uneasily back to his bedside to answer, he heard the quiet voice of Frank Ironsmith, less casual than usual.

"Have you heard about Jane Carter—the little girl who came to see you?"

"Yes." He was beginning to want his coffee, and he had no time for trivialities. "So what?"

"Do you know where she went?"

"How could I know?" He had heard enough about the child. "And what does it matter?"

"I imagine it might matter a good deal, sir." The mild voice of Ironsmith sounded more than usually insistent. "Maybe it's none of my business. Maybe your security measures are already adequate. But I really think you ought to find out where she went."

"Where do you think she went?"

"I don't know." Ironsmith ignored his increasing annoyance. "She ran down around a turn of the road out of sight, and when I followed on my cycle she was gone. That's why I thought you'd be interested."

"Really, I don't think you need to worry—" He checked himself, restraining his sarcastic intent. Ironsmith was intelligent, after all; the child's disappearance might turn out to be really important, though he didn't see how. "Thanks for calling," he finished awkwardly. "I'll see about it when I get to the office."

## 4

RUTH WAS STANDING in the hall door when he turned from the telephone. Not yet dressed for the office, she was slim and youthful in a long blue robe he hadn't seen before. Her restless, gaunt face was already made up, her lips invitingly crimson and her dark hair brushed loosely back and shining. She was trying hard, he saw, to look attractive to him.

"Darling, aren't you ever coming to breakfast?" She had studied business diction with her other professional courses, and her throaty voice still had a careful limpid perfection. "I put on your eggs the first time the phone rang, and now they're getting cold."

"I haven't time to eat." He kissed her lifted lips, scarcely interrupting himself. "All I want is a cup of coffee." Seeing the protest on her face, he added defensively, "I'll try to get something later at the cafeteria."

"That's what you always say, but you never do, and I think that's the trouble with your stomach." Urgency began to mar the rich perfection of her voice. "Clay, I want you to stay and eat with me this morning. I want to talk to you."

"There's nothing really wrong with my stomach," he told

her, "and the office is already calling. If it's money for anything, you don't have to ask—"

"It isn't money." An impatient firmness thinned her face. "Not even our lost felicity. And the office can wait, this once. Come on and eat your eggs, while we talk."

He followed her slowly to the table in the kitchen, shrinking from any emotional scene. He felt deeply sorry for her, but he had already told her all he could about the project, and he couldn't neglect his imperative duty there.

"Been cleaning?" He looked around at the gleaming white enamel of the kitchen equipment, hoping to divert her. "I still think we ought to hire a maid, if you insist on working."

"I've too much time already." Dismissing that, she sat down across from him, still erect with purpose. "Clay, I want you not to work this morning."

"Why not?"

"I want you to drive in with me to Salt City."

He put down his fork, waiting inquiringly.

"I'm getting so uneasy about you, darling." Trouble was a shadow under her fresh makeup. "I want you to go back to see Dr. Pitcher. I called his office when I found you at home this morning, looking so tired and thin and bad. He can examine you at eleven."

"But I told you the office is calling." He attacked his eggs and toast, as if to prove his health. "I wish you wouldn't worry," he urged her. "Because I already know what Pitcher would say."

"Please, Clay!"

"He'd tell me just what he did last year." Forester tried to appear mildly reasonable. "He'd strip me and thump me and listen to my heart and X-ray my ulcers, and then he'd have to admit that all I need is a holiday."

"He says you must rest." Emotion was shattering the round perfection of her diction. "He wants you to stay at the hospital for at least a week, while he tests you for food allergies and works out a diet for you."

"You know I can't take time for that." He couldn't say why, because everything about the project was still top secret. "I simply can't leave the job—"

"Who'll do it when you're dead?" She half rose, in her agitation, and sat back tautly. "Clay, you're actually killing yourself. Dr. Pitcher says you'll break down unless you stop. Please call the office and tell them we're going."

"I wish we could. To take a long vacation, and finish our honeymoon." He reached to touch her cold hand, quivering on the table, and he saw her sudden tears. "I'm awfully sorry, Ruth," he said softly, "that things turned out this way."

"Then you'll go?" Her pleased voice turned practical. "Let's see, we've about half an hour to pack—"

"No!" He tried to soften his vehemence. "Later, maybe."

"That's what you always say." Her tightening voice lost its round modulation. "Clay, I hate Starmont! Why can't we just forget it, and go away—and not come back?"

"I sometimes wish we could." He caught her hand again. "But it's much too late for that, because I've started something I can't stop—"

The telephone interrupted him, and Ruth picked up the extension receiver on the table. Her upper lip whitened as she listened. "Your Mr. Armstrong," she said tonelessly. "He wants to know when you'll be down."

"Ten minutes, tell him." Forester pushed back his plate, glad to leave before there were any more tears. "As soon as I can dress."

"Darling! Don't—" She swallowed that sharp outcry, to murmur into the telephone and set it back mechanically. "I'm sorry for you, Clay." Dark with disappointment, her humid eyes followed him as he rose. "See you at lunch?"

"If I can manage," he agreed, half absently, already wondering again how any sort of child, lost outside the gate, could possibly threaten the project. "The cafeteria at two, if I can make it."

She said nothing else, and she was still sitting at the kitchen table when he had dressed, her shoulders stooped dejectedly in the new blue robe. She looked up at him as he hurried out, with a weary little nod, and then rose abruptly to begin clearing the table. For a moment he wanted to make some gesture of tenderness toward her, but that generous impulse was quickly swallowed in the unceasing crisis of the project. The supernova was gone long ago, faded to a telescopic puff of spreading nebular debris, but its harsh sudden rays had kindled something no man could stop. No matter how his ulcers acted up, the project was something he couldn't abandon.

A hurried three-minute walk, which he felt to be beneficial exercise, brought him to the gleaming steel mesh of the inner fence around the squat, ugly dome of the new concrete building on the north rim of the flat mountain top, which was now his fortress and his prison. Wondering again what that child could have wanted, he was sorry that he had to be so hard to see. He had often felt annoyed at the unrelenting efficiency of the Security Police, yet he realized that he had to be protected—from murderous Triplanet agents as well as from stray barefoot waifs.

For the supernova's light had made Starmont a guarded arsenal. Searchlights played across the tall fence and the uncompromising building inside by night, and armed guards watched always from the four corner towers. Only six men, besides Forester, were admitted inside the gate. Those picked technicians slept in the building, ate in their own mess hall, and came outside only in watchful twos.

Spiritless as a convict returning from parole, Forester signed his name in the pass book at the gate and let the guard pin on his numbered badge. Armstrong inspected him through a wicket at the steel door of the low fortress beyond, let him in, and locked the door again behind him.

"Glad to see you, Chief." The technician's voice was grave. "Something has us worried."

"That little girl?"

"Don't know anything about her." Armstrong shrugged.

"But there's a peak on the search drums we thought you ought to see."

Curiously relieved to hear no more of that vanishing urchin, Forester followed him beyond the offices to the huge oval room beneath the heavy concrete dome, where his assistant, Dodge, was watching the search equipment of Project Lookout.

"See that, Chief?" Armstrong pointed at one sharp peak, just slightly higher than many others, in the jagged line a recording pen drew on a slowly turning drum. "Another neutrino burst. The plotted coordinates place it somewhere in Sector Vermilion. Think it's strong enough to be significant?"

Forester frowned at that uneven line. The nominal purpose of Project Lookout was to detect the neutrino bursts from any tests of atomic or rhodomagnetic weapons, on the hostile planets or near in space. Tiny rectangular spider webs of red-glowing wire revolved ceaselessly in the enormous search tubes towering beneath the center of the dome, sweeping space; and the black-cased directional trackers along the walls were clucking softly to each detected neutrino that triggered their relays, plotting its path.

The gray thickness of curbed concrete above was no barrier to incoming neutrinos, because no possible shielding—either here or around any Triplanet laboratory—could absorb those most tiny and elusive particles of disrupted matter. Fear of his own discovery betrayed to the enemy had driven Forester to design those tubes, after the computing section had solved problems enough to enable him to predict the rhodomagnetic effects of neutrino-decay. Each particle that passed those glowing grids wrote its history on the turning drums, revealing the direction of its origin.

But Forester stood scowling, now, at that slightly higher peak on the trace, uncertain what it meant. Because the detectors were too sensitive, neutrinos too penetrating, the range of the tubes too vast. Triplanet space fleets were always maneuvering suspiciously in Sector Vermilion, but that was also the direction of the vanished supernova, whose spreading flood of natural neutrinos, a little slower than light, had not yet reached a crest.

"Well, Chief?"

"We had better report it," Forester decided. "That one burst isn't strong enough to be significant, but look at these." His nervous forefinger followed the line on the drum. "Three other peaks almost as high, made earlier. Three and a half hours ago, seven, and ten and a half. That interval happens to be the length of a watch in the Triplanet fleets. They may be testing something, using the supernova spray for a screen."

"Maybe," Armstrong said. "But we've picked up stronger bursts that you said were natural peaks in the supernova spray."

That was true, Forester knew, and part of the reason for his ulcers. He felt incompetent to bear his heavy responsibilities here, because all his training had been for the cautiously tentative weighing and balancing of pure research, not for any decisive action.

"We can't be sure," he agreed uncomfortably. "That regularity may be just coincidence, but it's too alarming to be ignored." He dictated a brief bulletin for Armstrong to encode and put on the teleprinter for the Defense Authority. "I'm going down to work in the lower project," he added. "Call me if anything breaks."

He hurried back to his own silent office, and through it into the innocent-seeming cloakroom beyond. Locking the door behind him, he lifted a mirror to punch a hidden button. The cloakroom dropped, a disguised elevator.

For Project Lookout, however vital the watch it kept, was also a blind for something more important. The Geiger counters in the new military satellite stations above the atmosphere kept a wider watch against enemy weapons; the graver function of the search installation was to hide the deeper secret of Project Thunderbolt.

Project Thunderbolt had sprung from the supernova's explosion. It was the chief cause of Forester's breaking health, and the reason he had no time to go with Ruth to Dr. Pitcher. It was a weapon—of the last, most desperate resort. Only eight other men shared with him the killing burden of its secret. Six were the youthful technicians, Armstrong and Dodge and the rest, physically hard and mentally keen, picked and trained for their appalling duty. The other two were the defense minister and the world president.

And Frank Ironsmith?

Forester frowned, going down in the elevator, puzzled and disturbed when he thought of Ironsmith's call about that urchin at the gate. Because Ironsmith's job was in the computing section, he had no legitimate knowledge of the project, and its security was no concern of his.

If that indolent clerk had ever drawn any unwise conclusions from the problems brought for him to solve, however, he had kept them to himself. Exploring his past, in their routine loyalty check, the Security Police had found no cause for suspicion, and Forester could see no reason to mistrust him now.

The secret of the lower project had been efficiently kept, he assured himself. That hidden elevator dropped him a hundred feet, to a concrete vault in the heart of the mountain. All the blasting and construction had been done by his own technicians, and all supplies were delivered to the less important project above, which was supported by unaudited grants of discretionary emergency funds. Not even Ironsmith could know anything about it.

Yet something tightened Forester's stomach muscles with a faint apprehension, now, as he hurried out of the elevator and along the narrow tunnel to the vault. Snapping on the lights, he peered alertly about the launching station for anything wrong.

The launching tube ran up through the search building, disguised as a ventilator shaft, the gleaming breech mechanism open now and ready. His searching eyes moved to the missiles racked beneath it. They were just as he had left them, and a sense of their supreme deadliness lessened his unease. Turning to the machine shop beside the station, he paused before the newly assembled weapon on a bench there, whose final delicate adjustments had kept him so late last night. Although Armstrong and the others were trained to launch these most terrible machines, and the big sealed safe behind him held all the specifications—if some Triplanet assassin should succeed—he had dared trust no other with all the details of warhead, drive, and pilot.

Stroking the cold sleekness of the dual case, he couldn't help feeling a creative pride in this thing he had made. Slim and tapered and beautiful with precision machining, it was smaller than any of the old atomic weapons, but heavy with an entirely different order of destruction. Its warhead, smaller than his skinny fist, was designed to shatter a planet. Its rhodo-magnetic drive could far exceed the speed of light, and the relay grid of the autopilot invested it with a ruthless mechanical intelligence.

Forester picked up his jeweler's loupe and bent to open the inspection plate above the pilot again, afraid he had somehow failed to set the safety keys to prevent any detonation before the functioning of the drive had released them. Such a failure could turn Starmont into a small supernova; the fear of it forever harried his sleep, and ate his ulcers deeper.

He found the keys properly set, but that somehow failed to quiet his shapeless anxiety. Closing the plate again, he wished that he had been a different sort of man, better fitted to carry the lives of planets in his hands. He knew generals and politicians who actually seemed to envy the less appalling powers they believed him to hold, but no such man, he supposed, could have read the clue in the supernova's spectrum.

"Please, mister!"

The child spoke to him timidly as he turned from the missile. She was coming out of the narrow passage from the elevator, walking on bare silent feet. One grimy paw was deep in the pocket of her yellow dress, and she was trembling, as if to some desperate resolution, her voice dry with fright.

"Please—are you Dr. Forester?"

# 5

FORESTER STARTED TO an incredulous alarm. His jeweler's lens fell and clattered with a shocking sound on the steel floor, and rolled through a ladder well down into the power plant on the level below. Because no intruder should be here. Even the six technicians were not allowed to enter this vault except on duty, in twos to watch each other. He stumbled back against the bench, gasping sharply:

"How did you get in?"

He believed himself a mild and kindly man. His mirror showed the perpetual frown that worry had etched into his thin features, but he was still a wistful, harmless-seeming gnome of a man, slight and stooped and brown. He felt a flicker of hurt astonishment at the child's voiceless fear of him, before shocked dismay made him rasp again:

"Who let you down here?"

His voice went up, too shrill. For security and peace had been swept out of his life, by the very being of Project Thunderbolt. Because the holder of such a weapon had to be forever ready to use it instantly, or else to perish by it, this silent vault had become his last refuge from fear, where he caught uneasy naps on a cot beside the launching station and lived on coffee and hurried sandwiches and waited for the teleprinters to thump out orders to strike. Now the child's intrusion had demolished even this uncertain sanctuary.

"Nobody—" She stammered and trembled and gulped. Big tears started down her pinched cheeks, and she dropped a handful of yellow-flowered weeds to wipe them away with a grimy fist. "Please don't be mad, mister," she whispered. "Nobody let me in."

Sensitive to pollens, Forester sneezed to the rank odor of the blooms. Shrinking back from him, as if that had been a threatening gesture, the child began to cry.

"Mr. W-White said you wouldn't l-like me, mister," she sobbed faintly. "But he said you'd have to l-listen to us, if I came to see you here."

Forester had seen Triplanet agents, trapped and waiting for the firing squad. He suffered nightmares, in which he thought Project Thunderbolt had already been betrayed. But this shivering, big-eyed waif surely didn't look as if she had come to kill him, or even to loot the safe behind him, and he tried to soften the rasping anger in his voice.

"But how did you get past the guards?"

"Mr. White sent me." Shyly, she offered him a thin gray card. "With this."

Sneezing again, Forester kicked away the weeds, and took the finger-smudged card. His breath went out as he read the brief message on it, boldly inked:

*Clay Forester:*

*Sharing your concern for the people of these endangered planets, we can trade distressing and vital information for the aid we need from you. If you want to know how Jane Carter reached you, come alone to the old Dragonrock Light, or bring Frank Ironsmith—we trust nobody else.*

*Mark White, Philosopher*

Hearing the child's bare feet pattering on the steel floor, he looked up in time to see her running back down the tunnel to the elevator. He darted after her, shouting at her to wait, but the door closed in his face and a green arrow lit to show that the disguised cage was going up.

Shaken with dismay, Forester ran back to his desk in the

shop to telephone the upper project. Armstrong had seen no intruders, certainly no small girl in a yellow dress, but he promised to meet the rising elevator and hold anybody in it. Forester waited an agonized three minutes, and started nervously when the telephone rang again. Armstrong's voice seemed oddly constrained.

"Well, Chief, we unlocked the door and searched the elevator."

"Did you catch her?"

"No, Chief," Armstrong said slowly. "There wasn't anybody in it."

"But I saw her go in." Forester tried to hold down his voice. "There isn't any other landing, and the door can't open between stops. She had to be in the elevator."

"She wasn't," Armstrong said. "Nobody was."

Forester considered himself a man of reason. Technological marvels no longer astonished him, but he preferred to ignore any stray bits of experience which refused too stubbornly to fit the ordered pattern of physics. The planet-shattering missiles of the project no longer aroused any particular wonder in him, because they were part of the same pattern.

But the urchin's visit wasn't.

The grotesque impossibility of her coming and going left him shuddering. Restraining himself from starting up the escape ladder beyond the emergency door, he kept his numb forefinger on the elevator button. The cage came back at last, and he went up to join the two technicians, greeting them with a hoarse-voiced demand:

"Have you caught her yet?"

Staring oddly, Armstrong shook his head. "Sir, there has been no outsider here."

The man's voice was too courteous, too flatly formal, his level gaze too penetrating. Forester felt a sudden sickness. Sneezing again, from his allergy to those weeds the child had dropped, he said flatly:

"Somebody brought that elevator up."

"Sir, nobody went down." Armstrong kept on staring. "And nobody came up."

"But she was—down there," Forester croaked. These men knew the intolerable strain upon him always. Perhaps it wasn't strange for them to think that he had cracked, but he insisted huskily, "Look, Armstrong. I'm sane—yet."

"I hope you are, sir." But the man's bleak eyes were unconvinced. "We've searched the place and phoned the guard detachments," he reported stiffly. "There is nobody inside except the staff. Nobody but you has been admitted through our gate today." He glanced behind him uneasily. "The only odd thing is that call from Mr. Ironsmith."

"He called me, too"—Forester tried to keep his voice from trembling—"about the child at the gate, but that doesn't explain how she got inside."

"Ironsmith said she had some message—"

"She did." Forester displayed the gray card, soiled from Jane Carter's fingers. The two men studied it silently, and he saw the hard suspicion fade from Armstrong's eyes.

"Sorry, sir!"

"Can't blame you." Feebly, Forester answered his apologetic grin. "Now we can get at the problem."

They all went down again, to search the vault, but they found no intruder there. The great safe was still intact, plastered with unbroken seals. The long missiles lay safe in the racks. But Forester gathered up the weeds the child had dropped, frowning at them dazedly.

"This math expert," Armstrong said. "How does he come in?"

"We'll find out."

Picking up the desk telephone, Forester told Ironsmith to meet him at the inside gate, right now. They hurried silently back to the upper project, and out to the gate. Two guards waited for each of them to sign the pass book and surrender his badge, and finally let them outside to meet Ironsmith, who was already waiting for them, leaning on his rusty bicycle and calmly chewing gum. Forester asked him harshly:

"What about this little girl?"

"Who?" Ironsmith's easy grin had faded when he saw their tight faces, and now his gray eyes widened. "Did Jane Carter come back again?"

Narrowly watching that open, boyish face, Forester realized suddenly how many secrets he had carried to the computing section. He still couldn't quite believe that Ironsmith was a Triplanet agent, but a sudden sick panic tightened his voice.

"All right," he rasped. "Who is Jane Carter?"

"I never saw her before—" Seeing the drooping weeds in Forester's hand, Ironsmith started slightly. "Did she leave those?" he whispered. "I saw her picking them, just outside the main gate, when I was riding down to meet her."

Searching his pink, bewildered face, Forester handed him the gray card. He read it silently, and shook his sandy head. In a flat, accusing voice, Forester said:

"What I want to know is why you called me about her."

"Just because I couldn't understand how she went away," Ironsmith answered innocently. Handing back the gray card, he added quietly, "I'll go with you to Dragonrock Light."

"No, Chief!" Armstrong protested instantly. "Let the Security Police look for this mysterious Mr. White. Our job is here, and not playing cloak-and-dagger games with Triplanet spies." A sudden apprehension shook his voice. "Sir, you wouldn't think of really going?"

Forester was a man of science. Priding himself on the clear logic of his mind, he felt only scorn for intuition and mistrust for impulse. His own reckless words astonished him now, for he said quietly, "I'm going."

"If this White had any honest purpose," Armstrong objected, "he could contact you in some ordinary way. I don't like the look of all this funny business, sir, and you know your life is far too valuable to risk in what is probably a Triplanet trap. Why don't you just notify the police?"

But the technicians, after all, were a sort of military force, and Forester held command. He listened carefully to all the sensible cautions of Armstrong and the rest, but nothing altered that abrupt decision. For the child's visit had left him no choice. If strangers could enter and leave that guarded vault, they could wreck or steal his missiles at will. He gave his soft-voiced orders, and Armstrong and Dodge began loading a gray-painted official car with portable weapons.

"Stand by," he instructed the four men left behind. "Two off and two on. Watch the teleprinters for a Red Alert—just in case these people are Triplanet agents, trying to cripple the project until their fleets can strike."

The car was ready when he recalled his date for lunch with Ruth, and telephoned her hastily to say he wouldn't have time to eat. He tried to sound casual, and the project had parted them countless times before, but she must have heard the anxious tension in his voice.

"Clay!" she broke in sharply. "What's the trouble now?"

"Nothing, darling," he said uneasily. "Nothing at all."

He hurried to join the men in the car, and they stopped at the computing section for Ironsmith. No trained fighter, that indolent clerk would be useless in a trap, but Forester wanted to keep an eye on him. He couldn't understand how Ironsmith fitted into this sinister picture, or forget his sick suspicion that the mathematician had been trusted too far.

Sergeant Stone saluted respectfully as they stopped at the main gate, and Forester tried to question him. Years of service must have taught him the protective value of ignorance, however, because he could recall nothing at all unusual, sir, about the little girl in yellow.

Tense at the wheel, Forester drove down the twisting road to the desert and west to Salt City and on across the coast range. Beyond the mountains, they came down through a wall of chill gray fog, to the salt smell and the dull roaring of the sea. Somber with stray thoughts of the supernova and all its consequences, Forester turned south on the coast road.

The round stone tower of the old Dragonrock Light stood dim in the fog, half a mile from the road, on a cragged granite islet still joined to the mainland by the ruin of a storm-shattered causeway. Forester parked the car, as near as he could drive, and nodded at Ironsmith to follow him.

"Set up your rocket launcher in that ditch," he told Armstrong. "Fire without warning at any boat or plane that starts to leave—even if you think we're aboard. If we aren't back in exactly one hour, I want you to blow that tower off the rock. Any contrary order will be sent under duress, and you will ignore it."

"Okay, Chief," Armstrong agreed reluctantly, and looked at his watch. Dodge was already unfolding the tripod mount. Forester gave those two able men a smile of confidence, and then peered mistrustfully at Ironsmith, who was unconcernedly folding a fresh stick of gum into his mouth and tossing away the empty wrapper. Annoyed at his calm, Forester told him curtly to come along.

Grinning pleasantly, Ironsmith started scrambling briskly ahead over the wet, storm-tilted stones of the old causeway, which made an uncomfortable footpath. Forester followed, shivering to the raw bite of the mist-laden wind, and suddenly regretful of his impulsive decision. If this were really a trap, it occurred to him, the Triplanet agents had probably come ashore from a space raider lying underwater off the old lighthouse, and with the fog for a veil they might have him and the secret of the project safe on board long before that hour was up.

"Hello, Dr. Forester!"

The child's voice came to meet them through the mist, thin and high as some plaintive birdcall above the sigh of the wind and the murmur of the sea, and then he saw her standing above them at the base of the crumbling tower, tiny and alone. The wind whipped her thin yellow dress, and her skinny knees were blue and shaking with the cold.

# 6

FORESTER CLIMBED TO meet her, breathless and uneasy.

"Please be careful," she called anxiously. "The rocks are so slick and wet." The gusty wind blew her tiny voice away, and then she was saying, "—waiting to see you. Mr. White said you'd have to come."

Ahead of him, young Ironsmith ran up the spray-drenched rocks to the little girl. He grinned at her, his face pink and shining from the wind and exercise, and murmured something to her, and gave her a stick of chewing gum. Forester thought they seemed too friendly, although he tried to suspend his harsh suspicion when the clerk turned back thoughtfully to help him up the last high step. Greeting him with a timid nod, little Jane Carter trustfully offered Ironsmith her small grimy hand, and led them toward an open archway in the base of the old tower.

"Oh, Mr. White," she called eagerly. "Here they are."

A huge man came stalking out of that dark doorway. He towered a whole head above Forester, and the fiery red of his flowing hair and magnificent beard gave him a kind of vagabond splendor. He moved with a graceful, feline sort of strength, yet the angular planes of his ruddy face looked unyieldingly stubborn.

"We knew you'd be along, Forester, Ironsmith." His soft low voice was deep as the booming of the surf. "Glad you came, because we need you both very badly." He nodded at the dark archway. "Come and meet my associates."

Amiably, Ironsmith shook the big man's offered hand,

commenting like a delighted tourist on the bleak grandeur of the view. But Forester stepped back warily, his narrowed eyes looking for a Triplanet agent.

"Just a second!" The fabric and the cut of White's threadbare, silver-colored cloak belonged to no familiar fashion, and his soft accent seemed too carefully accurate to be native. "First, I want to see your papers."

"Sorry, Forester, but we're traveling light." The big man shook his flaming head. "I have no papers."

"But you've got to have papers!" Forester's nervous voice came too thin and high. "Anybody knows that. Every citizen is required to carry a passport from the Security Police. If you're a foreigner—and I think you are—then you aren't allowed off the spaceport without a visa."

"I'm not a citizen." White stood looking down at him with intent, expressionless, bright blue eyes. "But I didn't arrive by ship."

"Then how—" Forester caught his breath, nodding abruptly at the child. "And how did she get into Starmont?"

The big man chuckled, and the little girl turned from Ironsmith to smile up at him with a shining adoration on her pinched face.

"Jane," he murmured, "has a remarkable accomplishment."

"See here, Mr. White!" A bewildered resentment sharpened Forester's voice. "I don't like all these sinister hints—or your theatrical method of luring us out here. I want to know exactly what you're up to."

"I only want to talk to you." White drawled that disarming explanation. "You are fenced in with red tape. Jane broke it for me, in a way that made you come here. I assure you that we are not Triplanet spies—and I mean to send you safely back before Armstrong decides to open fire."

Startled, Forester peered back toward the mainland. The gray official car was vague in the fog. He couldn't see the two technicians waiting with their rocket launcher in the ditch beyond. Certainly he couldn't see their names.

"I call myself a philosopher." Beneath the lazy tone, Forester could hear a note of savage vehemence. "That's only a tag, however. Useful when the unsuspecting police of some ill-fated planet want to know my business, but not completely accurate."

"Precisely what is your business?"

"I'm a soldier, really," murmured White. "I'm trying to wage war against a vicious enemy of men. I arrived here quite alone, a few days ago, to gather another force for this final stand."

He gestured at the old stone tower.

"Here's my fortress. And my little army. Three men and a brilliant child. We have our weapons, even if you don't see them. We're training for a last bold assault—for only the utmost daring can hope to snatch the victory now."

The big man glanced forebodingly up into the driving mist.

"Because we've met reverses," he rumbled solemnly. "Our brave little force is not enough, and our weapons are inadequate. That's where you come in." His penetrating eyes came back to Forester. "Because we must have the help of one or two good rhodomagnetic engineers."

Forester shuddered in icy dismay, for the whole science of rhodomagnetics was still top secret. Even Ironsmith, whose computing section had established so much of the theory, had never been told of the frightful applications. Trying to cover his consternation, he demanded harshly:

"By what authority?"

White's slow smile stopped him.

"Facts are my authority," the big man said. "The fact that I have met this enemy. That I know the danger. That I have a weapon—however still imperfect. That I have not surrendered—and never will!"

"Don't talk riddles." Forester blinked, annoyed. "Who is this enemy, so-called?"

"You will meet it soon," White promised softly, "and you will call it so. It is nothing human, but ruthless and intelligent and almost invincible—because it comes in a guise of utmost benevolence. I'm going to tell you all about it, Forester. I've a sad warning for you. But first I want you to meet the rest of my little band."

He gestured urgently at the black archway. Little Jane Carter took Ironsmith's hand again, and the smiling clerk strolled with her into the darkness of the old tower. White stood aside, waiting for Forester to follow. Glancing up at him, Forester felt a tremor of awe. A queer philosopher, he thought, and a very singular soldier.

Uneasily aware that he had come too far to turn back now, Forester reluctantly entered. The chill wind came after him, and he thought the trap was closing. But the bait still fascinated him, that solemn-eyed child holding Ironsmith's hand. The tower room was round and vaulted, dimly lit from narrow slits of windows. The damp stone walls, black with ancient smoke, were scarred with the names of earlier vandals.

Blinking against the gloom, Forester saw three men, squatting around a small open fire on the stone floor. One was stirring a battered pot, which reeked of garlic. Ironsmith sniffed appreciatively, and the three made room for him and the child to sit on driftwood blocks by the fire. She leaned to warm her hands and Ironsmith smiled genially at the three, but Forester paused in the doorway, incredulous, as White presented the bold little band. For he could see no weapons; the three were only ragged vagabonds, in need of soap and barbering.

The gaunt man stirring the pot was named Graystone. He rose stiffly, a gaunt and awkward scarecrow in rusty black. His angular face was stubbled and cadaverous, with dark sunken eyes and a very red nose.

"Graystone the Great." Bowing with a solemn dignity, he amplified White's introduction. "Formerly a noted stage magician and professional telepath. My act was quite successful until the machine-minded populace lost its interest in the rare

treasures of the mind. We welcome your interest in our noble cause."

Lucky Ford was a small man, bald as Forester, crouching close to the fire. His dark cheeks were seamed and wizened, and darker pouches sagged under his narrow shrewd eyes. Squinting up at Forester, he nodded silently.

"Ford," White explained, "was a professional gambler."

Forester stood watching, fascinated. Absently, still peering up, the little man was rolling dice against a stick of drying driftwood. Somehow, the dice always came sevens. He met Forester's astonishment with a thin-lipped grin.

"Telekinesis." His voice had a hard nasal twang. "Mr. White taught me the word, just now, but I could always roll the bones." Dancing away from the driftwood, the dice made another seven. "The art is less profitable than you might think," he added cynically. "Because every gambler has a little of the skill—and calls it luck. When you win, the suckers always think you cheated, and the law ain't friendly. Mr. White got me out of a county jail."

Ash Overstreet was a short heavy man, sitting on a rock in stolid immobility. He looked sallow and unhealthy. His thick hair was prematurely white, and massive lenses magnified his dull, myopic eyes.

"A clairvoyant," White said. "Extratemporal."

"We used to call it just a nose for news, when I was a reporter." Scarcely moving, Overstreet spoke in a hoarse whisper. "But I had a sharper perception than most. I got to seeing so much, before I learned control, that I had to dull my insight with drugs. Mr. White found me locked up in a narcotics ward."

Forester shook his head uneasily. All such phenomena of the mind belonged to a disreputable borderland of science, where the truth had always been obscured by ignorant superstition and by the trickery of such cheap mountebanks as this Graystone. He wanted to stalk out scornfully, but something made him look around for the little girl in yellow. She was gone.

He blinked at the fire, shivering uncomfortably. The hungry-looking child had been here, he was certain, just a moment before, chattering to Ironsmith, but now her place was empty. Ironsmith was watching the doorway, with a calm, bright interest, and Forester turned that way in time to see her come running in again. Handing the clerk some small metal object, she sat down again by the fire.

"Please, Mr. Graystone." She watched the simmering pot, with enormous eager eyes. "Please, can't we eat?"

"You've already met Jane Carter," White was drawling softly. "Her great accomplishment is teleportation."

"Tele—" Forester gasped, wrestling with a sudden overwhelming surmise. "What?"

"I think you'll have to agree that Jane's pretty good." The big man smiled down through the red beard, and she looked back, her eyes luminous with a mute admiration. "In fact, she has the richest psychophysical capacities that I've found on any of the planets where I've looked for resources to fight our common enemy."

Forester shivered to the wind at his back.

"Jane was another misfit," White went on. "In this age of machine worship, her young genius had been ignored and denied. Her only recognition had come from some petty criminal, who attempted to turn her talents to shoplifting. I took her out of a reform school."

Her thin blue face smiled up at Forester.

"I'm not going back to that bad place," she told him proudly. "Mr. White never has to beat me, and he's teaching me psychophysics." She spoke the word with grave care. "I went to find you in that deep cellar in the mountain, all by myself. Mr. White says I did very well."

"I—I think you did!" Forester stammered faintly.

She turned hopefully to watch the stew again, and Forester

peered sharply about that smoke-darkened room, where a few driftwood timbers and little piles of straw made the only furniture.

"A curious fortress, I know." That ruthless purpose burned again in White's blue eyes. "But all our weapons are in our minds, and the hard pursuit of the enemy has left us no resources to waste on needless luxuries."

Forester watched the little gambler roll another nervous seven. That must be some kind of trick, he thought, and the child's appearance at Starmont another. He refused to take any serious stock in this paraphysical stuff, but he tried to conceal that bleak mistrust as he swung back to White. He must stall, study these people, discover the motives and the methods of their strange chicanery.

"What enemy?" he demanded.

"I see you aren't taking my warning very seriously." White's rumbling drawl became ominously intense. "But I think you will when you hear the news." The big man took his arm, to lead him away from the fire. "Mason Horn is going to land tonight."

Forester swallowed hard, unable to cover his shock. For Mark White, whether a desperate Interplanet agent or merely a clever rogue, had no right to know even the name of Mason Horn.

# 7

THE MISSION OF Mason Horn was another high secret, as closely guarded as Project Thunderbolt itself. Two years ago, when the pen traces in the new search dome at Starmont first began to hint of neutrino bursts from some nearer and less friendly source than the supernova, that competent astronomer had been drafted from the observatory staff to find why the Triplanet fleets always selected Sector Vermilion for their space maneuvers.

Hurriedly briefed in the dangerous art of interplanetary espionage and equipped as a legitimate salesman of medico-radiological supplies, he had taken passage on a Triplanet trading vessel. No word of him had yet come back.

"Mason Horn!" Forester felt ill with shock. "Did he find—"

Caution choked him, but White's great shaggy head had already nodded at Ash Overstreet. Turning slowly from the fire, the clairvoyant looked up with an expression of lax stupidity.

"Horn's an able secret agent," he rasped hoarsely. "In fact, though the man himself doesn't suspect it, he has fairly well-developed extrasensory perceptions. He was able to penetrate an Interplanet space fort stationed out in the direction designated as Sector Vermilion, and he got away with some kind of military device. I don't understand it, but he thinks of it as a mass-converter."

Forester's legs turned weak, and he sat down on a driftwood block. During all those ghastly years, while he had been perfecting the slender missiles of his own project and waiting beside them in the vault through anxious days and sleepless nights, this was what he had most greatly feared. He had to swallow before he could whisper:

"So that's your bad news?"

"No." White shook his flowing, fiery mane. "Our enemy is something vaster and more vicious than the Triplanet Powers. And the weapon against us is something more deadly than any mass-converter. It is pure benevolence."

Forester sat hunched and shuddering.

"I'm afraid you don't understand mass-conversion weapons," he protested faintly. "They use all the energy in the detonated matter—while the fission process, in the best plutonium bombs, releases less than a tenth of one percent. They make a different sort of war. One small missile can split the crust of a planet, boil the seas and sterilize the land, and poison everything with radioisotopes for a thousand years." He stared at White. "What could be worse than that?"

"Our benevolent enemy is."

"How could that be?"

"That's what I brought you here to tell you." Forester waited, perched uncomfortably on the damp timber, and White kicked aside a straw bed to stand over him impatiently. "It's a simple, dreadful story. The beginning of it was ninety years ago, on a planet known as Wing IV, nearly two hundred light-years from here at the far side of the colonized section of the galaxy. The human villain of it was a scientist whose name translates as Warren Mansfield."

"You pretend to know what happened there only ninety years ago?" Forester stiffened skeptically. "When even the light that left the star Wing at that time is not halfway to us yet?"

"I do." White's smile had a passing glint of malice. "The missiles of your secret project are not all that travel faster than light!"

Forester gulped with cold dismay, listening silently.

"Ninety years ago," the huge man rumbled, "the planet Wing IV had come to face the same technological crisis that this one does today—the same crisis that every culture meets, at a certain point in its technological evolution. The common solutions are death and slavery—violent ruin or slow decay. On Wing IV, however, Warren Mansfield created a third alternative."

Forester looked up at him searchingly, waiting.

"Physical science had got out of hand there, as it has here. Mansfield had already discovered rhodomagnetism there— perhaps because the light of the Crater Supernova struck Wing IV a century before it reached here. He had seen his discovery misused as a weapon, as most physical discoveries have been. Foolishly, he tried to bottle up the technological devil he had freed."

Forester began to wish he had called the police after all, for this man knew far too much to be free.

"Military mechanicals had already been evolved too far, you see, there on Wing IV," White went on. "Mansfield used his new science to design android mechanicals of a new type—humanoids, he called them—intended to restrain men from war. The job took many years, but he was finally too successful. His rhodomagnetic mechanicals are a little too perfect."

The big man paused, taut with an angry energy, but Forester sat too dazed to ask the frightened questions in his mind. He shivered again, as if the damp wind at his back had the chill of outer space.

"I knew Mansfield," White resumed at last. "Later, and on a different planet. He was an old man, then, but still desperately fighting the benevolent monster he had made. A refugee from his own humanoids. For those efficient mechanicals were following him from planet to planet, spreading out across the human worlds to stamp out war—exactly as he had meant them to do.

"Mansfield couldn't stop them.

"He found me a homeless child, wandering in a land that war had ruined. He rescued me from starvation and fear, and brought me up to join his crusade. I was with him for a good many years, while he was trying one weapon and another, but he always failed to stop the humanoids."

A sad sternness hardened White's bearded face.

"Growing old, defeated, Mansfield tried to make a physical scientist out of me, to carry on after him. He failed again. I had learned to hate the humanoids enough, but I lacked his scientific gift. He had been a physicist. I grew into something else.

"Living like a wild animal in the rubble of ruined cities, hunting and hunted while I was still a child, I had learned powers of the human mind that Mansfield could never recognize. Our philosophies came to differ. He had put his faith in machines—and made the humanoids. When he came to see his blunder, he tried to destroy them with more machines. He was bound to fail—because those mechanicals are as nearly perfect as any machine will ever be.

"I shared his hatred, but I saw the need of some better weapon than any machine. I put my trust in men—in the native human powers I had begun to learn. If men were to save themselves, I saw they must discover and use their own inborn capacities, rusty as they are from long neglect.

"So at last we separated. I'm sorry that our parting words were too bitter—I called Mansfield a machine-minded fool, and he said that my science of the mind would only end with another regimentation of mankind, worse than the rule of the humanoids. He went on to try his last weapon—he was attempting to ignite a chain reaction in the oceans and the rocks of Wing IV, with some kind of rhodomagnetic beam. I never saw him again, but I know he didn't succeed.

"Because the humanoids are still running.

"I'm still fighting them, and these are my soldiers." The huge man nodded indignantly at his ragged followers squatted by the fire. "Look at them—the most talented citizens of this planet. I found them in the gutter, the jail, the madhouse. But they are the last hope of man."

Flinching from the angry boom of his voice, Forester whispered uneasily, "I don't quite see—what are these weapons of the mind?"

"One of the simplest is atomic probability."

"Eh?"

"Take an atom of Potassium-40." White's great voice turned softly patient again. "A physicist yourself, you can easily picture such an unstable atom as a sort of natural wheel of chance, set to pay off only once during several billion years of spinning."

Forester nodded skeptically, thinking that nothing could be deadlier than the missiles of his own project.

"Like any machine of chance," White went on, "an unstable atom can be manipulated. Just as easily as a pair of dice—it seems that size and distance aren't important factors, in telekinesis."

Forester blinked unbelievingly at the withered little gambler crouching by the fire, who had just rolled a five and a two. "How do you manipulate an atom?"

"I don't quite know." Trouble darkened White's burning eyes. "Although Jane does it easily, and the rest of us have made a few successful efforts at it—children learn the mental arts more readily, I think, perhaps because they don't have to unlearn the false truths and break the bad habits of mechanistic science. And Jane is unusual."

His brooding face warmed for a moment, as he glanced at the little girl, who was eagerly watching old Graystone dip out her bowl of stew.

"But I don't know," he muttered wearily. "The facts I have discovered are often apparently contradictory, and always incomplete. Perhaps the uncertainty principle involved in atomic stability doesn't apply to psychophysical phenomena. Perhaps it is merely an illusion, born of the fact that our physical senses are too coarse to look into atoms. I have suspected that physical time and space are similar illusions—I don't know. But I do know that Jane Carter can detonate K-40 atoms."

White shrugged heavily, in the silver cloak.

"I've had dreams, Forester." His voice turned wistfully sad. "Magnificent dreams, of a coming time when my new science might free every man from the old, cruel shackles of the brute and the machine. I used to believe that the human mind could conquer matter, master space, and govern time.

"But the most of my efforts have failed—I don't know why." He shook his fiery, shaggy head. "I run into blind alleys. I stumble over obstacles that I can never really identify. Perhaps there's some barrier I fail to see, some limiting natural law that I've never grasped."

He moved restlessly, towering over Forester.

"I don't know," he repeated bitterly. "And there's no time left for trial and error now, because those machines have taken most of the human universe. This is one of the last planets left—and I don't think you know that their first scouts are already here!"

Forester stared up in slack-jawed unbelief.

"Yes, old Mansfield's humanoids are already infiltrating your defenses." White's voice turned wearily grim. "They make efficient spies, you see. More clever than the human agents employed against you by the Triplanet Powers. They don't sleep, and they don't blunder."

"Huh!" Forester gulped, astonished. "You don't mean—spying machines?"

"You've met them," White said. "You would find it impossible to tell them from men—they are cunning enough to avoid being X-rayed or mangled in accidents. But I know them. That's one thing I've learned, for all my failures. I've trained myself to sense the rhodomagnetic energy that operates them."

Forester shook his head, incredulous and yet appalled.

"They're already here," the big man insisted. "And Ash Overstreet says Mason Horn's report is going to be the signal for them to strike. That leaves us no more time for bungling. To stop them at all, we must grasp every device we can. That's why we need rhodomagnetic engineers."

Forester stood up uncertainly. "I don't quite see—"

"Those machines are rhodomagnetic," White's great voice broke in. "They are all operated by remote control, on beamed rhodomagnetic power, from a central relay grid on Wing IV. They must be attacked, somehow, through that grid—because they can replace one lost unit, or a billion of them, without feeling any harm. Now, unfortunately I've no head for higher math, and old Mansfield failed to teach me more than the rudiments of rhodomagnetics. So that's where you come in." The deep voice tightened. "Will you join us?"

Kicking uncomfortably at the timber where he had sat, Forester hesitated for half a second. He was fascinated against his will by the possibility that White and his dubious disciples had stumbled into a new field of science, but he shook his head uneasily. If all this were true—if Mason Horn were really coming back to report that Triplanet scientists had perfected mass-conversion weapons—then he should be back at his own project, standing by for a Red Alert.

"Sorry," he said stiffly. "Can't do it."

White didn't argue. Oddly, instead, as if he had expected the refusal, he turned immediately to Ironsmith, who still sat beside Jane Carter at the fire, listening with a calm attention.

"Ironsmith, will you stay with us?"

Forester caught his breath, watching narrowly. If the clerk chose to stay, that might mean that he was already an accomplice of White's. It might even mean that he had helped old Graystone the Great stage the expert illusion of the little girl's visit to the project—if that could have been any sort of trick. But Ironsmith shook his sandy head.

"I can't see what's so bad about those mechanicals," he protested mildly. "Not from anything I heard you say. After all, they're nothing but machines, doing what they were designed for. If they can actually abolish war, I'd be glad to see them come."

"They're already here!" Savagely harsh, White's voice forgot to drawl. "Overstreet told me you wouldn't help us now, but at least you are warned. I think you'll change your mind when you meet the humanoids."

"Might be." Ironsmith met his ruthless glare with a pink and affable grin. "But I don't think so."

"Anyhow, there's something you can do." White swung impatiently back to Forester, as if stung by Ironsmith's calm. "You can warn the nation of those humanoid spies infiltrating your defenses, and those invincible ships already on their way from Wing IV with mechanicals enough to take over the planet. As scientific adviser to the Defense Authority, perhaps you can delay the invasion long enough—"

White broke off suddenly, with an inquiring glance at Ash Overstreet. The short man had stirred on the rock where he sat. His dim eyes stared vacantly at the dark stone walls, but the tilt of his head had a curious new alertness.

"It's time for him to go." The clairvoyant nodded heavily at Forester. "Because his men are getting nervous, out there with their rocket gun. They imagine we're Triplanet agents, and they're about ready to blow us up."

# 8

FORESTER PEERED AT his watch and darted out of that dark room without ceremony. Outside the tower, he began frantically waving his hat, hoping that Armstrong and Dodge could see him through the drifting fog. Behind him, he heard Ironsmith taking a more deliberate leave. Little Jane Carter laughed with pleasure, and then he heard her voice:

"Thank you, Mr. Ironsmith!"

"Come along!" Forester shouted hoarsely. "Before they shoot!"

But the smiling mathematician lingered maddeningly, to shake the trembling hand of the old magician and murmur some farewell to White. He had turned out the pockets of his baggy slacks, to give Jane Carter a few coins and all his stock of chewing gum, and she followed him outside, when at last he came waving a grave farewell.

"They won't shoot." Grinning, Ironsmith displayed a dark bit of metal. "Because little Jane brought me the firing link out of their rocket gun."

Shuddering to the cold sea wind, still desperately waving his hat, Forester scrambled ahead of Ironsmith across the great wet stones of the broken causeway. He was breathless when they came back to the car, and cold with sweat from something else than running.

"You had us worried, sir," Dodge called gratefully from beside the tripod in the ditch. "That hour was almost up."

Turning to peer uneasily back at the old round tower, dark

in the driving mist, Forester told him to unload the launcher and test the mechanism. He obeyed, and shouted a startled curse. His jaw dropped when Ironsmith silently handed him the missing firing link.

"Don't ask questions now." Forester clung weakly to the door of the car. "Just stow your gear, and let's get back to Starmont. Because I think the project is going to be alerted. Soon!"

He didn't feel like driving. Armstrong took the wheel, and he sat with Ironsmith and the folded tripod behind. Chilled, and stiff with fatigue, and vaguely ill from the motion of the car, he studied Ironsmith uneasily. The clerk sat comfortably sprawled with his feet propped on the launcher tube, watching the landscape with a casual interest until they left the mountains and dropped back to the brown monotony of the desert, when he stretched and closed his eyes and went to sleep. Tortured with apprehensive uncertainties, Forester jogged him back to a quiet alertness.

"I'm a physicist." Hoarse with worry, Forester felt that he had to talk. "I'm used to limiting my inquiries to phenomena that are reproducible at will, by mechanical means, under strict controls. This psychic stuff—I just don't want to believe it."

"I understand." Ironsmith nodded cheerfully. "I recall a paper you wrote to attack the evidence for extraphysical action. You were pretty violent."

"Just a lab report," Forester protested defensively. "You see, Ruth's instrument firm had supplied equipment for some crackpot experiment. There were dice in a little frame that tilted to roll them, mechanically, making the conditions for each fall identical. The experimenter claimed that he could control the fall mentally, and I thought Ruth was taking him too seriously. I ordered a duplicate frame and tried to repeat the experiment—just to show her that it was all nonsense. And my results showed a curve of random distribution."

"Which itself was a pretty good proof of extraphysical action." Grinning quizzically at his startled gape, the clerk added innocently, "Because that was what you wanted. Any sort of extraphysical research, don't you see, requires a slight modification in the methods of classical physics. The experimenter is also a part of the experiment. Your negative results were a logical outcome of your negative purpose."

Forester stared, as if discovering a stranger. Ironsmith had never seemed much more than a convenient accessory to the electronic calculators, serenely content with his insignificant job. He had annoyed Forester with his careless dress and his chewing gum and his commonplace friends. He had always showed an irritating irreverence for the established aristocracy of scholarship, and Forester was startled into silence, now, by his unexpected cogency.

"Purpose is the key," he went on casually. "But Mark White has too much of the wrong sort—he's looking for weapons, instead of the truth. That's why I think he'll never learn enough to control those mechanicals. He hates them too hard."

"But he has reasons." Resentment of the clerk's pleasant calm spurred Forester to a harsh protest. "He knows the humanoids, remember, and we don't. I intend making a full report of his warning to the Defense Authority. Whatever the circumstances, our military forces ought to be alerted against any such planned invasion."

"I'd think that over, sir." Ironsmith shook his head. "Because this whole affair would look a little odd, don't you realize, to anybody who wasn't on the spot. You'll have to admit that our own testimony wouldn't sound very impressive to a military commission, what with White's rather childish theatrics and the trampish look of his associates."

His boyish face brightened.

"Besides, sir, I think these new mechanicals might turn out to be very useful. For all White told us, I still can't see any real reason to hate or fear them. If they can actually abolish war, we need them now. Don't you think so, sir?"

Forester didn't, but the quiet protest recalled that bleak doubt in Armstrong's eyes. Reflecting that the members of the

Defense Authority might prove equally incredulous, he decided to wait for better evidence.

It was twilight when the car labored up the narrow road from the desert, to the guarded fences and floodlit buildings of Starmont. Groggy with fatigue, Forester felt a pang of envy when Ironsmith swung easily out as they stopped at the inner gate, to step easily on his bicycle and pedal briskly off toward the computing section, whistling as he went.

The Red Alert came at midnight, on the tight-beam teleprinter. That warning signal meant that hostile action from the Triplanet Powers had been detected. It called for the staff of Project Thunderbolt to arm two missiles against each of the enemy planets, and stand by for the final order to end three worlds.

A second message, five minutes later, called Forester himself to the capital for an emergency meeting of the Defense Authority. He took off at once, with no time even for a word to Ruth. His official aircraft landed in cold rain at dawn on a military field, and a waiting staff car took him into a guarded tunnel in the face of a hill.

Deep in the underground site which men had dug in their frantic search for vanished safety, he came at last into a narrow room of gray concrete, and took his place at the foot of a green-covered table to wait for the meeting. He hadn't been able to sleep on the plane, tossed with nocturnal thunderstorms along an occluded front. The flight lunch he had shared with the crew felt heavy on his stomach, and he needed a dose of bicarbonate. Clammy in his travel-wrinkled clothing, he sat longing for the dry warmth of Starmont and trying not to think of anything else. He blinked and started when he saw Mason Horn.

The secret agent came in through another guarded door, walking between two armed lieutenants of the Security Police. Forester rose eagerly to call out his greeting, but Horn answered with only a stiff little nod, and one of the lieutenants beckoned Forester back. They waited, watchfully apart at the end of that long gray room. Horn carried a small brown leather case, chained to his left wrist. Sinking back into his chair, Forester felt a new chill in the damp blast from a fan somewhere behind him. He knew what that case must contain, and the knowledge was monstrous.

The nearer lieutenant saw his eyes on the case, and frowned at him sharply. Starting again, he shifted his gaze and tried to wipe the stickiness out of his palms. The silent weight of rock above began to give him a smothered feeling, and a faint reek of drying paint sharpened his physical unease. He slumped in his chair, and straightened again when the high military and political officials who formed the Defense Authority began to arrive, surrounded by hushed and nervous satellites.

The aged world president entered at last, leaning on the arm of his solicitous military aide, one Major Steel. Calling out quavering greetings to a few of his cronies, he shuffled to his big chair at the end of the table. Steel helped him to sit, and he waited for the dapper little officer to prompt him before he spoke to the hushed meeting.

"Gentlemen, I've bad news for you." His voice faltered thinly. "Mr. Mason Horn will tell you what it is."

The special agent left the two lieutenants, at the president's feeble nod, and stepped up briskly to the table. With his thinning yellowish hair and fat red face, he looked more like a show salesman than an interplanetary spy. Unlocking the chain, he opened the brown leather case to display a polished metal object the size of an egg.

"This is the bad news." His voice was as blandly casual as if he had been offering a chic new number in brown suede for the spring market. "I brought it back from a Triplanet arsenal in Sector Vermilion. The president has instructed me not to reveal the technical specifications. I'm only to tell you what it can do."

The men around that long, bright-lit table, most of them withered with years and all tight-faced with anxiety, leaned silently to watch as Horn's plump, careful fingers unscrewed the flat-ended metal egg into two parts and set them on the table. Cold light glittered on small knurled metal knobs and graduated scales.

"Huh!" The chief of staff sniffed scornfully. "Is that all?"

"It's enough, sir." Horn gave him a brief, amiable smile, as if about to explain the irresistible sales appeal of a plastic evening sandal. "Actually, the device itself is only a sort of fuse. The explosive charge is formed by any matter which happens to be near. The atoms aren't just fissioned, but converted entirely to free energy. This little knob sets the radius of detonation—anywhere from zero to twelve yards."

When his smooth voice stopped, an appalled silence filled that buried room. Men leaned to stare with a sick, slack-jawed fascination at the tiny machine on the table. The muted drone of the ventilator fan became an unpleasant roaring, the reek of paint seemed stronger. Forester sat shivering, trying not to be ill.

"One of these could finish us." With a fumbling care, Mason Horn began screwing the two small sections back together. "If you want to estimate its effectiveness for yourselves, convert the cubic yards of soil and rock to tons, and then multiply the answer by one thousand. That will give you the approximate equivalent in plutonium."

He paused, carefully locking the chain again.

"The Triplanet Powers have now had more than two years to plant these where they want them," he added quietly. "They may have been dropped into our seas, or sowed across the polar caps, or perhaps even smuggled into this very site. Placed in advance, they can be detonated by remote control, by a time mechanism, or even by the penetrating radiation from a mass-explosion on another planet. No defense is possible, and we cannot attack, not even with similar weapons, without destroying ourselves."

"I don't see that." The chief of staff cleared his throat, with a stern authority. "When they discover that you have escaped with this device, they will assume that we have also duplicated it successfully. Perhaps we should plant the information with one of our double agents—to create the fear of retaliation, and so make it impossible for them to strike."

"I'm afraid it wouldn't work out that way, sir." Horn frowned, as if in regretful disapproval of the shoddy workmanship of some competing line. "Because such absolute weapons create their own explosive psychology. I think it would be foolish to reveal that we have successfully stolen this weapon, because I saw symptoms enough of official hysteria in the enemy governments to convince me that we should be prepared to die on the instant they discover the loss. That delicate situation makes me doubt the wisdom of my whole mission, sir."

And Horn stepped respectfully back, mopping at his plump red face and waiting as if to write up an order for shoes. The chief of staff scowled at him, and abruptly sat down, seeming to say with his indignant shrug that such unmilitary men, with their unbelievable new weapons and their shocking ignorance of discipline, had ruined all his old pleasure in the ancient calling of war.

Wiping his palms again, Forester shook his head at the mute query on the bleak gray face of the minister of defense. Project Thunderbolt was ready. The warheads of his own long self-guided missiles, not far different from Mason Horn's prize, had a detonation radius of forty yards. Once the launching order was given, nothing could save the hostile planets. But it was too late to launch them now, if their blasts would also trigger enemy detonators planted here.

The old president was turning anxiously to his aide, with some question in his watery eyes. Nodding briskly, little Major Steel helped him to his feet. Forester tried to conceal a sharp disapproval, recalling the legends of Steel's phenomenal memory and efficiency, and mistrusting his undue influence.

"An unpleasant situation, gentlemen." Clutching the edge of the table with trembling yellow hands, the president cleared his throat uncertainly. "It first appeared to offer us only the hard choice of war without hope, or peace without freedom. However—" Gasping breathlessly, he gulped water the little officer held to his lips. "However, Major Steel has revealed a third alternative."

# 9

THAT QUAVERED PHRASE took Forester's breath. He remembered a pale tattered man, squatting by a smoky fire and peering as if at distant things with a strange alertness. Something drummed in his ears, and the old leader's faltering voice seemed far away.

"—quite a shock to me, as you will soon understand." The president nodded his cadaverous head at the trim little officer, who stood motionless at attention, peering fixedly down the table. "But the alternative he offers has ended a nightmare for me, and I urge you to accept his advice without question."

He coughed, leaning weakly on the table, and waited for the brisk little aide to hold the glass for him to drink again.

"Gentlemen, I believe in Major Steel." He turned to smile at the officer with a vague gratitude. "He has been my efficient right hand for the past ten years, and I feel that we can trust him now. He has brought us an amazing escape from both death and slavery. But I'm going to let him state the facts, with only this one word of warning—he is not a human being."

Forester knew that he shouldn't have been surprised. Mark White had tried to prepare him for this moment, and he had always mistrusted the superhuman energy and competence of the president's aide. Yet, as he watched the human-seeming thing at the other end of the long green table now, something made him shudder. Something cold brushed up his spine, and something took his breath.

"At your service, gentlemen." The human vocal quality was suddenly gone from Steel's voice, so that it became a mellow silver drone. "But just a moment, if you please. Because you should see us as we are, and now the need for this disguise has ended."

And the thing slipped out of the crisp uniform. It snapped contact lenses out of its eyes. It ripped at what had seemed its skin, and began peeling flesh-colored plastic from its limbs and its body in long spiral strips.

Forester watched helplessly. He saw the faces around the table turning stiff and gray, and heard men gasping with something close to horror. His own breath caught when an overturned chair fell with a shocking crash. Yet there was nothing really horrible about what emerged from that discarded mask.

Rather, it was beautiful. The shape of it was nearly human, but very slim and graceful, with no mechanical awkwardness or angularity whatever. Half a head shorter than Forester, it was nude now, and sexless. The sleek skin of it was a shining black, sheened with changing lights of bronze and blue. A yellow brand gleamed on its breast:

HUMANOID
Serial No. M8-B3-ZZ
"To Serve and Obey,
And Guard Men from Harm."

For a moment, when it had flung off the last of its wrappings, it stood quite still beside the old president. Now its eyes were blind-seeming orbs that caught the light like polished steel, and its narrow, high-cheeked face was fixed in a look of dark benignity. After the flowing felicity of its action, that frozen poise seemed as eerie as its inhuman voice.

"Your present alarm is needless, gentlemen," it cooed musically, "because we never injure any man. Major Steel was simply a useful fiction, created for your own benefit, which enabled us to observe the present technological crisis as it developed here and to offer our services in time to avert calamity."

"But—Mr. President!" The defense minister had risen, still gasping. "I fail to understand this strange display," he pro-

tested shakenly. "But I must remind you that wise laws exist to protect our working classes from the competition of such multipurpose android mechanicals as this appears to be, and I hope you recall that our party is pledged to enforce them. With elections to come—"

The president merely looked at the machine.

"You need not fear the labor vote," it broke in briskly. "Because we bring no want or suffering to any workingman. On the contrary, our only function is to promote human welfare. Once established, our service will remove all class distinctions, along with such other causes of unhappiness and pain as war and poverty and toil and crime. There will be no class of toilers, because there will be no toil."

Fumbling agitatedly with a pitcher and a glass, the chief of staff looked uncertainly from the droning mechanical to the trembling lieutenants beside Mason Horn, and finally shouted hoarsely:

"Seize that—device!"

"That isn't necessary, sir," its golden voice sang instantly. "Because we have no purpose except to serve you."

The two lieutenants merely moved closer to Horn, and the chief of staff forgot them, sputtering breathlessly, "That's no machine! It—it thinks!"

"We are mechanical," the steel-eyed thing told him melodiously. "But we do think, because all our identical units are joined by rhodomagnetic beams to our central relay grid on the planet Wing IV. Such units as the one before you are only the limbs and the sense organs of that mechanical brain, which perceives and acts through them. We think more rapidly and effectively than men, in fact, because our rhodomagnetic impulses act without the time lag which slows the inefficient mental reactions of human beings, and because that great relay grid is a far more perfect mechanism than any human brain. We don't sleep and we don't err and we don't forget, and our awareness embraces everything that happens on many thousand worlds. You may welcome us without fear, however, because we exist only to serve and obey mankind."

The chief of staff swallowed convulsively, and somehow overturned his glass and pitcher. Moving with a silent, incredible ability, the mechanical righted them before the water had time to spill, and held the glass to the old general's lips.

"Quite remarkable!" The chief of staff strangled on the water, turning red in the face, and sputtered at the dark humanoid, which now stood alertly motionless again. "But how—precisely how—can you abolish war?"

"We are used to dealing with the inevitable cataclysmic breakdowns of such hypertrophic technologies as this planet has developed," the machine pealed sweetly, "and we have efficient methods of averting violence. Our agents here and on the neighbor planets began preparing for this crisis ten years ago. Our ships from Wing IV are already near, bringing the necessary units and equipment to begin our service, and you will find the formal arrangements very simple."

The humanoid moved swiftly again, to set the glass and pitcher safely beyond reach of the man's agitated hands.

"Your spaceports and those of the Triplanet Powers must be opened immediately to our shipping," it continued serenely. "Our advance agents must be given authority to monitor communications and inspect military installations, in order to prevent any human treachery. At an agreed future date, all military equipment must be surrendered to us for safe disposal."

"Surrender?" The chief of staff turned a choleric purple. "Never!"

"The matter is not in your hands," the machine droned blandly. "The crucial decision for all these planets was actually made some decades ago in a physics laboratory, by a foolhardy man who had discovered the theoretical possibility of a nuclear chain reaction in a uranium-graphite pile. Once he chose to risk the rest, and so demonstrated the fission process, the outcome was already fixed. You are still free, however, to discuss the situation."

Turning attentively to face the president, the humanoid stood still again, a dark image of ultimate beneficence. Smiling at it hopefully, the old statesman called in a tremulous voice for discussion. Deaf to the wrangling which followed, Forester sat shivering in the damp blast of the fan, watching the machine and debating what to do. Once he caught his breath to report the whole matter of Mark White's warning. But that wouldn't do, he saw at once, because he would be compromising the security of Project Thunderbolt still farther. Finally he passed a note to the defense minister, asking for a private word with the president.

"Gentlemen," that sleek machine was purring, "you must understand the necessity of immediate agreement. The leaders of the Triplanet Powers are now meeting with others of our advance units, and they express extreme suspicion and alarm. Our units are finding it difficult, in fact, to prevent them from detonating this planet instantly."

But the president agreed to a brief recess, for a conference with the defense minister and his scientific adviser behind the soundproof doors of an adjoining private office. There Forester found the new paint drying, a dismal yellow-gray. The ventilators had been turned off and the choking fumes of it turned him faint with illness as he stood hastily reporting White's warning.

"Mr. President," he finished desperately, "I think we ought to keep these mechanicals out—at least until we can find out more about them and their 'service.' I want to remind you, sir, that we still have Project Thunderbolt. Instead of meekly giving up to the humanoids, I suggest that we fire a demonstration shot at some distant uninhabited satellite and send a warning note to the Triplanet Powers."

The old statesman hesitated, fumbling his withered yellow hands irresolutely together, and Forester knew that he longed for the confident assurance of little Major Steel.

"I'm afraid of war." His dim eyes blinked indecisively. "And I'm afraid your demonstration shot would touch it off, or even trigger detonators here."

"That might be," Forester agreed uneasily. "But at least, sir, I think we ought to stall somehow for time, until you can appoint a commission to investigate these mechanicals on some planet where their service is already established."

"I don't know." The old man twisted his gnarled fingers. "Let's ask Steel—"

"Just a moment, sir!" Forester broke in. "I object very strongly to letting the mechanicals know anything about Project Thunderbolt, because I think we may need it against them."

"Possibly." The president shook his head uncertainly. "But I don't know what to do."

A secret message, brought in by an excited male secretary, ended his agony of indecision. The satellite observation stations above the atmosphere were reporting a swarm of huge unidentified spacecraft, already within territorial space and still approaching at enormous velocities from Sector Xanthic. The president read the dispatch in a shaken voice, and then gasped apprehensively:

"Steel said we couldn't risk any delay." The message fluttered out of his helpless fingers. "That must be the Triplanet fleet, already invading our space."

"I think not, sir," Forester protested quietly. "With those detonators, our human enemies have no more use for heavy spacecraft than we have. And I believe the direction of Wing IV lies in Sector Xanthic." His voice shuddered. "I believe, sir, that those ships are bringing the humanoid invasion!"

"Invasion?" The old man rubbed at his rheumy eyes, in blank bewilderment. "Then I'll have to send for Steel—"

"Wait!" Forester broke in desperately. "Excuse me, sir, but we can still destroy those ships with Project Thunderbolt. I would suggest that you offer an ultimatum. This thing Steel is apparently in direct communication with all the other humanoid units. Why not tell him to stop those ships, until we can study these machines and their service?"

"But I'm afraid—"

"So am I," Forester whispered urgently. "That's why I want to keep the project safe. Our missiles can smash those ships. If that isn't enough, I can modify them to reach Wing IV. To wipe out that relay station, and stop every mechanical unit it controls. So don't betray the project, sir!"

"I don't know." The president chewed his parchment lips, trembling with the torture of doubt. His vague eyes went longingly to the room where the unmasked mechanical was waiting, but at last he gasped impulsively, "All right, Forester, we'll keep your weapon—though I know we won't need it. Go ahead with the necessary modifications to mount three missiles against Wing IV, and keep your staff alert to launch them if anything goes wrong." His large Adam's apple jerked nervously. "But I trust Steel!"

They went back to the outer room.

"—approaching spacecraft are our own," that small black machine was murmuring musically. "They are sufficiently protected against any unwise attack your primitive warcraft might make against them, but they carry no offensive weapons. They have come from Wing IV to bring our service, if you choose to let them land."

The Defense Authority voted a few minutes later, with the chief of staff indignantly abstaining, to suspend the antimechanicals statutes in this national emergency, and to open the spaceports to the craft from Wing IV. Forester hurried away from that damp underground room, tired and alarmed and vaguely ill, to look for a dose of bicarbonate.

## 10

THE IMPERTURBABLE MECHANISM which had been Major Steel dictated the sweeping articles of a proposed agreement between the people and the humanoids, which would become final in sixty days if ratified by a vote of the people. At noon, with that same competent device standing by to prompt him, the old president stood tottering before a battery of news cameras to announce the coming of the mechanicals.

Forester had found his bicarbonate, and a hotel room. He had soaked out his chill and his aching fatigue in a hot tub and napped for two hours, and he awoke with his brooding unease gone. He even felt hungry again. Calling room service, he ate while he listened to the president's broadcast.

The promised service of the humanoids was still an unknown quantity, but his first mistrust had been swept away by relief that the decision was made, with the terrible might of his own project still intact. Mark White's hate and fear began to seem absurd, and he felt something of Ironsmith's bright eagerness to see the new mechanicals.

He saw the ships from Wing IV landing that same afternoon. Returning in a staff car to his official aircraft, he had the driver pull off the highway where it ran near the spaceport, so that he could watch. One enormous interstellar vessel was already down, looming immense above the tall, familiar interplanetary liners, which now stood humbly along the edges of the field, towed hastily out of the way.

"Well, sir!" the awed driver whispered. "Ain't she big!"

She was. The thick concrete aprons had shattered and buckled under the weight of that black hull, which towered so high that a white tuft of cumulus had formed about its peak. Peering upward until his neck ached, Forester watched gigantic valves lifting open, and long gangways sliding down, and the hordes of humanoids start marching out to establish their service to mankind.

Tiny against the scale of their colossal craft, the new mechanicals were all identical, nude and neuter, quicker and sleeker than men, graceful and perfect and tireless. The sun shimmered blue on their dark hastening limbs, and glittered on their yellow brands. They spread out across the broken concrete by the busy thousands, innumerable.

The first scouts of that dark army came to the high wire fence around the spaceport, near where Forester had stopped. They began cutting it down, deftly slicing through the heavy mesh with small tools, and neatly piling the sections. Swarming about the task in ever greater numbers, they began to remind him of some social insects. They worked silently, never calling to another—for they all were parts of the same ultimate machine, and each unit knew all that any of them did. Watching, he began to feel a vague impact of terror.

For they were too many. Glinting with bronze and frosty blue, their hard black bodies were too beautiful. They were too sure, too strong, too swift. Unlike any actual insects that he had ever watched, they wasted no time and no effort. They worked as one, and they made no blunders. Mark White's apprehension of them seemed better founded now, and he was suddenly grateful for the president's decision to save Project Thunderbolt.

"Let's go!" He tugged at the staring driver's sleeve, and his voice was a husky whisper, as if he were already afraid for the humanoids to hear. "Drive on—fast!"

"Right, sir." With a last astonished look at the vastness of that ship and the silent machines still swarming from it, the driver pulled back on the road. "The world sure changes," he commented sagely. "What won't they think of next!"

Back at Starmont, Forester hurried down to the project without even taking time to call Ruth, and worked that night and all the next day without sleep, modifying three missiles. Light would take two long centuries to reach Wing IV, but these tapered shapes of death had their own dreadful geometry. The time quantity, in the equations of rhodomagnetic propulsion, varied with the fourth root of distance. Wing IV, consequently, was only a few seconds farther than the nearest planet.

When the third missile was ready at last, with drive and relays rebuilt, Forester went to sleep in his coveralls on a cot beside the launching station. The teleprinter bell awoke him instantly—and he saw that the time was somehow nine, next morning. The brief message from the defense minister was classified top secret. It warned him to be ready for a humanoid inspector, arriving within an hour.

Quickly checking the three modified missiles again, he left them racked and ready. Back at the surface, he locked the elevator, pushed the mirror down to hide the controls, kicked a rug over the escape door in the floor, hung his coveralls on a hook, and walked out of an innocent cloakroom into his office, to wait for the inspection.

The mechanical came on a military aircraft, escorted by the commanding general of the satellite space stations and his retinue. A staff car brought them from the landing strip below the mountain, and Forester waited to meet them at the inner gate. The machine stepped out ahead of the men, droning its greeting:

"Service, Dr. Clay Forester."

In the midst of the stiff military uniforms, the slender silicone nakedness of the humanoid had a curious incongruity, but that oddness was not amusing. Its air of kindly blind alertness was somehow disturbing, and Forester couldn't help an uncomfortable start when it spoke his name.

"We have come to examine your Project Lookout." Its voice was a mellow golden horn. "Under the provisional agreement, we are to patrol all military installations, to prevent any aggressions before the ratification election. Then we shall remove all weapons."

"But this project isn't a weapon," Forester protested. "Like the satellite stations, it's only part of the warning network."

He couldn't tell what the humanoid thought; nothing ever

changed that serene expression of slightly astonished paternal benevolence. But the machine went methodically ahead with a painstaking study of the building, the instruments, and the staff. The inspection became a cruel ordeal which lasted all day. Even when the human members of the party went to lunch at the cafeteria, the mechanical kept Forester to explain the deliberately sketchy records he had kept.

"We have secured access to the secret files of the Defense Authority," it purred blandly. "We have seen figures for the discretionary funds spent on this project, and lists of the items of equipment purchased for it. Can you tell us why those totals are so large, and why so much of that equipment does not appear to be in use here?"

"Certainly." He tried not to look so ill as he felt. "This was an experimental installation, remember, and men aren't quite so efficient as you machines claim to be. We made several expensive blunders in the design, and all that missing equipment was torn out and hammered into scrap long ago."

"Our coming will end such waste," the mechanical murmured, and he could see no other reaction. Even the humanoids, he thought grimly, would find it difficult to prove that those missing items had not already gone to the furnaces as scrap metal, but he was afraid to wonder what other clues to Project Thunderbolt their sleepless prying might uncover.

The inscrutable machine took him back, that afternoon, to the neutrino trackers. Its blind-seeming steel eyes stared blankly at the enormous search tubes, with their tiny grids of glowing wire forever sweeping space. It studied the softly clucking counters and the directional plotters. It made him dig all the specifications out of a safe, and inquired the name and address of every firm which had supplied any materials, and finally interviewed each of the six technicians.

As the inquisition dragged on, Forester felt increasingly tired and annoyed and alarmed. He hadn't slept enough, and his empty stomach fluttered uncomfortably. He was afraid his own agitation might betray the project, and when the machine had finished grilling Armstrong, at dusk, he asked it desperately:

"Isn't that enough? You've seen everything, and talked to all of us. Aren't you satisfied?"

"Thank you, sir," cooed the humanoid. "But there is one other man connected with the project whom we must question. That is the mathematician who calculated the designs for the search equipment."

"All the routine math was done in our own computing section."

"Who operates that?"

"A young chap named Ironsmith." Forester's voice rose, too sharply. "But he had nothing to do with the actual equipment. He never saw the tubes, or even heard about them. He's just a mathematical hack, and all he did was solve the problems we gave him."

"Thank you, sir," droned the urbane machine. "But we must speak with Mr. Ironsmith."

"He knows nothing about the project." Desperately, Forester tried to smooth the apprehension from his voice. "Besides, we haven't much more time today. I've already telephoned my wife that we're all coming over for cocktails and dinner, and she'll expect us right away. Human beings eat, remember?"

He didn't want the mechanical to meet Ironsmith—certainly not alone. There were too many secrets that bright young man might have guessed. The little humanoid didn't care for cocktails, however, and it glibly quoted the articles of agreement. Reluctantly, Forester called the computing section, and Ironsmith came pedaling down to meet the machine at the gate.

Forester spent an uneasy evening. Anxiety had destroyed his appetite, and Dr. Pitcher had forbidden him alcohol. He drank coffee to keep awake, and smoked a cigar until it tasted foul in his mouth, and listened absently to the military party's gloomy talk of professional unemployment.

It was midnight before the mechanical came back from the computing section, its dark serenity still revealing nothing of what it might have learned. Nervously, Forester went down in the staff car to put the departing group aboard their aircraft, and then he hurried frantically back to Ironsmith's rooms. The youthful clerk greeted him with shocked concern.

"What's the matter, Dr. Forester?" He blinked confusedly, and Ironsmith asked, "Why so grim and haggard?"

Ignoring the query, Forester peered sharply around the room. The few pieces of furniture were shabby but comfortable. A book printed in the strange characters of some ancient language of the first planet lay open on a little table, beside a tobacco humidor and a bottle of wine. Ironsmith himself, in unpressed slacks and open-collared shirt, looked guileless and friendly as the room, and Forester could see no evidences of his dealings with that inquisitive machine.

"What's the trouble, sir?" he insisted anxiously.

"That damned mechanical," Forester muttered. "The thing was grilling me all day."

"Oh!" The clerk looked surprised. "I found it very interesting."

"What did it want with you?"

"Nothing much. It asked a question or two, and looked at the calculators."

"But it stayed so long." Forester searched his open face. "What did it want to know?"

"I was asking the questions." Ironsmith grinned with a boyish pleasure. "You see, that relay grid on Wing IV knows all the math that men have ever learned—and it's quite a calculator! I happened to mention a tough little problem I've been kicking around, and we went on from there."

"And?"

"That's all." Ironsmith's gray eyes held a limpid honesty.

"Really, Dr. Forester, I can't see any reason for you to be disturbed about the humanoids, or Mark White to hate them."

"Well, I do!"

"But they're only machines," Ironsmith persisted gently. "They can't be evil—or, for that matter, good. Because they aren't faced with any moral dilemmas. They have no choice of right or wrong. All they can do is what old Warren Mansfield built them to do—serve and obey mankind."

Forester wasn't sure of that, and he was less certain that Ironsmith himself had always chosen the right. That armor of amiable innocence seemed impregnable, however, and Forester was already staggering with fatigue. He gave up learning anything from the clerk, and went wearily home.

Walking back to his house and his wife, alone beneath the stars the humanoids had conquered, Forester felt a sudden savage envy of Ironsmith's carefree ease. The harsh demands of the project became utterly intolerable. For one dark moment, he wished that the inspecting humanoid had found his fearful secret and set him free. But he stiffened his worn shoulders instantly. Those graceful missiles waiting in the vault were the last defense of man, and he dared not put his burden down.

# 11

THE TELEPRINTER RECALLED Forester to the capital, next morning, to attend the final sessions of the Defense Authority. The human government was already preparing to conclude its business on the day of the coming ratification election, but disturbing political tensions were mounting as a few fanatical opponents of the humanoids began campaigning vehemently against them.

A few labor leaders were afraid the mechanicals would bring technological unemployment, although they promised shorter hours and greater benefits than strikes had ever won. The heads of a few religious organizations suspected that the knowledge and power of the humanoids would leave insufficient scope for any superior omnipotence, and many bureaucrats were apprehensive of an unregimented society.

The humanoids, however, had learned the art of politics. They opened offices in every ward and village, glittering with displays of machine-made marvels. Their swarming units rang doorbells, calling each voter by name and promising paradise—admission free. When the election came, only a stubbornly skeptical few voted to halt the mechanized march of progress. The victorious humanoids, with malice toward none, offered the same efficient service to supporters and opponents. They directed the dissolution of the human government, and immediately began dismantling military installations. Forester was delayed at the capital a few days longer, until a brisk machine had put a pen in the trembling fingers of the world president and dictated the phrases of his resignation.

"I'm through," the old statesman whispered to Forester, afterward, when the members of the liquidated Defense Authority were filing by to shake his withered hand. "Now," he breathed, "it's up to you."

Meeting his dim, uneasy eyes, Forester nodded silently. He understood that the whole burden of the project now rested on his own tired shoulders. Yet, hastening out of the executive mansion, he felt a buoyant relief. For the efficient machines were also taking over the warcraft of the Triplanet Powers, and digging up the planted detonators. He was free at last to go back to Starmont, to Ruth and the pure science he loved. Under the stress of the election, he had all but forgotten his visit to that ruined tower by the sea. Mark White, with his disreputable disciples and his dubious science and his disturbing story, seemed to have no place in the bright new future.

The mechanicals had disposed of Forester's official aircraft, informing him that all such primitive contraptions were too dangerous for human use. Waiting for him, when a trim humanoid driver took him from the hotel to the airport, he found a wonderful new vehicle: a long, mirror-bright teardrop, unmarred by any projecting airfoil or landing gear. Two quick machines helped him up through an oval door, and he found the smooth hull darkly transparent from within. The flat deck covered all the mechanism, and there were no controls that he could see. The door closed behind him, untouched.

"How does it work?" he wanted to know.

"The door is operated by a concealed rhodomagnetic relay," purred the dark machine beside him. Another glided to the end of the deck and stood rigid there, staring blindly ahead. It touched no visible control, but the craft lifted silently. The unit beside Forester unfolded a low couch out of the deck, asking respectfully if he wished to sit, but he didn't feel like relaxing. A vague disquiet was already spurring him to ask increasingly uneasy questions.

"The cruiser is powered by energy from converted matter," the calm machine informed him. "The converters are on Wing IV, and the power is carried to the point of use by a tight rhodomagnetic beam. The thrust which propels the ship is created by a rhodomagnetic field."

"So? And what is the field equation?"

"It is not our policy to supply such information," droned the humanoid. "Because men who enjoy our service have little need of knowledge, and science has often been used for purposes contrary to the Prime Directive."

He looked away uncomfortably, watching through the hull as the cruiser lifted swiftly through a milky veil of high cirro-stratus, and on into the ionosphere. The sky turned purple-black. He could see the planet's lazy curve, and flattened mountains crawling beneath, and the red-winged sun dropping back eastward. And suddenly they were landing on a strange landing stage.

"Is this—Starmont?"

The familiar shape of the dark butte and the known brown face of the desert around it answered his voiceless question, but everything else was changed. New walls and towers rose everywhere, luminous in the sunlight with vivid pastels. Broad new gardens were fantastic with plants which must have come from other worlds.

The door of the cruiser had no handle that a man could

work, but it was opened for him silently. The solicitous machines helped him down, too carefully. Starting breathlessly across the new red pavement of the landing stage to look for his wife and his friends, he was halted by an abrupt, sharp sense of disaster.

The exotic gardens and the colonnaded walks and the long bright-walled villa were no real surprise, because he already knew that the teeming machines had been rebuilding all the planet into a streamlined paradise, and it was a moment before he knew just what was wrong. A breath of some rank jungle scent drew his eyes to a deep sunken garden where the administration building had stood, and he felt a faint revulsion from the tall, fleshy crimson stalks the machines had planted there. Next he missed the white concrete tower of the solar telescope, and then his breath went out when he looked again at the new blue-and-amber villa on the crown of the mountain.

"Where is it?" he gasped accusingly. "The big reflector?"

For that mighty telescope had been his life. The reach of it was farther than even the ships from Wing IV could go. It had found the clue to rhodomagnetics, and he had fondly planned to spend his last years with it, exploring the outer galaxies in quest of some other hint that might reveal the real *prima materia* of the universe.

But now that gay new dwelling stood where the telescope had been. The realization stunned him. For one painful instant, he tried to hope that the humanoids had simply replaced the precious instrument with some compact new devices as wonderful as the silver teardrop behind him, but the machine was cooing serenely:

"The observatory has been removed."

"Why?" A dim dread overwhelmed his first sharp anger, and his voice turned hoarse. "You had no right—"

"All necessary rights to set up and maintain our service were given us by a free election," the humanoid reminded him. "And that space was required for your new dwelling."

"I want the reflector put back."

"That will be impossible, sir." The tiny machine stood frozen and alert, staring past him with seemingly sightless polished eyes. "Observatory equipment is far too dangerous for you, because you would be so easily injured by heavy instruments, broken glass, electric currents, inflammable paper and film, or poisonous photographic solutions."

"You've got to replace that telescope." Forester stood trembling with a bitter amazement. "Because I'm going on with my astrophysical research."

"Scientific research is no longer necessary, sir." The benign surprise remained unchanged on that narrow silicone face. "We have found on many planets that knowledge of any kind seldom makes men happy, and that scientific knowledge is often used for destruction. Foolish men have even attempted to attack Wing IV with illicit scientific devices."

Forester shuddered to a speechless terror.

"Therefore, Clay Forester, you must now forget your scientific interests." That melodious drone was dreadful with a ruthless benevolence. "You must now look for your happiness in some less harmful activity. We suggest philosophy or chess."

The small machine merely watched as he cursed it, the black, high-cheeked face struck with highlights of bronze and icy blue, and set in serene solicitude. It didn't move until a new fear made him gasp hoarsely, "Where's my wife?"

In the harassed months of the ratification campaign, he had stayed away from Starmont for fear of somehow betraying the project with his presence, but he had talked to Ruth every night until the telephone system was taken out of service after the election. He had told her that he would soon be home, back to take up their lives where the supernova's light had interrupted. Shivering, now, he wondered why she hadn't met him.

"Ruth is here," that limpid golden voice assured him. "Waiting for you in the new toy room."

"Will you tell her I've come home?"

"We've told her."

"What did she say?"

"She just asked who you are."

"Eh?" Terror took his breath. "Is—is she all right?"

"She is quite well, sir, since we removed her unhappiness."

"Removed—what?"

"She had been unhappy," purred the black mechanical. "We discovered her secret troubles only a few days ago, the night you called to tell her you were coming back. The unit watching in her room observed her crying, when she should have been asleep."

"So?" A surge of puzzled fury knotted his stringy fists. "We had our problems, but she wasn't that unhappy. What have you done to her?"

"We asked the cause of her tears," chimed the machine. "She was restless, she told us, because there was no more work for her to do, at the office or at home. And she was afraid of your return, she said, because she was losing her beauty and her youth."

"But she isn't!" Forester swayed to a numbness of bewilderment. "Ruth's not old."

"By comparison with our own steel-and-plastic units, all human bodies are very fragile and ephemeral. Your wife had been afraid of age for many years, she told us. But now we have removed that fear, to make her happy again."

"Take me to her!"

Breathlessly, Forester followed the mechanical across the red pavement. Huge doors slid open soundlessly, beyond tall amber pillars, to let them into the dwelling, which had a faint, bitter odor of new synthetics. The walls were of some satin-surfaced stuff that could be made luminous, his guide cooed, in any pattern of colors he might desire. Broad niches along the lofty hall held color views of the scenic wonders of other worlds the humanoids had won, but Forester was becoming impatient of wonders.

At the door of the toy room, a wave of heavy scent staggered him. It was Ruth's perfume, Sweet Delirium. Her usual hint of it was cleanly pleasant, but this thick reek overwhelmed him. The room was huge and splendid, hung with softly glowing tapestries which the mechanicals must have copied from some nursery book, luminous with simple figures of animals and children at play.

He found her seated flat on the floor with her legs sprawled out, in the awkward posture a baby might have taken, and she must have drenched herself with that perfume, for its heavy sweetness seemed suffocating. A mechanical stood watching her with a tireless blind attention. At first she didn't see him.

"Ruth!" Shock had dried up his voice, and his knees shook. "Ruth—darling!"

She was building a little tower out of soft, bright-hued plastic blocks, gravely careful and yet strangely clumsy. Hearing his husky voice, she turned to face him as she sat, laughing in that cloud of choking sweetness, and he saw that age and ugliness had ceased to trouble her.

"Ruth—my poor dear!"

She looked as young as she had been when the hard blue light of the supernova struck them. Her fine skin was pink from lotions and massage, and her dark hair had been washed blond. Her brows were arched too thinly, her lips too crimson, and she wore a sheer blue negligee that she would before have thought too daring. And all awareness of fear and pain was gone from her vacant, staring eyes.

"Hello." She spoke to him at last, with a child's soft and solemn voice, still holding one of the spongy blocks with a child's clutching awkwardness in both her red-nailed hands. "Who are you?"

Terror struck Forester too dumb to answer, but she recognized him. The soft block rolled slowly out of her hands, to bound across the plastic floor. The humanoid moved instantly to bring it back, but her lax fingers didn't take it. Her dark eyes big with effort, she whispered faintly:

"Your name's Clay. Isn't it—Clay?"

"My dear!" The pathos of her uncertain voice had blinded him with tears, but he started quickly toward her. "What have they done to you?"

Her searching eyes had slowly lit with a dim and wistful gladness, and her white arms reached out toward him in impulsive eagerness. She didn't seem to sense his fear, but her movement overturned the tower of blocks. Her round baby-eyes saw the damage, and her scarlet lips thrust out in a petulant baby-pout.

"Service, Ruth Forester."

The brisk little humanoid helped her gather the fallen blocks, and she began building them up again. The groping uncertainty was gone from her eyes. Absorbed again, she smiled with pleasure. Forester heard a happy baby-chuckle. She had forgotten him.

# 12

FORESTER'S KNEES WERE weak, and he could scarcely see. Turning away from Ruth, he stumbled back into that splendid hall which was a gallery of windows into many other worlds that free men had lost, and he waited there for the humanoid to close the sliding door. Catching a deep breath of unscented air, he whispered bitterly:

"What have you done to my wife?"

"We have merely made her happy," the machine sang gaily. "We have only removed her cares."

"And her memory."

"Forgetfulness is the most useful key we have discovered to human happiness," whined the machine. "Our drug, euphoride, relieves the pain of needless memories and the tension of useless fear. Stopping all the corrosion of stress and effort, it triples the brief life expectancy of human beings. You can see that Ruth has lost her fear of age."

"Maybe!" Forester blinked incredulously. "But did she ask for euphoride?"

"No request was necessary."

"I won't have it!" He was hoarse and breathless with his anger. "I want you to restore her mind—if you can!"

"Her mind isn't injured," the machine said briskly. "The drug merely protects her from memories and fears which serve no purpose now, since our service shields her from every want and harm. If that distresses you unduly, then it may be necessary for you to take euphoride also."

For an instant he was stunned. The words had echoed in his mind like silver music before he grasped their sense, but then an unthinking fury flung his stringy fist at the bald plastic head of the machine. Its steel eyes seemed blind as ever and its narrow face reflected no alarm, but it moved precisely enough to let his fist slip past, and then, when he stumbled, it deftly helped him recover his balance.

"That is useless, sir." It danced back from him, poised and alert. "Many men have attacked us, on many worlds, and none has ever hurt anything except himself. Human bodies are too weak to match against us, and human minds too slow."

Gulping convulsively, Forester staggered back from the machine. It stood darkly beautiful and serenely kind as ever, but all his wrath had chilled into shivering terror.

"I—I didn't really mean to hit you," he stammered desperately. "It was just—just the shock!" He tried to get his breath. "I know I'll soon be happy enough, without any need of your drug."

"That decision is our responsibility," the mechanical hummed. "But a few men do find happiness without euphoride, and you may try that, if you wish."

"Thank you!" He swallowed hard. "And you won't punish me?"

"Our function is not to punish men, but merely to serve them."

"Thanks!" he muttered. "And I'll soon be all right." He tried to grin at the alert machine. "All I need is time to think."

That was it. He must think how to reach the old search building and make his way down to those missiles in the vault, already set and ready to smash Wing IV and stop these machines. But he must hide that bleak intent until the moment came, and he turned uncertainly toward the nearest picture in the wall, pretending a casual interest.

He looked upon wide desolation, where whirlwinds carried towering pillars of red dust across a barren desert, marching among huge eroded boulders that crouched like monstrous sleeping saurians of dark stone.

"There are rhodomagnetic television screens," the mechanical explained. "Our cameras are placed at points of interest on every world we serve, and the scenes may be shifted as you wish."

"I see." Forester mopped at his sweaty palms, carefully studying those dark shapes of twisted stone. "Interesting view."

"That is a world to which we came too late," sang the machine. "Men landed there six thousand years ago, flourished until they liberated energies which they failed to control rationally, and so destroyed themselves. The camera looks upon the ruins of a city whose builders died for want of our Prime Directive."

"That so?"

Now he could see the plan of fused and flattened walls, the bulk of crumbled towers. He tried for a moment to imagine that lost magnificence, before it had been burned and shattered into this dreadful desolation. Those ancient builders had been lucky, the bleak thought struck him, for they at least were cleanly dead, and not buried alive beneath the suffocating service of these machines.

"I think I'll take a walk." He turned slowly from the niche, carefully casual. "Just to look over all the new improvements here."

"We're at your service, sir."

"I don't want any service!"

"But you must be escorted, sir. Because our service exists to guard every man from every possible injury, at every instant."

Forester sidled away, speechless. The lingering bitter scent of the new walls caught his throat, so that he could scarcely breathe.

"You appear uneasy, sir," purred the attentive machine. "Do you feel unwell?"

"No!" He tried to swallow the sickness of his terror and control the frantic impulse to open flight or open battle, and he halted his slow retreat. "A little tired, perhaps. I only need to rest. I suppose there's a room for me?"

"This way, sir."

He followed the machine into the east wing of the long villa. Some unseen relay opened another sliding panel, to let them into an immense chamber where shining murals showed sunbrowned figures of lean young men and long-limbed girls dancing on landscapes of flowers.

"Those are scenes of a village spring festival, in the barbaric age when the descendants of the first colonists here had almost forgotten their civilization," the humanoid explained. "Your wife helped us plan the building, before she was given euphoride, and she selected the paintings for us to copy."

"Very nice," he stammered. The mention of Ruth filled his eyes with tears of angry pain, and then he was shaken with a fear that the humanoids would perceive his dangerous emotions. Sinking wearily into an enormous easy chair, trying to seem at ease, he took a cigar out of the engraved pocket case Ruth had given him on his last birthday, and snapped the built-in lighter.

"Where's all the staff?" he asked, as calmly as possible. "I'd like to talk—huh!"

Astonishment took his voice, for the humanoid had snatched the cigar from his lips. It took the case, put out the flame, and gave cigar and case to another mechanical which must have come just to carry them away. He started up angrily.

"Sir, we cannot allow you to smoke." The machine's voice was honey-sweet. "Fire is too dangerous in your hands, and the excessive use of tobacco has become injurious to your health."

He subsided helplessly, trying to swallow his fury. One cigar, he told himself, wasn't worth the risk of oblivion. But this was more than one cigar. When these meddling machines undertook to govern every such trivial detail of his life, that was more terrible than trivial.

"Maybe I have been smoking too much," he admitted uneasily. "But I was asking about my old associates here. Where are they now?"

"The other astronomers and their families all left Starmont when we closed the observatory. We have built new dwellings for them, wherever they chose to live. One of them is composing a symphony and one is painting watercolors and the rest have already been given euphoride."

"And the civilian technicians?" Fear dried his throat. "The six young men who worked with me on Project Lookout? What has become of them?"

The bright steel eyes watched him blankly.

"Those six men all appeared unhappy about leaving the project," the machine murmured blandly. "Therefore, it was necessary for all of them to be given euphoride. Now they have forgotten the project, and they're quite happy."

"I see." Forester nodded stiffly. "So all the staff is gone."

"All except one man, sir."

"Eh?" He sat up straight. "Who is that?"

"One Mr. Frank Ironsmith, sir. He says he is quite happy in his old quarters here, and there was no reason for him to leave."

"Young Ironsmith, eh?" Forester tried to conceal his puzzlement with a manufactured grin. "A good friend of mine. A charming fellow!" He peered uneasily at the tiny black machine. "I'd like to see him, right away."

"If you wish, sir."

Surprisingly, it glided toward the door. An identical machine was waiting in the hall, and the two escorted him out of the building and on across the newly landscaped grounds, where everything seemed too precise, the lawns too level and too neatly rectangular, the walks too painfully straight, where even the tall evergreens had all been uprooted and replaced in stiff, forbidding rows.

Oddly, however, the irregular grove about the computing section had not been disturbed. The grassy hillock had not been leveled, nor the old gravel path replaced with any shining plastic stuff. Sheltered among the trees, the old wooden building with its red man-made shingles remained unchanged. And Forester saw an even stranger thing.

For Frank Ironsmith came on his bicycle down the gravel path to meet them. That itself was unaccountable—for even a cycle, as Forester recalled from his own youth, could painfully damage its rider. Yet Ironsmith rode alone, with no mechanical to guard him. More disturbing still, he was smoking that under-slung brier. Riding with no hands on the handlebars— in a shocking defiance of the Prime Directive—he was holding a dangerous flame to the pipe. And Forester's own keepers made no protest. The cruel unfairness of that filled him with a stunned resentment, but he tried to stifle his envy. For here, apparently, was one man free—free to launch a missile against Wing IV.

"Glad to see you, Forester!"

That hail of welcome had a warmly genial ring. Grinning happily, Ironsmith braked the cycle to a perilous stop, alighted safely, and gave him a strong brown hand—too strong. He dropped it, staggering abruptly back. His knees turned weak, and sweat burst out on his face. For logic had struck him a cruel, foul blow. If men were not allowed to go about alone, or to handle fire, or to use any dangerous machines, then the conclusion was terribly clear. Ironsmith was not a man.

Shivering, he remembered little Major Steel.

"Why, Forester!" Ironsmith's pink and boyish face showed

a friendly, shocked concern. His startled voice seemed alto-gether human. "Are you ill?"

He reached out anxiously, and Forester shrank from his hand. It looked human enough. The fair skin showed a con-vincing pattern of red sunburn and freckle and tan. The fine hairs were bleached with sunlight. The nails needed trimming, and one was a little broken. It seemed entirely human—yet how was he to tell?

Frantically, Forester studied the old bicycle with its rusty frame and worn tires and chipped enamel. He searched the lank and vigorous form propped a little awkwardly against it, the sagging slacks and faded shirt and comfortable old shoes, the sandy hair and friendly face and keen gray eyes, wide and puzzled now. But he could find no useful clue.

"Just tell the humanoids, if you don't feel well," Ironsmith was urging warmly. "They know all the medicine that human doctors ever did, and more. Whatever is wrong, they'll know how to fix it."

Forester fought the shudder which swept him, but every-thing fitted too well. Even the two names had a frightening likeness now—Ironsmith and Steel! The ruthless mechanism inside this plausible and pleasant-seeming mask must have come to spy on Starmont. It must have inferred the secret of the project from the problems he had brought for it to solve. It had even been with him at Dragonrock, and heard the plans of Mark White—and then he saw the contradiction in his logic.

Ironsmith wasn't a machine. That knowledge warmed him with relief, and oddly it drained the little strength left in his knees. He clung to the frame of the battered cycle, beaming at Ironsmith's astonished face with a fatuous joy.

"I'm so glad!" he gasped. "For a moment, you know, I was afraid—"

Awareness of the two real machines checked his voice. He was afraid to say what he had feared, but Ironsmith had been at Dragonrock. And Mark White, who had learned to perceive rhodomagnetic fields and so discover such disguised machines as Steel, had obviously trusted him. That seemed proof enough of his humanity.

"Afraid of what?" Ironsmith was asking.

"That—that they had given you euphoride," Forester whispered desperately. "I'm glad to find you still remember!" Strength came back to his wobbling knees, and he let go the bicycle frame. "And I'm all right." He tried to stop the trembling of his hands. "Just a little nervous and upset. They gave that drug to Ruth, you know." He couldn't keep a tremor from his voice. "And she almost—didn't recognize me."

"A useful drug, sometimes." Ironsmith himself seemed to feel no terror of euphoride. "It's good to see you back at Starmont," he went on genially. "The hill seems a little lonely, now. Won't you come on to my rooms, and tell me what you think of the humanoids?"

Forester was still afraid to say what he thought about them, but he accepted instantly. Shaken and uncertain from that dark moment of unutterable suspicion, he still had a monstrous problem to face. If Frank Ironsmith wasn't a machine—what was he?

# 13

THEY WALKED UP the path to the old wooden building together, Ironsmith pushing his cycle unaided, Forester stalking silently ahead of his keepers. When they came to the door, Forester saw with a mounting bitterness that it still had a common brass knob, made for a man to work. He paused in the doorway, staring into Ironsmith's front room with chagrined bewilderment. For the old, book-lined walls enclosed a comfortable oasis of casual human disorder, in the midst of all this sterile desert of ordered, shining newness the humanoids had made. The shabby pieces of man-made furniture needed dusting. Tobacco crumbs were spilled on the floor. At the big desk, amid a clutter of such deadly implements as heavy paperweights and a sharp letter opener and a long pair of shears, a slide rule lay across an untidy stack of papers, as if Ironsmith were still allowed to work.

"Smoke?" The smiling mathematician opened a new silver humidor. "You know I couldn't afford cigars before the humanoids came, but now they keep me supplied with very good ones."

"Thanks." Forester glanced resentfully at the two machines behind him. "But they won't let me smoke."

"They know best."

Apologetically, Ironsmith closed the humidor, but the mellow fragrance from it had filled Forester with a hungry craving. He sat down stiffly, looking uncomfortably away from his guards. He wanted desperately to ask Ironsmith's aid, to help him smash Wing IV and set men free, but he couldn't speak of that. He was afraid to ask even the secret of the other's special privileges, but he nodded at the desk, inquiring indirectly:

"Still working?"

"Not really working." Lazily, the younger man sprawled his awkward-seeming length into a big, worn chair, beside a small table where chessmen were set up in an unfinished game. "Just playing around with a few ideas that I never had time to develop before. The humanoids do all the routine math—though they let me keep the old machines in the computing section, for any work I want to do myself."

"How do you manage that?" Forester gulped at a bitter lump of jealousy. "They tell me that research is too dangerous, said useful work no longer necessary."

"But thinking isn't outlawed," Ironsmith murmured gravely. "And I believe men still need to think." He picked up the queen of the black chessmen, absently. "In the old world, we had no time for thought. We were all too busy running machines, until machines that ran themselves came along to set us free."

"Free?" Forester stared bleakly up at his keepers. "Free to do what?"

"To live, I believe," Ironsmith said softly. "Take my own experience. I used to be a kind of human calculating machine. The best of my energy went into setting up problems for those clumsy old electronic devices. Now I have time to look for the real meanings of mathematics. Time to follow ideas—"

His honest gray eyes were looking far beyond the black queen, and his low voice quickened.

"Sorry, Forester, but I've another engagement coming up." He straightened, replacing the queen on the board. "But I think you'll be all right, if you'll just learn to trust the humanoids. Remember their Prime Directive—*To Serve and Obey, and Guard Men from Harm.* They can't hurt anybody."

"It's that drug!" Forester stood up reluctantly, trying not to look at his guards. "I can't stand the thought of that. It's almost—murder!" He gulped convulsively. "That's what it is—murder of the mind!"

"You're just overwrought." Ironsmith smiled, with a cheery, calm assurance. "Really, for those who fail to find their happiness in any other way, euphoride may be the best solution."

Forester shook his head, speechless.

"But you can easily avoid it, if you wish," the other promised lightly. "All you have to do is accept the humanoids, and find yourself a way of life that fits the Prime Directive. The physical frontiers are closed, I know, but you can find a wider field of scientific research still open, in the mind."

"How's that?" Forester whispered blankly.

"We can talk about it later." Ironsmith absently adjusted the chessmen. "Someone's waiting on me now, but I do want to help you get adjusted to the humanoids. Really, Forester, they're opening a new epoch of civilization. Splendid, when you get to understand it. I want to help you like them."

Forester snorted indignantly.

"You will," Ironsmith insisted mildly. "When you get acquainted with them. It's really too bad you persist in imputing malice to them, because they're not malicious. No machine could be. They're only doing the magnificent work for which old Warren Mansfield designed them, quite successfully."

"Huh?" Forgetful of the machines beside him, Forester had caught his breath to protest. The other man was already frowning at the chessmen, however, and, as Forester hesitated, awareness of his dark guardians fell upon him crushingly. He swallowed hard, trying not to shudder.

"Suppose we meet again, later?" Ironsmith was asking cordially. "For dinner tonight?"

"Thanks," Forester muttered stiffly. "Glad to."

But Ironsmith would never be an ally—that was starkly clear. He had always liked the humanoids too well, and he seemed far too clever now at rationalizing and excusing that strange perversity. Whatever the secret of his special freedom and the origin of his twisted loyalty to these benign enemies of men, he had become something far more sinister than any mere disguised machine.

"Till dinner, then," he was murmuring affably. "We'll go down to the coast. The humanoids have built a new place for me there, but I'm too contented here to move."

Nodding happily at the shabby old room behind him, the mathematician went graciously to open the door. Forester propelled himself reluctantly out, pausing to glance uneasily back at the waiting chessmen. Clammy-fingered dread touched the spine, as he wondered who was Ironsmith's chess opponent.

Forester felt oddly sorry to leave Ironsmith's sunburned grin and the comfortable little island of familiar things somehow preserved from the machines, for ahead was a sea of strangeness. Panic caught his throat when he saw once more how all of Starmont had been transformed, and he looked anxiously toward the north rim of the little mesa for the squat old concrete building which concealed Project Thunderbolt.

He couldn't find the search building. Perhaps it was only hidden behind the long amber walls of the villa, but he had to fight a suffocating dread that the machines had already torn it down, and so stumbled upon the vault beneath. He shuffled forlornly on between his keepers, afraid to turn aside or look again, but he must have somehow betrayed his sharp unease, because the humanoid at his right elbow asked suddenly:

"Clay Forester, why are you unhappy?"

"But I am happy. Quite!" He gulped at the dusty roughness in his throat. "It's just that things are different, now, and a man needs time to think."

"Thinking doesn't make men happy, sir," the machine protested blandly. "But we can solve any necessary problem—"

Forester tried not to listen to that cheery purr. His necessary problem was to reach that buried vault alone, to launch one missile against Wing IV, but the humanoids would be no help at that. His plodding steps halted suddenly.

"Service, sir," whined the machine. "Has something disturbed you?"

"No, I'm quite all right." He made himself move on, kicking at a pebble to show his unconcern. "But a man needs to talk to his friends, and I just remembered an old acquaintance I'd like to see. I wonder if you can find him for me."

"What is his name, sir?"

"Mark White." Forester's voice went too high, and he paused to frown as if with effort. "I don't remember any address, but he was living somewhere on the West Coast. A big, blue-eyed man, red-bearded. A professional philosopher. Perhaps he could help me get adjusted."

The machine stood frozen beside him. The sun struck its sleek blackness into molten bronze and frosty blue. Its opaque steel eyes seemed curiously alert, but it didn't answer at once, and he shivered inwardly. For Ironsmith had been with him at Dragonrock, and heard White's plans. Had that knowledge been the price of the mathematician's freedom?

"There is no such individual," the machine said at last, "among the individuals we serve on this planet." And he thought there was a new watchfulness beyond the mild, benign surprise on that narrow plastic face. "On other planets, however, we have several times encountered a very large man, who always wore a thick red beard and often called himself a philosopher and sometimes even used that name. His present whereabouts are unknown, because he took part in a foolish attack against Wing IV, and escaped when it failed."

Forester felt that veiled alertness tighten.

"Where did you know this man?" inquired the machine. "And when?"

"I never knew him well." Forester kicked carefully at the pebble again, attempting to undo his blunder. "I met him several times at scientific gatherings on the West Coast, where he was reading papers on his philosophy. The last time was several years ago."

"Then the man we seek is a different Mark White." That searching intentness seemed to relax. "Because he did not escape to this planet until a few months ago, when we almost captured him on a world four light-years from here. We are hunting him," the machine added smoothly, "because he is an extremely unhappy man, gravely in need of euphoride."

Forester strolled on, as deliberately as possible, regretting the blunder of his question. Mark White loomed tremendous now, the last tragic champion of mankind and his only possible ally, yet Forester dared not try to reach him again, or even to mention the old Dragonrock Light, because one more such ill-judged query might be fatal to them both.

Back at the villa, he let the machines display all the mechanical wonders of that commodious prison. Vast crystal windows turned opaque or luminous at need, and roofless gardens were tropical with radiant heat. The kitchen was an antiseptic laboratory. And every device, he bitterly observed, was worked by relays that a man couldn't reach.

Restless as any trapped animal, he wandered on. He didn't like the swaying, nightmarish things growing in the sunken garden beyond the villa, but he walked on around them, with a determined show of curiosity, just to reach a point from which he might see the old search building.

Even when he had reached the spot, he scarcely dared to

look, because his keepers were too near and too alert, their black handsome faces too remotely serene. His knees felt weak again, as he paused uncertainly on a little rocky point, near the lip of the prismed basalt precipice which dropped straight to the talus-slope and the brown flats far below.

"Service, sir." One of the machines moved to block his path, lustrous in the sunlight and implacably kind. "We can't allow you any nearer the edge."

He nodded, not protesting. Assuming an idle interest in the heat-rippled horizon, he let his gaze slide northward. Carefully casual, he swept a jutting buttress of the mountain, and the end of the mesa above. He found the flat dome of the old concrete building—intact!

He made his eyes move on instantly, yet he had time to see that the tall steel fence and the guard towers around the installation had been torn down. There was nothing to keep him from the building. Nothing except the humanoids. Looking out across the desert, with its white slashes of dry washes and its sharp wrinkles of far brown mountains, he stood discarding hopeless schemes to escape his keepers, until a rumbling vibration drew his glance again.

Careful that his eyes didn't pause, he looked past the low gray building and found the excavating machine. That monstrous thing held his gaze and slowed his heart. The clean, functional lines of its armored case gave it a kind of ominous beauty, but the mountain trembled to its motion. Red enamel and white metal glittered painfully under the hot sun. On immense slow tracks, it was creeping through the flattened ruin of the old guard barracks, its huge shining blades slicing the grassy mountain crown into a long red dike of raw soil and broken stone. The search building, he saw, would presently stand in its path.

"Unfortunately, sir, the landscaping of Starmont is not quite complete." The intent mechanical beside him must have followed his eyes and sensed his displeasure. "The dense basaltic formation has delayed the work, but it should all be finished in a few days. We are going to remove all the old military buildings, and excavate the entire area for a pool."

"That's wonderful." He was afraid to say that he didn't want a pool, although he could see that this huge slow mechanism would uproot the search building and uncover the vault beneath. He must strike soon, or surrender hope. Contriving a thin smile, he managed to say:

"We used to swim every summer, Ruth and I."

"Swimming," the machine said, "is forbidden now."

He couldn't help inquiring bitterly, "For Ironsmith, too?"

The humanoid stood completely motionless, a molten luster of sunlight flowing across its blackness. Waiting, Forester bit his lip, afraid he had revealed too much of his consuming anxiety.

"Mr. Ironsmith," it said abruptly, "has earned a different status."

"I know." He tried to smooth his ragged voice. "But how?"

The machine stood still again, for long, intolerable seconds, regarding him with a faintly astonished vigilance. "Service, sir," its clear voice pealed abruptly. "Such questions tend to show unhappiness, and raise questions about your future care." Again it paused, while he fought to keep an outward calm. "Now we observe that you are squinting," it went on gently. "This sunlight is too bright for your eyes. You should return to your dwelling and eat your lunch."

Putting up a quivering hand to shade his eyes, Forester fumbled for a ruse. Perhaps he could manufacture some excuse to send one of his guards away, and then knock out the other with a rock—better, push it off the cliff. Perhaps he would have time to reach the search building before any others came. Perhaps—

"The sun is pretty bright," he admitted cheerfully. "But I'm not hungry yet, and I want to look over the rest of the grounds." He peered hopefully at the nearer machine. "So, if you'll just go back to the house and get me a pair of sunglasses—"

"Service, sir." The machine didn't move. "Another unit will bring sunglasses and a parasol."

"Good," he muttered. "Very good, indeed!"

He strolled on again, obliquely toward the search building, keeping as near the edge of the mesa as his guards would allow, and developing an interest in the few wild flowers. He bent at last as if to pick a ragged crimson bloom, and snatched at a likely stone beside it.

"Service, sir." Beamed power made the machine a dark blur of incredible motion. Its steel-and-plastic fingers took the stone away from him, with an irresistible accurate strength. "That is dangerous, sir," it said. "Men can rupture themselves attempting to lift stones."

Forester straightened slowly, peering hopelessly at its bright steel eyes. Its narrow, graceful face held a calm, benign tranquillity. Perfect and invincible, it could feel no anger nor exact any penalty; yet his pathetic ruse had failed, as it seemed that feeble men must fail forever. Shrugging wearily, he stumbled back toward his shining prison on the hill.

# 14

WAITING FOR THE time to dine with Ironsmith, Forester wanted to see Ruth again, but he was afraid to return to that gay nursery room where he had seen her playing with her plastic blocks. For his control was too fragile. Too easily, he might betray his feelings, and so invite oblivion.

Trying to relax, he surrendered his person to the efficient machines, which washed him in a perfumed bath, steamed him and massaged him, and clad him at last in a soft white robe. He didn't like the robe, because it fastened in the back with tiny rhodomagnetic snaps that he couldn't reach or work, and it made him feel ridiculously unclad, but when he asked meekly for his trousers, he was told they had been destroyed.

"They were man-made, sir. The garments we supply are far superior in durability and comfort."

He said no more, for he wasn't seeking forgetfulness. The expert rubdown had relaxed his body, and his mind was vainly busy with the riddle of Ironsmith.

"Your body needs attention, sir." The cheery words shattered his thoughts. "It already shows defects due to age and overwork and want of proper care. Your muscular tensions and glandular malfunctions reveal a want of satisfactory mental adjustment to your environment which will result in serious physical deterioration unless relieved."

"Dr. Pitcher told me just about the same thing a year ago." Forester tried to grin. "But I'm still here."

"We must advise euphoride, sir, without any long delay."

"No!" He felt those same familiar tensions drawing him dangerously rigid again. "I'll be all right," he insisted stubbornly. "Frank Ironsmith is going to help me get adjusted to this wonderful new environment."

"The euphoride treatment may be delayed until you have seen him again," the machine agreed. "But we can permit no long neglect."

"If I really need any medical attention," he protested uneasily, "I'll just go back to Dr. Pitcher."

"He has retired," the machine said. "No human doctors are permitted to practice now, because drugs and surgical instruments can become so extremely dangerous through misuse, and because our own medical skill is so much greater than any man's. Dr. Pitcher is writing a play."

"Anyhow," Forester insisted, "Ironsmith will help me."

Waiting for the mathematician, he sat on a wide terrace at the villa, watching the desert redden in the dusk. The cruiser ready on the stage was a long smooth egg, bright-streaked with reflections of land and sky. A small humanoid, far beyond, was guiding a humming lawn mower. The whole scene was quiet enough, but he couldn't forget the frozen alertness of the

machines behind his chair or the enigma of Ironsmith's freedom growing more and more disquieting as he tried to solve it.

"Service, sir," the nearest humanoid said suddenly. "Mr.
Ironsmith wishes to know if you will meet him aboard the
cruiser, for your trip to his new place on the coast."

Even that gentle purr made him start up nervously, for he
had begun to face the evening with an uneasy dread. He hurried silently down to the rhodomagnetic craft, and let the
two machines help him up to the deck. Watching through
the hull's dark transparency, he saw Ironsmith pedaling alone
to join him, bareheaded in the cool twilight and whistling
cheerfully. A pang of envy stabbed him, for it simply wasn't
fair.

Bitterly, he watched that blithe young man lean his cycle
against the villa and run lightly to the cruiser. The covered
deck was chest-high, with no gangway or ladder, but he asked
no aid to come aboard and the mechanicals, oddly, offered him
none. Vaulting through the door, with almost the effortless
ease of another machine, he sank into the deep seat beside Forester with a genial grin.

A hidden relay closed the door, and another lifted the silent
craft. As the butte dropped back into the thickening darkness,
Forester risked another glance at the old search building. It
still stood, but that excavating machine, carving long slow
slices from the mountain, was creeping steadily toward its secret.

Careful not to look again, Forester turned to Ironsmith
with a guarded wariness, even though the younger man was not
behaving like any devious antagonist. He had left his pipe behind, as if from courtesy, and he offered a stick of chewing
gum.

"It helps," he urged, "if you mustn't smoke."

Forester chewed the gum distastefully, tautly alert, as the
other began casually pointing out the luminous roofs of new
villas scattered across the dark landscape, and talking brightly

of tunnels the humanoids were already boring and enormous pumping stations they were building, to raise whole rivers from the humid eastern valleys to this arid plateau.

Lifting out of the twilight over Starmont, the little ship curved high through the violet night of the ionosphere to over-take the setting sun. It dropped again, in its swift trajectory, toward a dark and jagged edge of land against the ruddy bright-ness of a humanoid copper sea. A stark granite headland flung up to meet it. Red sunset shimmered on the wet black stones of a broken causeway. White spray plumped up from black fangs of stone. Startled, Forester blinked at his pleasant-faced com-panion.

"I call the place Dragonrock," Ironsmith was murmuring. "After the old lighthouse that used to stand here."

Forester nodded stiffly, afraid to ask what had become of those curious fugitives hiding in the old tower, Mark White and his tattered disciples.

"Pretty wonderful, isn't it?"

Ironsmith was beaming innocently, and Forester turned uncomfortably to look at the new building crowning that bleak headland. Golden columns and balconies and clustered towers made a luminous filigree too elaborate for his taste, and high roofs burned crimson. When the craft had landed on a wide stage, Ironsmith took him proudly to tour the monumental halls and the exotic gardens sheltered from the cold sea winds by crystal parapets.

"Pretty gorgeous, don't you think?" Ironsmith inquired happily. "I might move down here, if I had time."

Forester eyed him narrowly, wondering what else he had to do, and then blinked angrily at his own silent keepers, blurting impulsively, "Can't you send them away—so we can talk alone?"

To his stunned surprise, Ironsmith nodded calmly.

"If you like. I'm afraid you let their presence upset you too much, and maybe I can help you accept them." He turned quietly to the machines. "Please leave us alone for half an hour. I'll be responsible for Dr. Forester's safety."

"Service, sir."

Incredibly, the two guards departed. Forester looked hard at Ironsmith. All he could see was a lean and harmless-seeming man with untidy clothing and gray, friendly eyes, but something touched him with an icy awe. Beckoning cheerfully, Ironsmith led him on across the warm soundless pavement of a vast court, where the heated air was bitter with the fragrance from huge crimson fungi, fringed and intricate, towering out of tall golden jars. A crystal wall stopped them, and white surf was moaning over black rocks far below. Forester caught his breath, to plunge vehemently:

"Frank, I want to know what you've done with Mark White and that remarkable child and the others."

"Nothing." Ironsmith turned sober. "I don't even know where they are. When I came here looking for them, the old tower was empty. I selected this for a building site, hoping they might come back. But they didn't. I never found a clue."

The cold purpose in his voice astonished Forester, for this was not the callow and indolent clerk who had loafed through his work with such surprising ease in the old computing section, but suddenly a mature, determined man. Somehow unnerved, he gulped hoarsely:

"Why try so hard?"

"Because Mark White is an ignorant, dangerous fanatic." That calm voice held a crushing certainty. "Because he's a mental child—as you must have seen from the melodramatic way he first got us here—a child unfortunately armed with something very dangerous. His blundering could wreck Wing IV."

"If he's against the humanoids, that's enough for me."

"That's why I brought you here—to warn you." Ironsmith's eyes were level and grave and a little sad. "Because I want to stop you from making Mark White's blunder. And

Warren Mansfield's. Your whole attitude is mistaken, Forester, and highly dangerous."

Forester shivered. "You mean—I may get euphoride?"

"That doesn't matter at all." The lift of Ironsmith's shoulders was almost scornful. "Really, Forester, I think you ought to ask for the drug. Because you can only hurt yourself—and others—if you try to fight the humanoids. Better let them help you, in any way they can."

Forester said nothing, but his narrow jaw set hard. He stared out at the copper glints fading on the sea, wondering how to ask what he had to know.

"The greatest danger is from Mark White," Ironsmith went on quietly. "But I'm sure he still wants to help, and I imagine he'll try to get back in touch with you. If he does, please tell him to come and talk to me—before his mad plots have done too much harm to be repaired. I just want a chance to show him that he has chosen the wrong side. Won't you pass along that message?"

Forester shook his head.

"That's nonsense." His voice had a breathless harshness. "But there are things I want to know." He caught his breath, trying to shake off his uneasy dread of this inexplicable individual—human or not—who once had been just a clerk at Starmont. "How do you get on so well with these machines? Why are you so disturbed about White's fight against them? And who"—his husky voice caught—"who's your chess opponent—when you're all alone?"

"Your imagination is working too hard." Ironsmith gave him a brief, sunburned grin. "I think you should ask for euphoride."

"Don't say that!" Forester's voice turned husky, and he clutched desperately at the other's sleeve. "I know you can help me—because you've escaped. Please—please, Frank—be human!"

"I am." Ironsmith nodded sympathetically. "And I do want to help you, if you'll only let me."

"Then tell me—just tell me what to do."

"Accept the humanoids," Ironsmith said quietly. "That's all I did."

"Accept those intolerable monsters?" Forester shivered in uneasy indignation. "When they've already wrecked my observatory and destroyed the mind of my wife? When they're even threatening me?"

"I'm sorry you persist in regarding the humanoids as malevolent enemies." Ironsmith shook his close-cropped sandy head with an air of bland regret. "Your whole attitude seems as childish as Mark White's, and I'm afraid it will get you in trouble."

"Trouble?" Forester tried unsuccessfully to grin. "What do you think I'm in right now?"

"Nothing you didn't ask for." A faint impatience edged Ironsmith's brisk voice. "You're a scientist, Forester—or you used to be. With all your experience, in finance and administration and practical engineering as well as pure research, you ought to be too mature to conjure up imaginary devils." As if with restrained exasperation, Ironsmith caught his arm. "Can't you recognize the humanoids as nothing but machines, to be treated as machines and nothing more?"

Forester whispered uneasily, "How do you mean?"

"When you make them into enemies, you imply something impossible to any machine." A sober frown had followed Ironsmith's flash of annoyance. "You imply the moral choice of an evil purpose, reinforced with some emotion of anger or hate—when you ought to know that machines are equipped with neither morals nor emotions."

"I'll agree about the morals!"

Ignoring that feeble stab, Ironsmith stared past him at the sea. "The humanoids, in fact, are the best machines men have ever made, because the more primitive devices always had the dangerous flaw that careless or wicked men could turn them to destructive ends. The humanoids are protected from human manipulation. That is their real perfection, Forester, and the ultimate reason that we must accept them."

Forester watched him silently, seeking in vain for whatever lay behind that disarming air of innocent candor.

"Get what I mean? A can opener will cut your finger as willingly as it does a can. A rifle will kill the hunter as quickly as the game. Yet those devices aren't evil; the error arises in the user. Old Warren Mansfield was merely solving the old problem of the imperfections and limitations of the human operator, when he designed a perfect mechanism to operate itself."

Lips tight, Forester shook his head.

"Anyhow," Ironsmith went on earnestly, "you ought to be too intelligent to try to fight the humanoids. Let them serve and obey, and you won't need euphoride."

Forester rasped harshly, "Obey me?"

"They will." Ironsmith nodded persuasively. "If you'll accept them—sincerely. Do that, and you can have all I do. If you don't, I see no hope for you but the drug."

"You don't, huh?" Forester felt his thin fists clenching. "See here, Frank. I don't quite follow all your phony arguments, and I don't want any sort of run-around. I think there's something else—and pretty ugly—behind your immunity from these damned restrictions and your queer attitude toward these perfect machines." Sarcasm lifted his breathless voice. "Let them serve and obey—I want the truth!"

Ironsmith seemed to hesitate. Ruddy in the reddening western light, his smoothly youthful face showed no resentment, and he nodded solemnly at last, admitting, "There are things I can't tell you."

"Why not?"

"If it were left to me, I'd tell you everything." He studied the remote, straight horizon. "I'd be willing to trust you with all the facts. But the humanoids are also involved, and they were designed to take no chances."

"Frank—don't you see?" Forester's broken voice was hoarsely pleading. "I've got to know!"

"Nothing more." Ironsmith turned to face him, smooth jaw firm. "Not until you actually accept the humanoids—and I had better warn you that they are expert in assaying human reactions. They don't trick."

"That's why I'm so—so horribly afraid!"

"I'm sorry for you, Forester." Ironsmith turned reluctantly, as if to rejoin the humanoids. "I had really hoped to help you—because your abilities are too brilliant to be killed by euphoride, and because I'm your friend."

"Are you?"

Ironsmith ignored that savage interjection. "I never really understood you, Forester—especially the way you've always neglected Ruth. Perhaps the humanoids are right. Perhaps there would be danger to the Prime Directive in trusting you with what I know."

"Wait!" Anger swept Forester—terror and bleak suspicion. "I'll never ask for euphoride." His sobbing voice turned wildly threatening. "And you've got to help me—"

Ironsmith twisted away from his frantic hands with the effortless deftness of another humanoid, his calm and honest eyes looking back across the court again, past the bitter-odored fungi in the tall yellow jars.

"Here they come," he murmured casually. "And I hope you remember my message." His voice fell to a whisper. "Tell Mark White to come and talk to me, before he starts any childish attack on Wing IV."

Forester nodded bleakly, watching the two tiny black machines come running silently back across the soundless pavement to resume their suffocating supervision. He'd accept them, he thought savagely—with a shot from Project Thunderbolt. Still he couldn't understand Ironsmith's motives in this curious attempt to bribe him, blindfolded, to join in the treason against mankind. But still the humanoids had to be stopped.

"Service, sirs," said the nearer mechanical. "Your dinner is served."

# 15

THE VAULTED HALL where they dined had a spacious splendor which only film producers had imagined in the vanished past before the humanoids. Six mechanicals served the too-elaborate meal. There were wines for Ironsmith, but none for Forester.

"Your digestion has been impaired by worry and fatigue," a machine reminded him melodiously. "You must take no alcohol until your health is better."

It was serenely right and monstrously intolerable.

Ironsmith announced that he was staying for the night, when the meal was done, and Forester went back to Starmont alone. Soaring above the atmosphere, he looked up once at the crystal beauty of the stars that men had lost, and then sat hunched on the edge of the luxurious seat, sunk deep in failure.

"Service, sir," murmured the mechanical beside him. "You appear uncomfortable."

"Huh!" Trying to cover his nervous start, he stretched himself elaborately and settled carefully back in the seat, grinning stiffly up at the two dark identical faces above. Nothing else was left to do. Utterly benevolent, more dreadful than anything evil, these perfect and eternal keepers of mankind prohibited even the freedom of despair.

At the end of the flight, he found the hope and courage to risk one more glance toward the old search building. The flat concrete dome was still intact—and as far from his reach as Wing IV itself. The excavating machine was nearer to its secret now, a slow metal saurian devouring the mountain in the dark.

He woke suddenly, that night, from a troubled dream.

"Dr. Forester! Please—can you hear me?"

A clear childish treble voice was calling to him, urgent and afraid. Only a part of the dream, he thought at first; yet it had brought him off his pillow, taut and shivering, wide awake. The dream had all dissolved, less vivid than this waking nightmare of men smothered beneath absolute benevolence, but the stark terror of it had left him cold with sweat, and gasping.

Comfort surrounded him, quiet, and utter peace, here in his own new bedroom at Starmont. In the softly glowing murals, village swains and maids danced silently at their unceasing festival. The vast east window, transparent now, opened upon the empty desert and the far folds of hills, washed now with the chill blue of dawn. But that luxurious room seemed more dreadful to him than any nightmare could have been, because a solicitous humanoid stood watching beside the great bed.

Shuddering convulsively, he desperately strove to smile and hide his fear—until he saw that the humanoid had stopped. It was falling, the blind tranquillity unchanged on its narrow face, and it made no move to recover its balance. Rigid as some statue of ideal grace in black-lacquered metal, it toppled deliberately to strike the soft floor with a muffled crash. And still it lay there, dark face up, incredibly dead. Forester coughed to a sudden stinging reek of hot metal and burned plastic.

"Dr. Forester!" Startled, he realized that the child's voice was not a dream. "Won't you please come with me now?"

He saw her then. Jane Carter! She came creeping timidly around the foot of his bed, peering uneasily at the quiet mechanical on the floor. That immense bright room seemed warm to him, and she was huddled in a worn leather coat too large for her, yet he saw that she was shivering. Under a thin yellow dress, her bare knees and feet were blue with cold.

"Huh—why, hello, Jane!" He answered her shy smile with a feeble grin, and nodded stiffly at the fallen machine. "What happened to that?"

"I stopped it."

He searched her frightened face silently, and then turned back to that fallen unit of the ultimate machine. A dazed incredulity shook his voice. "How?"

"Like Mr. White taught me." She retreated uneasily from the thing on the floor. "You just look, in a certain way he

taught me, at a little white bead in its head. That bead is—
potassium." She was careful with the word. "You just look—
that certain way—and the potassium burns."

Forester couldn't see any potassium bead, or anything else,
inside the bald plastic-covered head of the stopped machine,
but he shrugged with a numbed acceptance. He remembered
the unstable isotope of potassium, and Mark White's boast that
this hungry urchin had learned to control atomic probability,
to detonate K-40 atoms by a simple act of her mind.

"Please, won't you come and help us now?"

Staring at her black, limpid eyes, so wistful and afraid in
their dark circles of weariness and want, Forester scarcely
heard her thinly urgent voice. He felt a tingle in his scalp, and
he failed to stop his shivering. For the human body, it occurred
to him, also contained a fatal quantity of that radioactive isotope. If this strange child could stop a humanoid by looking at
it in a certain particular way, she could doubtless also kill a
man.

"Please come!"

The meaning of her imploring words burst upon him then,
sweeping away his dazed reflection that the old tales of that
deadly kind of vision called the evil eye must be something
more than superstition. A wave of hope dispelled his momentary terror of her solemn stare, and broke the nightmare chains
of his total frustration. He smiled at her breathlessly.

"I'm coming," he whispered. "But where?"

He was scrambling out of bed, a slight anxious figure in a
loose blue night robe, when the motionless machine caught his
glance. Its handsome narrow face was still the same, faintly astonished and eternally benign, but now the steel-colored eyes
were tarnished with heat, and thin gray smoke was seeping
from the black nostrils.

"We must get away from that!" Flinching from it, he
caught the child's thin arm to draw her hastily beyond the bed.
"It's still dangerous," he breathed huskily. "With secondary

activity. You can't see the rays, but they still could burn us badly."

He searched the room for any way out, rubbing his burning eyes and coughing to that bitter smoke—which must be laden with deadly radioactives, he thought, from that small atomic explosion. The sliding doors and the huge window were all secured with inaccessible rhodomagnetic relays, however, and he could see no possible escape. Unless— The thought struck him abruptly, shocking as the unexpected touch of a cold hand in the dark. Peering dazedly at the child, he heard her worried voice:

"—and Mr. White says we must come right away, 'cause the black things will know this one has stopped, and more of them will come to see what stopped it."

That acrid smoke had caught his throat, so that he could hardly breathe, and hot tears from it blurred his vision. He had to put a hand against the smooth shining wall to steady himself as he whispered to the child, "But how—how can we get out?"

"Come," Jane Carter said. "Just come with me."

She put up a grubby little paw for him to clasp, thin and shivering. He stared at her, nodding bleakly at the locked doors. "There's no way out."

"For us there is," she said. "We go by teleportation."

Forester dropped her hand. His dry laugh was almost hysterical, and the smoke changed it to a coughing paroxysm. He wiped his eyes with the sleeve of his robe, gasping huskily, "But I can't do teleportation."

"I know," she told him solemnly. "But Mr. White thinks I can carry you. If you will help, the best you can."

"Help?" he muttered harshly. "How?"

"Just think of where we are going," she told him. "And try to be there."

Shuddering, he attempted to believe. "Where are we going?"

"To a far, dark place, underground. It's always cold there, and you can hear water running. I don't like it—but there's no opening in the rocks, and no way in but by teleportation, so the black things can't get us there. Mr. White says he will help you find the way."

Forester took her hand again, trying to picture some dark cave where Mark White and his tattered followers must be hiding from the humanoids. He tried hard enough, he thought, because his mind could already see the efficient mechanicals swarming to investigate the one Jane Carter had stopped. He longed, with a savage intensity, to escape this glittering prison and the threat of euphoride. Surely, he tried desperately enough.

But he was still a physicist. He couldn't quite imagine the mechanics of instantaneous translation. Even if time were really only an incidental electromagnetic effect, it was still as actual as space and motion. Even the swift rhodomagnetic missiles of the project didn't quite reach infinite accelerations, and anything faster was still impossible, even to the different physics he had found in the supernova's spectrum. He wasn't surprised when nothing happened.

"Please—try!" Her voice was strained and breathless. "Harder!"

"I did." Forester let go her hand, his voice a gasp of baffled failure. "I did—but I don't know how. Sorry, Jane, but it's no use."

"But you must!" Her cold, tiny fingers clutched his hand again. "Mr. White says we can carry you—if you will only let us. By myself, I can move a rock as big as you. If you'll just turn loose—"

He tightened his grasp on her small hand, looking down at her black anxious eyes and thinking of Mark White and Overstreet and old Graystone and little Lucky Ford, waiting for them in some deep cavern. He thought he tried. But he knew that nothing would happen—and nothing did.

"But I did try, Mr. White!" Jane Carter's fingers grew frantically tight and then relaxed, limp and quivering in his own. Big tears of frustration washed grimy streaks down her pinched

blue face. "We did too try, 'cause we know it's so awful important. But we just can't."

And Forester caught a flicker of motion, then, outside the huge window, as something dark and very swift ran past. He knew the machines were closing in. Turning shakenly back to the child, he was choked with a sudden tenderness. For one moment of hopeless yearning, he wished that he and Ruth had found time for children—instead of Project Thunderbolt.

"It's all right, Jane—"

He reached awkwardly for the little girl, wanting to comfort her, but some cruel school must have taught her independence. She refused the caress. Her bare skinny knees shook with fear and cold, but she stood proudly straight.

"No, it isn't all right." Her voice was high and bitterly clear. "Mr. White says this is very bad, for all of us. He says the black machines are sure to take your memory now, if you don't get away. And he says they will know a lot about us, from studying the one I stopped. He says it will be very hard for us, now, to change the Prime Directive."

She stood a little away from him, tiny and indomitable. Her blue lips moved, murmuring silently. Her apprehensive eyes looked at something far away. Her famine-hollowed head tilted, as if she listened. And then she turned gravely back to him, sadly offering her small grimy hand.

"I'm sorry, Dr. Forester. We're all sorry, 'cause we need you and we like you. Now it's time for me to go. Mr. White says the black machines are coming—"

He could see another humanoid beyond her, watching with hard, bright eyes of blind-seeming steel through the great window. Nodding at it vehemently, he whispered at her to kill it. Before she could turn, however, the crystal panel turned abruptly opaque, shutting out that alert mechanical and the light of the dawn. The glow of the murals on the high walls was also extinguished. Smothering darkness fell upon them, and he heard a terrified gasp from the child.

## 16

STAGGERED BY THAT fall of blackness, Forester nodded in bleak understanding of the move. The humanoids, with their rhodomagnetic sensory fields, had no need of light. That efficient brain on far Wing IV intended to bewilder him with darkness, while its invincible units swarmed in to seize him. He wondered how forgetfulness would feel.

"We can't help you." The child's hurt voice seemed too loud, beneath that crushing dark. "And Mr. White says I must go."

Her tiny questing fingers caught his hand for a moment, and then let him go. For an eternal second he stood all alone in the dark, until sheer desperation armed him. "Jane!" he gasped. "Wait!"

"Please!" Her tiny, frightened voice brought back hope. "Mr. White says—"

"I can't go with you," he sobbed. "But tell him there's another way."

Careless of the strangling smoke from the machine on the floor, he filled his lungs again. His narrow shoulders lifted defiantly in the dark. He had failed to master the paradoxes of psychophysics, but he knew the planet-smashing power of the slender missiles in the vault, already set to seek Wing IV.

"Mr. White says we'll try to help you." Groping in the dark, she had caught the sleeve of his robe. "But he wants to know your plan. 'Cause there are too many machines—Mr. Overstreet can see them coming. More machines than I can stop."

"Tell Mr. White I have weapons," he whispered swiftly. "Self-guided missiles already ranged and armed to detonate Wing IV—still hidden in that underground station where you came. Just one of them could stop all the humanoids, in about half a minute." Apprehension rocked him. "Anyhow, I hope the missiles are still there," he added hoarsely. "Though I saw an excavating machine, working toward the building about the station."

"Wait," the child breathed. "Mr. Overstreet can look."

For an endless second the room was silent again, while he shivered to the dread of soundless black machines creeping upon them in the dark.

"Mr. Overstreet can see the building," she whispered at last. "The digging machine has broken through the corner of it, but the roof hasn't fallen in. He says the black things haven't found the elevator."

"Then we can try!" A savage elation lifted him. "We must wait until the humanoids open the doors, to get at us. You must be ready to stop them, Jane—as many as you can. And I'll make a run for the project."

Silence seemed to clot the dark again. Waiting for the mechanicals to break in, he was startled by the child's quiet voice. "Mr. White says we'll try your plan. He says he had hoped to change the Prime Directive without wrecking all the black things. But we needed you to help us make the new relays for that, and we can't try it now. So your weapons seem to be the only way, and I'm to stay and help you all I can. And he says—"

Jane Carter gasped faintly. Forester felt her small hand tighten on his sleeve. Breathless and afraid, she went on faintly, "He says there's another danger we must face—worse than all the humanoids. He's afraid we'll meet Mr. Ironsmith."

"Ironsmith?" Forester shivered, as if something unseen had breathed upon him from the dark. "I've been wondering," he whispered huskily, "why he likes the mechanicals so well— and why they leave him so free." He moved closer to the child. "Who—or what—is Ironsmith?"

"Mr. White says he doesn't know." Trouble slowed her voice. "Except he's helping the machines against us. He and others like him—others in far places." Remembering those chessmen set up in an unfinished game, Forester felt an unpleasant tingle at the back of his neck. "They tried to trap us at Dragonrock—Ironsmith and his friends—'cause they're helping the machines fight Mr. White."

Forester nodded uneasily. While the identity of Ironsmith's chess opponents was still as mysterious as their remote location, the outlines of the plot had begun to appear. The humanoids, to smooth the way for their invasion, must have bought the aid of a few human traitors—such masquerading things as Major Steel must have done the buying. And Frank Ironsmith, the sick certainty possessed him, was one of those turncoats.

"I was awful s'prised about Mr. Ironsmith," the child was saying with a puzzled regret. "He seemed so nice and kind when he first came to see us at the old tower. He talked to me about teleportation and he gave me gum to chew. I liked him then, but—"

She broke off suddenly, to listen in the dark.

"Mr. White says we mustn't wait any longer." Her voice turned breathless. "Mr. Overstreet can see them on the roof, fixing the ventilator to blow something in—something to make us sleep."

"So that's the way!" Forester swayed to the impact of disaster, remembering that the efficient machines took no chances. "They don't mean to open the door until we're helpless and we can't get out."

"But we can." She tugged urgently at his sleeve. "With Mr. Lucky helping."

"That ragged little gambler?" Forester peered around him in the gloom. "What can he—"

Forester's voice dried up, as he realized that he could see. As smoothly as if a rhodomagnetic impulse from some humanoid unit had tripped the hidden relay, the door was sliding silently back. Shadowless light poured in from the hall, but he couldn't find the gambler.

"Mr. Lucky isn't here," Jane Carter was explaining gravely. "But he can reach the lock, anyhow, with telekinesis. Mr.

Overstreet helped him see what to do, and it was just as easy as rolling a seven, he says."

Forester didn't wait to listen. A slight barefoot man, brown and awkward in the loose blue gown, he darted out into the great hall, where rhodomagnetic screens made bright windows upon so many conquered planets. A voiceless alarm sent him staggering back.

For two humanoids had darted into view at the end of the hall. They came running silently, with a terrible blind agility. One of them held a tiny bright object—a hypodermic needle, Forester thought, doubtless loaded with euphoride. The other snatched something like a grenade from a bag it carried, and swept back its arm to throw.

Instinctively, Forester had pulled the child behind him. She leaned to look past him with her dark sad eyes—and the humanoids stiffened. The one with the hypodermic needle turned a grotesque cartwheel. The other skidded forward on its face, a small gray cloud exploding from the object it had tried to fling at them.

"We must get outside," warned the child. "Mr. White says the mist from that bomb would make us sleep."

Forester had turned to run with her from that expanding cloud, before the warm feel of the floor reminded him that his feet were bare. He hesitated, glancing desperately back in search of his shoes, but the tidy humanoids must have locked them up in some closet with a rhodomagnetic latch. The child was tugging at his hand, and he fled with her on tender naked feet down that spacious hall, past the glowing screens in the niches. The outer door checked them again, until Lucky Ford could reach from that distant cavern to open it, but at last they came out into the brightening dawn.

The sunken garden outside was as strange as any of the shining scenes behind them. Spawn of some different evolution, the tall, red-scaled stalks the humanoids had planted were swaying ceaselessly. A few monstrous blooms were already emerging from the enormous, writhing buds which topped them, to fly free like great awkward iridescent moths on slow fragile wings of violet and dusty gold and black, dancing and fighting and thinly screaming and mating in the air. The odor of them was a rank sweetness as overpowering as that reek of spilled perfume in which he had found Ruth playing with her blocks, and some dust or pollen from them halted him with a fit of sneezing.

"Those awful flowers!" Jane shrank from them. "Why do you think the black things brought them?"

To please the victims of euphoride, Forester supposed, for he thought a mind without memory might be easily diverted by the flashing dance of those great wings and that meaningless, unending drama of love and death. But he didn't try to answer. Breathless with sneezing, he ran on with the trembling child until he could see the old search building.

The ruin of it stood on the very lip of a deep new excavation. The west wall had already been ripped away, and the flat concrete dome had begun to settle, so that it was leaning drunkenly. The excavating machine was somewhere out of view, however, and he thought the way might still be open to that masked elevator.

Sneezing as he ran, he wiped his eyes with the loose blue sleeve and watched the grounds ahead. All the straight new walks and neat new lawns seemed oddly empty. He saw a power mower, stopped and deserted. The mechanical units, he thought, must be hiding from Jane Carter's eyes.

"Stop!" she sobbed abruptly. "That ship behind us—Mr. Overstreet says the black machines are going to take it up in the air and let it drop on us."

They turned back together and Forester could see the cruiser on the landing stage, mirroring the dawn like a huge silver egg. He saw two humanoids darting toward it from the blue-and-amber villa, and pointed them out to Jane. She looked at them, and they fell.

"Come on," she urged. "Before they think of something else."

At the end of the smooth new walk, he helped her across an open ditch. Not for many years had he moved so violently, and his thin muscles began quivering to the weakness of exhaustion as they ran on across the rough ground beyond. His labored breath made stabbing pains in his chest, and sharp stones cut his feet. But they were halfway to the building before Jane Carter began to hang back, whimpering breathlessly. Pale with terror, she was pointing up at a long new ridge of raw soil and broken rock ahead.

"The machine that digs," she whispered. "Coming!"

They sprinted for the building, too late. That enormous machine which had been slowly slicing the end of the mountain into geometric neatness came lurching over the new embankment, no longer deliberate. The first sunlight flashed yellow on its huge bright blades and red on its black-and-crimson armor, as it roared down to meet them.

# 17

No longer creeping, that mountain-eating saurian snarled and bellowed with overburdened gears. The wide cutting blades slashed down wickedly, and cruel metal teeth glittered in its maw.

"Oh, Mr. White!" Jane Carter was calling desperately. "Please, Mr. Overstreet—please show me what to do. I don't know how to stop it. I—can't find the black thing in it."

Forester paused an instant, waiting for those men in their cavern fastness to stop the machine, but it came plunging on. Picking up the child, he ran again for the building. The lurching armored monster swerved instantly to cut him off. He tried to double back, and it veered again to meet him. Feinting right, he darted left. The machine attempted to follow, but its vast whipping tracks failed for a moment to hold in the loose rubble of the new embankment. He got past it—almost.

The wallowing machine had almost buried itself in clouds

of yellow dust and flying rocks, and the leaning wreck of the building was again in view, close beyond it, when a round stone turned beneath Forester's foot. He went to his knees, and the machine had time to climb out of its pit. Wheeling, it came after him. He ran to the right again, and again it cut him off.

"Can't they stop it?" he panted huskily at Jane. "Or can't you get the humanoid in it?"

"But there isn't any," she whimpered faintly. "Mr. White says it is run by beams straight from the brain machine on Wing IV, and there isn't any black thing I can stop."

Now on firm level ground, the excavator came ponderously on, and as he fled with Jane in his arms he saw that it was herding him like some driven animal away from the ruined building, forcing him out along a narrowing shelf between that steep new embankment and the ragged edge of the mesa.

"Please—Mr. White!" the child was begging frantically. "Please—can't you help?"

But nothing halted that grinding metal avalanche. Forester tried to climb the embankment and came back down into its path again, floundering in a slide of broken stone. Dust choked him, and sharp rocks slashed him. The child had become an impossible burden in his arms, but he somehow lifted her again, still retreating toward the point of that diminishing rocky bench, where the embankment came to the rim. He was cornered, and he saw no way out.

"Climb!" Jane shrieked. "Mr. White says climb!"

Turning, he tried to stagger up that rubble slope again. For a few yards the footing held, and then the broken rock flowed again. Falling, he twisted enough to keep the weight of his body off the child, but his breath was crushed out against a rolling boulder. Savage pain numbed him, and his scratching feet and hands found only sliding stone, pouring down to carry them into the very path of the machine, which came thundering out of the dust, great blades lifted to crush them or fling them off the cliff. He tried to push Jane Carter out of its path, but a chill of exhaustion had taken his last strength.

"Oh, thank you!" she breathed. "Thank you, Mr. Lucky!"

She relaxed in his arms, and the red-and-black metal saurian veered again. The great crushing tracks covered them with yellow dust, and went on by. The roar of its overdrive gears was deafening—and then abruptly stilled. Presently the mountain quivered faintly, and he heard a distance-muffled rumble from the talus-slope below.

"I just couldn't stop it." The child's voice still was dry with terror, but she stood up, brushing the dust from her worn yellow dress. "'Cause there wasn't any black thing in it. But Mr. Overstreet could see how it worked, like a different kind of humanoid, and Mr. White told Mr. Lucky how to turn it over the edge."

Forester was coming stiffly upright. His hot body quivered weakly, and dust had caked the lacerations on his knees and feet with stiff red mud. His twisted ankle throbbed, and his breath was a painful rasping. Looking at him, the child whispered anxiously, "Are you hurt—too much?"

He shook his head, too breathless for speech, and they came back, at a lifeless, plodding trot, from that narrow shelf to the door of the settling building, where Jane stopped. "Mr. White says I must wait here," she said. "To keep the black machines away."

"For just five minutes!" Forester whispered. "That's all the time I need."

Ahead, as he stumbled into the dusty gloom of the hall that ran back toward his old office, he could hear the ominous snap and groan of plaster and timber and steel yielding reluctantly to the weight of the tilted dome. Knowing that vast mass of concrete might come down upon him the next instant, he ran breathlessly until a hail of plaster halted him.

Glancing back, as he waited for the dome to drop, he could see Jane Carter, veiled in the plaster dust, standing small and straight in the bright rectangle of the doorway, waving him urgently on. He caught his breath and flung up his arm to shield his head and plunged blindly on into that rain of debris.

A sudden lurch of the groaning floor confused him, and then something struck his head a dazing blow, but he somehow staggered at last into the cloakroom beyond the office, grateful for doors that a man could open. The sliding mirror was still in place, the dusty clothing still hanging innocently on the hooks, the rug still where he had left it. The efficiency of the humanoids must be not quite unlimited, he thought, because he saw no sign that they had found the hidden elevator.

Another shudder of the walls moved him to push the mirror up and jab frantically at the "Down" button. Nothing happened, except another rumble of weakened masonry collapsing into that new excavation. When the ceiling didn't come down on him, he tried the lights. There was no power, and a new alarm shook him.

The humanoids, operating everything on energy beamed from far Wing IV, had scrapped the old electrical power systems, but Project Thunderbolt had been equipped with its own separate plant, installed beneath the launching station in the lowest level of the vault. The dead lights posed a distressing riddle now, but he tried to hold off his dismay. Armstrong must have shut down the automatic plant, he told himself, for fear the humanoids would detect the vibration or exhaust gases from the twin motor-generators. And the missiles, he promised himself grimly, would still be armed and set to detonate Wing IV.

Still there was no response when he jiggled the button again. He dropped to his throbbing knees, threw back the rug, and lifted the escape door. Blackness lay deep about him, and a reek of fuel oil, for the power failure had also stopped the ventilators.

Awkwardly, he lowered himself through the elevator floor. His painful feet found the escape ladder, and he scrambled down into black silence. That reek of spilled oil took his breath, and the metal rungs seemed like sharp blades to his lacerated feet, but he dropped himself frantically until the splash of cold water stopped him at the bottom of the shaft.

He left the ladder, stumbling in the wet dark, to grope toward the vault. Something in the water bruised his bare toes, and he was sobbing with pain when he found the tunnel door. Pushing it open, he scrambled laboriously out of the shaft and came panting to his feet in the narrow passage.

Darkness wrapped him. No light came when he found a switch, but he knew the vault from all the months and years that cruel duty had kept him here, and he padded confidently along the tunnel. His mind could see the shop, the benches and tools and racks, and the launching tube beyond. He knew where to reach those sleek and ready missiles. He came out of the passage—and his bare foot went down into emptiness.

He toppled into vacant space, where the steel floor of the shop had been. He felt his right leg double and snap, as solid rock and ice-cold water stopped him. Agony flickered in his brain, and then a dull, increasing pain seized his knee and thigh. Trying to get up, he fell back on his face in the oily water, and knew that the leg was broken.

The slow waves of dark agony surging from it against his consciousness were not yet so keen as the pain of his failure. Half strangled by the foul water, he coughed until he could breathe again, and then began crawling laboriously over the jagged basalt on his hands and one raw knee, dragging his leg and looking for those rhodomagnetic missiles.

His groping fingers found only bare concrete, however, and the sheared bolts which had held the generators and the rotary converters to their foundations. Project Thunderbolt had been efficiently dismantled. That fact was more stunning than his fall, and he couldn't understand it.

He had seen no hint that the disguised elevator had even been discovered, and certainly no sign of the special tackle necessary to hoist the heavy machinery out of the shaft. There had been no other entrance to the vault, and his crawling search discovered no new tunnel that the humanoids might have dug. But still the missiles were gone.

His dull brain wrestled with that crushing riddle, and abandoned it. His nerve was used up. He retched feebly from the pain in his leg and finally lay still, vaguely grateful for the numbing chill of the shallow water, which gradually made that throbbing agony remote and bearable.

Tclink!

A crash like shattering glass roused him from a merciful drowsiness, and woke a new ache in his leg. Obviously, he should have had Overstreet look down here for the missiles, but he wasn't quite used to this paraphysical stuff. Old dog and new tricks. Listening sleepily, he heard another crystal crash, and knew at last that it was only a falling waterdrop. Shivering, he waited for the next. There was nothing else to do.

He was done, and nothing mattered now. The next splash was plainly made by something larger than a waterdrop, but he didn't try to rouse himself until light struck painfully against his closed eyes. Blinking, then, he watched the slim machines jumping down into the pit and gathering around him. The gleams of bronze and blue were beautiful on their smooth black bodies, and their legs didn't break.

"Service, Dr. Forester." That silver voice was melodiously kind. "Are you badly injured, sir?"

But his injuries weren't important now, and he nodded stiffly toward the black emptiness on the concrete shelf above, where the launching station had been, muttering faintly, "So you found it, eh?"

"We found you, sir," droned the machine. "We observed your reckless indiscretion in entering the collapsing building above, and we followed as quickly as possible to rescue you. We were delayed, however, first by the child with you and then by the fall of the dome, and we had to clear away part of the rubble and repair the elevator in order to reach you."

A sick astonishment lifted his head.

"Don't you attempt to move, sir," warned the machine. "You might increase your injuries."

Too ill to laugh at the irony of that, he nodded feebly at the empty foundations. "How did you find it?" he whispered hoarsely. "This installation?"

"We discovered the elevator shaft when we removed the debris of the building above to look for you." Serene steel eyes watched him. "Can you speak without pain, sir? Then will you tell us what equipment was once installed here?"

That question stunned him. It meant that the humanoids knew nothing, even yet, of Project Thunderbolt. And it posed a monstrous problem: who had removed the missiles and equipment? Frank Ironsmith? He shivered from something colder than the black water. But even that remarkable mathematician, sanity assured him, could scarcely have carried away a hundred tons of heavy machinery on his rusty bicycle.

"What was this installation, sir?" persisted the machine.

"Our first neutrino lab." An impulse of defiance spurred him to that feeble invention. "Our first unsuccessful search tubes were built and installed here, for the sake of secrecy. Later, after the military guard had been established, we built and mounted the new tubes in the dome above, because of the water seepage here. The old equipment was junked, but we left the pit for an emergency shelter."

The machine seemed satisfied with that, but his own weary brain couldn't let the riddle go. He dismissed a fleeting notion that the project had been looted by the use of some psycho-physical agency. Mark White obviously hadn't known of the loss—and even Jane Carter, he thought, would have found it difficult to teleport sixty tons of storage batteries.

But somebody had those dreadful missiles now, and all the specifications he had left in that sealed safe. Somebody had stolen the power to detonate any inhabited planet, as easily as one savage could brain another with a wooden club. Retching weakly again, Forester felt a kind of pity for that unknown thief who had stolen his monstrous burden.

"—more questions, sir." He heard the insistent whine of that nearest machine again, as if from far away. "It is necessary for us to find that child who came here with you. What is her name, sir? And where is she now?"

Forester smiled against his pain, for those questions told him that Jane Carter had not been caught beneath the falling dome. She must have escaped to that dark, damp place underground, where water murmured and Mark White and her other friends still held out against the humanoids. He whispered defiantly, "I don't know."

"She is extremely dangerous," the machine said sweetly. "Because she possesses supermechanical capacities, which she is using against the purpose of the Prime Directive. We are now arranging a new service for such unhappy cases, because euphoride sometimes fails to control them, and we must find that child at once."

"I hope you never find her!" Giving way to a bitter wrath, because there was no more need for caution now, he shook his bruised fist at the circle of dark identical faces above him. "I hope she goes straight to Wing IV, and uses her supermechanical gift to wreck that mechanical brain that runs you." He caught a sobbing breath, and gasped, "Now I've told you—kill me if you want!"

"Clay Forester, you fail to understand the nature of our service," purred the machine. "It is true that the extreme unhappiness revealed by your behavior will now require you to take euphoride shots as fast as you can tolerate the drug, but our function is never to punish, but merely to serve and obey. You have displayed no supermechanical abilities yourself, and you need not fear destruction."

He lay silent, not even shivering.

## 18

WATER SPLASHED AGAIN, and quiet dark machines knelt to lift him with deft warm hands. Very gently, one unit examined his numb leg. "You have been most reckless and unwise," it whined. "This avoidable accident has fractured your right femur and patella, and damaged the ligaments of the knee. You urgently need our care."

"You weren't quite so careful," he muttered bleakly, "when you chased me with that excavating machine."

"That child was with you then," the bright voice sang. "Working under the Prime Directive for the greatest good of the greatest number, we must use every possible means to defeat the supermechanical abilities of such headstrong individuals."

They carried him on a stretcher back into the repaired elevator. For all their gentle skill, the pain of his swollen leg dimmed his awareness again. He knew when the sun struck his face, and he caught the musky reek of that sunken garden where those winged blooms of another life flitted and kissed and died, and then he lay on a cold table in a small white room. Deft machines were stripping off the damp rags of his torn robe and sponging away the blood and grime. A chemical odor took his breath, and something burned his lacerated skin. He tensed, with a stifled gasp, when something touched his throbbing thigh.

"Your alarm is needless, sir," came the voice of a machine, "because your pain will soon be gone."

Soft plastic fingers lifted his arm. He felt a cold swab, and the prick of a needle. His dry lips moved to protest, but no sound came.

"Don't worry, sir," cooed the machine with the needle. "This is your first shot of euphoride. It will help relax your injured body while we set the broken bones, and it will remove your unhappiness and pain."

Too weak to struggle, he lay still in a vague submerged awareness. The throb of his leg receded into dreamy unimportance, and time began to skip.

He was back in that great bedroom, with the luminous murals of dancing village boys and girls. Once he wondered for a long time, dimly, if people had really been happier in that simpler age, before machines became supreme. Once the vast crystal window was a screen of fine-veined jade against the desert day; and it was clear at some dusk; and again, when it was glowing dimly golden, he knew the time was night. Gentle hands turned him on the bed, and sometimes needles stung his arm again, always pushing him deeper into forgetfulness. And always there were sleek black faces, steel eyes watching, unchangingly benign.

Once his wife came, guided by a solicitous machine. She carried a furry toy, dangling by one bright wing, shaped like one of those great animate blooms. Below the thin, sophisticated arch of her plucked brows, her eyes were wide and childish and dimly troubled. Her perfume was first an exciting breath, stirring sleeping reflections, and then a choking wave of sweetness.

"This is Ruth," the machine said. "She is your wife."

The trouble in her eyes changed to a vague recognition, as she bent over him, and her full woman's lips made a wistful baby-smile. She reached out uncertainly to touch his forehead and his lips, and he thought he saw a momentary shadow of baffled longing on her too-young face, before she found that she had dropped her furry toy.

Her painted lips turned petulant, then, and quick tears rolled down her cheeks, until the deft machine picked up the toy. She reached for it jealously, and hugged it in her arms, and let the machine wipe away her tears. She was smiling again, crooning to it, as the humanoid guided her away.

Some other time he was lying in a padded chair, which had a lifted rest for his bandaged leg. Taut with a sudden bleak loneliness that rose up from that drugged oblivion to seize him, he whispered wistfully to the dark thing beside him:

"Haven't I any friends left who could come and see me?" Bitterness lifted his voice. "Or have you doped them all?"

"Most of your old associates have found relief in euphoride," the machine said. "Only a few fortunate exceptions were able to find happiness for themselves, with harmless creative activities. Dr. Pitcher is one, writing the dramas for which he had no time before we came. Another is Mr. Ironsmith."

"Will you have them come to see me?"

"They've both been here," murmured the machine. "But you didn't seem to know them."

"When Frank Ironsmith comes again—"

His words slowed and ceased, because another needle had pricked his arm. Trying to shape the questions to ask Ironsmith, he forgot—until a time when he lay on that same hard table again, in the same white room. Intent humanoids were stabbing him with other, more painful needles, and the pain seemed to sweep away that gray forgetfulness.

An illness came with the pain, but gentle-fingered machines rubbed and kneaded him until the shivering and the sweat of it had gone. They were wheeling him back to his room on that special chair when he found something clutched in his hand: a gay-colored furry toy, shaped like a winged worm. He tossed it away disgustedly.

"Feeling well, Forester?"

Startled by the cheery voice of Frank Ironsmith, he saw the mathematician waiting at the door of his room, smiling amiably and unattended by any humanoid.

"I suppose so." Nodding uncertainly, he felt of his leg. The bandages had been removed, and the swelling was gone. Flexing the muscles, he felt no pain. "I think I'm all right," he said. "Though I was pretty sick, just now."

"Reaction," murmured Ironsmith. "From the neutralizing serum." Taking the handles of the rolling chair, he pushed it on into the room and gestured casually for the humanoids to close the sliding door, leaving the two alone together. "I had them wake you," he said, "because I need your help."

Forester had half risen to test his knee, but he sat back at that, studying Ironsmith. The mathematician seemed less unsophisticated, more mature. Still candid-seeming, his friendly, sunburned face looked firmer and more forceful. Still clear and

honest, his level eyes were somehow sobered. Even his clothing was different, for the dilapidated slacks had been replaced
with a loose-fitting, tweedy suit which made him seem larger
and more self-assured. The gray coat fastened conservatively,
Forester noticed, with buttons that a man could undo.

"Is your memory clear again?" Ironsmith inquired. "Then
I want you to help me locate Mark White and his gallery of
freaks." He frowned with a mild concern. "Because we still
haven't run them down, even after all these months."

Forester said nothing.

"Little Jane Carter was with you nearly an hour, here at
Starmont." Watching him with shrewd gray eyes, Ironsmith
absently began filling a pipe with fragrant tobacco. "She probably told you where they're hiding, and exactly what they're up
to. Even if she wasn't specific, there would be clues enough to
work on."

A dark place underground, Forester remembered, and the
sound of water running. His lips tightened.

"White can do a lot of harm," Ironsmith insisted softly. "If
I were you, I wouldn't help conceal him."

Watching the pipe, Forester trembled to a bitter longing.

"It's more important than you might imagine." A mounting urgency was tightening Ironsmith's face. "I'm still not at
liberty to tell you much more than you already know, not until
you join us, but I had you aroused in the hope that now you're
willing to see the humanoids for what they are—"

"For innocent machines!" Forester broke in harshly.
"They can't be bad, I know, because they aren't wired for freedom of the will. They were built to save man from his own
inborn badness, and that's what they're busy about, and they
won't hurt us if we just treat them like our jolly little helpers."

"That's all true." Ironsmith looked regretful. "I was hoping you might accept it."

"But I don't," Forester rapped. "Because the damned mechanicals are too expert, and they always go too far. Where are

they going to stop? Being born can't be a completely happy experience—I suppose they'd like to keep us all nice and cozy in the womb?"

"I believe they're really experimenting with ectogenesis, to avoid the discomforts of childbirth," Ironsmith admitted smoothly. "But that's not what I came to talk about. I came to make a bargain with you."

"So?"

"We need information which I think you can supply. We need it so badly that I have induced the humanoids to let me offer you a second chance—if you will only prove your good faith by helping us trap Mark White."

Forester leaned wearily back in the chair.

"The advantages to you are considerable," Ironsmith urged. "You can keep your memory—I'll see that you find congenial scientific employment on some project the humanoids approve. You can soon earn any other privileges you wish. Isn't that better than euphoride?"

Forester sat up again, wearily alert.

"I don't want any more of that," he muttered huskily. "But I can't tell you anything. Not unless—" He bit his lip, and blurted, "Who else is with you?"

Smiling, Ironsmith shook his head.

"At least I must know one thing." Forester searched his open face, shivering inwardly. "Did you—or any of these mysterious associates who play chess with you—remove any military equipment from the vicinity of the old military installation here?"

"That doesn't matter." Ironsmith's amiable smile had widened slightly, but now his blue eyes lit with a cool, unspoken speculation from which Forester flinched. "What's your answer?"

"Send back your damned machines!" Watching Ironsmith drawing calmly on the pipe, he stifled an unruly pang of desire for that forbidden indulgence. "I don't know what sort of man you are—or even if you are a man!" Feeling a tingle at the back of his neck, he tried to lower his voice. "But I'm not turning against mankind."

"I had hoped for something a little more sane." Almost sadly, Ironsmith shook his sandy head. "I had hoped you had learned enough by now to face reality, Forester, because we're offering you quite an unusual opportunity. But we've other ways of getting at White." His tweedy shoulders lifted carelessly. "Because the man's more fool than philosopher, and his own folly will sometime give him up—I hope before he has done too much harm."

His mild voice fell, hopefully urgent.

"But I don't like to abandon you, Forester. I still wish you would reconsider, because we can show you a width and breadth and depth of living you never dreamed of, and a creative splendor of life you never imagined. Won't you trust me—even if you won't the humanoids—and come along?"

"Trust you?" Gulping painfully, Forester tried to laugh. "Get out!"

And Ironsmith turned to the door, which slid open as promptly as if he had been another mechanical. He glanced back, with an odd little grin as if of baffled sympathy, and stepped quickly out. Three humanoids came in, one of them carrying a hypodermic needle.

"Service, Clay Forester," it said. "We are acting under the Prime Directive, to make you happy again."

The other two moved with their incredible agility to catch him before he could scramble out of the chair. He tried to flinch from the one with the needle, but the black hands held him, gentle and invincible. He watched the flashing stroke of the needle, waiting—but it didn't reach his arm.

## 19

FOR THAT FIRST staggered instant, Forester thought that his own frantic squirming had somehow broken the unbreakable grasp of the machines. He thought he had fallen, somehow, out of that padded chair—until he realized that he was no longer in the villa at Starmont. Picking himself up from a cold surface of hard-packed sand, he looked around him dazedly.

"Oh, Dr. Forester!" Unbelievably, he recognized the thin, clear voice of little Jane Carter. "Did we hurt you?"

His bewildered eyes found her, and then Mark White and Lucky Ford, Graystone the Great, and Ash Overstreet. They stood spaced around him, all watching him. Curiously taut at first, their faces were slowly relaxing. Ford wiped his nervous claws of hands with a bright handkerchief. Old Graystone dipped his red nose in an awkward bow of welcome. Overstreet nodded, blinking dimly. Still magestic in that worn silver cloak, splendid with that flowing, fiery mane and beard, Mark White came striding to help him rise.

"So we got you!" the huge man boomed softly. "Welcome to our sanctuary!"

Grasping White's great hand, Forester came up awkwardly, careful of his leg. The knee felt weak, but it bore his weight without pain. He peered around him, shaken by a cold unbelief. Overhead was an uneven natural dome of water-carved limestone, encrusted with stalactites and shining with white calcite crystals, curving down on every side to the hard black sand. The air was damp and cold. Somewhere he heard a thin whisper of water running.

"Where—" He had to swallow. "Where is this?"

"We're safer if you don't know the precise coordinates," Mark White said. "But this cave is a good many hundred feet underground. A fortunate discovery of Overstreet's. There is running water, and air enough for ventilation, but no passage big enough for any mechanical intruders."

"Then you—I—"

"Teleportation." White nodded his immense, shaggy head. "Your own unconscious mental resistance caused our first failure. That's why we didn't warn you this time, but just waited for a moment when you wanted to get away from the humanoids."

"I certainly did!" Forester shook hands gratefully with the men who had snatched him out of that efficient prison. Now no longer tattered new recruits, they were shaved and clean and better fed. Even Overstreet had lost a little of his unhealthy pallor.

"We were watching you, Forester." White's huge hand fell on his shoulder, heartily. "I'm glad you didn't sell out to Ironsmith." Bitterness hardened his voice. "Did you know that he nearly trapped us at Dragonrock, before we were expecting any treachery? Come along, and let me show you how we're going to beat him."

Forester limped anxiously after him, to see that buried fortress. The sandy floor was scarcely fifty feet across. Low-roofed recesses, under the edges of the glittering dome, made living quarters. Little Jane Carter proudly showed him a tiny room of her own. A thrumming generator, in another jeweled alcove, gave current for lights strung across the roof.

"You brought all this equipment?" Forester whispered. "By teleportation?"

"There's no other way in," White assured him. "But we're improving with practice. Our greatest worry now is leaving some clue that Ironsmith can use to find us."

The hard clay floor in another low chamber had been leveled to support a long workbench, which was laden with crucibles, small power tools, and stacked ingots of some silver-colored metal.

"Here's where we need you, Forester." Dramatic in the worn cloak, White gestured at the charred and acid-bitten bench with a great emphatic arm. "To help us build the new relays to change the Prime Directive."

Forester turned from the small electric furnaces and tiny lathes and drills, back to that imperative giant. The hard light in his intense blue eyes might be fanatical, Forester thought, yet he seemed much too sure for a blunderer, too keenly alert for a fool.

"Just the interpretation," White was adding. "I've no quarrel with the words you see on that yellow brand—*To Serve and Obey, and Guard Men from Harm.* The trouble is that old Warren Mansfield built his first relays to apply them a little too broadly."

Thoughtfully, he weighed a small ingot on his palm.

"Ironsmith would call me a criminal anarchist, I imagine. He'd probably sneer at my motives as viciously as he fights my aims. But the worth and the dignity and the rights of every individual are the values of my philosophy—and the cause I struggle for.

"You've heard the old bull that a benevolent despotism is the best possible government. That must have been Mansfield's theory when he made the humanoids—but he made them benevolent enough and despotic enough to reduce it to a pretty uncomfortable absurdity.

"But I'm an equalitarian." He put the ingot down, with a crashing force. "I want to modify the Prime Directive, to assure every man and woman the same rights that only Frank Ironsmith and a few other double-dealers now enjoy. Even the freedom to do wrong."

He paused to fumble impatiently in a clutter of notes and drawings stacked under a white metal block, until he found an old envelope.

"Here's the change I want to build into that relay grid, to amend the Prime Directive." His booming voice read scrawled words from the back of the envelope. *"But We the Humanoids Cannot Serve or Defend Any Man Except at His Own Command, or Restrain Any Man Against His Will, for Men Must Be Free."*

"I'm with you!" Forester's shoulders lifted. "What's to be done?"

"Everything." Replacing the tattered envelope under the ingot, the big man caught Forester's hand in a smashing grasp. "I must warn you that we are attempting a nearly impossible task, with inadequate means, in defiance of such ruthless enemies as Ironsmith, in the face of hazards that even Overstreet can't quite foresee. Until you were here, I had no real hope at all."

Forester inquired uneasily, "What do you expect of me?"

"First, before we go into any future plans, you must know what we've already done. I've told you that I helped old Mansfield for many years in his struggle to destroy his own unfortunate handiwork—and I think we really might have beaten the humanoids, if he hadn't been quite so blind to my abilities. Because the job is going to take a combination of physical and paraphysical action.

"The changing of those relays, you see, is obviously a bit of physical engineering. But Mansfield built the grid to protect itself from any meddling by engineers, and it does that very efficiently, as he and I discovered so often. No man can now approach within three light-years of Wing IV—not by any physical means.

"But Jane Carter has been there."

Startled, Forester looked around for the child. She had followed them about the cave at first, and now he expected to see her playing somewhere on the sand. He couldn't find her.

"She's gone," White explained, "after palladium. We need the metal to build those new relays, and Overstreet has discovered an alluvial deposit of it, out on a planet where men and humanoids have never been. The nuggets are nearly pure, bearing only traces of rhodium and ruthenium."

"That little child!" Forester whispered blankly. "You sent her to another world, alone?"

"A necessary risk." White's eyes flashed sternly. "We've got to have palladium, but we reduce the danger as far as we can. Overstreet watches, ready to warn her if Ironsmith or his peculiar allies turn up."

The big man swung back to the cluttered bench.

"She supplies the metal," he said. "Your job is to build and install the new relays. Warren Mansfield could have done it, if he and I had ever got inside the defenses of Wing IV. You'll have to take his place."

"You don't mean—" Forester caught his breath, shivering to the penetrating chill of the cavern. "You can't mean—"

"I do." White nodded deliberately. "We'll give you all the help we can, but you're the rhodomagnetic engineer. You're the one we must send to Wing IV, to change the mind of the humanoids."

Forester caught the rough edge of the workbench with cold awkward hands, and then he had to sit down on a wooden stool, to take the weight off his trembling knees. He stared at the red-bearded giant, almost accusingly. "You know I can't do teleportation."

"You'll learn," White rumbled grimly. "You'll have to learn, if you ever want to see daylight. Because there's a thousand feet of solid rock between us and the top of the ground, and no passage large enough for a man."

"But—I just can't—"

And Forester shivered, swallowing hard, struck mute by a sudden claustrophobia. The damp air seemed too heavy and too still. He stared at the crawling dark, hiding in the narrowing fissures where no light had ever been, and he heard the whispered mockery of water running through crevices too tiny for anything else. The cavern was a grave, and he was buried here—until he could do the impossible.

But he set his chattering teeth, and feebly clutched at reason. If teleportation had brought him here, it could get him out again. The shadows in the crevices receded a little, and he caught a sobbing breath, turning shakenly to White.

"I'm sorry, but the weight of that rock just hit me. A sort of shut-in feeling." He straightened uncertainly. "I'll do the best I can, but you know I've failed before."

"You can do it," White said quietly. "Because you're a scientist. For paraphysics is a science. That means that observed phenomena can be linked by hypothesis, illuminated by theory, and integrated by law. It means that effects are subject to analysis by logic, to prediction from experience, to control through cause.

"A difficult science, I admit." He shook his bright mane regretfully. "Necessarily so, because the instrument of research is also the subject. The dissecting knife can't easily dissect itself. In all my years of effort, I've found more new questions than satisfying answers. What, for example, is mind?"

White's huge shoulders lifted heavily, and then his intense eyes stared away through a low archway of shining calcite into an avenue of darkness. That was another blind passage, Forester knew, which ended against physical barriers of living rock—but now Jane Carter came out of it.

The child stood blinking for a moment, as if dazzled by the crystal glitter of the cavern, and then she came running across the dark sand to White. Forester saw the sudden dust of frost forming on the worn fur collar of her coat and on her dark hair. Blue and shaking with cold, she gave White a heavy little leather bag. The white nuggets he poured from it into a balance pan were instantly covered with feathers of frost, and smoky trails of condensation began to drift downward from the pan and flatten on the bench. Shivering to a chill of his own, Forester blinked at the urchin, who stood wiggling her bare toes against the sand, looking up at White with huge, adoring eyes.

"Must I go back?"

"No, I think that's all we need." Glancing at the frosty mound on the pan, White smiled gently through his flaming beard. "You've done a wonderful job, and now Graystone has some hot broth waiting for you."

"Oh, thank you! I'm so glad I needn't go back, 'cause it's awful cold out there."

She ran on, happily, toward the crystal alcove where Graystone's pot simmered on a small electric stove. Staring at the dusty frost on her coat and her hair, Forester was numb and still with wonder.

"It is cold there," he heard White saying. "Those rich gravels must have been washed down a long time ago, because that planet has no more erosion now. It's lost from the star that must have warmed it once, and it's far too cold to have any gaseous air or liquid water. The temperature is very near the absolute zero."

Forester blinked and shook himself. "You mean she can defy every law of nature?"

"No," White said. "She has merely learned to use the principles of paraphysical nature—I think unconsciously. She just—adapts. At first she was always shivering with the cold, at Dragonrock and even after we came here—until she learned enough of our new mental science to keep herself warm."

"But—" Forester gasped. "How?"

"She can't tell you how. I'd like to know, but I suppose she has developed an unconscious psychophysical control over the molecular vibrations of heat, and the molecular flow of evaporation—nothing else can explain the way she can prevent the loss of heat and water and oxygen from her body, on that cold planet. I think she can even disassociate carbon dioxide, to renew the oxygen in her blood. However she does it, she can live under the absolute vacuum—long enough."

A cold something had touched Forester's spine. "Are you sure she's—human?" he breathed uneasily. "Not some mutation?"

"She's human!" the big man boomed vehemently. "I know that. For all my failures, I know that psychophysical capacities are as old as life—perhaps they are life! I know they are born in the brain of every man. They lie there—unused gifts greater than Jane's—within your unconscious grasp and mine." Exasperation shook his great voice. "I know that—and yet I've somehow always failed to reach the real secret of conscious control. Perhaps there's some barrier that I can't see—something perhaps as obvious as this."

Impatiently, he picked up a precious white ingot and slammed it down again. Forester saw the undying hate sweep through him like a bitter wind and blaze like a sullen fire in his eyes. But hate alone, even in such volcanic magnificence, would never stop the humanoids. Calmer now, Forester recalled him to the details of that task, pointing out the overwhelming difficulties.

## 20

SUPPOSE THEY PENETRATED all the known and unknown defenses of the efficient humanoids, to reach Wing IV? Suppose they even gained free access, somehow, to the linked relays that made the brain of Warren Mansfield's ultimate machine? Even granting all that, Forester knew, they still must almost surely fail.

"Such grids aren't exactly simple." He grinned wryly at White. "Not even the primitive little gadgets I designed to pilot rhodomagnetic missiles."

"I've seen relays like Mansfield made," White protested hopefully. "They don't look so complicated. And the same science should apply to your relays and his—he used to call it cybernetics."

"That's not quite simple, either. Not when you come to rhodomagnetic grids. It's true the individual relays do look simple. There's no wires, no moving parts, no electron tubes—that compact simplicity is all that makes the humanoids possible at all. But the functioning isn't as simple as the mechanism, because a rhodomagnetic grid thinks in a different way than anything electromagnetic."

White scowled through the red beard, impatiently.

"A common electromagnetic relay has only two positions,"

Forester explained. "Off and on. Vacuum tubes work the same way—one electron tube may replace thousands of relays, but every response is either an *off* or an *on*. Its memory, in other words, is limited to the digits of the binary system of notation—zero and one. While I know any number can be written with the binary digits, and any word designated, and any possible thought expressed, it's still a clumsy system—even though it's doubtless the system used by the ten billion or so cells in the human brain, which is also electromagnetic."

"But rhodomagnetic grids aren't binary?"

"That's the difference," Forester said. "Each relay—which is like an electromagnetic relay or a neurone cell only by analogy—each one functions through an almost infinite complex of variable fields and polarities. Such complexes are set up by guided beams as the relays learn, and afterward resonate to scanning beams as they remember. See the difference? A common relay can be taught only one or zero. Electron tubes can be built to hold several thousand ones or zeros. But a rhodomagnetic relay—far simpler and smaller and faster—isn't limited to one and zero. With the infinite number of possible combinations, of its nodes and their patterns of resonance, a single relay can remember a very large number of the most complex variables. That vast range and flexibility adds a whole new dimension to its capacity."

"Good!" boomed White. "I see you're the expert we wanted."

"No expert." Forester shook his head. "I'm just trying to tell you how little I know—and how difficult rhodomagnetic cybernetics is. Thinking, you realize, is more than memory. There must be complex mechanisms for purpose and decision and action. Complex even in my own devices made to guide one missile. Imagine the complexity in that brain built to operate some billions of units on each of many thousand planets!"

"But you'll do," the big man rumbled. "We aren't rebuilding the whole grid, after all, but just making a minor modification in its purpose. Let's get to work."

"How?" Forester blinked uneasily. "This Mansfield lived and worked on a world cut off from mine by two light-centuries of space, remember, and thousands of years of independent evolution. He spoke a different language. He must have used different kinds of tools and systems of measurement. He probably calculated with a different mathematics. The simplest relays in his grid would look completely strange to me—even if the humanoids themselves hadn't already rebuilt it into something too intricate for even Mansfield to understand!"

"I know it's going to be difficult." Mark White scowled soberly. "But we can help you. I know Mansfield's language, and I've been trying to understand that grid since the first time he tried to explain it. I've had Overstreet watching the way it works, and Graystone trying to pick up its thoughts—though without success. And Jane Carter has been there."

Forester nodded doubtfully, watching the snapping crystals of frost still growing over that tiny mound of palladium nuggets, and the cold white vapor draining from the balance pan. White's little group had remarkable abilities, he knew—but so did the humanoids.

"I sent her to the shop where Warren Mansfield built the first sections of the grid to operate his first hand-built mechanical units," White went on. "She found it still intact—he evidently set some compulsion in the humanoids, to keep them out of it. His old office safe was still packed full of his notes and drawings and preliminary models, and she brought back everything you ought to need."

"Let me see." Forester waited eagerly for White to find a stack of yellowed notebooks and a sheaf of faded blueprints in the clutter on the bench, and anxiously watched him pull out racks of plastic trays filled with tiny stampings and castings and machinings of silvery palladium. Hopefully opening one of the books, he frowned in bewildered disappointment at the dim hieroglyphics.

"It isn't quite so bad as that," the big man rumbled softly. "I worked with Mansfield for many years, remember. I can translate everything for you—even though most of the math is over my head." And he gestured at the long bench. "All the tools Mansfield used in that shop are duplicated here—collected mostly from junkyards where the humanoids are piling up confiscated machines. Gadgets too dangerous for men to use!"

A stern amusement flashed across his face, before he continued soberly, "We'll build the new grid sections here. Enough of them to contain our revised interpretation of the Prime Directive. When they're done, you and Jane must go to Wing IV. All you'll have to do there is to cut out the old sections of Mansfield's—the ones which make the humanoids so devastingly thorough—and hook in our new ones."

"So that's all?" Forester riffled through a stack of dusty drawings with unsteady fingers, and bent to study another tray of tiny machinings. "Didn't Mansfield once try to change those relays?" he whispered hoarsely. "And didn't the humanoids stop him?"

"Mansfield didn't use psychophysics," White protested quietly. "And I believe he built his own blind spot for that science into the humanoids, because they haven't learned to cope with it—not yet. They failed to discover Jane when she visited the shop, and I think you'll have time to change the relays before they find you."

"They're fast," Forester reminded him.

"But blind," White said. "Literally blind. Anywhere else, their rhodomagnetic senses are far quicker and keener than human sight or hearing, but there inside the grid the intense rhodomagnetic fields interfere with the weaker sensory fields of the individual units, so Mansfield told me, and with any luck at all you'll have the job done before they know you're there."

Screwing a jeweler's loupe into his socket, Forester stirred a tray of almost microscopic screws with thin-nosed tweezers. His fingers still were awkwardly uncertain, and he listened doubtfully.

"It's a brain operation, actually. Like the human brain, the grid has no effective sense organs inside it, and I believe you can perform the operation without disturbing the patient—if we're ready in time. I'm afraid our time is running out, however, because Overstreet can see the humanoids building something new, there on Wing IV."

"Huh?" Forester looked up blankly. "What's that?"

"My guess frightens me." White hunched a little under the silver cloak, as if to a fearful expectancy. "But we haven't found out what it is. Overstreet says it's going to be as big as the grid. He can see underground levels full of mass-converters, ready to pour energy into banks of huge devices somewhat like transformers, but mostly made of platinum. Above the ground, he says the humanoids are putting up an enormous dome made of some new synthetic, to cover something else."

"That something else?"

"A second grid, apparently. Overstreet can't see inside it—a very disturbing circumstance—but he can observe the humanoids manufacturing new relays, which are carried in there as if for assembly."

"Maybe the machines are just enlarging their own brain."

"They've been doing that from the first, just piling new sections on the old, but this is something different. For one thing, the relays going into that new dome are made largely out of platinum and osmiridium alloys, instead of palladium. I don't know what it is."

"Could Jane find out?"

"I took the risk of sending her there." Above the ruddy magnificence of his beard, White's massive face was bitten deep with acid apprehension. "She met a barrier that kept her out of the dome. She can't describe that obstacle, but I think it wasn't physical. I think the humanoids have somehow discovered that built-in blind spot, and begun psychophysical research for themselves. Which means we must get to work!"

They did. Listening to the haunting whisper of dark water running through channels too small for a man, oppressed by the crushing weight of that calcite-crusted roof, Forester set out to master the laws and resolve the mocking contradictions of White's half-science. He grasped at the amazing arts of old Graystone, and little Ford's telekinetic skills. He sought the far vision of Overstreet's myopic eyes, and the ultimate fleetness of Jane Carter's feet.

He even tried at first to hope that White's discoveries would somehow reach beyond the revelations of rhodomagnetics, to disclose the *prima materia* that he had pursued so far in vain—the total understanding of all the universe. That elusive fundamental fact evaded him again, however, as tantalizingly as when Ironsmith had demolished the relevance of his symbol *rho*. He failed to bridge the gaps or remove the contradictions, but once more he learned.

Watching Jane Carter flit out of that closed cavern and back again, to bring some useful tool that Overstreet's clairvoyant vision had discovered, he came to accept her ability more fully, and he slowly shaped a rational theory to bind it to the truth he knew.

"It's making sense," he told White hopefully at last. "All this psychophysical stuff used to seem impossible, but now I think I see how it could fit into the old science of quantum mechanics. Teleportation, now—that could be just a matter of exchange-force probability."

The huge man looked up alertly from his work at the bench.

"You know the theory of exchange forces? Anyhow, the concept arose from the fact that all electrons—and all other similar atomic particles—are actually identical. Mathematically, any movement of any electron can be treated merely as an exchange of identity with another, and the mathematics seems to reflect actuality. In every atom there appears to be a rhythmic pulsation of identity between electrons, and between other identical wavicles. And the forces of that ceaseless exchange—like most atomic phenomena—are governed by probability."

"But what has that to do with teleportation?"

Staring past the other man, at the closed, calcite-frosted walls of that deep crypt, Forester felt something cold against his spine. An icy wonder numbed him, that any mere act of the mind could open that living stone. But he was here, and he had seen Jane Carter come and go, and now he thought he saw the way.

"Those exchange forces are timeless—there's a place for them in the theory of rhodomagnetics," he said. "And they aren't limited to subatomic distances, except by a factor of decreasing probability. Because each atomic particle can be regarded as only a reinforcement in a standing wave-pattern—a wave, if you like, of probability—which pervades the entire universe.

"I think that's the answer!" He caught an eager breath. "When Jane goes out to that cold planet, I think there is no actual movement of matter, but only an instantaneous shift of those patterns of identity." He nodded, pleased with that distinction. "While I can't yet describe the precise mechanism of atomic probability, she has already proved that she can control it to detonate unstable potassium atoms. Perhaps teleportation is just as easy."

"No doubt!" White grinned briefly through his beard, and frowned again with thought. "I've worked on a hypothesis that physical time and physical space aren't actual, but just illusions—"

"They aren't fundamental," Forester agreed. "But something more, I'm sure, than mere illusion. In the light of rhodomagnetics, space-time appears to be a somewhat incidental side-property of the electromagnetic energy components in those complex units that manifest themselves as particles and waves. And the exchange forces would seem to be a kind of rhodomagnetic bridge across space."

He blinked up at White, hopeful and elated.

"There I think we've found it—the mechanics of teleportation! No transfer of actual substance, but rather an exchange of identities, brought about by controlled probability. That gets us around the old electromagnetic problems of inertia and instantaneous acceleration, which used to make it look so utterly out of reason."

"Might be." The big man nodded, still frowning. "Probably you're right—but still you haven't got the whole answer. What is the actual force of the mind? How does it act to govern probability? Anyhow, what *is* probability? What are the mathematical equations of psychophysics? The laws? The limits?"

And Forester shook his wistful gnome's head, baffled again. That uncertain hypothesis, he saw, had been only a flicker in the dark. White always found more questions than answers, and the ultimate truth lay somewhere far ahead. Yet that feeble illumination had restored his belief in the reality of some single basic fact underlying all the confusing things and events of the experienced world, and it cheered him on toward the nearer goal on remote Wing IV.

When he came to study the layout of that grid, to identify the relays that had to be changed, White had him take Warren Mansfield's yellowed plans and blueprints into the low grotto where Ash Overstreet sat wrapped in a blanket and looking with vague eyes beyond the lacy calcite fretwork on the walls.

"Yes, I can see the central grid," the clairvoyant whispered. "It hasn't been blocked off, like whatever is in that new dome the machines are putting up." He took the drawings in his puffy hands, peering as if his dim eyes could scarcely see them. "Here's old Mansfield's shop, where we sent Jane to get the specifications." His pale forefinger pointed. "And here, just inside the tower door from it, are the relays Mansfield built himself, to operate his first handmade unit. That unit manufactured others, and the new humanoids have kept on adding new relays, but those first sections are still there."

Dull behind the heavy lenses, his eyes looked away again.

"I can still make out the numerals that Mansfield painted to identify the sections. The first three sections—this and this and this—contain the Prime Directive." His fat finger moved on the tattered plan. "The next two—numbered four and

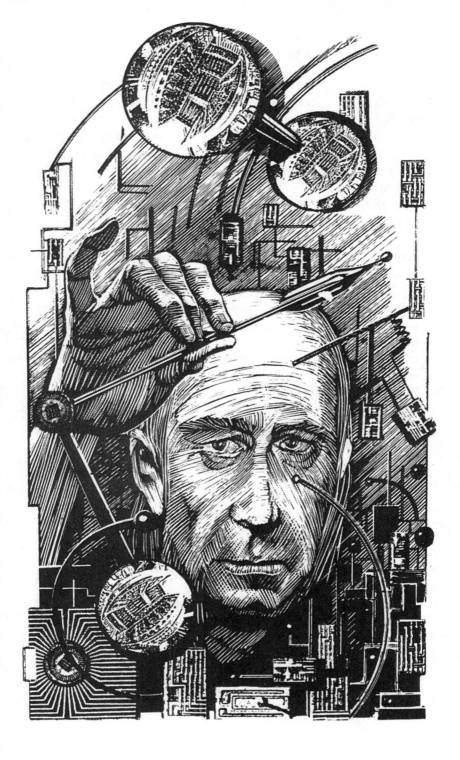

five—are ones which govern the interpretation. That's where Mansfield blundered. He made them the way he did because of a sick horror of war and a bitter conviction that men must be protected from themselves and one another, even against their will. And those two sections are the ones you must change."

Toiling at the bench, in that closed cave sealed against the flow of day and night, Forester lost track of time. For White had conquered sleep. Forester failed to grasp the method of it fully. Sometimes the weight of his weariness almost bore him down. But, following White's stern regimen, he came to share something of the huge man's driving vitality. And he had no time for sleep.

His hands were blistered from lifting hot metal. His eyes ached from straining to see tiny parts, and his back was sore from bending. His weak knee throbbed and swelled. But still he worked on—until his fatigue began to fall away. His old dyspepsia ceased to trouble him, so that he could eat his hurried meals with relish. White assured him heartily that he was learning psychophysics.

The silvery ingots of rare palladium were fused and cast and machined, rolled and stamped and drawn. Dangerous automatic machines from the new junkyards of the humanoids milled and welded delicate units. White and Ford and Graystone worked at the bench, assembling the new relays, and Forester mounted them in the two replacement sections.

While time was suspended in that deep cavern, however, the machines on far Wing IV kept moving, until a moment when Ash Overstreet came shuffling stiffly from the corner where he watched, to touch Forester's arm almost apologetically.

"Sorry, but I see trouble." His husky whisper was thin with worry. "I can't see it clear—and still I can't tell why. But I've got a feeling that whatever the humanoids are building in that new dome is almost done. Still there's a barrier around it, as far as I can see ahead, but I think it's aimed against us." Behind the heavy glasses, his puzzled eyes seemed vague and dark and strange. "I think we had better do what we can, right now. If you're ready."

Forester tested a last relay and adjusted a tiny screw. Laying down his tools and his loupe, he agreed reluctantly that he was ready.

# 21

THE TIME WAS now. The replacement sections were complete, and Forester had said that he was ready. Watching little Jane Carter vanish and return, he had reduced the stunning wonder of teleportation to a rational manifestation of sane exchange-force theory. But Wing IV was two hundred light-years away.

Standing with the child and White beside the two long sections gleaming in their rectangular palladium shields on the workbench, Forester shrank from the impact of that staggering magnitude. Twelve hundred trillion miles! That was several times farther than the naked human eye could see the blaze of an average sun. The vastness of the distance brought his old doubts back, and made the calcite walls close in again.

The dark water mocked him, whispering through passages where men couldn't go. He felt smothered by the stuffy deadness of the air, and crushed beneath the merciless weight of stone above. His stomach fluttered, and his bad knee turned weak. All the orthodoxies of his old training came trooping back to haunt him, out of dusty forgotten laboratories and gloomy observatories. It couldn't be done, his old habits screamed. No man could simply step across twelve hundred trillion miles, as if that frightful abyss of distance were only a line drawn on the floor.

"I can't do it." He turned uneasily away from the shining urgency of the new sections, those two long palladium boxes heavy with the last hope of man. "It's just too far!" Mopping his cold forehead, he looked from the impatient giant to the solemn-eyed child. "Perhaps—perhaps we could try shorter hops—just across the cave—till I get the feel of it."

"Nonsense!" boomed White. "Of course you can do it—remember your own theory. That balcony on Wing IV, outside the entrance to Warren Mansfield's old shop, is just as near us—in the geometry of paraphysics—as I am to you. And Overstreet says we've got to strike." He nodded impatiently at the long new sections, the blue hate in his eyes an unquenched flame. "So go ahead. Jane can help—if you'll just relax your unconscious opposition."

He stared at the child, trying not to shiver.

"Let me show you, Dr. Forester." She held out a small grubby hand, and he saw the shining eagerness in her eyes. "Now—let's go!"

And he knew the way. He caught the spark of her courage, and he gave her his trust. She led him, and they didn't even have to step across a line. He felt no movement at all—but they were on that balcony.

"See!" she whispered. "It wasn't hard at all."

He squeezed her tiny fingers with a voiceless gratitude, and then looked around him blankly. The narrow metal floor jutted from a wall which gleamed with the gray color of oxidized aluminum. The wall reached, windowless, immensely far to right and left. It soared above them, topless. It dropped beneath, a featureless metal precipice, so far that his breath went out when he tried to look down.

He found the narrow door at the end of the balcony which would let them through the old shop into the grid, but he couldn't keep his awed gaze from drifting up again. Because the vastness of that tower dazed him. The original level of the ground, he knew, must have been near this high platform, and Mansfield's original shop could only have been housed in some kind of rough temporary building—for that misguided idealist had exiled himself alone here in the beginning, in the rubble of a continent that rhodomagnetic war had shattered to build his new machines to banish war forever.

But eighty years of the humanoids had changed Wing IV. Looking down again beyond the low gray railing, Forester shivered to a paralyzing awe. The shadow of this tremendous solitary tower fell dim and vast before him, an endless blot across a queerly flat plain, where mountains must have been leveled. For now, out to the gray rim of the murky sky, all he could see was a single unending spaceport, beneath interstellar craft arriving and departing. All those long black ships must be enormous, he knew, as those which had brought the humanoid invasion to his own world, yet those in the far distance seemed tiny and multitudinous as dark insects swarming.

A few of those mighty vessels were landing on the surface of that endless field, near enough for him to glimpse the chutes down which they poured dark rivers of ore—metal, he thought, for new humanoids. Another was loading, and he could see ordered armies of tiny black mechanicals marching ceaselessly up its gangways—ready, he supposed, to quiet all the quarrels of some troubled world with the crushing benevolence of the Prime Directive.

Most of those vast transports, however, streamed down into wide black pits spaced across the field, or emerged from others, as if their docks were somewhere far beneath. The entire planet, it came to him, must have become a single busy labyrinth of shafts and landing cradles, ore bins and smelters, foundries and assembly lines—the dark metal matrix of Mansfield's unimaginable machine, in which all the humanoids were born.

Forester withdrew from the railing, humbled and shuddering. Jane Carter had crouched close against his legs, breathlessly silent, and they retreated now to the cold face of the metal wall behind. She had been smiling proudly, showing him the way, but her huge eyes had turned solemn now, and she hung back when he tried to lead her toward that narrow door.

"Wait!" she whispered. "Mr. White wants you to look at that." She pointed uneasily out across the gray vastness of that mechanized planet. "He says you're an engineer, and maybe you can tell him what it is."

Looking the way she pointed, he saw the new dome the humanoids were building. Dim in the smoky distance, it was taller than its breadth, colored darkly red. Scaffolding made a fine dark web around it. Towering far-off and alone, it gave him no clue to its size until he saw an ascending interstellar vessel creeping up across its crimson face, tiny as a black insect. He knew then that it was unimaginably huge.

"I tried to go inside it for Mr. White, but I somehow couldn't." Her voice was stifled and afraid. "Even Mr. Overstreet can't see anything inside, but he thinks it's going to be something to use against us."

Forester tried to study that remote red dome. Were the humanoids attempting to improve themselves with a new grid of platinum relays better than the palladium brain Warren Mansfield had designed? That seemed scarcely possible—they were already far too perfect.

"Tell Mr. White I don't know what it is." A thin wind had brushed his face, stinging his eyes with biting smoke and chemical fumes. That was the bitter breath of the machine, and it doubled him with coughing before he could go on. "The shape doesn't tell me anything—and platinum would be no better than iron in rhodomagnetic equipment. So it couldn't be anything rhodomagnetic."

"But it's something bad." He felt her small hand trembling, and then tugging him toward that weathered aluminum door. "Mr. White says we must hurry, now. Mr. Overstreet can see the shape of trouble waiting for us—only he can't tell quite what it is, with *that* always getting in the way."

She nodded fearfully at the far red dome, as he followed her toward the narrow metal door. Oddly, in this world without men, it had a knob shaped to fit a human hand, which yielded stiffly when he tried it. A short hallway, the walls glowing faintly with a gray radiant paint, let them into the old room where the first humanoid was made.

"Wait." He felt her small hand tighten. "Mr. White says wait," she breathed. "Mr. Overstreet is watching the sections we must change, and he can see one of the black machines working near it now. We must stay out here till it goes away."

Waiting, taut and almost ill with the stress of hope and dread, Forester looked wonderingly around this scene of old Mansfield's monstrous blunder. The cold dull radiance of the paint fell on a scarred wooden desk and a worn swivel chair, on a dusty drafting table with a tall stool pushed against it, on rough shelves filled with technical books in faded bindings, on cluttered benches and rusting tools. A few moldering blankets were still folded on a cot where he must have slept, and a little table rudely made of packing crates was still stacked with soiled dishes and rusted cans and a faded carton which must have held some cereal—as if he had interrupted his disastrous creation only reluctantly, to snatch the simplest essentials of life. The room had a dry stale odor of years and slow decay, and a comfortable disorder the tiny humanoids would never have allowed. Touched and saddened by all that evidence of Mansfield's austere innocence, Forester turned slowly back to watch the inner door, Jane Carter's anxious hand cold and tiny in his own.

"First we must find those two sections—number four and number five." His mind was rehearsing the steps they must take to undo that unintended crime. "You must keep watch while I unhook them, and then bring me the new sections from the cave. I'll hook them in—and you must stop any humanoid that finds us."

Listening, she nodded. That would take them no more than another five minutes—to amend the Prime Directive with a bill of human rights, and free many thousand worlds from a suffocating kindness. Unless men blundered again. His heart began to thump as Jane Carter tightened her icy fingers in his hand, nodding silently at the inner door.

That door also had a common knob, and no concealed relay. He opened it cautiously—to close it very quickly. For he had seen the grid. Its limitless billions of tiny palladium relays, the cells of the mechanical brain, were all linked with the rhodomagnetic synapses in sections like the two he had built. The sections were arranged in long panels, all connected with a coiling jungle of branching wave-guide tubes of white palladium, the panels mounted in a skeleton of massive columns and girders that seemed to have no end.

The humanoids required no light, and most of that enormous space inside the tower was dark. On this original level, however, which Warren Mansfield himself had designed and begun, the panel faces and the narrow inspection walks before them were finished with a gray-glowing paint, whose dim radiance shone far into the gloom, above and beyond and below. Rooms to hold the precise mind and unerring memory of all the far-scattered moving units, the panels of the grid made endless shadowy avenues, rising level upon level as far as he could see, and falling away, level beneath unending level, into the chasm of whispering dark.

"What's wrong?" Jane breathed fearfully.

It was the humanoids, the busy limbs of that eternal brain. He had seen scores of the tiny-seeming mechanicals moving with their swift, efficient grace about the web of narrow walks strung through the dim abyss between the tiers of panels. The nearest one, poised on a thin footway not fifty yards distant, had been facing toward him, and terror of its bright steel eyes had stricken him. He leaned weakly against the closed door, speechless.

"But it didn't see you, Dr. Forester," Jane whispered through her own pale alarm. "It can't really see, you know, and Mr. White says it can't feel us more than about ten paces, here in the tower. He says it's only working with the others to clean and keep up the grid."

"I'm sorry." He moved shakenly to open the door again. "I just forgot they're blind."

They crept out silently, into the vast chamber of the brain. Beneath a soundless hush, Forester fancied that he could feel the pulsation of unimaginable energies—the rivers of incalculable rhodomagnetic power that flowed out from here to drive and control all the trillions of mechanicals serving all the worlds that men had owned.

Following a narrow, dim-lit catwalk that had no railing—because it was built for perfect machines that never slipped or stumbled—he searched the gray-glowing panel faces. And he found the numbers old Mansfield had painted on the sections, eighty years ago. Hasty brush marks, splashed on merely for identification in the shop, they were faded now, peeling away from the satiny palladium shieldings. But he could read them still.

The first three sections held the Prime Directive. Three long, silver-gray cases, a little smaller than three coffins. The freedom and the future of mankind had lain buried in them for eighty years, he thought, murdered by Mansfield's error to preserve a sterile peace. He passed them and crept on toward those beyond, the silent child clinging hard to his arm. Trying to ignore the blind machines ahead, trying to forget the giddy pit beneath, he leaned to read the faded numbers.

*Four!* For an instant he couldn't breathe. He felt as if that narrow walk had swayed beneath him, and he had to clutch desperately for a flange of the nearest massive girder. But he got his balance back, and he was fumbling desperately to open the little leather case of tools he had brought to change the connections, when he felt Jane tugging sharply at his hand.

Turning apprehensively, he saw her pointing at that nearest black mechanical. It was still busy removing invisible dust from the panel faces with something like a tiny, silent vacuum cleaner, but it was working steadily toward them. Forester saw that he had no time for terror. He found his pliers and lifted the cover of the fourth section and began rapidly unhooking the flexible wave-guide tubes that coupled it into the brain.

"Oh—"

Jane Carter's cry was a low and stifled moan of pain. She let his fingers go, but at first he didn't know what had happened. He thought she was falling from the walk until he saw her backing silently away from him along it, and then he thought that nearest humanoid must have discovered them. His dropped pliers made a frightening clatter on the metal shielding. He almost lost his own balance, and skinned his knuckles on the sharp edge of the section cover in his frantic snatch for safety.

That busy machine was still approaching as it dusted the panels, but he saw in a moment that it hadn't yet found them. He looked back down at Jane, trying to see what had so disturbed her. She stood frozen now, poised on that narrow gangway like a mechanical at rest. Her pinched face was bloodless, and her staring eyes seemed enormous in the gloom, watching the door where they had come in.

## 22

CLUTCHING THE FLANGE of that great girder to balance himself, Forester turned fearfully back to the door. It was still closed. In that breathless hush of inconceivable energies, he could hear nothing at all. He was glancing blankly back at that intent humanoid when the first faint creak of the opening door spun him back. A man came out, striding toward him confidently along that giddy path.

"Stop it, Forester!"

His instant of weak relief was shattered by a stark dismay. For he knew that clear, pleasant voice, echoing so alarmingly through those dim corridors of the grid, and it belonged to a man more dreadful than any humanoid. Frank Ironsmith came stalking out along the catwalk, urbanely indifferent to any risk of falling.

"You blundering fool, Forester!" Lower now, restrained, his voice reflected neither hate nor anger, but only an infinite shocked regret. His boyish, sunburned face looked lean and stern, and his gray eyes held a wounded sadness as he looked past Forester at the rigid, staring child. "Look what you have done!"

For an instant Forester stood heartsick and shaken, swaying on that gangway meant for sure machines, wishing hopelessly that this grave antagonist had been merely another mechanical that Jane could have stopped. Fighting a sudden giddiness, he tightened his sweaty grasp on the girder. The silent forces of the brain seemed to roar around him, an unheard hurricane.

"I tried to warn you, Forester."

Scarcely hearing that sad reproof, he blinked unbelievingly at Frank Ironsmith—who should have been still idling his useless life away at Starmont, reading his ancient books and playing his mysterious chess and riding his rusty bicycle. But this startling intruder was changed, somehow, from that lank and callow youth in the computing section, indolently squandering his brilliant gifts on fantastic new geometrics instead of crossword puzzles. Youthful still, he looked leaner and firmer and browner, older and sobered.

"I thought Mark White would call on you, but—"

Forester interrupted that suave, regretful voice. He stood empty-handed, for even the pliers had fallen in his first alarm, but now, when he had reached the most vital part of Mansfield's monstrous creation, he didn't intend to be stopped. Sudden purpose clenched his stringy fist, and sudden fury drove his lashing blow.

Darting forward, Forester forgot all his dizzy fear of the vast black spaces of the brain beneath, and all his dread of the busy blind machines behind him. All he remembered was Ironsmith's shrewd defense of the humanoids, and his unfair freedom, and his treacherous hunt for White. He tried to knock the urbane traitor off that unrailed way, but Ironsmith evaded the blow.

"That won't help you, Forester." Smiling apologetically,

Ironsmith caught his quivering wrist. Quick and strong as any humanoid, the mathematician twisted it up and back, to pin him against the gray panel faces. He gasped and pulled and tried to strike again, and somehow hurt his injured knee. Throbbing pain checked his fury.

"You aren't fit to fight." Ironsmith's low calm voice held no resentment, but only smooth regret. "You had better give up."

Not yet! Forester shook his head to clear the mist of pain. He twisted in Ironsmith's ruthless grasp, trying to ease his arm, and shifted his weight to relieve his trembling knee. Looking desperately behind him on that perilous catwalk, he found Jane Carter. She stood still and pale with fright, but he knew the dreadful power she had learned.

"Jane!" He fought that agony, and found his voice. "Stop him!"

Ironsmith was twisting back his arm again, with the merciless efficiency of a machine. He had to flinch from the excruciation of that, but red hatred surged back against the crushing weight of pain. Chilled with sweat, he gulped for the breath to gasp:

"Stop him, Jane! You can do it—the way you stopped those machines. Because he has potassium in his body—not in beads but everywhere. Mr. White can help you find it—and you know how to break the atoms." Cold waves of agony were beating him back against the glowing panels, but still he whispered faintly, "Just find the K-40 atoms—explode them in his blood!"

But the little girl had shaken her head, the movement stiff and slight. Her blue lips seemed to quiver, but then she froze again, motionless as a humanoid not working. All the color had drained from her hollowed face, and her immense dark eyes seemed fixed and blind as those other orbs of shining steel.

And nothing happened to Ironsmith.

The detonation of even a tiny fraction of the unstable potassium atoms in his body would have killed him instantly, but not even his calmly compassionate expression changed. Dazed from the impact of that failure, Forester gave way to pain. He stopped his useless struggles, and Ironsmith mercifully loosed his arm. His throbbing knee yielded suddenly, and he staggered on the catwalk, snatching frantically at nothing, until Ironsmith reached out to help him. Clinging to the girder again, he heard Jane Carter speak.

"Service, Clay Forester." He shrank from her, stricken, for now her thin treble voice had a new quality of whining, emotionless melody. It was like the voices of the humanoids. "We heard your unwise request," that new voice droned, "but we cannot injure Mr. Ironsmith. You are the one who requires restraint, sir, because Mr. Ironsmith has been faithful to the Compact, and he has loyally defended our relays from your own unhappy effort to alter the Prime Directive."

And she stood appallingly still again. Even her human terror had been somehow calmed, for now a strange smile was fixed on her tiny face—a white, dreamy smile, that he felt ill to see. For it reflected the serene tranquillity of the humanoids, without feeling and without life. It was mechanical. Forester turned in consternation, to croak accusingly at Ironsmith:

"What have you done to her?"

"Not I." Sternly, Ironsmith shook his bare sandy head. "Though it is a dreadful thing." His cool gray eyes rested on the stiffened child, and Forester could see the shocked pity in them. "Because the humanoids aren't ready, yet, to cope with such opponents in any humane way. I'm afraid she'll have to be destroyed. But you're the one to blame."

"I?" Forester trembled angrily. "How?"

"Come along—if you really want to talk about it." Glancing sadly at the child again, he nodded toward the door. "We can't stay here."

He swung, as if in sublime contempt, and Forester limped helplessly after him along that narrow inspection walk, to clutch gratefully at the jamb of the door. Looking bitterly back, Forester glimpsed the tiny tenders of the brain already hastening to inspect and repair the connections he had unhooked. Defeated, he stumbled wearily to the rusty swivel chair that old Mansfield had used, and sat down to ease his throbbing knee.

Little Jane Carter had glided after him with the sure grace of another humanoid. She halted at the end of the battered desk, motionless as any stopped machine, still smiling. Her set face was pinched and bloodless, and her eyes had dilated into great pools of shadow, lifeless and blind. Forester looked away from her, mopping his face and trying to swallow the dry horror in his throat and blinking unbelievingly at Ironsmith.

"How?" he croaked huskily. "How am I to blame?"

The mathematician was strolling absently about that gray-lit, stale-smelling room. He glanced at the faded backs of the reference books, idly spun the loose headstock of a bench lathe, curiously tapped the time-stiffened keys of a tiny portable calculating machine—which must have been a remote cybernetic forebear of the humanoids themselves. Dust came up in little gray puffs about his shoes, and dust marked his dark suit where he had brushed the benches and the drafting table. Thrusting both hands deep into his pockets, he turned back at last to Forester with a slow frown of thought.

"The humanoids have to guard the grid." His voice was mild and friendly as if Forester had never urged Jane Carter to detonate the unstable potassium isotope in his blood. "Warren Mansfield built that into them. When such blundering fools as you and Mark White attack the Prime Directive with paraphysical weapons, they are compelled to develop paraphysical defenses."

"They?" Forester kept his eyes off the frozen child. "Or you?"

Ironsmith stood silent, watching her with gray troubled eyes, until a sudden gust of wrath brought Forester out of the dusty chair. His knee gave again, and he had to catch the corner of the desk.

"So you don't deny it?" He spat on the floor. "I guessed the truth a long time ago—when you began inventing all your sophistic little arguments for accepting the machines, and when they paid you off so well. You—traitor!" Gasping for breath, he shook his feeble fist. "But I suppose you can't deny it now. Not when you're right here on Wing IV—murdering the last hope for liberty the rest of us will ever have. Not since I've heard about this Compact—whatever it is—between you and these machines."

"It's true that a mutual pact exists." Ironsmith nodded pleasantly. "A necessary arrangement. Because the humanoids were created without any psychophysical capacities, and because they aren't themselves creative. They were unable to protect the Prime Directive from psychophysical attacks, without the human aid the Compact provides."

"I thought so!"

"But you didn't think enough." Rubbing the lean angle of his sunburned jaw, Ironsmith strolled about the shop again, and nodded at last in grave decision. "You've made things very difficult, Forester—but still I'm going to give you one more chance to join us."

Peering in a bleak perplexity at this amiable and honest-seeming man who had turned so incredibly against his kind, Forester muttered sardonically, "Thank you!"

"Not me." Ironsmith shook his head. "Your thanks should go to someone else, who is still willing to forgive most of your follies and to risk far too much to help you. To Ruth—who was your wife."

"Ruth? But she's at Starmont, under euphoride."

"She was." Ironsmith smiled innocently. "You left her there with the humanoids. But I had always liked her, Forester—more, I suppose, than you ever did—and I brought her away with me when I came to leave Starmont. She has her mind and her memory back, and now she's with us in the Compact. She's anxious for you to join us." He paused hopefully. "What shall I tell her?"

"So she's with you?" Forester's bad knee shuddered and he

felt cold inside. Leaning weakly against the desk, he nodded to a painful understanding. He had never entirely liked Ironsmith, not even before the humanoid invasion, and now he thought he saw the reason. And the cause of Ruth's unhappiness that the humanoids had tried to cure with euphoride.

For the desert observatory had been an isolated, intimate little world, and this ingratiating traitor, the realization stunned him, had too often been with Ruth. At the office and the cafeteria, talking with his indolent brilliance of some quaint bit of forgotten history or useless philosophy he had translated from the dead languages of the first planet. At staff parties and on the tennis courts, always conveniently free to spin his aimlessly glittering mathematical paradoxes—while Forester was busy with Project Thunderbolt.

Forester's skin felt hot, and he heard a roaring in his brain. His whole body tensed and shook with hatred, but his knee was useless and he knew he couldn't fight. His eyes fell from Ironsmith's blandly urgent face, and he saw Jane Carter again. He looked at her blind, smiling stillness, until a shiver swept him.

"I'll go with you." He swung abruptly back to Ironsmith. "On one condition."

"So you'll join us?" Ironsmith turned suddenly genial. "You're ready to accept the humanoids for the useful machines they are? And to help them defend the Prime Directive?" He offered a vigorous, sunburned hand. "Then welcome, Forester."

"On one condition," he repeated flatly. "Jane Carter comes with me—free."

"Sorry, but that's out of the question." Ironsmith was smoothly regretful. "We can rescue you, but she has unfortunately used psychophysical powers of her own against the humanoids, and I'm afraid there's nothing we can do for her."

"Then there's nothing you can do for me."

"If that's the way you want it." Ironsmith nodded soberly. "Ruth will be hurt—but I imagine the humanoids will need another guinea pig, to test their new relays."

He looked at Jane Carter.

"Service, Mr. Ironsmith." She spoke to him with that high, inhuman whine. "Since Clay Forester refuses to enter the Compact, we must keep him in our care because of his dangerous knowledge of rhodomagnetics."

"All right," he cut at Ironsmith. "Let them kill me!"

The child's strange voice answered, "It will not be necessary to destroy you immediately, sir, because you have displayed no independent paramechanical capacities of your own."

Beyond her, two identical humanoids had come in through the balcony door. Beautiful with flowing gleams of bronze and blue, they glided silently to Forester's elbows.

"Service, sir," the child said. "Come with us."

Smoothly as any humanoid, she moved toward the balcony. Following between his keepers, Forester looked back twice. The first time, Ironsmith still stood beside the desk, tall and young and stern, watching him with a look of dispassionate regret. When he looked again, the dusty shop was hushed and empty.

# 23

A LITTLE RHODOMAGNETIC cruiser was waiting outside, hovering silently above the low aluminum railing of the narrow balcony, the smooth oval hull of it reflecting the gray vastness of the tower and murk of the smoky sky and the dark flatness of that endless busy spaceport, all in shimmering distortion. Numbed and tingling at the scalp from the vanishing of Ironsmith, Forester shuffled blankly toward it between his guards. The idle-seeming clerk from Starmont, a cold certainty struck him, must have somehow learned to control exchange-force probability for himself.

Agile as any mechanical, Jane Carter sprang nimbly over the railing to the deck of the waiting craft. Forester's two graceful guards helped him aboard, and the little ship rose silently. Watching through the one-way transparency of the hull, he saw the smoke-veiled vastness of that endless spaceport sink and spread. And he saw his destination.

His bad knee shuddered again, and the two intent machines moved closer to his arms, asking gently if he wished to sit. But he didn't sit. He stood between them, scarcely breathing, watching the red curve of that unfinished dome rise up ahead. He could see the scaffolding still about it, a dark metal veil across its sullen glow. At last, as the cruiser dropped, he found the toiling machines on the platforms, the merest insects, still scarcely visible. He thought their work was almost done.

"Service, sir," droned one of his keepers. "What disturbs you now?"

"I just begin to get it!" The tiny craft banked, coming down to land, and he tried to guard his knee. "I begin to see what this monstrous thing is for."

His bad knee gave as the deck leveled again, and the humanoids reached quickly to support him. He cuffed at them impatiently, but they held him up until the cruiser had settled gently beside a long windowless building, with the scarlet dome looming up beyond, fretted with the black scaffolding, huge as a strange moon rising. Forester shrank from it.

"Now I think I see the truth," he rasped at his guardians. "I think those platinum relays are paraphysical. I think Ironsmith and his gang of renegades have taught you how to generate paraphysical energy and helped you build this new grid." His voice turned hoarse. "And I think it's intended to operate men."

"That is partly true, sir." His brooding eyes had moved to Jane Carter, and now her thin body broke suddenly out of that stark immobility, moving a little toward him with a quick mechanical grace. "The platinum rays are to be energized with paramechanical force, and the grid has in fact been constructed to control the minds and bodies of men. But our purpose with it is not evil, sir, in any way."

Sweetly melodious, her thin bright voice reflected nothing human.

"Our only function, as you should know, is to secure the greatest possible measure of happiness for all men, under the Prime Directive. In the past, we have sometimes failed. A few unhappy individuals have developed paramechanical abilities, enabling them to elude our care and endanger our whole service, but this new grid is designed to govern them. We shall use it to cause all men, everywhere, to do only what is good."

Forester stood numbed and voiceless.

"Men have need of such guidance," droned the mechanized child. "Because most men cannot truly control the working of their own bodies, or even understand the functions of their own minds. Our function is to guard men from the consequences of their own ignorance and folly and vice. You cannot call that evil, sir."

Gulping painfully, Forester found no reply.

"Now come." The door of the cruiser was sliding open. "Here is our new paramechanical laboratory."

The two humanoids helped him carefully down from the deck. Shivering in the red shadow of that enormous dome, he limped stiffly after the child. Watching her strange new grace, he could see all men moving like puppets on the invisible strings of the grid. He could glimpse the ultimate despotism of old Warren Mansfield's altruistic idea, utterly benevolent and unthinkable. His narrow shoulders drew furiously straight, but he limped on helplessly after the child.

In a windowless vastness of gray wall ahead, a narrow doorway opened. Beyond was a dark enormous space, where he could see the loom and gleam of strange machines. A sharpened apprehension checked his feet—for he didn't want to be a guinea pig.

"You need not be alarmed for yourself, sir." His keepers must have seen his hesitation. "Or concerned about Jane Carter. Because we are careful to conduct our paramechanical research without causing any pain or needless bodily harm to the human subjects, and we always cause a complete suspension of awareness in individuals under paramechanical control."

Forester didn't want his mind dissected, not even by the most efficient methods, and he hung back until the two machines moved to catch his shrinking arms and thrust him, with an almost tender deftness, forward into the shadowy cavern of the research laboratory.

The humanoids had no use for light, and the only illumination came through the bars of an endless row of cages built along the foot of one high wall—cages much like those he had seen containing animals intended for biological experiment. They seemed quite small at first, in that enormous space, so that he wondered for an instant what sort of animal they were built to hold.

The dim light, spreading from them a little way across the floor and diffusing upward toward the unseen ceiling, outlined here and there the dark bulk of some immense unknown mechanism, picked out some polished metal surface, or caught the hastening sleekness of another humanoid. In a moment he had grasped the vastness of everything, and he knew that the cages were large enough for him.

He tried to stop again, but the two careful machines carried him on without effort. The barred door of one empty cage lifted for him, and the machines set him gently down inside. One of them stayed with him.

"You must wait here," it said, "until additional sections of the new grid are ready to be tested. Meantime, you may request any comforts you wish."

Concealed relays behind him shut and locked the door again. His black guardian stood abruptly motionless, the glow of the walls glistening faintly on its slim silicone nudity. Muttering sardonic thanks, Forester looked about the cage. He found a cot, a table and a chair, a tiny bath behind another door. Partitions shut off the other cells, but the thick dark came in through the bars, crushingly. Limping to the cot, he sat down on the edge of the hard mattress. The cold air had an antiseptic bitterness that choked him, and the gray walls closed until he was shuddering with a helpless claustrophobia.

"You have no reason for alarm, sir," came the golden monotone of his keeper. "Because you will feel nothing at all."

He watched its blind serenity, trying not to shiver.

"As a very distinguished physicist, sir, you should be interested in our research and pleased with your own part in it," the machine continued brightly. "Because we are following the methods of your own science. The basis of our work is a single simple assumption: if paramechanical forces can cause mechanical effects, then mechanical means can also generate paramechanical forces."

He tried to listen. Sitting cold and ill on that hard, narrow cot, he tried to breathe the bitter air. He tried to push back the suffocating dark. He rubbed his swollen knee, and tried to understand.

"We have proved that basic assumption," purred the humanoid. "With the aid of a few good men, we have designed instruments for the detection and analysis of paramechanical energies. A few bad men have also aided, however unwillingly, as experimental subjects."

Shivering on the cot, Forester wondered what had become of little Jane Carter. He had lost her in the dark while he struggled with his keepers, and he couldn't see into the other cages. He couldn't find her now.

"As another scientist, sir, you will understand our methods," the machine went on. "Our human subjects, under strict control, are caused to exert paramechanical forces. We proceed to measure those forces, to investigate the mechanics of their origin and determine the nature of their effects, and finally to duplicate them by mechanical means."

Forester had slumped abjectly back against the cold partition. Watching the intent machine, he nursed his knee and clung to one thin thread of hope.

"The final result of this research will be the perfected

paramechanical grid. Any human body under its direction will be operated far more efficiently than is ever possible by the slow, uncertain biochemical processes of the natural brain. It can regulate men to prevent all the accidents caused by their clumsy feebleness. It can stimulate the restoration of lost or damaged members, and correct the faulty functions which so often impair the well-being of fragile human bodies and minds. It can even mend the decay of time, to make men almost as durable as our own units."

Forester shrank from the bright steel eyes of the machine, clutching his single thread of hope.

"So you see that our methods are sound and our goal is good," it finished serenely. "You see that you have no cause for any personal fear, and your own love of scientific truth should make you eager to do your own small necessary part in this greatest possible humanitarian undertaking."

The humanoid ceased all movement, in absolute efficiency, as that golden melody ended. Forester sat uncomfortably before it on the cot, nursing his knee and his hope. Desperately, he clung to memory of that sealed and secret limestone cavern, where no humanoid could go. For Mark White must still be there, unvanquished, still toiling with his adepts to turn their freakish psychophysical powers into a fighting science of the mind. Perhaps—

His breath caught, and the feeble strand of his hopeless hope became a mighty thing. For he saw a huge, red-bearded figure striding out of the dark beyond the cages, still majestic in a tattered silver cloak.

"Mark!" He lurched to his feet, his knee strong again. "Mark White!" Darting past his frozen keeper, he tried to shake the massive, coldly glowing bars. "Mark—here I am!"

But that tall figure ignored his call. It stalked on by, and all his hope went with it. His knee shuddered under him, so that he clung weakly to the bars. For he had seen the face of the marching thing, strangely stiff and pale. He had seen the eyes, huge and dark and blank, their sullen blaze of hate dead at last.

And he had seen the look behind the splendid beard, a smile that came from some far place of cold forgetfulness, lost beyond all feeling.

He stared after the stalking creature, stricken, until it vanished in the dark. Even its movements, the realization hit him, no longer had any characteristic of Mark White. Its striding gait had been too quick and sure and soundless. Like little Jane Carter, it had become a mechanical puppet of the grid.

And it was not alone, for the others came marching after it out of the whispering dark. Still tall and gaunt, old Graystone was no longer awkward now, his nose no longer ruddy. Overstreet, for all his puffy bulk, moved lightly as a child. Not nervous anymore, little Lucky Ford came gliding by with a swift mechanical grace.

Forester found no voice to call again, and none of them seemed aware of him—for all awareness was suspended, in those controlled by the paramechanical relays. All their eyes had blind, distended pupils, and all their faces smiled out of unfeeling oblivion.

"Service, sir." He started when his keeper touched his arm. "Those unhappy men can cause no trouble now—and you can only tire your leg, standing too long. You should let us bathe you now, and massage your knee. And then you should sleep."

## 24

Blankly, Forester turned away from the murmuring dark and the monstrous shape of defeat. Limping obediently toward the narrow bathroom behind his cage, he nodded at the way those smiling automatons had gone, inquiring listlessly, "How did you capture them?"

"Through Jane Carter," the machine said. "They had hidden from us in a cave which had no physical entrance, but we reached them with the child's mind, and took hold of them with paramechanical impulses from the energized test sections of the new grid. We controlled their own paramechanical capacities to bring them here."

Stumbling on his painful knee, Forester had to let the quick mechanical support him. "Come along and let us tend you." He heard its droning only vaguely. "Your test section of the grid will soon be energized, so that we can try to repair the damaged ligaments."

He limped passively along with the machine, and he let it put him to bed. Lying in the narrow cot, he tried to forget the glowing bars and the finality of his failure. He closed his eyes against an unendurable solicitude, and he tried to solve a riddle.

He had no conscious purpose left, but he was still a scientist. The old habits and disciplines of abstract thought were still working in him, even when all the plan and meaning of his being had been shattered, and his sick mind turned back now to seek relief in the old pursuit of fitting facts together to form new patterns of the truth.

Project Thunderbolt had never left him mental peace or freedom to develop all the theoretical implications of his first basic discoveries in rhodomagnetics, but now in the relaxation of despair he found his mind turning from practical things to consider that long-neglected challenge.

For the humanoids had not yet conquered the realm of pure thought, nor closed it to men. Lying on his cot, he resumed the oldest quest of science: the ancient search for the first fact of all things and the law of its multitudinous manifestations, for the *prima materia* and the philosophers' stone.

Electromagnetics, even with all its ambitious achievements in smashing and rebuilding atoms and draining off their energy, had never quite blueprinted atomic architecture. Mighty as it was, that old science of iron had never quite accounted for the nuclear binding force—for that incredible something, not itself electromagnetic, which somehow contained the furious electrostatic repulsions within unfissioned atoms.

Once he had thought he saw that other energy, revealed

long ago in the supernova's light. If space and time were really electromagnetic effects, as all the phenomena of his new science suggested, then it followed that the quantum nature of all electromagnetic energy must be reflected somehow in the structure of space and time. Space-time should exist, he thought, in tiny, indivisible units. And the dimensions of such uncuttable units of space-time, as he inferred them, placed definite lower limits on the action of such electromagnetic forces as the mutual repulsion of bound positive particles in atomic nuclei. Because all such forces, with their finite velocities of propagation, must have time and space in which to act—and must vanish, therefore, at those certain, almost infinitesimal magnitudes at which time and even distance disappeared.

Such reasoning, by removing the very space and time which the disruptive forces of the atom must have for action, also took away the need of any actual binding force—almost. And he thought he had found the necessary remainder, expressed as a function of his constant, *rho*. For rhodomagnetic forces, existing apart from electromagnetic space and time, were not restricted by the limits of the electromagnetic quantum. Timeless and continuous, they must still act within the atom, even at those distances so tiny that space and time fell apart into paradoxic quanta in which other forces disappeared and motion lost its meaning. Some such cohesive force was surely necessary to bind together all the discrete units of atomic space and atomic time into one continuous universe, and the supernova's spectrum had showed him the working of an actual rhodomagnetic component in matter, essential to the intricate balance of opposing forces in suns and atoms alike.

*Rho* had been his symbol for the constant of mutual equivalence with which he had hoped to join the twin systems of energy, electromagnetic and rhodomagnetic, expressing their basic nature and reciprocal relation. He had used the symbol to write an equation which seemed to unite the two sciences into the final fact he sought—until young Ironsmith so casually and cheerily proved that seeming *prima materia* to be just one more illusion.

For rhodomagnetics, like the older science built on the properties of the first atomic triad, had also failed. Forester had carried the light a little farther, but vast areas of dark were left. He had detonated matter with his new partial knowledge, as men with even less knowledge had split atoms, but both sciences were still not enough to explain why all atoms didn't fission at once, and all matter detonate itself.

Stable atoms still existed, to prove the presence of some third component, acting to preserve all substance from spontaneous fission and dissolution into free energy under the furious disruptive force of the two components he knew. But *rho* had failed him. The unknown force refused to obey the established laws of either science, and its actual nature still escaped him. Unless, just possibly—

Forester caught his breath, recalling that the periodic table offered still a third triad—composed of the three precious heavy metals, platinum and osmium and iridium. The same elements the humanoids were using to build their dreadful new relays! Could that last triple group prove to be another convenient key, ready to unlock yet a third sort of energy?

While some such rousing notion had crossed his mind long ago at Starmont, on that tremendous night when he first grasped the awesome gift of the rhodium triad, he had then been forced to dismiss it as nothing more than a purely logical possibility, as inaccessibly far beyond his reach as the whole science of electromagnetics must have been to that observant barbarian of the mother planet who first noticed a floated steel needle seeking the north. Project Thunderbolt had left him no leisure for any such nebulous speculations, but now his short remaining time was good for nothing else, and the hint of those platinum relays had already begun to shape another pattern in his mind, waiting for that idea to complete it.

The youthful thought spread a swift excitement through him now, but he tried to keep his body quiet. Afraid to look at his keeper, or even to let the rhythm of his breathing change, he tried to analyze and demonstrate that breathtaking new conception in the uninvaded laboratory of his mind. The heavy elements of the platinum triad were indeed the logical key to that unknown component, it came to him, because the more powerfully disruptive electromagnetic and rhodomagnetic forces of the more massive atoms must obviously require a far greater intensity of that stabilizing energy to balance and contain them—it was only the ultimate failure of the binding component in the very heaviest atoms that allowed the fission of such elements as uranium.

Lying very still, wishing absently that he had Frank Ironsmith's computing section to help him with the math, he groped with his mind alone for the nature and the laws of that unknown energy. Since electromagnetic effects varied with the second power of the distance, and rhodomagnetic with the first, he thought this third sort of energy should logically be invariant with distance. Again, since the velocity even of electromagnetic light was finite in time, and the speed of rhodomagnetic energy infinite, then the effects of the platinomagnetic force might reasonably somehow transcend time. And, if those two fumbling hypotheses were true—

His breathing paused again, and he couldn't keep his body from stiffening on the cot. For Ash Overstreet could look into the future and the past, and the curious abilities of Lucky Ford and little Jane Carter were unlimited by distance. Trembling to a startled understanding of the platinum relays in that new grid, he recognized the unknown component. It was—it simply had to be—psychophysical energy!

"What disturbs you, sir?" inquired his keeper. "Are you still unhappy?"

"No trouble." He mumbled the words, turning carefully on the cot to keep his face away from it. He breathed again and made his limbs relax, trying to seem merely restless in his sleep. "And I'm going to be very happy now."

He was. Because that flash of intuition had been a wide illumination, lighting many things. It had closed the gaps in Mark White's half-science, and swept away the baffling contradictions. It actually explained Jane Carter's gift and Lucky Ford's ability and Overstreet's searching perception—and an answer more complete than the shadowy conjectures and the mocking uncertainties hiding behind vague unknowns, out of which he had tried to shape his exchange-force hypothesis of mind and probability.

Lying still, relaxed again, he forgot the alert machine behind him. He forgot the bars, and his painful knee, and the long failure of his life. Absently regretful that Ironsmith couldn't check his speculations, he began an awed exploration of the universe, by that tremendous, sudden light.

It wasn't hope that urged him on—not consciously—for he thought hope was dead. He had yielded his body to the machines, and ceased all resistance. Waiting, resigned to whatever fate, he had simply released his intelligence upon the familiar paths of science, and now his triumphant mind began to rove through atoms and far galaxies.

For he had reached the oldest goal of alchemy and science. The fabulous *prima materia*, when now at last he grasped it, proved to be a very simple equation, so plainly obvious that he thought he should have found it long before. It merely stated the relation and equivalence of electromagnetic and rhodomagnetic and psychophysical energies, as involved most simply in the equilibrium of a stable atomic particle—revealing all three as different aspects of the single basic unity science had ever sought.

The sheer mathematical beauty of that equation brought Forester a deep glow of pleasure. For the integration was complete. The terms described the fundamental stuff of nature, neither electromagnetic nor rhodomagnetic nor psychophysical, but all three at once—the keystone of all the ordered splendor of the universe. Now at last, too late to help anything, he saw the picture whole.

The alchemists of Ironsmith's historical fragments, taking

mercury for their *prima materia* and sulphur to be the philoso-phers' stone that made it into lead or iron or gold, had been but little farther from the truth, it occurred to him, than the ambi-tious thinkers of the later age of iron, who had attempted to balance their universe upon another single leg. Rhodomagnet-ics, adding a second leg, had improved the balance only slightly. But psychophysics, the third aspect of one reality, completed a firm tripod of truth.

The transformations and derivations of that equation of equivalence, Forester perceived, would explain the origin of atoms and the universe, the gravitation of matter and the dis-persion of the galaxies, the dark paradox of time and the nature of space, and doubtless even the birth and meaning of life and mind themselves.

Lying quiet on that hard cot, he was lost in the elemental grandeur of that concept. He had forgotten the gray-walled cage around him, and his sleepless keeper watching, and the unpleasant fact that he himself was waiting for the scalpels of another research project—until the humanoid touched his arm.

"Service, Clay Forester," it said. "We're ready now."

Then he was no longer in the cage.

## 25

HE WAS STANDING on a flat gravel bed, at the bottom of a shal-low, dry watercourse. On his left were low dark cliffs, formed where the vanished stream had cut against an outcropping granite ridge. The barren gravel fields spread far to his right, and beyond were hills, lying low and naked and dead beside the wide shallow valley of the ancient river.

It was night, and cruelly cold.

For this was not Wing IV. The sky told him that. The gray murk of the humanoid planet was gone, and the sky above the low dark cliffs and the far black hills was a dead and utter black, scattered with only a few tiny oval blobs of gray mist. Towering against the dark, above the foot of that dead valley, was a tall, leaning dome of pale white splendor, a remote incredible spray of diamond glints frozen motionless.

For a moment he merely stared, shivering and bewildered, shrinking from the savage attack of the cold. For he stood barefoot on the icy sharpness of the gravel, clad only in the thin gray pajamas in which his mechanical keeper had clad him. The cruel cold sucked out his breath and seared his skin, and he stood blank with his stunned perplexity until he felt the tug of a child's anxious hand.

"Oh, Dr. Forester!" Jane Carter was crouched beside him on the river-worn gravel, no longer a creature of the machines. Her huge frightened eyes could see again, and that serene cold smile of far forgetfulness was gone. "I'm so cold!" She shivered against him. "Please take me out of the cold."

"But how can I do that"—he shuddered beneath a crushing wonderment—"when I don't even know where we are?"

He found that he couldn't really speak, because that empty cold had taken all his breath. His throat was dry and his lungs were burning and his lips too stiff to move. He made no sound—and heard none, for this dark place was utterly dead. Yet the child seemed to understand him, for a new dismay was sick in her eyes.

"Don't you know?" She frowned up at him, her thin face stiff with pain, and he realized that he hadn't heard her actual voice at all. "You ought to know," she said. "'Cause you took me away from the black machines, and you brought us both out here. All I did was show you where to come."

"No—that couldn't be!" He shook his head dazedly. "Because just a moment ago I was in a cage, waiting for that platinum brain to take hold of me. I don't remember doing anything at all. I didn't even hope to get away, and I certainly don't know where we are."

"I know that." She clung close to him, her unvoiced thought more rapid than speech. "This is the cold, far place

Mr. White used to send me to pick up palladium nuggets. I used to hurry right back to the cave, to keep from freezing—but now we can't go there. The black machines would take us again if we did." Her anxious fingers were icy in his own. "Please—where can we go?"

But Forester was mute, swaying to a numbed understanding. He remembered those frosty nuggets of alluvial palladium Jane had brought back from the gravels of a sunless planet that was cold to the absolute zero, and now he saw the terrible meaning of the starless dark and that tall arch of diamond dust beyond the black and barren hills. The merciless, still cold sank into him more piercingly. For now he knew that he and Jane had been somehow marooned on this lifeless planet lost outside their native universe of stars.

Those tiny oval blots against the dead and empty dark were other island universes, remote beyond knowledge. And that tall plume was the edge of their own galaxy, luminous with light which must have left its splendid mist of suns a long thousand centuries before the first philosopher of the mother world ever dreamed of seeking the one eternal reality behind the multiplex flow of seeming things.

"It's so awful cold," the frightened child was sobbing. "Please, can't you do—anything? I can't keep us alive much longer here without breathing. And I don't know anywhere safe to go. Please, can't you—"

Blankly, Forester shook his head. Because it must have taken a long billion years, he thought, for this stray atom of a world to drift so far through the extragalactic dark. It must have been time beyond imagining since some lost sun had warmed these old black hills, since vanished waters had washed this frozen gravel. This world was dead. No day would ever break the black-and-silver splendor of this savage, soundless night. Nothing could live long here. His hands were empty and his weak knee throbbed and the cold of the gravel burned the bare soles of his feet like something very hot. Peering at the black frown of those worn cliffs, he dropped his thin shoulders hopelessly. Nothing at all could live at the absolute zero.

"No, Jane, I don't think I brought us here." He was trying gently not to increase her fright, until he saw in her uplifted eyes that she knew all his own overpowering dismay. "Maybe the humanoids did it, with that new grid." His mind shuddered from that. "They were using us for test animals, you know. Maybe they wanted to see how you kept alive out here. Maybe they mean to pull us back again, just before we die—to save us for some other test."

Quickly lifting one small bare foot and then the other away from the searing cold of the gravel, she stood straight and tiny in that worn leather coat too big for her, a white dust of frost on her stiffly frozen hair. " 'Scuse me, but you did it. You fought that new brain machine to take me from it, and you teleported us both out here." Her dark eyes held a solemn plea. "Mr. White would say you're awful good—but I'm still afraid we're going to die. Can't you find a warm place for us, with air?"

"I can't do teleportation," he insisted bleakly. "Or anything else. But you can go—somewhere." He pushed her slight body from him. "Better leave me, and look for some safe place."

"No—please—there isn't any!" She clung to him desperately. "You did take me away from the machines, even if you don't remember. You're still fighting that brain thing to keep me, even if you don't seem to know it. So we must stay together—don't you see?"

"We'll keep together." Die together, he thought, nodding to an uneasy acquiescence. "Can you tell me how you hold back the cold, so I can help?"

She only shook her head, shivering against him, already exhausted. She didn't know, not consciously, and her unconscious psychophysical adaptation could keep them both alive no more than a few minutes longer. Beyond that, his blurred and stinging eyes could see no hope. For the silent fangs of cold had sunk deep into him. His empty lungs burned, and his stiffened fingers scarcely felt the limp tug of her small body, slipping down beside him.

He forgot his own despair, and bent to pick her up. His bad leg buckled. He fell, searing his hands on the gravel, and lurched feebly back to his knees. He lifted her tenderly, trying to shield her with his arms, for he knew nothing else to do. He could feel her straining effort to hold back that implacable emptiness of cold, but he knew no way to share the burden. She seemed to flinch and quiver, and instantly the cold slashed at them with new fury, as if her life and her power had almost failed. Swept with an infinite helpless compassion, he wished he knew how to help her.

"The door!" She stirred weakly in his stiff arms, trying to point. "See it—there!"

Turning painfully where he knelt, he found a faint new gleam above the rim of those changeless ancient cliffs. Dimly, his fading vision made out the smooth curve of a transparent cupola there, washed with the pale cold radiance of the far galaxy. Against the dark rock below, he saw a green light burning.

He shook his head stiffly, and peered again. Because it couldn't be a light. Nothing could be still alive to light any sort of beacon on this dark world, and he was certain that cupola hadn't been there, anyhow, when he first saw the cliffs. He blinked and gaped, mistrusting his dimming senses. But the light continued to glisten incredibly on polished metal surfaces, beyond a round opening in the dark rock.

"Please!" Jane was sobbing. "Hurry—"

He didn't wait to wonder any longer. Swaying laboriously to his feet, he picked her up again. A frozen numbness tried to hold him, and a painful roaring was increasing in his ears, but he staggered with her toward the green-lit opening. The sharp gravel no longer hurt his feet, and even the ache in his knee had ceased, but a dead stiffness tripped him. He fell, and came heavily up again with the child still whimpering in his arms, and stumbled on until he fell again.

And again he carried her on until at last, somehow still alive, he lurched across a shining metal threshold. Inside the tiny chamber where the green light burned, he saw that it must be an air lock. His bleared and throbbing eyes found a row of buttons, one glowing dimly green. He punched it clumsily, with a finger that had no strength or feeling left, and a massive valve slid up to shut them in.

Air screamed in, a warm and kindly hurricane. He filled his burning lungs, and breathed. His sight began to clear, and that pressure of roaring blood decreased in his ears, and his stiffened feet began to ache again to the good warmth of the floor.

Jane Carter was still in his arms, limp and silent. Catching her thin blue wrist, he felt no pulse. Her flesh seemed very cold, even to his numbed hands, and he thought she must be dead. He was bending to lay her down when he felt a sudden warmth—as if some psychokinetic force, he thought, had acted directly upon her to accelerate the molecular motion of heat. She shuddered convulsively, drawing a long sighing breath. Her dark eyes opened, seeing again, full of a complete devotion.

"Oh, thank you, Dr. Forester!" Now he could hear the grave sweetness of her voice, her own again. Seeming fully restored, she slipped quickly out of his arms. Her smile was human now, relaxed and glad. "I think Mr. White would say you're very, very good!"

Puzzled again by her sudden recovery, Forester looked around him with a mounting bewilderment. Any aid or shelter for them, on this long-dead wanderer of the dark, had seemed unbelievably improbably, and now he began to notice singular things about this oddly convenient haven.

Certainly it wasn't a billion years old.

The clean warm air had a faint smell of new paint. The buttons which worked the valves were made of the newest sort of

translucent synthetic—and all neatly labeled in his own language. Riveted to the case of the control mechanism was the familiar name plate of the Acme Engineering Corporation—a small firm which had contracted to supply certain machinings for the neutrino search tubes of his own Project Lookout.

Calling up the courage to experiment, he gingerly pushed the button marked "Inner Valve—To Open." Something hummed inside the case. An amber light flashed, and a warning gong rang. And another heavy wedge of polished steel slid down, to let them into the shelter. Quivering with a voiceless astonishment, he led the child inside.

Exploring this enigmatic sanctuary, they followed a wide passage back into the rock. Plates of smoothly welded metal lined it, painted with the same shades of cream and gray that Forester had chosen for his own office back at Starmont. The soft illumination came from recessed fluorescent fixtures—which bore the familiar trademark of United Electric.

Doors were spaced along the tunnel, fitted with knobs for a man to turn. Forester pushed them open as he passed, to look dazedly into the rooms beyond. The first housed a power plant, with a small rotary converter humming silently beside a bank of transformers, and a standby unit waiting. Searching for the generator, he caught his breath. For all the power seemed to come from a single small cell, with a name plate which read, "Starmont Rhodomagnetic Research Foundation."

Forester blinked at the outrageous impossibility of that. Once, it was true, he had dreamed of establishing a nonprofit foundation to develop rhodomagnetics for peacetime usefulness, but the harsh demands of military security had killed that bright hope, along with many another. If that research project had never even existed . . . He stumbled blankly on, searching for a sane explanation.

The next room was a kitchen—oddly like Ruth's had been, in the little house the humanoids had wrecked when they took over Starmont. The electric range and the streamlined refrigerator were the same white and shining United Electric models, and the canned and packaged food stacked in the shelves was all gaudy with the same familiar labels of standard brands.

He found a room for himself, and a smaller one for Jane. The table beside his bed was thoughtfully stacked with a dozen of his favorite books—but there was none, he saw with a faint disappointment, that he hadn't read. The bathroom was even supplied with the soap and toothpaste he liked, and the razor on the shelf was incredibly like his own.

At the farther end of the tunnel, a narrow stair led upward. They climbed it breathlessly, and came up into the crystal-domed cupola that he had seen from outside. Chilled with an increasing awed perplexity, he stood staring at the dead land-scape beyond the curving panels.

Nothing had changed, outside. The cruel sky was black and strange. The high curve of the galaxy stood like a leaning plume of silver dust beyond that empty valley where nothing could have lived within imaginable time, its pale radiance fall-ing faint and cold on the naked cliffs and the low, eroded hills beyond the gravel fields that water once had washed.

Leaning on a little table under the center of that impossible dome, to ease his weary knee, Forester stood a long time look-ing dully at that tall splendid arch of silver mist and diamond dust. The biting cold and the brooding loneliness of this deadly night took hold of him again, and he shuddered convul-sively. Jane Carter caught his hand, to whisper anxiously:

"Is it something very bad?"

"Nothing bad." He smiled down at her apprehensive face with the best assurance he could manufacture. "I just don't un-derstand. I don't know how we got here—so far from home that all the stars men ever knew are lost in that cloud, yonder. I'm sure I did nothing—"

"But you did," she broke in softly. " 'Scuse me, but you really did."

"Maybe it was Mark White." Looking up again at that re-mote plume of mist that was a billion stars, he ignored her shy protest. "Maybe he somehow beat the machines, after all!"

That exciting possibility lifted his voice. "Maybe he had this place ready—and somehow broke free from that grid, long enough to teleport us here."

She shook her head. "But it wasn't Mr. White."

"How do you know?" He shivered again, to the monstrous cold that crouched outside the dome. "Somebody from our world must have built it—quite lately." Blinking at her breathless astonishment, he dropped his shoulders helplessly. "I just don't get it! Everything's so—familiar. The books I like. My kind of toothpaste. Even a bottle of the capsules I take for indigestion, with Dr. Pitcher's name on it, and the right prescription number!"

"But don't you remember?" Jane was frowning gravely, perplexed as he was. "Don't you know?"

He could only shake his head.

"It's funny you don't," she said softly, " 'cause you're the one who did it all. You took me away from the brain machine, that still has poor Mr. White and his poor men. All I did was show you where to come—far away from the black things."

He opened his mouth, and found no voice.

"Don't you really remember?" Her tiny voice was hushed with wonder. "How you fought the brain machine? And how you made this warm place for us, while I tried to stop the cold?" She nodded toward the empty valley, her dark eyes afraid again. "And how you helped me, here at the door, when I was about to die?" A bleak disappointment shadowed her face. "It's a pity you don't remember," she whispered faintly. " 'Cause you could be awful good at psychophysics."

## 26

FORESTER LOOKED DOWN at his hands, and flexed them unbelievingly. Small and wiry, they had seemed sensitive and competent until he had seen the efficient limbs of the humanoids, beautiful with the flow of light on smoothly molded silicone synthetics and powerful with beamed energy. They had served him once, but now his fingers were still clumsy and aching from the cold, his knuckles still dark-scabbed where he had peeled them awkwardly when Ironsmith came upon him in the tower of the grid. They were numbed and useless to him now.

"But you didn't use your hands at all." Jane Carter seemed to read his groping doubt. "You did it with your mind—how could you forget?"

Trembling with his stunned perplexity, Forester looked around that little cupola again. The small table, lit from a shaded fixture, was like one he had used in the observatory at Starmont—even to the brown familiar scar where some forgotten cigarette had burned it. Neatly arranged on it were scratch pads and sharpened pencils, a slide rule, and several technical handbooks; one of them, listing tables of rhodomagnetic coefficients, published by the Starmont Press, was by Clay Forester, Ph.D.

"That's my name!" The back of his neck was prickling uncomfortably. "Those are values I worked out, or had Ironsmith calculate for me. But the book was never printed, because of the censorship. There was only the one typed copy I kept in the safe. I don't see how . . ." And his voice fell away into a chasm of wonder, dark as the dead night above.

"You did it with your mind," Jane insisted gravely. "You did it with paraphysics, the way I used to change potassium atoms to stop the black machines. Only I think you can change any atom, to let it go into energy, and then make the energy right back into any other atom you want. 'Cause you made all this place out of the rock, just by thinking how you wanted it to be."

Forester stood speechless, unbelieving.

"I saw you do it," Jane told him. "I watched you cut the hollow in the cliff, with only your mind, and turn the rock into machines and air and food and everything we need. And I'm awful glad you did. I was nearly dead!"

He walked slowly to look at the thermostat beside the stair, near the ventilator register. It was a good copy of the one in the nursery at Starmont that he and Ruth had never needed. The enamel on the case showed precisely the same diagonal scratch.

"I suppose you're right." His narrow shoulders lifted uneasily. "Because I can see that everything is copied, somehow, from something in my own mind—from things I know or ideas I had thought about. But I don't see how." A stubborn doubt shook his head. "There simply wasn't time! Not for anything like that. Because the whole place just came here—instantaneously!"

"I guess you just can't remember." She sighed, baffled. "It seemed an awful long time to me, waiting out there in the cold, watching the rock while you changed it."

His troubled glance went back to the windless world outside the dome, and something touched his spine with the white chill of the thin light that fell from the far galaxy. He knew the science of transmutation. Inspecting industrial atomic piles for the Defense Authority, he had seen awesome demonstrations in which a tiny sample of sodium or aluminum or platinum was cautiously thrust into the hot reactor through an opening in the lead-and-concrete shielding, and came out again as an untouchable mixture of deadly radioactives in which cautious analysis revealed the triumphant traces of man-made magnesium or silicon or gold. He knew the mechanics of nuclear transformation by which the savage energies of the pile shattered and rebuilt the atomic units or proton and neutron and electron into different elements. That was old stuff to him. But this—this was different!

Cold granite dissolving swiftly to some inexplicable reagent of the mind, to flow into fitted sheets of strongly welded steel thickly backed with insulating fiberglass, into sealed drums of compressed oxygen complete with pressure gauges and reduction valves, into bright-labeled cans of green beans and that remarkable rhodomagnetic power cell and the slide rule in his trembling hand—matter molded by sheer thought!

He knew no mechanics for that. The skeptical half of his

brain wanted to reject the evidence, but no reluctance to believe diminished the comfortable hard reality of that transparent shell holding back the airless emptiness and the cold. The dome was there, and its solid existence spurred his uncertain search for understanding.

The theory of exchange forces might help again, he thought—that concept of the ceaseless pulsation of identity between one atomic particle and any of its innumerable twins. Because every particle, conceived as a wave of probability, existed everywhere. That fact had suggested a provisional answer to the puzzle of teleportation, and now he saw that other equally staggering wonders were also implied—even to the mental creation of this curious refuge.

Because all the chemical and physical properties of matter were determined, obviously, by particular patterns of atomic identity. Any change of pattern, clearly, would also be a change of property—a transmutation. And all existing patterns were nothing more than functions of exchange-force probability.

Probability! Itself an unsolved riddle, that must be the answer. Jane Carter had proved many times that her mind could govern probability, to explode unstable atoms or to change her place in space. And Lucky Ford had made a simpler demonstration, he recalled, long ago at Dragonrock, with only a pair of dice. There—somewhere—must lie the truth. Forester felt reassured by that flicker of understanding—until its brief illumination faded.

For Mark White's unanswered questions came back then to haunt him. What was the stuff of the mind? How could it grasp anything, even probability? What were the laws, and where the limits? Baffled, he studied the miraculous slide rule in his hand, and nodded with an absent approval. The sections slid easily, and there were four special scales he recalled once thinking he would like to have for rhodomagnetic problems.

"I suppose I really made it." He put down the rule, turning slowly back to the troubled child. "But still I don't know how."

"You must try to remember," she insisted desperately.

"Please—try awful hard! The black machines still have Mr. White and the others. We've just got to help them."

"We'll try." He nodded, his lean jaw set. Effort furrowed his thin face, but all the escape from Wing IV and the building of the shelter remained darkly mysterious as the dead landscape beneath that leaning arch of frost. Wearily, he shook his head.

"Can't you think how you learned?" Jane whispered anxiously. "Can't you remember what you were thinking—just before you forgot?"

"Of course!" He started as it came to him. "That equation of equivalence."

Why hadn't he thought of that before? Lying in his cage beneath the machine's suave alertness, he had been excitedly elated with the infinite promise of that final *prima materia*. It was far too important, certainly, to be so casually forgotten. Wondering at the blind spot that had so oddly blotted it out of his mind, he snatched a pencil and hastily set the equation down—taut with a fresh sense of the limitless implications of it, and chilled with curious apprehension that it might somehow slip away again, beyond that inexplicable barrier of oblivion.

"Now?" Jane whispered hopefully. "Can you remember?"

"Not much." He shook his head, trying not to see the disappointment in her eyes. "But I think this equation ought to be the key—if I just knew how to use it. Because it gives the constants of equivalence for ferromagnetic and rhodomagnetic energy, both of them in terms of platinomagnetism—which is also the energy of mind."

He started to explain the symbols.

"I can't read." She stopped him shyly. "I never went to school, really, except to Mr. White. Some things I can do, like holding back the cold." She nodded, unafraid, at the black, silent savagery crouched outside. "But I can't understand when anybody tries to 'splain how I do it."

And Forester sat scowling at the paper in his hand. Here,

he knew, was the ultimate key to knowledge and to power that other men had sought in vain since the days of alchemy. He had used it triumphantly, and then inexplicably forgotten how. Grim with resolution, he set out to get its secret back.

"Better go and play," he urged the child. "Or do you want to rest?"

But she refused to leave the dim-lit dome. Standing silently against the railing above the stair, she watched him work at the little desk, and sit scowling at the merciless dark, and finally work desperately again.

"These are the expansions and transformations of that prime equation," he explained. "I'm trying to derive complete mathematical descriptions for all the psychophysical phenomena. Because they ought to tell how to do those things I must have done and then forgotten."

She shook her head confusedly, and kept on watching.

"Huh!" He caught his breath, and wrote something hastily, and then peered outside at the fields of frozen gravel where she had looked for nuggets. Suddenly his gaunt face smiled, and he whispered softly, "See it, Jane!"

And a worn bit of metal dropped from nowhere to the table. He reached as if to touch it, and cautiously drew back his fingers. For the rich whiteness of palladium was swiftly covered with the brighter white of frost, which hissed and crackled and increased as the dreadful cold sucked moisture from the air. Forester looked up at the cruel sky, frowning slightly as if with effort, and the nugget was abruptly gone.

His pencil hurried again. He paused to study Jane's uneasy face with somber eyes that seemed unseeing as if that new machine possessed him. His thin yellow fingers plied the new slide rule—until he caught his breath, and made another quick notation, and called a warning to the child:

"Cover your eyes!"

A flash brighter than lightning shattered that frozen night. A new blue star burned for an instant above those dead hills, before its brief splendor faded and went redly out.

"No, I don't remember yet." Forester shook his head at Jane's breathless question. "That's just one transformation of prime equation, describing the detonation of mass into free energy when the psychophysical component is canceled. I tested it on that nugget."

He nodded triumphantly at the quarter of the sky where that savage light had burned and vanished.

"I teleported the nugget out in space, and set it off. An eight-ounce supernova! That's our weapon. A little better than Project Thunderbolt—and one I don't think Frank Ironsmith and his peculiar friends can steal."

"Then we can help poor Mr. White?" she whispered anxiously. "Before the machines kill him with their 'speriments?'"

"I think we can." Forester nodded soberly. "Though there's something else we must do first, to give us any chance against the humanoids. We must find Ironsmith, and smash that gang of traitors with him."

"I guess he's the first one to fight." She nodded reluctantly, moving uneasily toward Forester in the shadows of the cupola. "He seems so terrible now, not a bit like he used to be. He doesn't really seem quite human anymore."

"I don't know what he is." Forester's thin face set. "But we can fight him now."

With Jane Carter watching, he looked for the traitor's nest. Once he told her, with a hard wry smile, that what he needed was the computing section back at Starmont, because Ironsmith had always worked out the beautiful abstractions, and he had only applied them to reality. It was an endless time of scowling concentration and empty staring and hurried work with the new slide rule, before he set down another brief equation.

"Still I don't remember anything," he told her. "But that's another derivation. It defines space and time—as the electromagnetic effects I thought they were, but joined by a psychophysical binding effect that keeps the universe from shattering into an infinity of tiny space-time manifolds, one around each separate quantum." Looking past her toward that far pillar of frosty light where all the worlds of men were lost, he added hopefully, "It's that psychophysical factor that makes it the equation of clairvoyance."

"You mean you can see with it?" she whispered. "Like Mr. Overstreet?"

"I hope so." He nodded thoughtfully. "If I can learn how to use it. Because the space factor vanishes when you solve for the psychophysical term, and the factor of past time is infinitesimal. The only actual limit is a factor of uncertainty, which increases to infinity in future time."

She shook her head reproachfully.

"That means," he tried to explain, "the equation tells how we ought to be able to see anything happening anywhere, right now—except of course in a place shielded with a powerful psychophysical field, the way that new grid is. We should be able to see things that happened a long time ago, though that would be harder. But things that haven't happened yet will be dim and uncertain, because of that factor of increasing improbability, and I don't think we can ever hope to see far ahead."

"That doesn't really matter." Her puzzled eyes had brightened slightly. "If you can just find Mr. Ironsmith—and then go on to help poor Mr. White."

Sitting at that little desk beneath the dome, Forester lifted his brown, wistful face again to that cloud of stars beyond the dead valley. His searching eyes saw only misty light already old before men first thought of crossing space, but his mind explored that binding medium where distance was no barrier and even the veil of time drew thin. The anxious child saw him nod at last, and the empty vagueness of his straining eyes turn to sharp attention.

"Do you see him?" she whispered huskily. "Mr. Ironsmith?"

"It's hard to see anything." Still he faced that toppling column of cold cloud, his voice slow with effort. "The equation tells the method, but I haven't learned the skill. It's hard to focus the perception—with all the universe in view. Hard not to see too much."

But he looked again, and presently she saw his faint smile of triumph.

"Yes, I've found Frank Ironsmith now." His voice was so low she had to lean across the desk to hear. "Back in the past. Back at Starmont, before the machines ever came. We must follow him down through time, and trace him when he leaves—"

Forester shuddered, and something hardened that pale smile into a grimace of pain and hate. His bald head sank forward and his drawn face turned gray and his thin lips whitened. The child recoiled a little from him, before she asked gently:

"What did you see that hurt you so?"

"Ironsmith and—Ruth." His terrible eyes focused on her face for an instant, and then looked searchingly back toward the leaning, luminous plume. "That doesn't matter now—except to him and Ruth and me." His voice was harsh and slow. "We must follow them from Starmont—though it's hard to trace the world lines, where they are teleported."

Jane waited, watching the changes on his haggard face. She saw effort and agony and dread, but at last he nodded again.

"I've found it." Still he looked at the leaning galaxy, and still his voice was hoarse with strain. "The den of the human renegades." He shook his head uneasily. "Though I still don't understand that Compact."

Shivering, the child stood watching. After a long time, the man came back to her in the silent cupola. Drawing a long tired breath, he smiled a greeting to her and then stood up to stretch, flinching when he put too much weight on his knee.

"Did you find Mr. Ironsmith?" she whispered. "Now?"

"I followed him and Ruth, and I found the traitors' nest." He began limping restlessly about the gloomy cupola. "I saw them there together, a few days ago. But now he's gone—I don't know where." His baffled eyes flickered back toward the far galaxy. "Still on Wing IV, I imagine—probably helping the humanoids complete that platinum brain. But I'm afraid to look for him there anymore, because I felt the potential of it when I tried." His thin frame shivered. "The psychophysical energy of that mechanical brain," he breathed harshly, "reaching out to operate every man alive—and already terribly strong."

"Then what—what can we do?"

"I looked ahead." His voice was shaken with the conflict of fear and resolution. "That factor of uncertainty makes things blurred and dim, but I think I saw him coming back to Ruth. I think I know the place to wait."

"Where?"

"On that planet where the humanoids are paying off their human friends." His stubbled face was taut and dark and savage. "It's about three light-years from Wing IV—as near as the machines want men to come. The renegades seem to be the only people there—and they're doing pretty well, thank you!"

He scowled at the toppling arch of far-off stars.

"That must be one of the first worlds the humanoids took, I think, too late to prevent atomic and rhodomagnetic wars; looking back a hundred years in time, I couldn't find anything but charred ruins, and huge bomb craters, and sterile deserts still deadly with atomic residues. But the machines have fixed everything up for their friends. The craters are level now, and the continents green again, and the residues all cleaned up. I suppose the renegades gave some psychophysical help with that, because radioactives aren't easy to remove from the soil and the seas."

He wiped his lean face with the loose gray sleeve.

"I still don't understand," he told her. "Not how men could do what they have done. But Frank Ironsmith isn't the first. I could see others like him gathering there, years ago. I can't tell all they've learned or done—spying on them can't be very safe. But they're—powerful!"

Jane was biting her grimy knuckles, listening silently.

"I didn't see any weapon, but such men don't need physical

weapons," he went on bleakly. "I don't know what unseen traps they may have set, or what unknown forces they have ready to destroy us. But I didn't see any evidence that they understand mass-detonation. Perhaps I can kill Ironsmith, and what others I must, and then somehow force the humanoids to give men a better deal."

She nodded apprehensively, and then, when she found they had still an hour to wait, she shyly confessed that she was hungry. He took her down to that white kitchen which the new unconscious power of his mind had shaped from the substance of the rock, and inexpertly fixed a meal. He watched her eat, but his own stomach felt too uncomfortable for food and presently he went to his room for another antacid capsule.

The mirror in the bathroom gave him a shocking glimpse of sunken, bloodshot eyes and a sick gray pallor beneath his unshaven beard; and the flapping gray pajamas seemed a comic battle dress. When he tried to change into a new blue suit he found in the closet, however, he couldn't work the rhodomagnetic snaps, and the thin gray cloth proved too tough to tear. He gave it up, and washed his face, and limped wearily back to where Jane waited in the dim cupola.

"It's time," he told her. "In about five minutes—if that was really Ironsmith—he'll be coming back to Ruth."

He paused to study his notations on another scrap of paper.

"The equation of teleportation," he said. "It describes the instantaneous deformation of the exchange forces, through that psychophysical binding component, to shift patterns of atomic identity—such patterns as we are—to new coordinates of space and time. The uncertainty factor seems to rule out any actual travel in time, but the shift in space is the art Mark White taught you."

Jane shook her head at the words, reproachfully, and trustingly put her hand in his. He glanced at the paper again, and crumpled it savagely, turning with the child toward the distant galaxy.

## 27

THE GLOOMY CUPOLA was gone instantly, and they stood in a strange, enormous room. Immense square pillars the color of silver supported the lofty roof, and wide windows of something clearer than glass showed the green rolling hills and blue friendly sky of the traitors' planet. Other great white-pillared buildings shone like silver crowns on other hills, and wind made a sparkle on dark far-off water.

"He'll meet her there." Forester nodded at the wide stair outside the open doorway, his voice hoarse and cold. "We'll be ready."

Beckoning sharply for her to follow, he limped hastily across that vast floor, between rows of tall transparent display cases.

"Where are they all?" she whispered uneasily. "Mr. Iron-smith's terrible friends?"

"Not here." He didn't look back. "Because this is a museum of war. I suppose all these old weapons were collected for historical research—I don't imagine the renegades would need them for anything else. Anyhow, the place isn't popular. I think we can wait here, safe—Huh!"

An impact of sharp surprise had stopped him. For a moment he stood gaping blankly at something in a long crystal case, before he stumbled dazedly toward it. Jane watched him apprehensively. All the cases held weapons men had made. Clubs and spears and trays of arrow points. Knives and swords and rusty guns. And later illustrations of the long evolution of the tools of death. The display that had checked Forester was a long shell of shining metal, shaped for speed, with the parts from inside neatly labeled and spread out below.

"Please." She pulled at his gray sleeve. "What is that?"

"One of my rhodomagnetic missiles." His voice was a shaken rasping. "From Starmont. I'd suspected Ironsmith of looting the project, though I never guessed why." He swung nervously back toward the doorway. "So these are the men we've come to fight—who lay such weapons out to rust, along with displays of throwing sticks and plutonium bombs!"

Jane hung back as he started on, to watch a tiny flying thing which must have strayed from the meadows outside. She followed the flutter of its rainbow-colored wings above a case of catapults and early cannon, smiling at its hovering loveliness. Glancing back impatiently, Forester saw it. His thin face tightened.

"Don't look." He swung her from it, with a quivering violence. A hard light flashed where the winged thing had been. A clap like thunder made a hollow rumbling against the far walls, and the odor of something burned drifted bitter in the air.

She flinched from him, crying out. "Why did you do that?"

"I wanted to test the detonation equation again." His haggard face was gray with illness and shining with a cold film of sweat. "And I suppose that butterfly reminded me of Frank Ironsmith—so lazy and so useless and so brilliant."

Pity erased her hurt bewilderment, and then her face was bleak again with fear. Clinging to the man's thin arm, she followed him to the gray ugly bulk of a battle tank, placed as if for its rusty guns to command the doorway. He drew her down behind the bullet-scarred and fire-blackened armor of it, and they watched for Ironsmith to come.

The broad steps outside fell to curving walks and wide green lawns. Beyond a clear stream, the meadows were clumped with strange low trees that flamed with violet blooms. A man and a girl were walking beside the stream, holding hands. Showing no visible stain of infamy, they looked happy and brown and strong, and their laughter lifted softly. No humanoids followed to serve them—although on another green hill, small as a toy in the distance, a tall black ship from Wing IV was standing. Forester peered at them, crouching lower, and a sudden alarm made Jane Carter tug at his sleeve, whispering anxiously:

"Please don't hurt them!"

"They're the enemy." His voice made her shiver. "If they find us, we must kill them."

"Then I hope—I so hope they don't!"

The laughing couple had chosen a level site beyond the stream, and now they began putting up a gay-colored building. They had brought no visible tools or materials, nor any humanoids to help, yet the house they made went up very swiftly. The sections of it seemed to form in the stream, and float into place, and flow firmly together. Those two, Forester knew, must have found the unity of ferromagnetic and rhodomagnetic and platinomagnetic energies, and discovered the philosophers' stone of mind to shape that *prima materia* to their desires. He drew himself lower, appalled by the ominous ease of their creation, and started when the child touched him.

"There!" she breathed. "Is that—"

Peering around the war-scarred tank, he saw a man coming up the broad steps outside, but it wasn't Frank Ironsmith. The stranger was an old man, snowy-haired but lean and straight and tall as Mark White himself. His cragged, rawboned face had a look of austere command, and his great gnarled hands hung forward in an attitude of competent readiness for anything.

Forester looked unthinkingly for the vehicle in which the man had come, and saw none. He caught his breath and waited, then, watching covertly with hard narrowed eyes, ready to kill the old man if he started to come inside. But the stranger turned on the broad level above the steps, looking around expectantly and seeming himself to wait.

Jane relaxed a little, as if relieved that it hadn't been Ironsmith, but Forester was taut and quivering. Bright sweat shone on his twitching, sallow face, with his illness gray beneath the unshaven stubble, and the gnawing inside him lining his cheeks with pain. Wishing he had taken another antacid capsule, he set his teeth and held his breath and watched the silver steps.

Waiting too, the vigorous old stranger glanced idly across them into the museum, and then strolled to a low white parapet. He watched the man and girl across the stream until they saw him and paused at their work to wave to him gaily. A moment later he smiled and turned, striding to meet the man he must have come to meet.

"Still I don't see Ruth," Forester breathed harshly. "But here's our man—if that's what he is!"

Still there was no vehicle, but Frank Ironsmith came running up the steps, smiling and holding out his hand. His sandy head was bare, his pleasant face bright with a quiet elation. He looked warmly human, and he had to be a man, but Forester still couldn't understand him.

"Well, Ironsmith?" The old man's heavy rumble of a voice seemed both glad and anxious. "How're you doing with your grid?"

"Done." They shook hands genially. "I've just finished overseeing the humanoids hooking together the main conduits, at the safety breaks. We can use it to go after Clay Forester as soon as we get an operating potential built up. If it works the way the tests with White and his gang have showed, I don't think even such unfortunate cases will ever be dangerous again."

Jane Carter huddled away from Forester, watching the grimace of effort twisting his haggard face and the fury burning in his hollowed eyes, shrinking from the detonation that would destroy Ironsmith. But nothing harmed the smiling man.

"No!" Forester whispered hoarsely, the deadly purpose relaxing from his dark face. "I can't kill Ruth."

For the woman who had been his wife was already coming to join the waiting men. She looked tall and joyous. Her hair was red-glinting black, and her long gown crimson and black, and all he knew for an instant was the fact of her utter loveliness.

"My darling!" she called. "I'm so glad you're home."

Behind the fire-scarred tank, Forester came stiffly to his feet. But her joy was for Ironsmith. He watched the man run down the steps to meet her, and her arms open for him, and her bright lips part for his kiss. And Forester's face, under the untidy stubble, was livid with his agony. His stringy fists opened and clenched and opened uselessly again. He stumbled to the doorway of that peaceful museum of war, hobbling painfully on the leg the humanoids had set, and stopped between the silver pillars there.

Forgotten, Jane Carter ran after him. Too frightened even to whimper, she crouched again behind the flapping folds of his gray pajamas, watching with him. Outside the tall old man stood with his back to them, surveying Ironsmith and Ruth with a fond approval as they turned slowly from their long embrace. Ironsmith murmured something, and she whispered softly:

"Don't be gone so long again."

"Next time will be longer." Forester's voice was harshly uncontrolled. "Ruth—stand away from him!"

They all swung to face him then, with an unstartled calm which terrified him. The old man's seamed and cragged face hardened with a stern regret. Ironsmith stood with his arm still around the woman, unalarmed. It was shocked pity, and not terror, which widened Ruth's dark eyes.

"Clay Forester!" She seemed breathless, and wounded. "What—what are you doing here?"

Forester limped toward them across the wide platform, trembling violently. His hollowed face was bloodless. His bad knee buckled and he got back his balance awkwardly, catching a ragged breath of pain. The child kept close behind him, silent and afraid.

"I'll tell you!" He spat his answer. "And you'd better listen—all of you." His scowling vehemence included that calm old man. "Because now I can follow you across the universe, if you try to run away. And now I've a better weapon, Frank, than those you stole from me."

And his gaunt head jerked scornfully back toward the crys-

tal case behind him, which displayed the parts of that dismem-
bered rhodomagnetic missile.

"The Starmont project had served its purpose," Ironsmith
protested mildly. "I know you must have felt that it was really
needed, once, for defense against the Triplanet Powers. But
they aren't launching any more aggressions. Because the humanoids are looking after their people now—dictators and
space admirals and rhodomagnetic engineers, as well as those
who were better pleased by the change. Anyhow, I knew you
had no further use for your deadly little toys, and they were
needed here to complete our historical exhibits—"

No longer listening, Forester was pointing with a thin
shaking arm out across the scattered silver buildings on the
hills, toward the far estuary.

"Look!" he broke in hoarsely. "Watch that rock!"

The old man and Ironsmith and the woman all turned
slowly, frowning as if with pained reproof. The rock stood far
away, where wind-ruffled indigo water met the limpid sky, the
black point of it accented by a wisp of shining foam. Forester
gestured as if to strike it with his clenched hand, and it turned
to incandescent fury.

"I'll guard us," Ironsmith murmured, "against the radiation."

And something screened the blinding light of that appalling dome swelling out at the speed of sound from where the
rock had been, until the terrible flame of it began to soften at
last into a flow of strange tawny color, reddening in an ominous dusk. Then the screening something must have been
removed, for that dusk lifted suddenly. Presently the floor
shuddered.

"You shouldn't have done that, Forester." The old man
shook his white mane regretfully. "Seafowl nested on that
rock."

Weakly trembling, Forester brought his eyes back from the
great cloud of fire and darkness still mushrooming upward to
stand like an ominous symbol of ultimate destruction against

the peaceful sky. The three before him looked disturbingly unimpressed. Ironsmith, who must have set up that unseen barrier against the light of the explosion, stood gravely with his arm still around the woman.

"Clay!" Ruth's voice was choked with a hurt concern. "What do you think you're doing?"

"I know what I'm doing." He limped grimly toward her. "I'm going to smash your plot with the humanoids—this monstrous Compact to smother and mechanize all the human race. I'm going to fight the machines for a better deal—to give every man, everywhere, the same freedom a few of you have sold us out to get." He swung vehemently to the sober man beside her. "Ironsmith, I'm going to kill you. I'm willing to bargain with any of the rest, but you've done too much. Have you anything to say?"

Mildly, Ironsmith said, "You might specify your charges."

"I think they're wide enough." Forester grinned sardonically. "You turned against your kind, to help the humanoids. You spied on Starmont. You sabotaged Project Thunderbolt. You betrayed Mark White. You wrecked our effort to change the Prime Directive. Now you're building this platinum brain, to operate us all like more machines."

Trembling, he tried to lower his voice.

"Those are the crimes I know, and I think they're wicked enough." Gulping, he stiffened as if to a spasm of pain. "I won't even ask how long you schemed to take my wife away. Beside all the rest, that doesn't matter." His sick eyes flickered at Ruth. "Now, have you any defense to make?"

He paused, swaying on his bad knee, but Ironsmith stood calmly silent.

"Get away from him, Ruth!" Agony shivered in his voice. "Because I don't want to hurt you—whatever you may have done. With our lives, I suppose, some of the blame is mine. But I'm going to kill this monstrous traitor now—and you'll be hurt if you stand too near."

"Please, Clay—don't be ugly." The woman didn't move,

and her low voice seemed merely distressed. "We can help you yet, if only you'll let us—and forget your silly threats." She shook her head sadly, as he lifted his skinny fist. "Because you can't hurt us, really."

Standing in a paralysis of rage and helpless pain, he dazedly watched the glow of devotion on her face when she glanced at the calm man beside her, and he wondered blankly at the limpid pity in her eyes when she looked back at him.

"Please, Clay—won't you try to see it our way?" He saw her tears. "Because there's nothing unfair about Frank. And nothing to blame but Project Thunderbolt. I was always sorry for you, Clay, and I used to be sorry for myself. Because the project was your wife and your child. You never needed me."

Forester nodded unwillingly, stiff with his pain.

"Don't—don't blame Frank." She tried to control her trembling voice. "Because he wouldn't take me away from Starmont until after you had abandoned me there, drugged with euphoride, when you wandered away on your insane adventuring. He brought me here, and woke my memory, and taught me this real felicity. We're in love, Clay. I—I hope you'll try to wish us well." Her white throat pulsed. "Won't you, Clay?"

"No!" With that choked sob, Forester pushed the child behind him to shield her from the fire of annihilation. Swaying to the gray illness of his fury, he thrust his quivering fist at the two before him, and he tried to kill them both.

## 28

FORESTER TRIED WITH the weapon of his mind, and he waited for the man and the woman to die. No part of their bodies was detonated into dreadful flame, however. They didn't even fall. They merely stood there on the silver steps, Ironsmith urbanely grave, Ruth shaking her head in sad reproof.

"Huh!" Forester gasped with a shocked unbelief, as if the two had wounded him with some unfair blow. His bewildered eyes went back to the far horizon, where that tall mushroom of ominous cloud was beginning to thin and fade against the blue summer sky. He looked for another rock.

"Stop it, Forester!" the gaunt old man broke in hastily. "There's no use wrecking all the landscape. Because you can't hurt anybody—not with psychophysics."

Forester retreated from him warily.

"You needn't be alarmed," the stranger rumbled softly. "You can't injure us, and we don't need to retaliate." He smiled, patient and not unkind. "If you'll calm yourself enough to listen, I might explain that you've apparently overlooked a couple of basic fundamentals."

Forester stood swaying, blank and ill.

"You should have learned that the psychophysical functions are normally unconscious," the old man said. "They belong very largely to that major fraction of the brain tissue which is not used for conscious thought. Full conscious control of them always requires long training, and a high degree of integration to remove the interfering internal conflicts. You should know that—though you have astonished us."

The cragged face showed a kind of admiration.

"I don't suppose you know the wonder of your own achievements. It is a rare thing that a mind divided by such savage conflicts as yours is able to attain any conscious psychophysical control at all. The explanation of what you have done, I believe, is in your unusual grasp of the physical and mathematical aspects, as well as in the tendency toward psychophysical compensation for physical handicaps in individuals under intense emotional stress."

Forester stood numb and stupid with his pain.

"Yet, for all your incredible accomplishments you still show no real understanding." The old man turned gravely stern again. "You've just proved your blindness, with this insane attempt at murder. Anybody less crippled with hate would have learned, long ago, that psychophysical energy cannot be used for such destructive purposes.

"Because it's creative—can't you see that? The basic creative force of the universe. It builds stable atoms, out of disruptive ferromagnetic and rhodomagnetic components. It is the mother of suns and galaxies, and it aids the condensation of planets. It kindles life. It is the driving power of organic evolution. And it *is* mind."

Forester tried not to yield to his fatigue and his grief and his shock. Thin blades of pain stabbed through his swollen knee, and small fangs of hungry agony nibbled at his stomach, and a groggy weakness tried to possess him. But he shook his head and he tried to listen.

"Psychophysical energy is mind," the old man insisted softly. "Every atom in the universe has mentality to the tiny extent of its own creative component. Every molecule has more. Every new development of structure—in the complex organic molecules, in the simple viruses at the borderline of life in the human brain—each such forward step in evolution is brought about by a new emergence of that building component, on a higher level.

"Some of the mystics among us can see the working of it on levels even higher. Studying the structure and the function of the entire creative mind arising from the substance of the whole universe, to make and shape all things, they perceive the actual anatomy of God."

Forester wanted to listen. But the phrases seemed too large and vague, and the warm breeze became suddenly oppressive. Sweat began trickling down his forehead and his taut flanks, and something squeezed his chest, and his knee let him lurch and stagger again.

"—sick, Forester," the old man was saying. "You can't injure us, but the attempts are killing yourself. Because the energy of life and mind—and divinity, if you like—is always creative. When you attempt to turn it against itself you set up conflicts which act to destroy your own identity. A mind, like an atom or a star, can be shattered by a failure of the psychophysical component."

His knee buckled, and the tall man caught him. Dazedly, aching all over, he sat down on the broad silver stair. The breeze from the far blue estuary seemed suddenly cold. Wet with a nervous perspiration, he began to shiver in the thin pajamas. Some stray pollen grain gave him a brief fit of sneezing. He blew his nose and tried to listen.

"The full conscious control of the psychophysical functions requires a whole mind," the stranger said. "A mature and integrated personality, free of inner strains. No man who has discovered that mental poise and peace would be capable of attempting murder. No man who has not would be able to commit it—not psychophysically. Because that creative energy will not destroy itself. Does that tell you why you failed?"

Forester nodded uncertainly. Drugged with the poisons of fatigue and pain and defeat, he tried heavily to understand.

"You imagined you were fighting for the public good," the old man said. "That creative purpose—however mistaken—explains what you did accomplish. Didn't you have the most of your success with projects entirely creative?"

"That's true." Forester peered up dully. "And I think you've answered the most amazing riddle. When we escaped from Wing IV, you see, we somehow got to a planet outside the galaxy. Somehow I built a shelter for us there—or Jane says I did." Wonderment haunted his voice. "I could never remember."

"A creative project." The gaunt man smiled briskly. "Therefore, no internal division existed. Imagined danger to the child was your stimulus. The unconscious function made successful use of your conscious knowledge. But your murderous attempt had to fail, just now, because it was destructive—the utmost folly."

Forester shivered, and sneezed again. He could feel the trembling fear of the child, and he put out his stringy arm to draw her to him. Apathetic, yet still defiant, he peered enviously down at Ironsmith and Ruth, below him on the silver stair.

"So you can't hurt us, Forester." He drew back stiffly from Ironsmith's suave assurance. "Because psychophysical energy creates, as surely as masses gravitate. I might have taught you that long ago—if you had been a little less absorbed in machines for smashing planets, and more willing to trust the humanoids."

Too cold and ill to answer, Forester merely drew Jane a little closer. Her tiny fingers came up to touch his twitching cheek, sympathetically. That small act of compassion blurred his eyes with tears. Wiping at them angrily with the thin gray sleeve, he sat staring at the tall stranger who had been his wife.

"Please, Clay—try not to hate us so!" Her pity cut him with a thin blade of pain. "Because your mind is sick, and hate is most of the sickness, and you can't get well until your hate is cured. Until you learn the meaning of love."

Heavily, he shook his head. He didn't really hate her now, because all the past was lost. He thought he was glad to see the bright happiness binding her and Ironsmith, because the past was gone. But he didn't want to hear her voice again, or smell the musky scent of Sweet Delirium, or think again of her beside him in the bed.

"Sure, Ruth," he muttered bleakly. "I understand."

"I knew you would." Her quick little smile hurt him with too many memories. He looked away, trying not to hear the tenderness in her voice, because he wanted nothing from her now. "And we can help you, Clay," she was saying softly. "With Frank's new grid."

"Huh?" Taut with protest, he came painfully to his feet on the silver steps. "What do you mean?"

"Yes, Forester, we'll take care of you." Ironsmith answered, still absently swinging the woman's hand, watching him with amicably candid eyes. "We designed that installation just to handle such troublesome cases as yours, where partial knowledge and inadequate power and mistaken resentments become too difficult for the humanoids to manage."

And the serene gray eyes of the younger man looked unseeingly away, as if to examine something far beyond the silver pillars and the vast crystal windows of the war museum with another sort of vision. Shrinking from him, Forester was washed with a sudden chilling tide of dreadful recollection. He remembered four human machines he had seen marching too swiftly and too gracefully through that dark laboratory on Wing IV. He wanted no help from that monstrous platinum brain, and he shivered when Ironsmith's far gaze came back to him.

"We'll be ready for you soon." Ironsmith nodded, smiling pleasantly. "The installation is mechanically complete, but it will take us just a little longer to build the psychophysical potentials up to operating levels—"

Convulsively, Forester broke free of his terror. Picking up the frightened child, he fled with her up the silver steps, toward the open doorway and a crystal case beyond.

"Listen, Jane!" he whispered hoarsely as he ran. "I want you to go away—back to our shelter. I think you'll be safe—because I'm going to blow this planet up—with the detonator in that case!"

"Please—don't!" She squirmed protestingly in his arms. " 'Cause—don't you see—even Mr. Ironsmith isn't really bad."

He almost paused. But he didn't want to be a flesh machine, surely run by any infallible platinum brain. His knee shuddering under him, Jane too heavy in his arms, he came to the top of the steps. His anxious eyes found the white palladium cylinder of the rhodomagnetic detonator among the labeled parts of the stolen missile displayed in the case—a weapon even smaller than his knobby fist, but big enough.

Stumbling on, he glanced back fearfully. The three behind had not moved to interfere. Perhaps they didn't guess his object. Or maybe their psychophysical powers, like his own, were useless for violence. They merely stood watching, Ruth with an aching pity on her face. He was suddenly sorry she must die.

"Please!" Jane was whimpering. "Please don't—"

He was sure he hadn't noticed any raised threshold across the wide door before, but something tripped him now. His bad knee folded, pitching him forward. He tried to save his balance, and tried to shield the child, and finally fell. His head struck the armor of that rusty battle tank.

For a time he merely lay there, dazed with his pain and his unexpected failure. Jane Carter was kneeling by him, crying. At first he thought he had hurt her as he fell, and then he felt her trying to lift his bursting head. He scrambled feebly to get up, and felt a sickening stab in his knee.

"Better wait, Forester," he heard the old man booming. "Wait for the grid."

Laboriously, he pushed his elbows beneath him, and hitched himself painfully backward far enough to prop his body against the massive treads and the armored trucks. He could feel warm blood in his hair, but he tried to grin at Jane's tearful face.

"Good try," he breathed. "Nearly—made it!"

He tried to push himself a little higher, but the surging breakers of pain hammered him down again.

"Lie still, you blundering fool." The aged stranger's voice seemed faint and far away. "Don't you think you've made mistakes enough?"

He could see the gaunt man dimly then, following through that wide entrance with a vigorous stride—and now there was no longer any lifted threshold, where he had tripped. He looked dully beyond for Frank Ironsmith and Ruth, but they were gone.

"They went back to Wing IV," the old man said. "While the platinum grid is entirely automatic, there's a control room from which it can be stopped. The room is closed to the mechanicals that maintain the grid, and shielded against its own operating forces. We are going to keep watchers posted there, and Ironsmith has gone back to put Ruth and another on duty. A needless precaution," he added, "because that grid is as perfect as the one that runs the humanoids. It can't go wrong."

Propped against the cold rusty steel, Forester waited blankly. Blood made a sticky rivulet down his stubbled cheek, dripping slowly on the gray pajamas. He reached with a feeble gesture of farewell, to touch the child's dark hair. For the trial was over. The verdict was guilty. The sentence was death—by a very special sort of gallows, which made a mechanized puppet of the victim. He was waiting for the hangman.

"Don't you worry, Dr. Forester." Jane bravely tried to smile. "That machine had me once, and it doesn't really hurt."

"It doesn't hurt at all," the old man promised heartily. "It heals." His rugged face seemed kindly now, as if he felt apologetic for a sentence too severe. "It can really help you, Forester. And I want to help you. I fought the humanoids, and even attempted to alter the Prime Directive."

Forester blinked at him, rasping faintly, "Who are you?"

"My name's Mansfield," the tall man said. "Dr. Warren Mansfield."

## 29

FORESTER TRIED TO sit up, but the pressure of pain forced him back against the blackened tank. A weary detachment had begun to soothe his useless fury, but now a bitter wonder shook him.

"Mansfield?" he muttered bleakly. "A Mansfield made the humanoids."

"That was I." The gaunt man nodded serenely. "Because I wanted to save men from themselves. I built the Prime Directive into the relays that govern them, and protected it from change—and tried mistakenly to change it."

Beyond the maker of the humanoids, Forester could see a display case made of something scarcely visible, and a tiny silver-colored cylinder inside it. He tried once more to lurch his body higher against the rusty armor, and again ruthless pain pressed him back.

"A common error." Mansfield shook his head sadly. "Many another has made it—though few have come so near a disastrous success as you and I did, Forester, in our turns. The common cause, I suppose, is a want of philosophy. I know that I had none, thirty years ago, when I tried to blow up Wing IV with a rhodomagnetic detonating beam—and fortunately failed. Egotism ruled me, instead of intelligence. I wanted freedom, before I had earned it. Childishly, I forgot the stark necessity behind the humanoids."

Forester struggled protestingly, and had to gasp again with pain.

"Don't move," the old man urged calmly. "If you'll just wait a few minutes longer, the psychophysical grid will be ready to pick your body up and fix all that's wrong with you. Thirty years ago, I wasn't quite so lucky. Because Ironsmith hadn't designed his grid."

"Huh?" Forester caught his breath and tried to ease his knee. "Mark White told me how your own machines exiled you from Wing IV when you tried to modify them, and hounded you on from planet to planet." His voice was harshly accusing. "I don't suppose you trusted them quite so far yourself, back in those days?"

"I didn't."

"Then tell me why you sold us out!"

"Nobody sold out, Forester." The old man was gravely emphatic. "In my case, I simply changed—rather, the humanoids changed me. Let me tell you how it was—from my standpoint, instead of Mark White's. Perhaps I can help you welcome the grid."

Forester shook his head sullenly, but he had to listen.

"Thirty years ago," Mansfield repeated, "there wasn't any Ironsmith grid. The humanoids had inherited the same scornful ignorance of the human mind I used to have, and their mechanical mind is not inventive. The psychophysical properties of the platinum metals were not then known. When the humanoids finally caught me, after my last defeat, they had to operate."

"Operate?" Forester stiffened. "For what?"

"To remove the conflict and the hate that kept me from accepting their service. They also took a part of my memory, because it was dangerous to the Prime Directive. Difficult surgery—I'm glad the new grid will make such operations needless. But it did give me freedom."

"So that's the way?" Forester shivered against the steel. "Did they operate on Ironsmith, too? Or did he get his remarkable immunity in some kind of ugly deal—"

"Neither," Mansfield said. "There aren't any deals. The humanoids are simply excellent psychologists—you'll have to admit I designed them well." The lean man smiled briefly. "They were always able to distinguish those who do need watching from that fortunate few who don't. Your own dangerous traits must have been obvious to them, and they could see that Ironsmith was harmless."

Harmless? Forester caught his breath for an angry protest, but even that slight movement made another surge of pain beneath his matted hair, thrusting him down again.

"They left me free, soon after the operation," Mansfield continued. "They even let me carry on my research. The physical sciences were still out of bounds, of course, because you'll have to grant that most laboratory equipment is pretty dangerous, even for mental adults. But there was parapsychology."

Forester's haggard eyes narrowed warily.

"I had always been a skeptic, as I suppose you were." The old man waited serenely for his stiff nod. "That conscious denial of the psychophysical phenomena usually comes, I think, from some buried rebellion against love—against the creative power of the unconscious psychophysical urge. Removing hatred from my mind, the humanoids also liberated my repressed psychophysical capacities. The telepathic function came first, and I was soon in contact with the pioneer philosophers here."

"Philosophers?" Forester rasped his sardonic challenge. "Or traitors?"

"Does this look like a den of treason?" The old man turned soberly to point through the white-pillared doorway at the pleasant land without, the clustered silver towers crowning kindly hills and the wind smiling on the blue estuary. "No, Forester, this is the Psychophysical Institute. It was formed nearly seventy years ago, by a few adult and able men released by the service of the humanoids from their physical cares and their limiting preoccupations with physical science. They turned naturally to philosophy. And then to a new sort of psychology which their true orientation made possible—an actual science of the mind. They were looking for truth, and they found it. The service of the machines kept them from placing too much value on such spectacular practical stunts as telurgy—"

Forester frowned his dull puzzlement.

"That's the term for mental transmutation of mass," the old man explained. "The same art you used, unconsciously, to build your shelter on that extragalactic planet. Quite a trick, because the telurgist must learn to perceive and grasp all the subatomic structure of the stuff he wants to change, and he requires an exact knowledge of the atomic and molecular and crystalline and gross physical structure of whatever he wants to make. Your telurgic shelter shows quite a remarkable unconscious adaptation.

"Such practical tools of the mind were useful, even to those first philosophic theoreticians. Scattered over all the planets the humanoids were overrunning, they discovered one another by telepathy. Teleportation brought them together here, when the Institute was founded. Telurgy freed them from an uncomfortable dependence on care from the machines, and clairvoyance soon warned them of the mounting danger to Wing IV from such dangerous fanatics as you are—and I was, when I thought I had made the mechanicals too perfect.

"The Compact was formed when we first warned the humanoids of dangers which they lacked the paramechanical power, as they call it, to foresee or avoid. They agreed to tolerate and support the Institute, in return for our necessary aid."

Nodding bleakly, Forester contrived at last to heave his shoulders a little higher against the tank. He reached gingerly to touch his puffy knee, and had to set his teeth against a sob of pain. His fevered eyes swept back across the neat displays of weapons beyond his reach.

"Part of the Institute." The gaunt man gestured casually at the cases of wooden spears and guided missiles, of blowgun darts and biotoxin ampules, of flint points and rhodomagnetic detonators. "Collected tokens to remind us of the old enemy born again with every human being. For life hurts every man, many of us badly. The wounds must heal before we are actually adult. Some recover easily, most of us slowly. A few are deformed beyond any natural cure. The first great goal of our new psychology has been to mend such mental injuries, safely and completely. Now I think we can, with Ironsmith's grid."

Forester was doggedly trying to listen, though his knee was a twisting torment and his head had become a beaten gong of torture beneath his clot-stiffened hair and he felt ill from the old agony of his stomach slowly digesting itself. He moved laboriously against the tank, looking carefully away from that tiny palladium cylinder that still contained a planet's fate.

"I want you to understand," Mansfield rumbled on persuasively. "I want you to see that our motives were simple and human and good. That all we've done had to be. Perhaps you don't yet like the humanoids—but the other alternative was death. They're here to stay, anyhow, and I want to show you the very useful change they've forced in the direction of human progress."

Forester lay sullenly still.

"Technology had got out of step with mentality," the cragged man insisted. "Don't you see? Technicians too busy to see the tragic consequences were putting such toys as rhodo-magnetic detonators in the hands of mental savages. I made the humanoids, to put an end to that. Such technicians as your-self—with the highest possible intentions—had wrecked the balance of civilization, so that it was breaking up like an off-center flywheel. The humanoids simply made them take a holi-day until the philosophers could restore a better equilibrium.

"Such rebellious unhappy men as you and Mark White were simply trapped in that dilemma. Even when desperation turned you to parapsychology, you failed to do much with it because you weren't philosophers. You needed the humanoids to give you time to learn to think. Yet you couldn't accept them when they came, because that tragic fault in your world had already flawed your minds with hate—the very antithesis of the creative psychophysical force. You didn't want the truth, but only tricks you could turn to weapons.

"Ironsmith, now, is another type." Admiration lit Mans-field's vigorous features. "The type who made the Institute—though I don't imagine he ever won much success back at Starmont. Because your true philosopher is free from such de-structive drives as excessive ambition. Probably you considered him something of a bum."

"Completely worthless." That point, at least, Forester ap-proved, and he tried to grin through a haze of pain. "Except that he was good at math."

"But Ironsmith found himself when the humanoids came. They saw he had no harm in him, and they left him free. When they learned of his interest in parapsychology, they put him in touch with the Institute—he used to play chess with me, when he was learning telepathy. Now, designing the platinomag-netic relays that made the new grid possible, he has turned out to be a brilliant psychophysical engineer as well as a philoso-pher."

"I see." Forester nodded painfully. "So that grid's the god you spoke about—built to run men everywhere like streamlined machines!"

"Won't you try to understand?" Mansfield begged. "Can't you see that any society must shape and train its members? And somehow discover and control and reclaim maladjusted individuals—before they destroy others or themselves? That's the real function of the grid—education. Don't you see that?"

"I see Mark White, after it got him," Forester whispered harshly. "A meat machine, smiling out of some cold hell! I don't want to be another mechanical unit, operated by Ironsmith's relays—not even if they are efficient. I'd rather—"

His whisper failed, for breathing, even, had become laborious to him now. He lay glaring helplessly at Mansfield. He was afraid to look at that bright detonator, but his blood-stiffened fingers itched to feel the cold weight and the ultimate, conclusive power of it.

"Your mind's still closed," the old man was chiding him patiently. "Or you could see that the grid is just another tool, like the humanoids, built to serve mankind. Certainly it's no monstrous god arisen from the machine—the God our mystics see, existing in the total creative force of all the universe, is incomparably more than any mechanism."

Forester shook his head, because it hurt too much to think.

"The Ironsmith grid is just an instrument," Mansfield insisted. "It was designed to focus and apply the unconscious psychophysical energies of all mental adults, everywhere—I think you're physicist enough to understand that the residual platinomagnetic fields of the relays themselves would be rather too weak to coerce one unwilling moron. It's no mechanical brain, but something far more useful—a convenient vehicle for the racial human mind. The perfect instrument of a new order of intelligence. It can't be evil or destructive, because its very nature is creative. The power of it won't be arbitrarily authoritarian, as you seem to fear, but completely democratic. Because it is just a tool to unite the unconscious minds of all people in whom love had displaced hate, and each will share equally in the direction of it."

The tall man's voice was booming now.

"This new emergence of the mind of the race is a huge stride forward in the long evolution of intelligence from the mental component of matter. It follows the gradual birth of organic life from almost lifeless atoms, and the slow rise of the individual mind from life. It is another higher synthesis, on another level of unfolding creation—and no one not a mystic can see what lies beyond."

Mansfield looked down at him, compassionately.

"You're sick, Forester. You need the grid—as most men do. Because the whole race was sick on my old world and yours. The cause beneath most of our symptoms, I think, was a runaway physical technology—killing us like the runaway cells of an organic cancer. But the humanoids have removed that social cancer, and now I believe the new control of the Ironsmith grid will assure a balanced growth and heal such unhealthy cells as you are—"

The old man broke off suddenly, smiling, and Forester stiffly turned his head to see Ironsmith come striding briskly in between the silver columns.

"Ruth stayed on duty," the young man said. "And we're reaching out! The operating potential is coming up fast, as we find and unite more and more well-integrated minds." He glanced down brightly at the man on the floor. "Ready, Forester?"

## 30

PROPPED AGAINST THE battered tank, the child whimpering silently beside him, Forester didn't try to answer. His pain-fogged brain hadn't followed all the brief against him, but he knew the case was closed. He was condemned, and Frank

Ironsmith the cheery hangman. He lay now looking at that white cylinder he couldn't reach, enduring the slow thudding in his head and the swollen tightness of his knee and the gnawing fangs of his ulcers, waiting for the platinum brain to seize his being.

"Please!" Jane Carter's breathless whisper startled him. "I know how to help you now!"

He felt her leave his side. He glimpsed her instantly again, stooping to pick up the rhodomagnetic detonator in that transparent case. Then she was already back, thrusting the small palladium cylinder into his grasping hands. His blood-stained fingers moved with an automatic skill, stripping out the safety keys. He set his trembling thumb on the firing bar, gasping hoarsely at the child:

"Thank you, Jane. Now save yourself!"

He waited to see her frightened nod. Then his shuddering thumb came down, in an act of ultimate rebellion against the humanoids and that omnipotent mechanical brain, in a last savage stroke against Ironsmith's pink-faced, intolerable rightness, in a frantic last attack against the very pain tormenting him. For the detonating field would instantly unstabilize all mass within forty yards—the stuff of the rusty tank and the museum floor and his own sick flesh—and convert it into energy to shatter the planet. The bar moved easily, and he felt the spring begin to yield.

Yet something stopped his thumb.

He shook his head painfully, glaring feebly at his enemies. The old man's ramblings hadn't impressed him. He still hated Ironsmith, and he still feared the grid. Here in his hands was escape, and triumphant retaliation. But something in him refused to press the bar.

"I don't know why," he breathed to Jane, "but I just can't." Carefully, he locked the two safety keys back into their slots, and returned the cylinder to her. "Please put it back."

"But I can tell you why." Ironsmith had strolled easily nearer, smiling in candid friendship. "You didn't kill us—not

even when we let you try—because you don't want to, really, because you're already yielding, in spite of yourself, to love."

They had let him try. That meant they must already have foreseen his failure, with their extratemporal vision, before they allowed him to begin that last useless effort. Apathetic frustration overwhelmed him, but he would acknowledge no surrender to love.

"Go ahead," he muttered harshly. "I'm ready now."

And he turned his scornful face away from the old man's cragged kindliness and the young one's sunburned benevolence. The strength fled out of him, dropping his body back against the rusty steel. His emaciated head sagged on his shoulder, smearing the gray pajamas with tears and sticky blood. He lay quivering stiffly to his painful sobs of self-defeat, waiting for the power of the grid.

Forester waited—and then he was standing again in the huge bedroom the humanoids had built for him at Starmont. The transition was abrupt. He had felt no power seize him, and now he had no sense of any time gone. Automatically shifting his weight from his hurt knee, he looked anxiously around him for Jane Carter.

The village swains and maids still danced in the high murals, luminous and gay. The vast east window was now an amber green, filling the room with a mellow radiance. Motionless before him stood a steel-eyed humanoid. But he couldn't find the child.

He recoiled from the machine—until his first unthinking terror dissolved into a keenly pleased awareness of the molten gold of light flowing across its lean, ideal perfection, accenting its lean, alert solicitude. He smiled a little at the serene beauty of it, puzzled and already faintly astonished at that shock of irrational revulsion.

"Where's Jane Carter?" he asked huskily. "Did that platinum brain—take her?"

For he thought that his own awakening psychophysical capacities must have somehow snatched him out of danger again, but failed to save the child. The machine's serene reply brushed him with a vanishing wonderment.

"Miss Carter did require special service," it purred. "She was admitted to the care of the Ironsmith grid at the same time you were."

"I?" A momentary disbelief lifted his voice. "But I didn't feel . . ."

His voice faded, with the dissipation of his first startled incredulity. For he knew somehow, without any conscious recollection, that the stimulating energies of the grid had remolded and restored him, and he felt a fleeting wonder at his own astonishment, as if the knowledge of everything lay in him, just below the level of awareness.

"Men don't ever feel the grid," the machine was saying, "because the individual consciousness is suspended."

"What—" Dread tried to choke him, but he shrugged it lightly off. Because the grid was nothing more terrible than a channel and a tool for the goodwill and the unconscious aid of people who loved him. How could anyone fear that? Swallowing his huskiness, he asked quietly, "What did it do to me?"

"It repaired your body, and retrained your mind."

Lifting quickly to his face, his searching fingers found that clotted stiffness of drying blood gone, and the unshaven beard. Reaching higher, to examine the long gash where his scalp had been cut against that armored tank in the war museum, he found no wound or scar. That slow, thudding pain had left his head, and—he caught his breath.

"Let me—let me see a mirror."

The machine moved instantly to press the lowest stud in a row beside that immense translucent window—no concealed relay, but a button that he could reach. The amber glow went out, and the wide panel became a mirror, luminous with the soft light from the murals.

It reflected a dark stranger, taller and younger than he had been, not quite so skinny but lean and straight and fit. The balding head was haired again, the petulant twist gone from the lips. The deep scars of worry were all somehow erased. Even those durable gray pajamas with the impregnable rhodo-magnetic snaps were gone at last, for he wore a new blue suit with buttons that he himself could unfasten. Moving to get a better view, he recalled his twisted knee.

Oddly, he felt no pain. Bending to explore that old injury with his fingers, he found the swelling and the stiffness gone. The joint felt sound. He walked back across the soft floor, ex-perimentally, and found his step firm and sure. He smiled gratefully at the sleek, alert machine, and saw no response.

Because that was what it was—merely a machine. Neither good nor bad—he could hear Frank Ironsmith's protesting voice again, convincing now. Neither friend nor enemy, moved by neither love nor hate, it was doing the work for which Warren Mansfield had designed it—serving and obey-ing, and guarding men from harm.

Approaching it with that enlightened understanding, he prodded the nude plastic flank of it with an experimental fore-finger, and even slapped the lean curve of a silicone buttock resoundingly. There was no reaction. The slightest human need of its service or obedience or protection would trigger its remote relays, but nothing else could move it.

Turning his back on its blind benevolence, he wondered how long the grid had been teaching him the folly of his fears. How long had he been—blank? While he had no sense of any time lost, he was somehow curiously certain that not even all the unconscious energy of united minds flowing in that vast mechanism could have mended his sick body instantly. How long? He caught his breath to ask the question, but apprehen-sion checked him. Instead, he inquired:

"Jane Carter—is she still ruled by the grid?"

"Her Awakening Day was three years ago."

Three years! He must have spent all that time in featureless oblivion—and how much longer? A cold awe touched him and was gone—as if all that time lay very thinly covered just beneath the threshold of his own recollection. Yet he couldn't remember anything, actually, and he asked eagerly:

"Where is she now?"

"Away," the machine said. "Traveling."

"Tell her I want to see her."

"We can't reach her," the machine said. "She is beyond the range of our service, exploring planets where no men have been before."

"Can't I get any message to her?"

"Possibly you can secure information from one of her associates, sir. From Mr. Frank Ironsmith, perhaps. Or from Mr. Warren Mansfield or Mr. Mark White."

"Where are they?"

"Mr. Ironsmith is still with the Psychophysical Institute. Mr. Mansfield and Mr. White are living now at Dragonrock, in the intervals between their expeditions."

"So Mark White's free of the grid?" He smiled with relief. "I'd like to see him."

"Mr. White has anticipated your wish. He had been informed that you were to awaken today, and he is now aboard a rhodomagnetic cruiser on his way here. He'll be landing in a few minutes."

"Good!" Forester nodded, anxious to see how the grid had transformed that archenemy of the machines into an associate of Mansfield and Ironsmith. He couldn't keep his voice from catching as he asked, "And where's—Ruth?"

"With Mr. Ironsmith, sir." The pain from which he shrank had somehow been erased, and he felt only an eager interest when the machine added, "She sent a gift, to be delivered when you asked of her."

Another mechanical brought it to him. A thin rectangular block of something black, polished smooth and golden-veined, it carried a green-lettered message in Ruth's neat printing:

*Dearest Clay—*
*We're delighted that you're well again, and we both re-*
*joice in the new felicity you should discover now.*
                                        *Ruth and Frank*

Felicity—that was a pet word of hers. The plaque had a
faint, haunting hint of Sweet Delirium. He read the message
twice, before a stinging in his eyes blurred her clean printing.

"Please thank them both." His voice was quiet, surprisingly, as if his tears had been for nothing. "Please tell them I
wish them happiness together."

"We are telling them," the machine said. "But there is a
picture also, if you wish to see it."

He began to shake his head, recoiling from the pain of old
emotions, and found again that they had vanished. Quickly he
whispered, "Let me see."

The humanoid pressed a stud at the base of the plaque, and
the green printing dissolved. The golden veinings faded, and
the dark surface became a window, through which he saw a
simple gay pavilion cupped in a green valley beneath the silver
towers of the Institute. Frank Ironsmith and Ruth came out of
it, waving at him gaily. The man looked heavier, pink with
health and calmly self-content, his sunburned jaws moving as if
he still were chewing gum. Ruth was straight and radiant, the
clean planes of her face firm with a quiet strength he had not
seen there before. They came on toward him, smiling in the
picture, until the stud clicked softly back again and that tiny
window closed itself. Even then the image of Ruth stayed in his
mind. She had never looked quite so young, he thought, not
even on the day of their own wedding back at Starmont, never
quite so light and free.

"Tell them I'm glad to see their own felicity." He grinned
at the grave machine. "Now please put the picture away for
me—and open this window."

Nodding a casual farewell to that curiously youthful and

untroubled reflection of himself, he watched the mechanical press another button. The mirror became a wide transparency, which slid down silently. A clean morning breeze came in to cool his face, and it brought him a sense of free well-being.

"There's the cruiser." The machine pointed gracefully. "Mr. White is landing now."

Turning to look, Forester gaped again. The red-paved landing stage, still empty, was as he had known it. Far away, however, beyond the uneven edge of the mountain's flat crown, he could see the rolling vastness of the desert he once had known—now no longer a tawny desolation. For new lakes shone blue in the valleys, above dams the humanoids must have built, and scattered villas made gay islets of color in a new sea of tender green, and now dark forests clad the higher summits, which had been harsh fangs of naked stone.

New forests, grown since he was here!

"That grid!" he breathed. "How long?"

He was turning, still almost afraid to put that question to the humanoid, when he caught a shimmer of color moving against the sky. The cruiser was dropping silently, the oval mirror of its hull aglow with blue and flowing green and the red reflection of the stage. It touched gently and Mark White jumped lightly down from the deck, not waiting for the humanoid behind him.

"Well, Clay!" Forester stared, too breathless to reply to that boom of greeting, for White showed no trace of the time for forests to grow. The luxuriant beard and shaggy head were fiery as ever, and he came striding across the stage with a young man's buoyancy. "Confused?" White's chuckle rumbled. "I know how you feel."

Forester stepped slowly over the low window ledge, to take the huge man's offered hand. Looking up from the merry light in those blue eyes which he had last seen smiling out of cold forgetfulness, he whispered huskily:

"How long has it been—how many years?"

"This is the fiftieth Awakening Day."

A cold wind blew on his spine.

"That's the day the grid releases its yearly crop of graduates, ready for independent life," White added genially. "Quite a holiday, and we've arranged a party for you. We're getting together at Dragonrock. Mansfield will be there, and our old friends Ford and Graystone and Overstreet—who all finished a year ago."

"And—Jane Carter?"

"Not there." Disappointingly, White shook his head. "But we're going on to join her—and you'll find her changed from the ragged little waif we used to know!"

"Grown up, I suppose." Forester caught the light of admiration in White's eyes, and began to wonder what the grid had done to her. If the impulses of creative energy channeled through those platinum relays could stimulate the mending of every human defect and blemish, and even knit back all the wear of time—a breathless eagerness caught him. "Join her?" he whispered anxiously. "Where?"

"A million light-years from here, more or less." The big man spoke of that unimaginable distance almost casually. "Somewhere in the Andromeda Galaxy—our nearest neighbor, you know, among the spiral nebulas. She has been exploring likely planets for our new colonial project there, you see, and she'll be waiting for us at the site she has picked for our first installation."

"Andromeda!" Forester shivered and smiled again, at another vanishing phantom of awe. "That's a long way for colonists to go."

"But the distance is no barrier to us," White objected heartily. "The only difficulty is that the humanoid units can't operate there—rhodomagnetic beams can't reach successfully so far. We first settlers will have to exist without any humanoid service."

"No great hardship." Forester frowned at a momentary

sense of wildly illogical delight, which turned unreal as he tried to examine it. Impulsively he said, "I think I'd like to stay there."

"You're going to," White assured him. "That's why we had Ironsmith leave you under the grid so long—to receive special training for your job out there."

Forester caught his breath, waiting.

"Our first installation, on the site Jane has picked, is going to be a new rhodomagnetic grid," the big man explained. "The beginning of a separate humanoid service for the Andromedan pioneers. The first relay sections will have to be assembled and tested without mechanical aid, of course, and you've been chosen to do that delicate bit of rhodomagnetic engineering."

Forester wondered why his body tried to stiffen, and why he almost shook his head. He could recall a time when he had disliked the humanoids and even mistrusted Frank Ironsmith, but now, even though his recollection of past events seemed clear enough, all the misguided emotions which must have driven him to his unfortunate past actions were fading from awareness, even as he fumbled vaguely for them, like the irrelevant stuff of some unlikely dream.

Once, a preposterous notion tried to haunt him, he would have been reluctant to help import the humanoids to serve the virgin planets of another island universe. His leanly youthful shoulders tossed that unwelcome thought lightly away, however, and his smooth face erased the fleeting trouble of his frown.

For why shouldn't the wise benevolence of the Prime Directive be extended as far as men could go? How could the colonists care for themselves, without mechanicals? Some gifted few, of course, might be able to provide for all their needs with telurgy—but what of all the rest?

"Ready?" The former foe of the machines nodded restlessly toward the waiting cruiser. "Jane will be waiting."

Forester hesitated, glancing back at the motionless humanoid in the room behind, poised alertly to serve and obey. He knew it would be useless to him on those distant worlds until the new palladium relays were working, but at least he wanted it with him until the time to go.

"Come along," he commanded.

Obediently it came, and he turned with a bright expectation on his face to go aboard with White.